MW00882287

PROMISE TO LOVE YOU

J. SAMAN

Copyright © 2021 by J. Saman

All rights reserved.

No part of this book may be reproduced in any form or by any electronic or mechanical means, including information storage and retrieval systems, without written permission from the author, except for the use of brief quotations in a book review.

Cover Design: Danielle Leigh Designs

Photography: Wander Aguiar

Editing: My Brother's Editor

Proofreading: Danielle Leigh

❀ Created with Vellum

PROLOGUE

HENRY

Blue. If I had to guess, that would be the color I would pick. They're not iridescent enough to be green and so far from dark there is no way those beautiful irises are brown. The heavy house bass coats me in its never-ending torrent of sound, quickening my pulse and heating my blood.

Silently, I live for this.

The freedom of the room. The darkness of the shrouding anonymity. The static zing of sexual energy as it swells without restraint, filling the warm, sticky air with a spicy flavor and erotic texture. Down here is my escape. And not once have my bandmates, my lifelong best friends, ever questioned my flying solo as I do it. They might not understand it, but they do understand my need for it.

Even if they don't, and never will, know the reason behind it.

But this woman... the one I'm staring at... the one I've been staring at since I stepped into this enormous, gyrating body-filled room five minutes ago and instantly spotted her... she ignites my blood. Makes me hard.

And best of all... she's alone.

Like me.

Gorgeous. That's not even a question. But she's more than that.

She has an aura.

Something unique, exotic, and captivating as hell. I can't even place what it is about her, but I haven't been able to look away for a second.

I waited. I watched. She's a slave to the music as it flows through her body, calling her muscles into action. Arms above her head, hips swiveling, eyes now closed. She's not here for the men who have come up to her, demanding her attention and body.

And there have been plenty.

They see what I see. However, where they all failed, I already know I'll succeed.

She's here for me tonight, whether she knows it or not.

I don't question my motives as I slide through the ménage of bodies.

I don't hesitate as I lower my mouth to her ear and whisper, "Want to dance with a stranger in the dark?"

Her eyes flash open, ready to explain in explicit detail all the ways I can fuck off since my hands are now on her waist and my face is right before hers. Instead, her pithy retort dies on her tongue, her eyes filling with recognition as those deep blues cast about my face.

"How did you know?" she replies playfully, inadvertently drawing closer.

The high of the show we played tonight hasn't abated. It still hums along my skin and spears my lips with its smile. And right now, I'm thankful for that. Otherwise, the smile she's reflecting—the one I've seen on a thousand other women when they look into my eyes and see a world-famous rock star—would seriously turn me off.

Still, the disappointment that she clearly recognizes me doesn't stop me from snaking my arms deeper around her back, guiding her gorgeous body into mine. Something foreign and heavy floods my chest when she's finally seated against me, staring up into my eyes. I lick my suddenly dry lips, trying to ignore whatever this is, desperate for this brand-new sensation to remain unnamed.

I start to move us, grinding into her in sync with the beat of the music.

She sucks in a gasp of air, those heavy-lidded eyes growing wide with shock. Her head frantically snaps about, eyes scanning like she's afraid we're going to be caught by someone.

"Do you have a boyfriend?" I ask, because I don't do that. I don't share. Never and not even close.

"N-no," she stutters and then shivers, reacting to the glide of my hands up her back and into her long, brown mane of hair. "It's just that... I never thought... you... this. You're touching me and looking at me and..." A self-deprecating laugh chokes past her full lips. "Never mind. I'm gonna shut up now."

"Do you wish I wasn't touching you?" My fingers descend, dragging down her neck and along the smooth, exposed skin of her arms that feels almost electric beneath my touch. "Looking at you?" My face drifts closer, our eyes locked and only inches away. My breath catches in a way it never has before. *Goddamn...*

She licks her lips, her eyes bouncing back and forth between mine. Like she's trying to read me. See what my intentions are with her. I don't hide my want and when she realizes it, her eyes come to life with a heat that makes my cock twitch.

"I like you touching me. I love the way you're looking at me. I don't want you to stop. I guess I just assumed you'd be upstairs. Not down here with everyone else. With me."

She's referring to the private floor, and all I can do is shake my head. The women on the private floor do nothing for me. They're all the same. Not an ounce of real outside or in between any of them. They're agenda-driven. They see money and fame and zero in.

I can't stand any of them. Not even for a night.

"Are you down here alone?" she pushes, peeking around me once more.

"Looking for someone else?"

Her eyes snap back to mine. "Not when you're the one I've

always wanted. I'm just making sure we won't be interrupted by anyone we wouldn't want to find us."

"We won't be."

"Well then," she murmurs, her smile growing. "In that case, sure. I'd love a dance in the dark with a stranger like you." She snakes her arms around my neck, her fingers boldly coiling into the strands at my nape. Yet her eyes are guarded, her movements hesitant, almost as if she's waiting for me to push her away. "Is it off-putting if I say I've always dreamed of this but never in a million years imaged it would happen?"

"With me?"

"Yes." She laughs the word like I'm crazy for asking. "With you, Henry Gauthier. Though I think you already knew that."

"You're beautiful. Any man would be lucky to dance with you. Many before me have tried."

Her arms fly up above her head, her head tilting back as her eyes fall closed, moving with me to the heavy house beat. I lied just now when I told her she's beautiful. She's so much more than that. And looking at her like this, in my arms, she's robbing me of my ability to breathe. The temptation to throw caution to the wind and kiss her here, run my hands all over her body, reach up under her short dress and make her come with hundreds of people around us is so compelling I have to bite my lip to staunch the tenacious need.

"Other men have tried. But I haven't wanted any of them."

"Why's that?"

An impish grin curls up the corners of her lips. "Because they're not you, are they?"

Her body plunges backward, forcing me to dip her, trusting I won't drop her. Fingertips scrape the floor before she rights herself, her eyes glowing, her cheeks bright, and her lips parted with her breathy laugh.

"That was fun. Do you have moves, Henry? So far I'm doing all the leading."

"*I* approached *you*."

"That doesn't make you special."

Fuck. I like this one.

The nerves she had when I first approached her are gone. Now she's a siren. A sexy, confident force of nature. Wild, sinful trouble I want to drown myself in.

"It makes me the one you said yes to."

But the more I study her face, the more something familiar niggles at the darkest recesses of my mind. I can't place it. I feel like I know her somehow, yet I'm nearly positive I've never met this woman before.

Or maybe it's just that I'm more drawn to her than any woman I've encountered lately.

She hikes up on her toes, her body seductively pressing into mine. The scent of her skin and hair hit me hard. Something light and soft and irresistible. Something that makes me want to lick every perfect inch of her.

"What exactly do you think I'm saying yes to?" she whispers in my ear.

"Me. Now. Here. Tonight."

Her breath hitches as my tongue sneaks out, swiping at the line of her jaw. My hand glides up her thigh, my thumb dipping into the softness of her inner thigh. Those pretty blues grow impossibly dark with a hunger that matches my own.

"Tell me no right now or this is happening."

"I want this to happen. Now. Here. Tonight."

"That's all it will be," I warn.

"I know." I don't miss the touch of sadness in her tone. The hint of longing. But her gaze is unwavering as it holds mine.

"You sure?" I ask, studying her.

"Yes. I understand why it's only tonight, and even though one night isn't my style; I've wanted you for too long to ever say no."

Taking her hand, I intertwine our fingers, dragging her through the crowded club to the dark alcove I already scoped out. I never kiss women in public. Sure as hell never touch them in a way I wouldn't be okay with being photographed.

I spin her behind the black curtain that separates the main part of the club from an emergency exit, press her into the wall, cup her face in my hands, and crash my lips to hers. She responds instantly, her hands gripping my triceps, hauling me infinitely closer. Demanding full contact. Our lips move frantically, our tongues seeking, playing, dancing.

She tastes so fucking good; I can't help but angle my mouth, deepening the connection and groaning into her.

She's small. Petite with similar curves, just the way I like 'em.

My hands roam from her face, capturing her breasts over the thin material of her dress before quickly tugging it down. She gasps as my lips flee hers, stealing one taut nipple in my mouth and sucking it in. Greedy hands fist my hair, her neck arching away from the wall as I devour her breasts while skimming a hand up her inner thigh.

"Yes," she hisses on a throaty moan, half her sounds being absorbed into the chaos of the club just steps away. Normally, I feed off of this. Allow the impersonal nature of it to be my guiding force. But something about this woman makes me want to hear all her sounds. See every sweet inch of her flesh. Watch every ounce of pleasure I'm about to give her.

"What is it about you?" I murmur into her skin, knowing she can't hear me. The question is for myself because from the second I saw her, instinctively, I knew it was something. Some bewitching magic she exudes that floated through the club and snaked directly into me. It's holding on tight. Making me greedy and ravenous. Making me want to break all my rules and keep her just a bit longer.

My fingers find the smooth satin of her panties, gliding back and forth over the thin strip covering her pussy, gathering moisture. She's so wet, and she feels and tastes so good my head is spinning.

I release her nipple, working my way back up her neck with deep, open-mouthed kisses until I find her lips again. Pushing aside the satin, I explore her, rubbing her clit and toying with her opening. She bucks against me, grinding, searching for more. Her breathy pants and delirious moans float into my mouth, forcing themselves inside me as I strain to hear each and every note she produces.

"Trouble," I growl into her, gnashing my teeth into her bottom lip and biting down just enough to let her know I mean it. "You're fucking trouble."

"Good. I never wanted to be easy for you. I always wanted to twist you up as badly as you always have me."

I shake my head at that, not quite understanding her meaning. More hints of recognition spark to life but are just as quickly snuffed out as I push two fingers inside her. She rips at my shirt. Trying desperately to undo it. I use my other hand to stop her.

I can't go upstairs after if this is missing buttons.

"I want to see you. I want to touch you," she pleads.

"Not here. Not enough time."

She thunders in frustration, digging her nails into the back of my head and dragging them down my neck, marking me, no doubt. "I hate you," she seethes, emotion clouding her voice as I continue to work her.

For some inexplicable reason, I understand her sentiment. I hate her too. I hate all that she's doing to my insides. All that I've never had to fight before that I'm suddenly fighting here, now, with her. I'm a hot second from saying, *let's go to my hotel room instead.*

But I can't. Not with a girl like this.

The kind of girl who wants more than I can give her.

I'd blame it on the Rockstar. On the lifestyle. Only that couldn't be farther from the truth or reality of it. And where there will never be a future for any woman in my life, it's best to not to live beyond the present.

"Let's see how much you hate me. Unzip me."

She shoves me back, my hand slipping out from between her legs, and just when I think she's about to end it, her blue eyes hold mine as she goes for my zipper. My fingers find my mouth, craving a taste of her. I haven't gone down on a girl in forever, and right now, I'm burning up with the desire for it. With the desire for her.

"You feel it too, don't you?" she accuses, toying with me. Like she knows just the idea of *feeling* something with her will piss me off. Newsflash: Already there.

I nod my head in agreement, words clogging at the back of my throat.

She smiles at that like an evil temptress.

With my dick in my hand, I roll the condom on, lining myself up to her opening. She hitches her leg up and over my hip before leaning back into the wall, helping our angle. My thumb coasts along her bottom lip. "You're so beautiful," I tell her.

"I bet you say that to all the girls," she muses, a light smile on her lips, her eyes dark with lust.

I blink at her, momentarily stunned. "Actually, I don't. I never say that." Then I slide inside her, burying myself to the hilt. Her back arches and she lets out a loud cry. My mouth takes her, stifling the sound. "People will hear and think I'm killing you."

She laughs. "I think you just did. Jesus. Size thirteen shoe really does correlate."

I hold myself still. Giving her a second to get used to me, sure, but how does she know my shoe size? That's hardly common knowledge. Only the guys and—

"Move. Please, I need you to move."

I do. I clear all thoughts from my head and start to pound into her. One hand on her hip, the other tangled in her long, thick hair as I take her over and over again. Her hands are all over me. In my hair. Digging down my shirt. Scraping along the fabric over my chest, abs, and arms. Her eyes are closed, her head is back, her mouth is open, and I'm looking at her. I'm watching her.

Yet another thing I never do. What the motherfuck is going on?

"Harder. Yes. Holy hell, Henry, just like that."

Her eyes flash open, locking on mine. That with the combination of my name on her lips does something to me. It drives me into her harder. Deeper. I press against her and I consume her mouth. Our bodies move in sync, our rhythm increasing and Jesus it's perfect. Just so ungodly perfect. I feel her body start to convulse around me, her moans turning into cries as she writhes in pleasure, coming without restraint. I follow her over the edge, the air sucked from my lungs as I grunt and groan and growl, losing my mind as flashes of light dance behind my eyes.

My forehead lands against hers, our breathing ragged.

Bemused laughs slip past her lips as she lowers her body back to the ground. I only now realize I had lifted her up. "Well, that was unexpected."

It absolutely was. In the best of ways. I stare down at her through a fan of lashes, wanting to lick at her smile. Maybe I can stretch this a bit longer? Break my rules just this once? All I know is the idea of walking away from her and never seeing her again feels—

"I certainly didn't think that would happen when I came here tonight to meet up with you guys."

That pulls me up short. "You came here tonight to meet up with us?"

Her eyebrows furrow as she adjusts her clothes, putting everything back in place. "Of course, I was. Why else would I be here?"

Dread pools low in my gut as horrible pieces of the puzzle start coming together. I tie off the condom, sticking it into my pocket, and tucking my dick back inside my pants, zipping up. "What's your name?"

"My name?" she parrots, pain flashing across her face quickly followed by anger. "You don't know who I am? Are you fucking kidding me?" She stares at me, waiting for me to laugh or tell her I'm joking. She puffs out an incredulous burst of air. "You really didn't know who I was, did you?" She scrubs her hands up and down her face. "I can't believe this. I thought..." A humorless laugh escapes her lungs. "How stupid. I thought after all these years, you finally wanted me back," she murmurs that last part, more to herself than to me, but I hear it all the same.

"I'm sorry..."

Her hands fall and her eyes—narrowed slits of fury—ensnare mine. "Eden Dawson. You know, your *bandmate's,* your *best friend's,* little sister. You remember me now, right?" she spits, vitriol dripping from each syllable. "You've only known me my entire fucking life."

"Eden." I choke on her name. Keith's baby sister. How could I have...

Guilt and remorse clog my throat. I reach for her and she shoves me away.

"Don't touch me. You're such a piece of shit. How could you not have known?!"

"God, Eden. I'm so, so sorry. I didn't realize. I haven't seen you in a few years and you look so different. Nothing like Keith or your other sisters. I swear to God, I didn't know. I would never have touched you if—"

She smacks my face. Hard. Flashes of pain prickle across my cheek, a trail of burning heat closely follows. I stare into her blue eyes, not even the slightest bit stunned. I deserve so much worse than that. She's right. I am a piece of shit. The absolute worst sort.

Because I didn't recognize her. In fairness, I made a point never to notice Eden Dawson or any of Keith's sisters. The last time I saw her, she was sixteen and looked like she was twelve. She was not this woman standing before me.

Christ. Her brother will murder me where I stand. Deservedly so.

"Just go."

I shake my head, trying to touch her again only to drop my hand at the last second. I don't deserve her touch or forgiveness. Still... "I can't. Eden—"

"Don't say my name. You bastard, just go. Now I really do hate you."

I stand immobile.

"Go," she screams, shoving at me with all her might. This time I listen. With my heart in my throat and my stomach churning with every nasty emotion I can throw at it, I walk away. I just fucked my best friend's baby sister in the middle of a club like any other meaningless woman. Only she's not meaningless, and not because she's Keith's sister.

She was more before I even knew her name. Knew who she was.

For that reason alone, I should be relieved she slapped me while spitting venom in my face. I should be...

Something inside of me stirs uncomfortably.

I need to fix this.

Need to see her again.

Only... I have no idea how I'm going to do that. Not when her brother will kill me if he ever finds out what I just did to his baby sister.

ONE

EDEN

Three years later

"HARRY, you know I love you, but I just can't do this anymore," I tell the man standing before me, his eyes earnest, hopeful, but it's just not gonna work. There is no way.

"Eden. My love. I know you can make this happen. Lyric would want it that way."

I fight a grin at the way he tosses my boss's name out like that. As if it's meant to induce nerves in me, the newbie on the street. It doesn't. Lyric is the one who passed this directive on to me.

"We are tightening up the last song on your album. The album is..." I sigh dreamily, not even caring if I'm stretching here a bit. "It's perfect, Harry. Just perfect. One of your best. One of Cyber's Law's best. It's a hit and the song you think we need to add to this perfect album will only weigh it down."

Especially since the fucker is already twenty tracks deep.

He studies me for a moment, his gaze scrutinizing but steady. I don't intimidate easily. Try being the youngest of six with Keith

Dawson as your big brother. Nothing scares me. It's why Lyric passed Cyber's Law onto me. She's been producing their albums for years, and I think finally had enough. Plus, Harry refused to finish recording in New York, and that's where Lyric is now primarily based.

"You're honestly telling me we can't squeeze one tiny little new song on?" He's trying for incredulous and falling way short. But I like his English accent enough to keep this conversation going. Even if it's done.

"That's exactly what I'm telling you. But the wonderful thing about that is you already have a killer song to kick off your next album."

He considers this for a moment, his eyes sweeping about the studio we've been toiling in for the last eight hours straight. Hell, for the last three weeks straight. We even have food delivered and I think I've only used the restroom like once a day. That's how hard we've been working. His bandmates too, but they're holding back comment on this new song.

I think they're as done with this album as I am.

"Alright luv, you've won me over yet again. We'll push the new track onto the next album. How about we celebrate with dinner tonight?"

"As I've already explained several times, Harry, I don't date the people I work with." Or more specifically, I don't date you.

"But we've just established that we're done working."

A pointed eyebrow slides up my face.

"Ah, you're trouble. But gorgeous trouble, so I'll keep working on wearing you down."

Trouble. Why does everyone think I'm trouble? A couple of piercings and some purple hair dye and you'd think I was out purse-snatching old ladies.

"You're doing our next album, yeah?"

"If it floats your boat, I'd be honored to do your next album. But my answer on dating you won't change." With that, I sling my purse over my shoulder, throw them all a parting wave, and head for the door before he can waylay me further.

This man could talk for hours if I let him.

And despite Harry's propensity to flirt with any young, attractive female who crosses his path, working with him is an experience I didn't think I'd be afforded so early after starting my career as a producer at Turn Records.

It is insanely cool I was given the chance to work with Cyber's Law. I mean, *the* Cyber's Law, right? I remember a million years ago when my brother's band, Wild Minds, opened for them. Now my brother is headlining world tours, playing to sold-out stadiums. It's seriously a trip.

All of this is.

This new job. This new life. This fresh start I needed like nobody's business.

Shutting the door behind me, I head for the elevator that will take me down to the garage. It's Friday night and after the long weeks spent here, I intend to celebrate the completion of this album with a steady flow of margaritas, pajamas, and Netflix. I'm also contemplating making a spread of enchiladas to go with it.

How's that for trouble?

Bounding toward the elevator, my finger a hairsbreadth from hitting the down arrow, I stop dead in my tracks at the sound of voices. But not just any voices. Familiar voices. Familiar voices that belong to my brother and his friends.

Crap in a jar of mustard. He can't find me here.

Frantically, my head swivels left and right, and for a fleeting second, I debate hitting the down button and taking my chances. But those voices... they're close. Growing louder. And I'm out of time.

Something tall and green catches my eye and I rush behind it, practically knocking the freaking plant over in the process. It sways dangerously and I have to grab it by the thick stalks, yanking it back before it goes crashing to the floor. As it is, some dirt spills over onto the pristine carpet and the flimsy fronds sway.

I can only hope no one notices that or me as I cower behind it like the coward I am, hiding from my brother. Well, and Henry too, since I'm sure he's with Keith. But let's be real here, he's the last man I want to see. I'd take Keith over him any day.

Just as I get myself settled in a position I hope renders me invisible to human eyes, my brother, Jasper Diamond, Gus Diamond, and Henry Gauthier step into view, flanked by their manager Marco Morales. They're all laughing and shooting the shit as they head for the elevator I was so nearly on.

I thought they were still on tour.

I must have miscalculated my days. Dammit.

If they catch me here, the jig is up, and I do not want the jig to be up. At least not yet. It will change everything. And not in a good way.

Since I started working at Turn Records last month, I've been avoiding my brother and his bandmates like the plague. Between my overprotective brother who does not see me as anything other than his baby sister that he partially raised and freaking Henry who had to go and ruin me the last time I saw him, this duck and cover routine is a necessary one.

I know I'll have to face Keith eventually.

I know I'm being childish about that.

But this is not the moment for it with Henry right beside him.

I hate the gorgeous bastard. Hate him more than I hate crab, and I'm deathly allergic to crab. My main problem with Henry is not that he screwed me or even that it was only going to be a one-and-done deal. I had accepted that when I accepted his crude offer. The problem was that I thought he finally *saw* me.

And he didn't.

Childhood crushes are a nuisance like that, and mine stems back a long way. The one good thing my brother's asshole best friend did by fucking me in a public place like the nameless side piece I was to him was to finally cure me of my lifelong, insufferable obsession with him. Silver lining, right?

Random bits of conversation and laugher flitters over to me and I slink down farther, wedged between the plant in the wall in the most uncomfortable of ways while doing my best to be silent and unobservable.

And forcing myself not to look at Henry.

Not to feel the same, familiar swarm of butterflies I always feel in his presence.

Not to notice his simple white tee that clings like a second skin to his large arm muscles and smattering of colorful tattoos, making him look deliciously, dangerously bad ass. To ignore the way his dark, low-slung designer jeans fit so stupidly perfect it's beyond annoying. To pretend his face isn't cut from stone, sculpted by God, and sent to Earth from the hottest depths of hell.

Asshole!

They hit the button for the elevator, all of their backs to me and I watch with bated breath as the doors open and all five men step on, turning to face the front of the elevator—and me—at the same time.

I scan their faces, one by one, hoping, praying I remain undetected. But just as the doors begin to close, I catch Marco's eyes narrowing, his head tilting as if he's trying to discern what the dark mass behind the plant is.

Our eyes meet and his searching expression morphs into one of puzzled amusement.

Raspberry-tinted lips curve in an amused smirk, and I violently shake my head, holding my hands in supplication, silently begging him to keep quiet. He subtly shakes his head in return like I'm too much, but he doesn't say anything, mercifully, and returns to conversation with Jasper, effectively ignoring me.

The doors finally close and the guys are carried down into the bowels of the building and away from me. Relief hits me square in the chest in the form of a deep sigh as my head sags back against the wall behind me.

That was damn close.

I know Keith's more than aware I live in his city. I'm positive it was our mother who ratted me out despite my asking her not to. I don't think my sisters would, though one never knows with them. Being the baby of the family and chronically treated like one is nice when you're six. It sucks when you're twenty-two, trying to start your own life, and your family's only explanation for continuing to baby you is old habits die hard.

Keith calls a lot and that was never something he used to with this much frequency. He leaves angry messages and texts, demanding I speak with him. I love my brother dearly and I don't want him angry with me. I'm excited beyond measure that we're living in the same city again and can hopefully become closer than we have been in the years of our distance.

But I need more time before that can happen.

The real kicker is my friendship with his fiancée, Maia. She sought me out, hunted me down, and sweetly informed me that we were to become best friends. Clearly Keith isn't as clever or tenacious as his better half. Something I genuinely love about her.

I didn't argue with her because she's going to be family, and the more I get to know her, the more I like her, so it's a win-win. Besides, a girl can't have enough sisters on her side. Especially ones who treat her as an equal.

My one caveat was that I wouldn't tell her what I do for a living or where I live and she couldn't ask.

She didn't even balk.

Pulling myself up and out from behind the plant, I count to twenty and then go for the elevator, dialing up Lyric Rose, my boss and the CEO of Turn Records, as I go.

She picks up quickly, as I knew she would. "Did you convince Harry to push the song off?" she asks without preamble, but I really don't want to talk about Harry Evans right now. No, my mind is running wild—seriously, no pun intended—all over a different set of rock stars.

"Yes. All I had to do was compliment him and the album. Worked like a charm."

Lyric laughs. "Glad to hear it. He's a pushover for a pretty face and harmless, but if he oversteps with yours, let me know."

"He's nothing I can't handle."

"That I already know. Doesn't change anything. Work is work and these boners seem to forget that not all women are there for their dicks' pleasure."

"He asked me out. I said no. He let it go. There was no boner touching involved." I step onto the now empty elevator and hit the button for the garage. I gnaw on my lip, hoping my brother and his friends are already in their cars and racing out into LA traffic. "I thought Wild Minds was still on tour."

"No. They returned home yesterday. Why do you ask?" she continues cautiously.

I bluster out a breath, leaning back against the wall as the car descends. "Because I had to hide behind one of your spiny plants in the hall to avoid my brother." *And Henry!*

She laughs. Kinda loud, actually. "Eden, you could just tell him you work for me. He'll find out eventually and no matter what he says or thinks, he's not the reason I hired you."

"I know that." At least I think I do. But Lyric has been close friends with my brother and his bandmates for years. Has produced their albums for years. And even though I don't want to trade on his name, I know he's the reason I got the summer internships with her while I was in college.

I'm grateful to him for that, but I need this job to be about me. Not him.

And I know that if, *when*, my brother finds out I'm working here, not just interning, he'll think I'm taking advantage. I need to earn my stripes before that happens and finishing Cyber's Law's album and having it be a success is the first step.

"Good. Because I've been following your work with Cyber's Law and it's good. Really good. The two songs you produced are every bit as well-honed and polished as the ones I did with them on the rest of the album. Monday, I want you to shadow Steven who is working with one of our solo hip-hop artists. Watch and learn the way they create the background instrumentals and how they pair that with her voice."

"Okay. That sounds great. I'm really excited to learn that side of things."

"That," she says. "That right there. Your enthusiasm and willingness to take on whatever I throw at you is why I hired you. You remind me of me when I first started interning for Robert Snow. And to be fair, he was friends with my father and how *I* got the job. So I understand your position and your trepidation. But just like how I earned my way up, you are too. You've got this job, Eden. You truly do. Wow yourself, wow me, wow the industry with your talent, and no one can touch that."

I smile so big my cheeks hurt. "Thank you, Lyric. I won't let you down."

We disconnect the call and the smile on my face and the giddy flutter in my chest carry me all the way down. I'm not a musician like Keith is. I can't sing a note.

But I know how to create music. How to blend it and arrange it.

How to make it more than just voices and notes.

I know how to make it come to life.

I just need to believe in myself. To hold on to my courage and convictions.

To never let anyone hold me down or back again.

Stepping off the elevator, I head toward my car and immediately my jubilant smile and steadfast thoughts crash to the ground, shatter, then scatter like pieces of broken glass across the cement floor of the garage.

I stand frozen, immobile for a beat too long before I regain my composure, realign my mask of cool indifference, and saunter toward the man leaning against the passenger side door of my car, not so patiently waiting for me with an icy reception.

TWO

EDEN

One of the cruelest power trips of nature is our inability to bend time to our will or change the course of our hearts when our minds truly know better. I don't bother asking what he's doing here. It's obvious he saw me and with that realization, humiliation creeps up my face in the form of an inconvenient blush. I was, after all, hiding behind a freaking plant.

I hold his gaze anyway, refusing to back down.

"How did you know this was my car?" I ask instead of addressing anything else.

Henry doesn't smirk, smile, or even speak. He just stares at me with an indecipherable expression, large arms folded casually over his equally large chest as he watches me draw closer and closer. He's alone, which is a relief, and it isn't. I'm glad Keith is not with him because one confrontation at a time is plenty, but I almost wish there were a buffer to dull the mounting tension swirling between us.

I shrug up a shoulder when he doesn't answer, feigning indifference. Keith bought me this car as a graduation present, and since all the members of Wild Minds are practically lovers they're so close it shouldn't surprise me that he knows this is my car. I doubt they take a piss without consulting each other and sharing pics of the event.

Hitting the clicker, I get in, doing my best to ignore the man still poised against the door, angering me the way only he can.

Three years ago, when I saw him in the club and he approached me, I had never been happier in my life. I was no longer a little girl. I was a woman, nineteen, and all grown up.

He started talking to me. Flirting with me. Then he propositioned me. And when he kissed me in that dark corner with a passion I wasn't expecting but delighted in all the same, it was a dream come true. It was more than just sex to me, as I knew it would be, but there was a connection. A spark. It all felt too good, and I knew I wasn't alone in feeling that. I freaking knew it!

Then, when I realized he didn't know who I was, I was heartbroken. No, my heart was so much more than broken. It was annihilated. It was as if every piece of girlish hope that had ever resided inside me died, leaving me cold, empty, and humiliated. I told him my name when he finally got around to asking it and watched as the gears clicked into place. As his eyes filled with recognition and then... regret. Revulsion.

The bastard said he wouldn't have touched me if he had known it was me.

God, could anything hurt worse after what had just happened between us?

The sear from his rejection burned me deep, leaving irrevocable scars. Scars that lasted. Scars that lead and fed into other things that lead to scars of their own.

Only his are infinitely more resonating, indelible, destructive.

I've spent the last three years of my life avoiding Henry Gauthier. Not so easily done when he's your brother's best friend and chronically attends family functions and holidays with us. I forced myself to get over him. To not think about him. Now he's here and there is no avoiding him since I'm on his turf, in his city, and working for his record label.

Now he's seeking me out. This time knowing full well who I am. Only I'm no longer the same girl he treated like trash that night. And if he thinks I will follow him around, the way I tried to when I was just a girl, he's got another thing coming.

The car starts up, The Cure's "Just Like Heaven" pulsing loudly from my speakers, and I blare the horn, starting to lose some of the cool I was hoping to cling to a little longer. "Move."

He does, but not the way I want him to.

Instead, he twists around in a blur of motion, opens the passenger side door and slips inside like I invited him in.

"That's not what I meant when I said move."

Green eyes, hard as the coldest emeralds, stare unabashedly in my direction, his body angled along with them and in a car this small, it's like he's everywhere.

"How long have you been stalking me?"

"What?" bursts from my chest, and I twist to finally look at him, utterly incredulous and indignant. "Stalking you? Are you fucking high right now?"

"I saw you, Eden," he accuses. "Upstairs. I saw your skinny ass hiding behind a plant like that would somehow cloak you from me. Hell, I smelled your weird perfume the moment we stepped out of the studio. So again, how long have you been stalking me?"

"How do you remember what perfume I wear?"

He cocks an impatient eyebrow at me, his eyes unapologetic as they demand my answer.

"God," I snort out a strained laugh. "I seriously cannot stand you. You're nothing but a loathsome, arrogant prick. Were you always like this and I just didn't realize it? A boyband reject who doesn't know he's been kicked out of paradise. How disappointing."

"Huh? That doesn't even make sense. Eden—"

"I'm not stalking you, loser. I work here."

He shakes his head like that makes no sense. "No. Keith would have told me. Lyric would have told me."

I roll my eyes. "Why? Because you're so big and important in my life that people have to report to you on what I do and where I work?"

He stares hard, nonplussed. Screw him.

"I'm still calling bullshit. What could you possibly do here at a record studio? And why this one if you're not stalking me?"

The way he says that, with so little faith that I could actually do anything real...

My fists clench as I fight the swell of emotion his hurtful words drive up in me. "Get out of my car, Henry. I didn't stalk you. Stalking implies interest and where you're concerned, I have none."

A confident smirk hits his lips as he takes me in. "We both know that's a lie. But you didn't answer my questions. I'm not going anywhere until I have some answers." He sits back, getting comfortable, and right now, I just need him to go. It's been a long week. A long couple of weeks.

And doing battle with Henry is exhausting.

"I'm an associate producer. I graduated with a degree in music production, which I know you know, so shut your shit about it not making sense that I work here. I've interned in New York for Turn Records every summer for the last four years, which I also know you know. So, a job here shouldn't be all that much of a shock to you."

"Why California? Why not New York again?"

My reasons for why California over New York are most definitely not something I want to discuss.

"My reasons are my own and they do not involve you," I state flatly. "That said, Keith doesn't know about my working here, though I have no doubt once you open your big, ugly mouth, he will. Lyric didn't tell you punkholes because I asked her not to."

"Why would you ask her not to?"

I growl out an aggravated breath. I just want him to go. I just want him to get out of my car so I won't have to look at his face that unfortunately still makes my belly swoop in that annoyingly girlish way. So I won't have to inhale the scent of his cologne that is earthy and spicy and infuriatingly wonderful.

Being insanely attracted to someone you loathe is the absolute worst.

"Last I checked, I'm a grown woman who doesn't have to explain herself, her job, or her life choices to her brother or his lame friends. Now. Get. Out!"

He doesn't move. Of course, he doesn't.

In all the years I've known Henry Gauthier, he's never once done anything I've wanted him to. I curse in frustration, running my hands through my hair.

He watches me intently, his voice softening. "If you didn't want us to know where you work, why pick Turn Records? You had to know I would hear about this. That I would see you again, Eden."

"What's that supposed to mean?"

His eyes flitter about my face before he subtly shakes his head and redirects. "Keith's been calling you. He's worried. Why don't you want him to know you're here?"

I sigh, my forehead falling to the steering wheel, my eyes closing. "I don't mean to make him worry. I didn't realize he was. It's just that sometimes being his little sister is exhausting. I want to be seen as Eden Dawson. Not Keith Dawson's little sister." I twist, opening my eyes to find him. "Can you understand that, Henry? I know you boys all think the world rotates because you're living on it, but I'm tired of my professional world revolving around my relationship with Keith. I'm good at this job and I don't want you or my brother or anyone else interfering or impacting it."

His eyes do battle across my face. Like a triumphant warrior, plundering all he can as quickly as possible. Gentle fingers reach out and capture a lock of my purple hair and my breath hitches before I can stop it. He toys with the tresses, staring at my nose ring before dropping down to my dark-stained lips, black T-shirt, peek of my tattoos on my arm, and jeans.

"What happened to you, Eden?"

I push his hand away from my hair. "Since when do you care?" I bite out.

"I don't. You just didn't look like this the last time I saw you."

I snort out a humorless laugh. "You mean when you didn't recognize me? Yet, somehow, you did today. I'd call that a win but really I think that falls more into the loss category."

He continues his inspection, but my accusation lit a fire in his eyes that wasn't there before. "I hadn't seen you in years. Not since you were a child. And let me tell you, that night, you didn't look like a fucking child. So yeah, I didn't know who you were when you came onto me—"

"When I came onto you?" I bark out, my voice loud, the sound carrying through the car. "Please, the second you walked into that club your eyes were all over me. Sort of how they've been since you got in my car today."

His eyes scour over every inch of me, almost like he's mocking me as they drag lazily, clinging on places like my legs, breasts, neck, and lips until he reaches my eyes once more. He licks his lips and clears his throat, but he doesn't look away.

"I'm only staring because I'm shocked just *how* much you've changed. So again, what happened to you?"

I blow out a silent breath, trying to calm myself and my thundering heart down. Only that's nearly impossible when I think about the last couple of months. "You've got it the wrong way around. *This* is who I am." My hands do a sweep over myself. "That other girl was not. If you don't like it then I guess I did something right."

"I didn't say I didn't like it. I'm just not sure I understand it."

"Lucky ducky for me, I don't need you to."

The air in the car shifts. Grows even more unsettled. The Smiths play and our voices fall silent, but somehow the tension seems to grow instead of dissipating. He's not getting out, if anything he's ingratiating himself further into my space and head as he stares directly into my eyes with an intensity I feel everywhere. I can't stand it. Any of it.

He has too much power where I'm concerned. He always has.

I jerk my head back, sitting up straight and leveling him with a look that hides none of my ire. "Out, Henry. I have somewhere to be that doesn't include you."

His teeth gnash, a muscle in his jaw tics, and I take only a small amount of joy in his reaction. "Are you still mad at me?"

"What are you, six?"

Finally, that smirk I knew was hiding beneath his layers, cracks. "Maybe." He leans in, getting right up in my face. "I'm sorry I didn't recognize you that night."

I roll my eyes which just fluffs my nutter more. I have no witty or snappy retort this time. I'm grateful he didn't apologize for the sex again. That hurt a hundred times more than him not recognizing me. I shouldn't still hurt over what happened that night. But I do. I was hopelessly, childishly in love with this man. I may not have stalked him today or at this job or even in this city, but I did internet stalk him for years prior to that night like a girl obsessed. And I'd be lying if I said that when I went to that club, dressed how I was dressed, my single, solitary goal wasn't Henry Gauthier.

If I snark back to his half-baked apology, he'll see it all over my face. I've never been adept at hiding my emotions. It's a work in progress, but he doesn't need another front-row showing.

"That's not why I'm angry."

"No?" he questions in disbelief. "Enlighten me. Because this feels infinitely more hostile than our last interaction."

"Out. Seriously. We're done." I point past his face in the direction of the window. "One lousy fuck doesn't make you my boyfriend or my BFF. I owe you nothing. Our worlds work better when we pretend not to know each other." I try to hide the bitterness from my voice, but I'm positive some of it leaks out anyway.

"I never pretended. I just fucked up is all. And you can call me a lousy fuck all you want but I had you moaning into my mouth, crying out my name, and starving for more." He inches closer, his minty breath fluttering over my lips. "We both know you loved every second of it."

"Wow, men really are dumb as rocks. I highly doubt the women you hook up with are very forthcoming. They think you're some hotshot celebrity, right? Some big musician?" I lean in, same as him, until our faces are inches apart. His eyes darken, dropping to my lips, watching them as I speak. "Newsflash, Henry: Women lie. We do it all the time. We fake our orgasms and bullshit about how you men all rock our worlds. But really, we do all that so you'll finish quicker and we can get ourselves off since you failed to and return to whatever we were doing before that was infinitely more pleasurable than getting it on with you."

An unstoppable smile lights up his face, his eyes on mine, my lips, then back up to mine. "Is that so?"

I nod, but he picks this moment to move in even closer and I have to swallow hard before my nerves get the better of me. As it is, my hands are trembling and my heart is beating so loud and so fast I'm positive he can hear it. His nose glides against mine before he angles his head, layering his lips with mine, and for one painstakingly impossible moment, I think he's going to kiss me.

Worst part? I don't even know if I'd have the strength to push him away.

But the thought dies just as quickly as he rights his body, his smile turning smug when he notes the flush on my cheeks. "You're as beautiful when you lie as you are when you come. I'd love nothing more than to call your bullshit card, but you're not something I can take on again, are you? Despite how much we both know you want me to." He throws me a wink and then gets out of the car. "See you soon, Eden." He slams the door behind him and walks off in the direction of a huge white Escalade. I look away, refusing to track his every move.

I hate that he just did that. Unsettled me completely. Wrangled me in in no time flat.

That was your one freebie, Henry Gauthier.

Next time it won't be so easy for you.

THREE

EDEN

The door slams shut behind me with so much force the picture hanging beside it teeters before crashing to the floor. "Shit." My purse slips from my shoulder and I drop down, picking up the broken frame and pieces of glass.

"What was that?" my roommate Jess calls out as she makes her way to me from her bedroom.

"Your painting." I look up, meeting her pale green eyes with a mournful frown. "Jess, I'm so sorry." I glance back down, staring woefully at her broken picture. It's one her father painted for her and it's her favorite.

She waves me away as she crouches down, helping me carefully pick up the remaining pieces. "It's fine. It was just the frame."

It's not fine though. This was just the icing on a crappy end-of-day cake. "I'll replace it. I swear. Thankfully the picture looks unharmed."

"Take a breath. I'm not mad. As long as the painting is okay, the frame is meaningless. Why were you slamming the door like the bitch had it coming?"

I glower, sagging like a girl who's lost her way. Walking over to the trash, I dump everything into it. "Long day dealing with the perfection that is Harry Evans and his band." I peek over my shoulder in her direction. "Then Henry found me."

Jess throws out the glass in her hand and sets her prized painting down on the counter in the kitchen before hoisting herself up so she can sit beside it. "What do you mean, Henry found you?"

I heave a breath, leaning my back against the opposite counter in our galley kitchen. Our apartment isn't big. This is LA, after all and if you want to live in a decent neighborhood in a decent building then apartments are expensive as hell. Keith is insanely rich and generous beyond measure and I'm so grateful for all he's done for me. He paid for my college tuition so I wouldn't graduate with heavy loans and bought me a car, but that's where it stopped.

I'm done letting him pay my way.

"When I was leaving work, just before I got on the elevator, Keith and his band were exiting another studio."

She's smirking now, a sparkle in her eyes. "Let me guess, you tried to hide."

"Hey, don't judge."

Her hands spring up, palms toward me but she's still laughing without restraint. "I'm not at all. I just know you."

I fold my arms over my chest, smiling a little despite myself. It is kinda funny. "Fine. I hid behind a plant. Not well obviously because their manager Marco saw me, as did Henry."

"Not Keith?"

"No. But I'm sure by now he knows everything because Henry was waiting for me at my car."

"Did you talk?"

"Fought mostly. He got in my car and proceeded to accuse me of stalking him. It got worse from there."

Jess gives me a sympathetic half-frown. She knows all about me and Henry and not just what happened in the club. We've been best friends since we were little. Went to college together and now we're living together in LA while she attends law school at UCLA.

"Whatever, it's done and it's probably better that I got it out of the way. I've been spending time with Maia, so it's only a matter of time before Keith knows all I'm doing anyway."

"I've said this before, and I'll say it again. I think Keith will be proud of you. I know you keep saying you want to prove yourself before you tell him, and I understand why you think you need to do that, but you don't have to prove yourself to anyone other than you."

"Now you sound like Lyric."

She cocks an eyebrow at me as if to say, *yeah, duh*. I release a silent breath, my body deflating along with it.

"You're right. I know you are. It's just that Keith still treats me like his baby sister, with a heavy emphasis on baby. He's loving and supportive and wonderful. I just want to do this on my own and he would have unintentionally made that difficult in the name of helping me."

"And you think Henry will tell him?"

I snort at that, rolling my eyes derisively. "I know he will. Those boys do not keep secrets. It's like some kind of pact. Ever since everything that went down between Jasper, Gus, and Viola, they hold nothing back."

She gets a wicked gleam in her eyes as she leans forward, planting her elbows on her thighs and intertwining her fingers. "Oh, I don't know about that. I think the fact that Henry devoured you in a club and still wants to drink you up like a fine wine is still very much a secret."

I scoff bitterly, giving her my back as I go to the fridge and grab a bottle of water. I offer her one, but she shakes me off. Twisting the cap, I take a large pull, but her challenging eyes haven't left me. I groan, setting the bottle on the counter. "Yes, I'm sure Keith doesn't know about what happened in the club. But trust me, Henry is as done with me as I am with him."

She points a stern finger at me, matching it with a cocked eyebrow and a who are you kidding expression. "You said he was waiting at your car? Why do that if he didn't want to see you? He could have pretended he didn't see you when he was getting on the elevator if that were the case."

I play with the paper wrapper on the water bottle. "He thought I was stalking him, Jess. He wasn't exactly looking for a repeat."

"You forget I was there that night. I saw the way he was watching you. He couldn't keep his eyes off you and then he was all over you," she says, tilting her head, her knowing smile spreading like the Cheshire Cat.

"That was before he knew who I was. Add to that, I look very different now than I did that night."

"Agreed. You look better. Did he at least apologize?"

"Yes. He said he was sorry he didn't recognize me that night. But seriously, I don't want to talk about Henry anymore." I take another swig of my water.

"Fine. All I'm saying is if a guy doesn't want you, he wouldn't wait for you at your car just to accuse you of stalking him and then apologize."

I shake my head at that, refusing to acknowledge her point.

It's nothing but detrimental to my resolve to hate him for all eternity. Any affection I ever harbored for Henry Gauthier died three years ago.

Besides, Henry is irrelevant.

I'm done with men. All men. Especially the too good-looking for my own good cocky ones.

"Hot purple hair, I don't care," I tell her, making her laugh. "With any luck, I can dodge him like a bullet and won't have to see him again for at least a few months." I clap my hands together, rubbing them back and forth. "Now, onto better things. What are we doing tonight? I finished Cyber's Law's album today. My first official solo produced songs on it. I'm thinking lots of good alcohol, homemade Mexican food is a must, and an overdose of Marvel's Chrises."

Jess taps her bottom lip, pinning me with me a look I know too well. It makes my heart instantly gallop into a sprint.

"What? Why are you staring at me like that?"

"I'm debating the wisdom of showing you something after you've already had a long day and a run-in with the guy you've been obsessed with since you were five who you now claim to hate. Or at the very least, maybe I should get you drunk first?"

"You realize you now have to show me this very second, right?"

She purses her pink lips to the side, watching me carefully.

"Jess!"

"Ugh. Fine." She slaps her hands to her thighs. "But I warned you. That's all I'm saying. After we go down this dark and stormy path, we will drink. And you'll cook because that's your second happy place. And watch all the movies."

Oh boy. This isn't going to be good.

She hops off the counter, determined steps leading her to the family room. I follow, already jittery and sick even before my eyes zero in on a box on the coffee table I hadn't noticed previously. "This came for you today. I was tempted to bash it like a piñata and then throw the fucking thing in the trash chute. Say the word and I'll do that now. Happily. I'll even let you take the first swing with the bat. I have my daddy's Louisville under my bed."

I glance up, meeting her eyes for a fleeting second before nervously returning to the box.

It's big. It takes up half of our goddamn coffee table.

It's also a present. Not the sort of thing that is delivered in the mail or by UPS. This big white box with the perfect black satin bow was hand-delivered.

Black. The color he hated me wearing most. "It might not be—"

"You know it is."

I nod. I do know it is.

I try to swallow past the lump of emotion clogging my throat but it's futile. Those slimy bastards have already been choking me all evening. Now this. Why is he doing this to me? Upping the ante this way? He's still calling and sending me texts. Now this present...

"He didn't—"

"I don't know," she says. "It was just sitting outside our door when I got home from class."

"Christ. This day." I scrub my hands up and down my face, trying to muster the courage I do not feel. "The hits just keep on coming. One asshole after the other. Why can't men learn how to fuck themselves and leave us out of it?"

"Now you appreciate why I was reluctant to show you." She squeezes my shoulder. "Trash chute or opening it?"

I don't know. I should throw it out and never look back. I don't return his calls or texts. Ever. But I do read the texts and listen to his voice messages. Each and every one if for no other reason than to remind me why I made the right choice.

A choice that still hurts like hell.

"Open it. But I need a shot first."

"That's my girl. Vodka or tequila?"

I pop a 'are you for real with that question' eyebrow.

"Right. Tequila. What was I thinking?"

I continue to stare until she returns with the bottle of Patron from the freezer and two small juice glasses. She pours us each a shot plus a little extra for the devil to join in my pity party and then we down them in one swift go.

"Crumb bars, that's rough. Wooh!" Jess wipes her mouth with the back of her hand. I don't even taste it. I can drink like a sailor on leave mixed with that chick from the first Indiana Jones movie who goes shot for shot. I have no limit.

She plops down on the couch, reaching out and drawing the box closer to her as if she expects me to follow her lead. I do but mostly because I'm not sure I can stand anymore. Suddenly my legs feel numb, which I don't understand since my heart is beating so fast.

"This was hand-delivered. How does he know where I live, Jess?"

"He's Chad Mason," she states simply with a half-shrug.

I snicker mirthlessly because it's true. Dumb question. There isn't anything my ex can't get if he sets his mind to it. His family is sports royalty and he's following along in their regal footsteps.

Money, women, fame, it's all at his fingertips and he eats it up with his golden spoon.

And for two years, I was the one he wanted.

The woman on his arm. The one he doted on and made feel special. We planned a future together. Had it all mapped out.

Until it all went bad. Real bad.

"Do you think Marni's decapitated head is in here?"

Jess glances over to me, her eyebrows knit. "Like in *Seven*? I think that's a bit too dramatic for him. He likes to profess his love in much subtler ways."

I scoff at that, bristling hard. Like so hard my whole body hurts. "Yeah. Like by fucking Marni behind my back."

"Like that. Though we don't know they actually fucked." I glare and she shrugs, pushing on. "But it can't be Marni's head because she didn't move out to LA with him like you did. She's in New York."

"Thanks for the reminder," I grimace.

Chad and I were ecstatic at the draft when LA took him in the top ten. It all felt so perfect. So meant to be. Lyric said LA or New York. My choice. He got drafted and I picked LA. Now I'm here and so is he but we're not together because he's a lying, cheating piece of shit.

She nudges the box with her knuckles. "This won't open itself."

"I'm going to need a lot of alcohol tonight. And greasy food. I want to cook a feast, but I'm not sure I'm up for it anymore. I might want to do takeout."

She gasps. "No." Her hands go to her chest. She's mocking me now.

"Shut up." I laugh lazily.

"I'm thinking you're absolutely perfect and no man should drive you to drink or do takeout. But if that's what you need, I'm in because that's like my faves candy on Halloween."

I breathe out a laugh, leaning over and kissing my girl on the cheek.

Then I go at it.

The perfect satin bow falls gracefully away with a gentle tug. The white lid so easily removed. There is no tissue paper inside. Just a stack of things I find myself staring stupidly at.

"It's his jersey," I mutter bewilderedly.

"Both college and NFL from the looks of it."

"I burned the college one I used to wear."

"He's replacing it. There's a note, but we can get to that later. I'm kinda hung up on the jewelry box."

Yeah. Me too.

With a shaky hand, I reach in for the small rectangular box. I already have a good idea what it is, and knowing it's not *the* diamond, I open it, hating that I was right. It's the necklace he gave me on our one-year anniversary.

It's our names in delicate script overlapping in platinum and diamonds. When he gave this to me, I cried and vowed never to take it off. Until I caught him cheating. Then I ripped the thing from my neck and threw it in his face. He obviously had it repaired, as the platinum chain is once again perfect.

"Does he honestly expect I'll wear these and not have a bonfire with them as the guests of honor?"

Jess taps her bottom lip in contemplation. "I think this is his alpha way of saying you're still his."

"Funny, I didn't get that impression when I found Marni's lips wrapped around his dick."

It was more than that though. So much more than that betrayal.

Setting the necklace back inside the box, I close it up and shove the whole damn thing away. I'm not that girl anymore.

I turn to my best friend and meet her worried gaze. "Forget what I said about takeout. Let's get dressed up and go out."

"Hell yeah!" She springs off the couch like a cattle prod just lit up her ass. "Let's do this. Girls' night out. No men allowed. We're going clubbing. I know the perfect place."

FOUR

EDEN

Chilled tequila slides effortlessly down my throat, the mild bite on the backend welcome as I lick my lips and set my empty glass down. The pulsing beats of the brilliantly spun techno and trip-hop pulses across my skin as the tequila warms it from within. My eyes momentarily close, listening closely to the way the DJ mixes this particular track.

He's good. I was watching him for a while when we first got here.

"Just go and introduce yourself to him already," Jess yells so I can hear her.

"I will. Not yet though. Never interrupt a DJ in the middle of a set."

"Words to live by," she snorts. "Shit, I'm buzzing already." I open my eyes and fix them on my friend who is clinging mercilessly to her lime like it's her saving grace before smacking her lips. "Whoa! I should have had more to eat."

We both likely should have. We split an order of nachos and each had a taco salad. Well, and two margaritas. My stomach was still in knots over the afternoon I had, and Jess is on a student budget. I didn't cook. Cooking is my thing but instead, we went out and I don't think that was in either of our best interest.

"Which reminds me, why are we doing shots?" she asks.

"Because that's all I do in clubs as you know. I don't dance with drinks in my hands that someone can spill all over me or slip something into. Plus, they're always insanely watered down. If I'm going to pay these kinds of prices for a drink, I want alcohol in it."

"That makes so much sense, it's almost frightening I never asked you before. But only one more and then I'm done. I can't drink the way you can."

"That's a good thing, my friend. And your liver thanks you for it."

She laughs. "Hashtag truth."

My drinking prowess was legendary in college. High school too actually, but we don't talk about my teenage drinking heroics anymore. In college, it became a bit of a thing. It's actually how I caught Chad's eye in the first place. I was drinking two of his teammates, his much larger offensive linemen teammates, under the table to the tune of a hundred bucks each. I mentioned the chick from Indiana Jones and I was not kidding.

I'm not sure if it's a Dawson thing or a high metabolism thing or what, but all of my siblings are like this. Alcohol hits us slow and burns off quick.

I flag down the bartender and wave my finger in the air, using the universal sign for one more round.

"Another tequila, ladies?" he asks, giving Jess a sly flirtatious grin. I have no doubt he gives that same smirk to all his female patrons, hoping they'll flirt back, drop a number, and a back-room BJ all the while over-tipping him.

"Yes," Jess exclaims. "But two for her and one for me." I throw her a side-eye, and she winks at me before turning back to him. "You're cute," she states with the slightest hint of a slur as she blinks rapidly, slightly wide-eyed with a flush on her cheeks. "Are you single?"

His smirk turns into an adorable smile complete with twin dimples, and I think Jess might just fall in love with him tonight.

"I am. But I don't make a habit of getting numbers or giving out mine to just any of my customers." He gives her a slow once-over. "Then again, I'm thinking I'd like to make you the exception."

Oh damn. That was a seriously good line. And judging by the expression on Jess's face, it worked perfectly.

"Here," I tell him, leaning over the counter and grabbing a cocktail napkin. I tug a pen from my purse and write down her name and digits. "She's really smart though. And driven. And a vegetarian. So, if you can't deal with any of those things, don't take it." I wave the napkin in front of him.

Jess's ears turn a bright pink, her telltale sign of total embarrassment as she smacks at me. "Bitch."

He snatches it out of my hand without a second's hesitation. "I like smart, driven, beautiful women and since I'm vegan, I have no problems with vegetarian."

Wow. He might be so full of shit with all of this, but right now, he's playing it just right.

"I'm Ben."

"Jess."

"Here, ladies." He pours me two shots of Patron—one a freaking double—and then Jess her single. "This round is on me because I'm hoping you'll stick around until the end of my shift so we can talk some more."

Jess is all wonderful, happy smiles. "I think we can manage that."

I start with my double and then my single. Like bam freaking yes ma'am. Smart idea? Likely not. Do I care in this moment? Not a whip. While my BFF is making her love connection, I'm trying to forget all of mine.

I lean over and give Jess a kiss on the cheek, whispering into her ear so only she can hear, "I'm going to dance. You stay here and talk to hot bartender Ben. Be safe and be smart and no more alcohol, only water. I have my phone and I won't leave until you're with me or I know you're good."

She gives me a kiss in return. "I'm good. Promise. Love you."

"Love you," I tell her as I pull back. "I'm going to dance," I announce so Ben can hear. "Hold my place at the bar."

Jess grins and I point a finger at Ben. "She's a goddess. Treat her like one or I know people who will cut up your body and dump you in so many places even a dentist won't be able to identify you. Get my meaning?"

Ben looks stunned for approximately three seconds before he pulls himself together and nods. "Got it."

Right then. Time to dance.

All around me, drunk gyrating bodies move in the darkness, arms over their heads, hands swaying. My body moves with them as I meander my way through the fray into the heart of the floor. My pulse climbs to the beat as I start to lose myself in the hypnotic sound.

This is exactly what I needed.

No thoughts. No men. No nothing.

Just my body and music.

My heart. My heaven. My life's blood.

No sooner are those thoughts in my mind than a large hand meets my waist. My eyes snap open only to be immediately greeted with a man so close you'd think he was sewn to my shirt. I shift back, removing his hand and shaking my head no. He scowls but smartly moves on quickly.

I spend the next I don't even know how long dancing alone, pushing off unwanted suitors, and occasionally checking on Jess who is getting cozier and cozier with Ben the bartender. She's rocking a big beaming smile that says I was right about her falling in insta-love tonight.

My view of them is cut off as a tall, dark body shifts directly in front of me, forcing my eyes to cast up and my legs to take a step back. The guy grins down at me, inching in a little closer to me despite my blatant head shake. Grabby hands reach out at me when two others firmly grasp my waist, spinning me in place.

I don't need to see his cold green eyes to know who it is.

I smell his cologne before he even rights me in front of him.

"She's with me. Shove off," Henry orders at the guy who is now behind me. Henry menacingly stares him down for another long beat and then the guy must do as he's told because Henry's frigid, dark gaze falls on me.

Ugh. There have to be hundreds of clubs in this city. Why is he here at mine?

"This is supposed to be a man-free night, Gauthier. You can shove off too."

"Stalking me again, Dragonfly," he muses, ignoring my request.

"Clearly, since I was here first," I deadpan, rolling my eyes. Hell, I'm not even an eye-roller but this man just brings out all my bad habits and multiplies them. Wait... "Dragonfly?"

"Yeah, you know, big eyes. Colorful. Long body. *Bites*."

"Put a lot of thought into that nickname, did you?"

Instead of saying something dickish in return, he wraps his hands around my waist, resting them confidently on the crest above my ass as he draws me in. His eyes hold mine as he starts to move us, tossing me back into a swing of a dip that has my hair and hands skimming the floor before snapping me upright just as quickly.

Just like I forced him to do with me that night three years ago.

A breathless laugh escapes before I can stop it, but it dies instantly on my tongue as he presses our bodies seductively together. "What are you doing?" I gasp.

"Dancing with you." As if it's that simple when it's anything but.

One hand slides up through my hair, lifting the heavy sweaty strands from my neck. The other roughly grips my hipbone. His face hovers over mine, his head angled down until our noses practically touch. He's daring me to stop him. To tell him no.

And I should.

But we both know I won't.

That cocky take-no-prisoners smirk curls up his face as he presses in. He doesn't grind or swivel. He just sways, moves in perfect synchronization with the beat, my body a helpless vessel tagging along for the ride. A tirade of angry expletives and snarky words swirl through my mind but just as quickly slip away.

I forgot how well Henry can move.

Add to all this hot as all fuck dancing, he hasn't removed his eyes from mine. Not once. Not even for a moment to get lost in the music. He holds me prisoner. A willing captive. While his lips remain sealed, his eyes are open wide.

"Such a pretty pest, aren't you?"

His words are an angry growl as his forehead drops to mine, his hand tickling the exposed skin of my lower back. I shudder against him, trying to stifle it down, but there is no hiding the way my body responds to his. He licks his lips, his eyes dipping to mine, and I'm about eighty-six percent positive Henry is hard for me. A number I quickly confirm and then add to as I grind my pelvis against his.

"This dance won't end the same way the last one did," I promise. "Despite what you said earlier, I was not daring you into a repeat."

"Sometimes a dance is just a dance, Eden." His hand comes up, his thumb roughly dragging across my lower lip. "Still, I don't need words to know you want me. It's written all over you."

My eyes narrow. "I can say the same about you. Lucky for me, I hate you a hell of a lot more than I want you."

"And if I were to lean in and kiss you?"

"You won't," I snarl, though I practically swallow my tongue at the way he's touching me.

He grins impishly, but it doesn't quite reach his eyes. "You're right. I won't. This dance is already a hell of a lot more than I should be doing with you."

"So why are you then?"

"Good question," he breathes so light I'm not even sure I heard him correctly.

Behind all the dark, lust-fueled temptation is a tormented anger.

Henry is attracted to me and he loathes himself for it. He's disgusted by it. It's the same look I saw in his eyes three years ago, and I simply can't do it again.

"Why are you here?" I continue, attempting to pull away but his grip in my hair tightens. "Let me go. I'm done dancing with you."

"You've become a magnet for my eyes," he tells me, his voice harsh as if he hates this beyond measure. "You hide behind a stupid plant; I see you instantly. You dance as one of hundreds in a dark crowded club; I zero in on you. Not once, but twice. Explain that to me, because it makes no sense."

I shake my head, not understanding him.

He shakes his in return, frustrated.

"I didn't ask you to come dance with me, Henry."

"No. You didn't. And I stood about ten feet away watching you for who knows how long before I even came over."

"Then go back to your cave of seclusion. If I wanted company, I would have it."

His expression grows menacing as he presses himself closer.

"Not on my watch, Eden."

"So that's why you stepped in? Didn't like watching all the men in here coming up to me. Touching me. Trying to dry hump against me as they felt me up. Such a fucking hypocrite. I don't need you to cockblock for me. I'm more than capable of doing that myself."

"Saving yourself for someone in particular? I thought you broke up with the boyfriend. What happened between you and him anyway?"

The boyfriend? I smirk tauntingly. "None of your business." Because if I tell him what happened and Keith finds out, he'll kill Chad. And while I don't care so much about Chad on that end of things, I do on Keith's.

"Must still be your juvenile obsession with me making you turn all the boys away then. If you're over the boyfriend the way you're playing."

"Considering the sight of you now makes me want to reach back in time and smack that silly besotted little girl upside the head, I'd go with no."

"You're a liar. A damn poor one at that. You're all over me, Dragonfly." He tugs my hair, yanking me into his hard chest. He speaks against my mouth, his sweet tequila-tinted breath mixing with my own. "Always have been."

"This must be so *hard* for you." I grind into him, proving my point. His eyes flare. "You can't fuck me—though we both know you want to—and you can't stop me from fucking someone else." I make a show of looking around. "Hmmm... maybe you're right. Maybe a rebound after the boyfriend is exactly what I need tonight. I should find someone. Take them home and fu—"

He grasps my chin, forcing me back to him. "You're not taking anyone home tonight, and you sure as hell aren't fucking any of them either. I'll cockblock you all night, sweetheart."

I shove against him. "Go away, Henry. I don't like you on a good night, and since you showed up, it's turning into a bad one."

"How about you come with me instead."

I don't even get the chance to argue before he releases my hair and grabs my hand instead. My head flies over my shoulder to Jess who is watching me with a strange look I can't read until it turns into a smile and a wave. My eyes narrow at her and she laughs. Traitor. What happened to best friends and man-free zones?

I twist back to Henry, smacking at his shoulder as he shoves me into a waiting elevator.

He backs me up into the corner, hitting the button for five. The private floor. The members only floor. It dawns on me that despite his solo appearance downstairs, he didn't come to this club alone.

He never does.

I grin up at him, licking my lips seductively. I reach down and cup his hard cock through the thick fabric of his pants. He grunts and I take a little too much enjoyment in that sound. "Better get this under control before your best friend sees it and knows all the dirty thoughts you're having about his little sister."

His face dips in, skirting along my cheek until he reaches my ear. He breathes against me and I shudder involuntarily. "Doesn't matter, Dragonfly. He knows I'd never *knowingly* act on them."

Jerk!

He takes a deep inhale of my skin, nips at my earlobe, and steps away from me, smirking like a devil as he does in fact adjust himself to hide the large bulge. The elevator doors part, and he gives me a wink. "Time to face your brother."

I suck in a deep inhale. *Shit.*

FIVE

HENRY

Once upon a time, things were worse than they are now. Day was night. Night was a million times worse than day. And despair mixed with longing turned to resentment, turned to hate before my very eyes.

I was young when it started. But that didn't mean I was immune to its effects. If anything, it was worse because of that. I learned the reality of what love is truly capable of. The power it can wield. The devastation it can reap. The lives it can ruin without breaking a sweat.

How cruel indifference can be.

What a hateful monster jealousy is.

It changed me. I like to think for the better.

Like a blow to the head or a badge of honor. Call it what you want, survival and pleasure became my only game. Pain and love my nemesis. And I was good with that. It felt right and safe and just. It held me together when some days, I wasn't sure anything could.

When I was twelve years old, I made a promise to myself that I would never be them. That I would never fall in love. That I would never—and I mean fucking ever—let a woman get her hands on my heart or my soul.

Then I saw *her* dancing in a club one night.

A woman I can never have. A woman I do not deserve to touch. Hell, a woman I simply do not deserve. So even though hurting her felt like the worst thing ever, I persevered where others would have succumbed.

Pretend was my fortress. Denial my battlefield. Acceptance a place I never found sanctuary in.

That last one was my downfall.

Let it be known this very instant.

My inability to hold firm on this despite my rhetoric is what ultimately acts as my handicap. Only this is no golf game where no one gives a shit. This is learning, knowing, owning boundaries and sticking to them because that's the kind of guy you are, and you discovered long ago nothing else matters but that.

Lust is simply a weapon. Terms for manipulation.

That's all this is, I remind myself. Lust.

I step back and allow Eden to exit first. I'm not being a gentleman. A gentleman wouldn't be as hard for her as I am. No, I'm a piece of shit deviant who needs a second to get his dick under control before he delivers his best friend's little sister to him.

Still, that threat has yet to stop me from acting where she's concerned.

It's no joke that Keith is an overprotective bastard when it comes to his sisters. He's pointblank warned me off Eden in the past when I've tested the waters by joking with him about me and her. So what the fuck am I doing waiting for her at her car? Grinding with her in a dark club and allowing her to touch my cock like they're about to get intimately reacquainted?

They're not.

They never can.

I scowl before I can stop it, and once I realize I am, I straighten my features, going for indifference and impervious and some other words that start with "i" that I can't think of right now.

Keith is so much more than my best friend. So much more than my bandmate. He's the brother I never had, and I will not risk that. Not for anything or anyone.

"You could have warned me."

I shrug dismissively.

"I'm surprised he sent you to get me," she continues, her eyes casting over her shoulder for a beat before returning to the private floor of the club.

"He didn't. I always hit up the main floor on my own first. That's when I saw you."

She stops dead in her tracks, spinning around to face me. Her head tilting and her eyebrows scrunched in stunned confusion. "But he knows you saw me earlier today, right? He knows where I've been working?"

I shake my head. "I haven't told him yet."

"For real?"

"You need to be the one to tell him, Eden. Not me."

"Oh boy." She emits a breathy laugh. "That almost makes this worse, though I think having the element of surprise on my side will go a long way." With a skip in her step, she spins back around, scanning the dance floor, the tables, then booths for her brother.

I chuckle under my breath, doing everything I can not to stare at her in the outfit she's wearing. A white lacy crop top that shows off her smooth, toned stomach and black jeweled bellybutton ring. It has cups like a bra, and they push her small but perky tits up perfectly. Add to that tiny, skintight black short-shorts and cute little leopard print flats. She's revealing more than she's covering, and my hands and eyes certainly appreciated every inch of smooth bare flesh when we were dancing.

She looks so different than she did three years ago.

Her hair is no longer its luscious flowing chestnut brown. Now it's some version of purple, deep and rich and silky looking sure... but now it's shoulder length and she has bangs that flirt with one eye. Between her purple hair, nose ring, the scattering of colorful tattoos, this girl is so far removed from the sweet little thing who looked deeply into my eyes that night with a smile that robbed me of my senses and breath.

My eyes drag lazily over her...

Quit it! This chick is numero uno on my do not touch list.

And then she shows up like this.

Doesn't she know what dressing like this, what looking like this, is doing to me?

"I don't know what you're so afraid of with him," I muse. "He's a kitten wrapped in a giant teddy bear."

She laughs at the imagery. "That's not quite how I picture him. But we'll see if all my fears are for naught..." She trails off, spotting our large private setup along the far wall and heading that way.

She can talk all the shit she wants but the second she spots Keith; her face erupts into an all-encompassing, excited smile.

Bursting across the room at a sprint, she launches herself directly onto Keith's lap, tossing her arms around his broad shoulders and squeezing the life from him. He jolts upright, surprised at the sudden intruder and ready to throw her off until he realizes who she is and then he wraps her up in an equally as crushing hug.

I hear him scolding her as I approach but the look of delight on his face isn't selling his harsh words. "Where the hell did you come from? I've been calling and texting you non-stop, Eden. No one tells me anything. Not Mom. Not even Maia, who I know you've become friends with. What the hell?"

Eden draws back, laughing at Keith's pathetic attempt at ire. She scoots off his lap and sits beside him, dropping her head against his huge arm. I'm forced to take the seat beside her since the rest of the U-shaped booth is occupied by Jasper, Gus, and Keith. Naomi, Gus's fiancée; Viola, Jasper's wife; and Maia are out on the dancefloor, laughing and dancing in their own private bubble.

"I came here tonight with Jess. You remember her, right?"

Keith nods, taking a sip of his signature Jack Daniels. "Yeah. Jess Hill. You've been best friends forever."

"Well, we live together now. She's at UCLA for law school starting this fall but she's taking summer prep classes."

"You're a brat for living in my city and avoiding me."

"I didn't have a choice, Keith."

"That's total crap, Ede. How did you get up here anyway?"

Eden juts her thumb in my direction. "This guy found me dancing downstairs and dragged me up."

Keith's eyes track up to mine, shining bright with gratitude as he sticks out his fist for me to pound. If I didn't feel like shit before, I certainly do now.

I pour myself a glass of tequila only to have Eden steal the thing directly from my grasp before taking a large sip. "Help yourself," I deadpan.

"I already did, thanks." She winks at me, licking her lips.

I stare, mesmerized. Those lips. I remember those lips. How they felt against mine. How they tasted—like cherries with her gloss and a hint of tequila since that's what she drinks. Like I do.

I clear my thoughts and turn away.

She takes another sip finishing it off and then tries to grab at the bottle from my hand next. Brat. I snatch it back, smacking at her as she attempts to fight me for it. "Goddammit, this is mine." I don't even care if I sound like I'm five. This girl drives me up a wall like no one else.

"Just pour me some and stop being a dick."

"How about you stop being a brat and maybe I will."

Keith's eyes dance suspiciously back and forth between us and I feel my gut twist. I pour Eden some more and then slide away from her, as far as I can without falling off the edge of the stupid bench, taking the bottle with me.

"Why you hidin' from me, Ede?" Keith asks, drawing her attention back to him. That's when Jasper starts to laugh under his breath.

All eyes swivel to him, the casual motherfucker leaning back and sipping whatever the hell he's sipping as he stoically watches everything with the astute eye of an eagle. Even Gus, turns to stare at his fraternal twin with a bemused expression, so whatever Jasper knows, he's not in on it.

Jasper's green eyes lock on Eden as she growls in resignation, slumping back dramatically into the stiff cushioned bench. She throws one leg over the other, using the toe of her shoe to point at Jasper. "I should have known you'd know. You know everything. You always have. Even when I was eight and accidentally broke Keith's favorite drumsticks and then blamed it on Joy."

"That was you?" Keith barks, and Eden shrugs at him, grinning while trying to appear innocent. "Shit. I yelled at Joy for like an hour."

"Yeah. I felt a little bad about that." She shrugs again and then turns back to Jasper. "For real, how do you know?"

Jasper's smirk says sorry not sorry while the rest of him stays locked in that half brooding, half impervious mask he's perfected over the years. "Harry has been blowing up my phone for over a week now about you."

"What?" Keith, Gus, and I all burst out at once. "Harry Evans?" Gus finishes for us, though there is only one Harry we all know.

"Why didn't you tell me?" Keith snaps at Jasper who just rolls his eyes and shakes his head dismissively.

"Because you're like this." He points at him. "And really, it was up to Eden to tell you. Not me."

Keith pivots back to Eden, jutting his chin in her direction while eyeing her accusingly. "You're at Turn? I thought you were thinking Sony or some other label."

She wolfs down the rest of the drink I just poured her and shifts in her seat, squaring her shoulders as if she's readying to do battle.

And for the first time since hearing she's been ghosting Keith; I finally understand why.

He doesn't look proud or delighted. He looks pissed.

"I was. Kinda. I didn't want them though. They only offered me unpaid internships. Lyric offered me a real job as an associate producer. She offered it last summer after I finished my internship with her. I didn't say anything to you for this very reason, Keith." She points an angry finger into his stern face. "Can you see why I couldn't say yes to those other crap gigs? Why this was a real shot for me? Or are you just gonna be pissed I'm at *your* label?"

His jaw locks at her mocking tone. "What's that supposed to mean?"

She throws her hands up in the air. "It means your face says it all. You have no faith in me, and you never have. I *earned* this job myself. You didn't help me get it."

"How can you say that when you're working for our producer at our label?"

"Because I'm good at my job!" she yells, not even caring if others around us are looking, which they're starting to. She plants her hand into his chest, not shoving but holding him steady, letting him know she means business. "Maybe I got the initial internship four years ago because of you, but I kept it because of me. I got this job because I'm talented. Because I know what the fuck I'm doing." She jams her fist into his chest as she levels her brother with a glare for the ages.

"Harry said she's the real deal," Jasper jumps in, defending Eden who smiles gratefully at him and smugly at Keith. Keith shifts, looking like he's ready to get into it some more when Jasper asks, "Do you have any of them?"

"What?" both Eden and Keith snap.

"The songs you were working on with Cyber's Law? Do you have any of them I can hear?"

Eden blinks at Jasper a few times, momentarily speechless. "Y-yes." She clears her throat. "Yes. I have one of them on my phone."

Jas holds out his hand expectantly, palm side up. "Give it here. If it's shit, I'll be the first one to tell you."

She laughs nervously because even though Jasper would never

tell her *that*, he will be honest, and she knows it. "Thanks," she grumbles, but starts fishing through her small purse to retrieving her phone and her AirPods. She calls up the song and then hands them both to him. "You might have trouble hearing in here."

He shakes his head as he places the buds in his ears, cupping his hands over them as he hits play. We all stare dumbfounded at Jasper, waiting for the verdict as he closes his eyes and listens intently. Three minutes later a pleased grin cracks his lips, and he hands the pods and phone to Gus. "Listen to this, brother," Jas commands, tapping his finger on the screen of the phone. "You'll like the hell out of it."

Now it's Gus's turn and not even a full minute in, his eyes pop open to meet his twin's, nodding in sync to whatever beat he's hearing. "Yeah, man. Did you catch the sweet break after that G?"

Jasper grins, rubbing the back of his neck. "I knew you'd like that."

"That was my idea," Eden offers confidently, sitting up a little straighter as she recrosses her legs. "There needed to be a pause after so much build."

"Totally agree." Gus continues to listen and then when the song is over, removes the pods and hands them to me. Evidently, we're punishing Keith and making him wait. "Killer tunes, Ede. Nicely done, girl."

Eden tries to contain her triumphant gleam as she nods her appreciation at Gus.

"You really did some songs for Cyber's Law?" Keith asks just as I place the pods in my ears and hit play. The sound of their voices and the beat of club music drowns out as Cyber's Law blasts through my ears, Harry's soft voice a constant juxtaposition to the hard sound of their music. I listen for that break Gus was talking about and when it comes, it's... flawless. But this song is more than that. The flow of it, the synchronization of the instruments...

I stop listening before the track ends, having already heard enough.

"As much as I hate to admit it, they're right. It's legit."

"Thanks so much," Eden snarks at me. "I know those words must have really burned your ass to say. You okay? Should we call an ambulance?"

I flip her off and she bats her eyelashes, blowing me a kiss.

"Knock it off. I mean it. It's legit."

I hand off the phone and AirPods to Keith. He takes his turn listening, staring directly at Eden, his expression now depicting nothing but awe. "You did this." Only it's not a question. It's a statement. "Hell, Ede."

"I told you," she boasts. "My job there has nothing to do with you. This is why I waited. I didn't want to tell you where I was working until I could prove to you that I had earned it."

Keith looks like he just swallowed a bug that crapped in his mouth. "I'm sorry I said all that. I was wrong, babe. Seriously wrong. You did good. I'm insanely proud of you."

He gives her a hug, planting a kiss to the top of her head as they whisper things back and forth that no one else can hear, smiling and laughing like it's all just so easy for them.

And for a moment, I can't look away. I'm hypnotized. Entranced. Jealous...

I've always known how close Keith is with his sisters. He helped raise them while his parents worked long hours. Hell, I lived with them for the majority of my high school life.

But it's something else entirely to witness it before me when I haven't in years.

Yet another reminder of how different my *family* is than Keith's or even Gus's and Jasper's. They grew up with loving parents. With siblings who love them.

And me? That's nowhere close to what I had.

"Well, now that we know Eden is a kick-ass producer, this makes my little impromptu band meeting a hell of a lot easier," Jasper announces, a sparkle to his wicked smile as he claps his hands together, rubbing them like an evil genius. "Eden, how do you feel about taking on the production of our next album?"

Her breath catches high in her chest, staring at him with wide, unblinking eyes. Her hands fall to her lap and she grips her knees, utterly astonished and completely speechless.

Jasper grins. "Don't get too excited yet. There's a catch."

SIX

HENRY

"What's the catch?" Eden asks, finally finding her voice and completely ignoring the ridiculousness of producing our next album. An album we haven't even started yet.

Jasper casually takes a sip of his drink while dropping his other arm along the top of the booth. "The catch is that I need this album done in the next two-and-a-half months. Three weeks of that will be while on vacation. Adalyn is starting kindergarten this fall. Once that happens, I plan to take a break from touring and producing albums and be with all of my girls. Kindergarten is going to be a huge transition for Adalyn."

I fall back into the cushion of the seat, stupidly floored. I gulp down the rest of my drink, when what I really want to do is chuck it across the room to watch the glass shatter. What is Jasper up to? Offering something so monumental up in such a thoughtless, cavalier way?

I knew this was coming.

Not the Eden part, but the break part. That I knew was coming.

It's something we as a band have discussed a lot over the last year. Adalyn with her autism has trouble with transitions. So much trouble with any alteration in her routine. She doesn't like new experiences. She doesn't like new people. She thrives on consistency and has been surrounded by Jasper and Viola practically non-stop. Us too, but it's not the same.

Kindergarten is going to push her and it's going to push Jasper and Viola.

Add to that Maia is pregnant, and Gus and Naomi are going to be starting fertility treatments—

"I finished writing this last album on our last tour and I need it to be done by September first. If Lyric were in LA, we could likely pull it together quickly even though the music isn't done, just the lyrics. But not only is she not in LA, and can't be so for recording any time soon, my lovely wife has informed me that she and Naomi have gotten their pretty heads together and planned a three-week vacation for all of us in Hawaii."

"Hawaii," Eden parrots. "And you said you want to record during this trip?"

"Yes. We won't have a choice with the time constraint I'm imposing."

She glances around at each one of us in turn, her gaze ghosting mine. "When are you leaving for Hawaii?" she questions as if giving this some serious consideration. And that just cannot happen. None of this. Her doing our album. Her vacationing with us. No. Absolutely not.

"Two weeks or so."

I choke on my drink, the tequila hitting the back of my throat at the worst possible second, making me cough and gasp while the alcohol burns like a son of a bitch. "Two weeks? A fucking vacation, Jasper?" I grunt out, bolting forward with my elbows digging into my thighs as I stare my friend down.

Gus laughs, saluting me with his drink. "Dude, you were the one who mentioned a private island for all of us to vacation on."

My hand finds the rough grains of my stubble. I *was* the one who suggested that. But that was seven or so months ago and mostly I was just musing about it. I didn't think... it was meant to be in the future. Hypothetical. I really didn't think...

"I know, but..." I can't finish my thought. None of this is what I had in mind.

"My wife wants a special vacation before Adalyn starts kindergarten. Naomi wants a special vacation before she starts treatments. Maia wants a special vacation before she pops out a kid and walks down the aisle."

And I'm the single guy out, the bass player, so I don't really get a say.

That's what they're saying and not saying.

Truly, in fairness, I never cared before. I was always fine with saying yes. To going with the flow because I had no reason not to. Until now.

"And you want Eden to do this?" Keith blusters, just as incredulous as I am.

"She's got the talent," Jasper states. "She's an associate, which means she does whatever Lyric says, and she'll still have oversight. And we need this album done quickly. Even on vacation. If the songs need some more polishing, that can be done after we've finished laying down the main tracks."

Christ.

I scrub my hands up and down my face and then grab my goddamn bottle. I down a few gulps only to have Eden attempt to steal it once again from me. This time I let her. She does the same, downing large gulps with a panic-stricken look splitting her features in two.

"You're serious with this?" She stares at Jasper, bewildered. "Jas..."

"I just heard your work, Eden. Both songs actually, not just the one you played for us tonight. Harry sent me the track you finished today to me earlier this evening. I spent the last ten days listening to Harry brag about how perfect you are. I understand I have to put it to a vote since that's how we roll as a band, but from my point of view,

I'm offering you the job of producer for Wild Minds' next studio album."

"That makes me too," Gus adds, because if Jasper says he wants her and has confidence that she can do this, Gus is in. Hell, that's usually enough for all of us. That's how much we trust our front-man's judgment on things.

Keith meets Eden's eyes with a smile that tells me I'm the last man standing. "I'm sorry I wasn't by your side from the start. I get shitty and weird when it comes to this stuff. But you're my sister, and I absolutely believe in you. You can do this, Ede. If you want it, it's yours."

She coughs out an astonished laugh, overwhelmed by the way this night has turned for her. She takes Keith's hand. "If you're for real and you get Lyric to sign off on this, I'm in. It would be a dream come true to produce one of my brother's albums. Add to that your faith that I can do it. I'm honored and humbled and would never ever let you down."

I can't stop my mind from going a million miles a minute. What the hell is happening? They're offering Eden a job as our producer for our next album? She's as wet behind the ears as it gets. One or two decent songs does not a producer make.

Jasper wants this done in two-and-a-half months, three weeks of that while we're on some vacation in Hawaii? That means she'd come. With us. On vacation. In Hawaii. Sunshine and beaches and... bikinis.

"We just released an album this year," I argue. This cannot happen. Surely, he has to see how nonsensical this idea of his is.

"Marco thinks we should hold on to this new one until next spring or summer and release it then for Grammy and sales reasons," Jasper clarifies. "But for the sake of Ady and my girls, the sooner we get this finished the better. In truth, I think we could all use this upcoming time off. We've been going non-stop for a decade, Henry. Ten years and seven albums. Soon to be eight."

Jesus. This is just...

"And you think we can record an album while on vacation?" I'm skeptical. And a fucking wreck. And hoping he sees that's just lunacy.

"I'm thinking if we spend fifty percent of our time recording this album in the three weeks we're there, we can get at least a few songs of it done."

He's got this all mapped out. All nod in agreement because they're on the same page. Keith glances over his shoulder at a pregnant Maia dancing on the dance floor. Gus is staring at Naomi too, obviously thinks about the tough road they are about to venture down with regards to their own baby-making dreams.

Me? I'm thinking about the fact that our little girl, our Adalyn, is going to be starting kindergarten and needs all the love, support, and attention to be on her. I blow out a silent breath, forcing myself to focus on the only brothers, the only real family I have in this world, and let out another slow, steady breath.

"If this is what you need done, I'm in," I tell them because how I can be anything but.

It won't be as bad as I'm making it out to be. I can ignore Eden Dawson easily enough. There will be plenty to distract to me. My friends. Their wives. Adalyn and baby Cora. Music. Fucking Hawaii. Yeah, I can do this.

Eden won't even enter into it.

That's the vow I silently make to myself. Eden won't distract me. I won't let her. It's an attraction that ends here and now.

I quickly stand, ready to get the hell out of this club. Away from this girl who is staring up at me with bright blue inquisitive eyes that I cannot meet. Playtime's over. Hell, playtime never should have begun.

"I'm gonna head out." Jasper, Gus, and Keith scrutinize me with questioning looks I refuse to answer. I'm never the first to go home. I'm always the last and whenever I do leave, I'm rarely alone.

This woman is already messing everything up with me.

"No woman tonight, Henry?" Keith teases, but there is no humor in his eyes.

"Who says there wasn't already? Just because you're sitting here like a pansy on a stick waiting for your girl to come over and give you some attention doesn't mean that's how I roll."

Gus snickers under his breath. "You speaking for all of us then, bro?"

"Nah." I grin at him. "Only the dickmonger giving me shit. You can feel free to watch your woman all night long, brother."

"So... was there a girl then?" Keith presses, and I know what he's doing. I don't even bother trying to lie.

"Yup," I tell him, staring straight into his eyes because he didn't ask me if I fucked one. Just if there was someone. Nuances, but I'll take it. "Am I allowed to leave now Dad, or do I have to fuck my way through the club before you'll let me? Or do you need details so your wifed-up ass can live vicariously?"

Keith laughs. "Dude, did you look out on the dance floor? Do you not see the three hottest chicks in this place dancing? Yeah, now you know why we're wifed-up." He gestures to Jasper and Gus. "Ain't nothing better. Trust me on that. Wouldn't kill you to do the same. Club pussy gets old, man. They" —he points back at their women dancing— "don't."

"Actually, I think you have that reversed. Club pussy I believe stays around the same age. One of the benefits of it."

"You men are fucking pigs. It's seriously a wonder we allow you access to not only our bodies but our hearts." Eden rises, turning to me. "Will you drop me at home?" she questions, her voice soft and her tone filled with nerves I instinctively know have nothing to do with asking me for a ride.

No. No, Eden, I will not drive you home. Because being in a car alone with you not only makes my dick hard, it will permeate my goddamn leather with your scent. With your warmth. It will fill my head! And my head being filled with you is worse than a fucking migraine.

How does she not see that?

Only all eyes are suddenly on me, and I have no choice. Once again.

"Yeah. Sure. Whatever."

I do the bro shake/hug with my guys and wave to the ladies still having the time of their lives on the dance floor—though they were watching us the entire time and not very good at hiding it—and don't glance over my shoulder to see if little miss trouble is following.

I don't care if she is.

"You don't think I can do this," she murmurs after she catches up to me and we approach the elevator.

"Your brother and the guys seem pretty convinced you can."

"But not you."

I lean back against the glass wall of the elevator, staring out at the club below as we slowly descend to the first floor. "It doesn't matter what I think. Does your friend need a ride too?"

"No. Jess is sticking around with the bartender she met earlier. I already texted her letting her know I was leaving."

I don't say anything, just force myself not to look at her as we exit the club and wait for my car to be returned from the valet.

"For the record, you're not my favorite person either," she announces as she clicks the buckle for her seat belt, the valet shutting the door for her.

"No?" I laugh under my breath as I pull away from the curb and out into the Los Angeles night.

"No," she states simply, adjusting her position until she's facing me instead of looking out the windshield or the passenger side window as any normal person would do. "You used to be. When I was little, I used to plan our wedding. You wore a traditional black tux and my white gown looked like Cinderella's—"

"Is there a reason you're telling me this?"

I catch her smiling out of the corner of my eye. "There is actually. Since that night you treated me like a whore at the club—"

"I did not treat you like a whore," I snap, gripping the steering wheel so tight my knuckles turn white. "I never treat any woman like a whore, and I never think of them that way either. Women are entitled to seek pleasure and take it wherever and whenever they choose. That's on them. I am always honest about my intentions as I was with you that night. You agreed, readily. I fucked you thinking you were someone else only to find out you were you. That part was on me."

"Who did you think I was?"

I laugh mirthlessly, dragging a hand across my jaw and around to the back of my neck. I glance in her direction, staring into her cerulean eyes in the dark. "Not Eden Dawson."

"That's exactly my point." She runs her finger along the leather stitching of her seat, watching me, and I look back to the road. I can't even with this chick.

"I have no idea what you're getting at."

"You wanted any other woman than me and all I had wanted was you. So now you understand why I've spent the last three years hating you."

I do understand it. I understood it before she laid it out for me. I don't blame her either. I saw it in her eyes that night. I broke her heart. I always thought her infatuation was adolescent in nature and that since she'd grown up and went to college, it was done. Truth, I didn't give it much consideration because she was a kid.

But that night... her eyes... part of me broke right along with her.

That's the one thing with all of this that makes no sense to me.

I've hurt women before. They've gotten attached when I told them not to. They thought they could change me. That they'd be the exception. Only no woman is, and no woman ever will be.

But Eden lingered with me.

It was like when I broke her heart, a piece of it found its way into me. Imbedded itself.

That still doesn't change the reality as it stands: Her brother would kill me if he knew what I did to her. What I still want to do to her. Despite the sassy hellfire that rages from within her, she's a good, sweet girl who deserves to be loved and cherished like the stunning, perfect creature she is.

But I will never be that man for her, Keith notwithstanding.

I will never get attached to a woman nor desire anything above the physical here and now with them.

"I never meant to hurt you, Eden. Never. But you should hate me," I tell her. "It will make all this easier for both of us. Your adolescent fantasy of me will never be a reality."

"Except I want to do this album, Henry. And hating you is exhausting. Keith won't understand it either without explanation. I'm over you. That ship sailed away three years ago. So how about you stop being an asshole and I'll stop being a bitch and we just focus on our jobs."

A strange ache suddenly pierces my chest, making it cave in on itself. I rub my fist over it, desperate to wipe whatever the hell it is away. I clear my throat. "Is this your way of trying to call a truce?"

"Yeah. I think it is. Do you see any other way?"

I think on this for a moment and realize that she's unfortunately right. If I'm a dick to her, Keith will wonder why. He'll want explanations, as she said. Explanations I can't give. It appears I'm stuck with Eden until I can shake her loose once more. "Fine. Truce. But if I ignore you, just deal with it." It's the only way this can go with us.

SEVEN

HENRY

"All I'm asking is how you found her." Keith feigns nonchalance as he flips a pancake wearing a fucking apron and a bullshit smile.

"I told you already, I just did."

"In the dark amongst hundreds of other people? Was that before or after you were with this random mystery woman?"

That smile is so misleading. He's readying to slide a butcher's knife out of the block by his right hand and slice my neck open with it.

"Yup," I tell him. "She was on the bar side of the dance floor. It was serendipitous."

Keith sharply cuts away from his frying pan, eyeing me harshly. Likely because I've never used a word like serendipitous in my life. But that doesn't change the Spanish Inquisition style of this questioning. The fact that I'm not already shackled up by my balls is a wonder. We are talking about Eden Dawson after all. Keith's precious baby sister.

"And then what?" he asks, returning to his pan.

"And then he brought her upstairs, dickwad," Maia chimes in, trying to be helpful. "Shut up, already with this. I'm hungry.

Growing your kid is no joke. I don't understand how I'm eating every-thing I see and yet I'm still hungry."

I would get up and hug Maia if I could, but I think it's pretty damn clear why I can't. I can never let Keith know I'm grateful for the distraction she's trying to present. As if I require the distraction. Like I'm guilty of something.

"Breakfast is almost ready. And I'm telling you, we're having twins."

Maia adamantly shakes her head, gearing up for battle. "They only heard one heartbeat."

"Then they missed the second one. I have twins in my family. It's twins, Pandora. I know it. But I also know what you're trying to do, and I'm not done questioning my friend here."

I groan loudly, scrubbing my hands up and down my face and pushing annoyance out of every pour. "Come on, man. You're making this into so much more than it has to be."

"And you're getting the best goddamn breakfast ever, so deal with it. We're talking about you and Eden," Keith brusquely reminds me. "I am entitled to my line of questioning."

"You're not entitled to anything if it keeps me from my breakfast. And truth, Eden is a grown woman, older than I am."

"She dated a douchebag who didn't appreciate her," Keith protests, pointing the end of his spatula at Maia.

"Haven't we all," Maia retorts, rolling her eyes. "That has nothing to do with Henry. Back off this already. And I'm telling you now, Keith Dawson, if you point that spatula at me like that again I will declare my boobs a no-go zone."

"No, you won't."

"I wouldn't try testing me. I'm hungry. Can we be done with this now?"

Keith grunts, but instead of letting it die, his anger only grows, demonstrated by the harsh scrape of the spatula under the pancakes and the hard flip onto the plate beside him. Then the spatula goes right back, pointed directly at Maia. "Who says this has nothing to do with Henry?" The spatula waves in my direction before swinging back to her. "Henry's been talking about how much he wants my sister for years now."

I slam my fork down, garnering both their attentions. "Nothing is going on between me and Eden. That was just me fucking with you. Now let it drop."

His eyes narrow into twin slits of accusation. "Then why did you refuse to look at her last night? Why did you act all weird and shit when you brought her upstairs? You were quiet. And drinking more than you normally do. And—"

"You were watching him pretty closely," Maia chirps. "You sure you're not in love with him instead of me?"

I reach under the counter and squeeze her hand. She squeezes back because Maia and I talk. Sometimes a little too much. Sometimes about things I should absolutely not talk about with my best friend's fiancée, baby mama. But she and I get each other. We're cut from the same cloth. Our upbringings, though different, have some surprisingly awful similarities.

"My love for Henry is well established. Now stop trying to change the subject." He practically stomps, throwing a toddler-size fit. "I know what you're doing, Maia. I'm on to you."

"Maybe I should go while you two hash this out," I suggest, partially rising up out of my seat. Both their eyes cast over to me, Keith's growing more recriminating. I likely should have kept my mouth shut.

"No. Sit. Speak."

"I'm not a dog, asshole," I snort, hiking up on the rung of the barstool, taking matters into my own hands and reaching to grab a pancake off the plate they're cooling on beside the pan. I drop it onto my plate, lick my fingers, and start lathering the fluffy cake with butter and the good maple syrup before Maia polishes it all off.

The room falls uncomfortably silent and just as I'm shoveling the perfect bite into my mouth, I can resist no longer. I peek up to find Keith and Maia facing off in a silent fight.

"Will you two stop," I grouse through a mouthful of food. "You're getting like Jas and Vi."

Maia scoffs at that, grinning smugly at Keith. "No way. We fight way better than those two."

Keith not so casually scoops a stack of pancakes onto a plate before handing the mammoth thing to Maia. Then he thrusts his spatula at me as if it were a sword. "Did you kiss Eden when you took her home?"

"No. Of course not." Though I absolutely wanted to. It's a problem, but not an insurmountable one. I chalk it up to the whole forbidden fruit thing. Her name says it all, right? I want a woman I can't have simply because I can't have her. But just sex for me could never be just sex for her, so we're back to baseline. "Again, nothing is going on between me and Eden!"

He lowers his current weapon of choice and goes about pouring more batter into the pan. And for a few moments, the only sound in the room is sizzling and popping as the batter cooks and browns. Maia is chowing down. I should be, but I can't remove my eyes from my friend.

Keith is frustratingly still as he stares blankly at the pan, lifting a corner of a pancake before flipping it with skill and precision.

"Keith?"

He doesn't answer me at first and my heart starts to jack up. Keith is never this still. Rarely this quiet. He's a drummer, for fuck's sake. He is an in-your-face guy in case you missed this whole encounter. The endearing bastard is lovable to a fault. But he also tends to bottle shit up in his head and that's what scares me most about him. He's been suffering from PTSD for more than a decade after the death of his high school girlfriend, Amy. So the silent Keith is an ominous Keith.

Finally, he turns on me and the force of his eyes pulls me back upright.

"What?" I push out. "Dude, just say it."

"I'm going to sound like a dick."

His somber expression holds any potential retort frozen on my tongue.

"I don't want you to think..." He puffs out a breath, turning off the stove, dropping his fists—spatula still clutched in one—to his hips. "I don't want you to fuck my sister."

Well shit. There it is.

"Who said I was planning to?" But with those words, something inside of me drops.

"Planning to, maybe not. Wanting to, absolutely. You've been talking about Ede since she came to that club after our concert in Bama three years ago. I saw the way you weren't looking at her last night. I know you, Henry. I've known you my whole goddamn life. You want my sister."

I do, so I can't deny it.

In truth, I'm not exactly sure why I've been talking about Eden all these years, other than she was stuck on my mind when no woman ever has. I knew nothing would come of it. I knew I'd never act. I always understood Eden was above my pay grade. Maybe I was simply testing just how deep his not wanting me near his sister went.

Newsflash: It goes deep!

Which is why his words should resemble something very close to relief for me. What if he had said, yeah, sure, Henry, go for it. I give you my blessing. What then? I will never allow a woman to own me, and Eden is the type of woman who could do it without even breaking a sweat.

"Relax, big brother. It's not like that with me and her." I fork up another bite of my now cold pancake, forcing it into my mouth so I don't say what I'm actually thinking.

"Henry?"

"Keith, let it go," Maia snaps. "You spanked me in an elevator and went down on me in a bathroom at a party."

"Um. I think I'm going to throw up."

Maia rolls her eyes at me like I'm being a child before turning back to Keith. "I'm proving a point."

"And that is?" Keith snaps, plating two more pancakes for himself and placing two strips of deliciously crisp bacon that I didn't get on Maia's plate.

"Can I have some bacon?"

Keith flips me off without sparing me a glance. Awesome.

"My point is that you're in no place to judge," Maia clarifies. "Eden is a grown woman. She is smart. She is capable. She broke up with the douchebag and that's all there is to it. If she decides to mess around with Henry—"

"She's not messing around with me," I roar, growing more flustered by the second with this conversation and the goddamn incessant cycle it's stuck on. "Can we just quit it already?"

Keith brushes Maia off and turns to me, staring me dead in the eyes. "You are my brother and I love you. But Eden is my baby sister, and you are admittedly not a guy who wants the life Jasper, Gus, and I have chosen. Am I missing something? Has that changed?"

I pause, fork in mid-air.

"You barely date, and whenever you do, those relationships—if you can even call them that—are purely physical. You don't get involved. You don't give a shit. I'm not judging, okay? I'm not. Hell, I was worse before I found Maia. But the point is, I found her, and I stopped because other women no longer appealed. You have no intention of doing that. Tell me if I'm wrong here."

"No." I clear my throat. "You're not wrong."

"Care to finally tell me why that is?"

"No."

It's the one secret I have. The one thing I won't discuss with anyone. The one thing I've never discussed with anyone. Not even when I was a kid and living through it and had to rely on my best friends to get me through. I hid everything from everyone because I knew no one would understand. Hell, I didn't understand. Now it's just the way I choose to live my life and I have no plans on changing that.

Not even for a certain purple-haired goddess.

"If you never plan on falling in love, Henry, then please, for me, for our friendship, keep your hands to yourself. If we end up working with Eden, then I know you can't stay away from her completely. But keep your distance. She fancied herself in love with you growing up. She just got out of a long relationship that I suspect ended with her getting hurt. I'd hate for any dormant feelings she has for you to resurface only to get her heart broken again."

I stare at my best friend and swallow thickly as I think on his words. His warning.

I picture Eden in my head and my chest clenches. I don't want her to get hurt again. I never want that for her. I hurt her once already and the idea of doing it again makes me physically ill.

A painful gust of air pushes past my lungs.

I force down everything in me that's telling me not to make this promise.

And I lie. "Eden doesn't even register on my radar."

Maia's head flies in my direction, her lips pursed, and her expression poised in a 'I'm calling bullshit' position. I ignore that too. My eyes flash to hers and she quickly reads me. A little too quickly and a lot too accurately, but Maia is like that, and I knew that before I met her unrelenting gaze.

I turn back to Keith who looks mollified.

"Well, that's a relief. Let's keep it that way."

Maia frowns, and I stare down at my plate, trying not to.

He's right and I know it. Staying away from her is the only play I have where she's concerned. Now I just have to figure out how to keep my promise.

EIGHT

EDEN

Everything that has ever seemed too good to be true, always is. Isn't that what they say? A universal life rule or Murphy's law? I keep waiting for the other shoe to drop. For someone to pinch me and I wake up angry and frustrated that my dream, *my freaking dream*, isn't real.

But as I sit in a huge corporate, stuffy boardroom at Turn Records, the walls anointed with framed gold and platinum records, I start to hold on to a glimmer of hope that maybe, just this once, I won't wake up. That my dream is a reality and it's not too good to be true.

Lyric flew in for this Monday morning meeting. And believe me, Lyric Rose hates to fly in unless she has to. Lyric, who is now pregnant with her first baby, likes staying in New York with her husband Jameson and her best friend Ethan, who incidentally flew in as well since they clearly can't do anything without the other.

"Can someone explain to me why this couldn't be done over Zoom? Do you know what a redeye flight does to the complexion?" Ethan grouses, checking his reflection in his phone's camera, tilting his head this way and that. "These bags are bigger than the ones Winona Ryder tried shoplifting out of Sacks 5th Avenue."

I snort out a harsh laugh before just as quickly tucking it back.

"Everyone forgave her once she starred in Stranger Things."

Ethan cocks an eyebrow in my direction before just as quickly dismissing me and returning to his face. "No one is forgiving these blotches, honey. I will never fly overnight again."

This room is filled. Way beyond just the members of Wild Minds, me, Lyric, and Ethan. No. It's like the crew all decided to get together and do this gang-style because Marco, Viola, Maia, and Naomi are all here as well. You'd think this was some serious business meeting, but I don't think anyone in this room, well, maybe other than Jasper and Maia, does serious.

"I wouldn't either if I were you. It makes you look like an old woman with big pores, bags under her eyes, and wrinkles. So, *so* many wrinkles."

Ethan flips Naomi off who is smirking like she just nailed his number.

See what I mean? Nothing serious going on here.

"These are wisdom lines," he retorts brusquely, though his tone has no bite. "Not wrinkles. Just wait until you're my age, peaches and cream. You'll look like an ancient Prada bag with all the sun you expose your face to when you surf."

Naomi cackles out a laugh. "Damn. I was going for Hermes, not Prada."

Ethan grins. "You better start anti-aging your shit now or there won't be a laser out there to help you."

"Oh snap," Marco snorts. "He did not just go there." He looks to Naomi. "Come on, love. Go all Naomi Kent diva on his ass. He's just a jealous bitch because he's all bags and SPF and you're all sunshine and radiance."

Naomi throws Marco a wink before returning to Ethan, throwing her hands up in exasperation. "Get over your PMS. Your complexion is perfect and so is mine. You missed me. You can admit it, everyone here knows it already." Her hands span about the room, a gleam in her eye. "Play it however you want but you only flew in to see me. And to produce the song I just wrote. I'll let you have it if you play nice."

"Bitch, I'm always nice," he barks, slamming his phone face down on the table.

"Not when you call me a bitch."

"Fine." He throws his hands up in surrender. "You're a goddess and I'm drooling for this song, so let's go and make it snappy." He stands, pointing a not to be ignored finger at Naomi. "My pumpkin hit midnight somewhere over Omaha and I am not Fashion Famous right now. We're doing this song on the ASAP and then cosmos at Lavender on you." He throws a quick side-eye to Maia. "Sorry, love. I know that must sting. They did fire your ass."

Maia scoffs indignantly. "Um, only because I had a broken arm. And no sting anymore since I'm starting college full-time this fall and am still working as the band's PA. But if you want to eat the E. coli beef and the salmonella chicken they tote, by all means."

"Damn. My girl is fierce." Marco high fives Maia.

Gus grabs Naomi and kisses her soundly on the lips. She staggers back a step when he releases her, her cheeks flaming red. He stares Ethan down. "I will let you have her today. But only today. Tonight, if you play nice, I will take us all out for dinner. That's sorta my plan that I haven't announced yet because it didn't occur to me until Ethan mentioned it. But not to Lavender. I'm thinking some really good southern food is in order." He winks at Naomi and she simpers a smile, so I'm guessing this is some inside thing they have.

I don't know.

I'm too nervous to think too deeply about anything these lunatics say.

It's like I'm watching some reality TV show. Rockstars in Paradise... oh wait, that episode is yet to come. As long as I'm not the one who gets multiple STIs and pregnant, I think I'll survive. Maybe.

I feel like the emo/punk chick with the small boobs is always the first to get voted off.

"Right. Well, this took a weird turn," Lyric announces, though her eyes and one hand are on her phone, her other hand is stuck to her large pregnant belly.

"When has it ever not with this crew?" Keith questions.

"True. I think I've been in New York too long. Maybe it's the lack of vitamin D making me a cranky bitch. Or maybe it's the fact that my freaking back hurts and I'm carrying a pumpkin around where my stomach used to be. In any event, I've got something like three months before I'm meant to deliver this kid and I will tell you all this, if I don't get back to New York soon, Jameson will call my father. Does anyone want to deal with Gabriel Rose? Show of hands."

The room falls deadly silent.

"Yeah. Didn't think so."

I've never met Gabriel Rose, lead singer of Blind Tears, and Lyric's father, but I've only heard good things. Evidently when it comes to his daughter, those good things go out the window.

"We're here to discuss if you feel Eden can do our album. Or at least as much of it as she can while we're on vacation," Keith announces as Naomi and Ethan leave and Lyric sets her phone down.

"Talk Lyric. Tell us your thoughts. You're the only one who has ever done our albums and worked consistently with Eden," Jasper adds.

Lyric pins her hazel eyes on me and my heart accordingly starts to pound in my chest. Because Lyric can espouse all the glowing praise she wants. She can even throw me a song or two on a mostly produced album. But to start from scratch on a new album by one of the world's largest bands? Yeah, that's no fucking around territory.

I try not to squirm. I try to hold steady and look tough and capable and formidable. I think I might even be somewhat close to pulling it off. But damn, does *everyone* in the room have to stare at me like they're waiting to see if I'll crumble like a Chips Ahoy and break down in tears?

"I think Eden can do it," Lyric finally announces. "I think she'll bring a fresh and unique take on the production side of this for you. I think she will deliver a new take to your existing sound by adding her own style to your work. She's shadowed me long enough that she knows how I operate and if she's in over her head, I expect her to be professional enough to admit."

"Of course," I state clearly for all to hear.

"Then I guess it's sink or swim time, Eden. But something tells me you are the shark in these waters and will swim brilliantly. Even if it does mean your brother has to trust your judgment and listen to your guidance." Lyric smirks, cocking an eyebrow at Keith who laughs under his breath.

Dammit, Lyric. I beam a full-on, no-holding-back smile for the ages before I can stop it. "Thank you, Lyric. I swear, I will never let you down. If the idea of letting Keith down stings, letting you down burns like a bitch."

She laughs, her hand returning to her belly. "I have no doubt and no doubt in your talent. These are my boys. But more importantly, they're yours too."

It's true. They are her boys, she's been producing their albums since their start, but they are mine as well. I would never do anything to hurt my brother's career. To hurt the careers of the guys who have been his lifelong best friends, his brothers when he only had sisters.

Maia catches my eye with a prideful sparkle in hers. "On that note, let's go get... something. I don't know." Maia yanks on Marco's collar, dragging him up and out of his chair like a wayward child. "Now, Marco." They're gone in the next breath, out of the room despite his protests that he's the band's manager.

"Us too, Lyric," Vi states, folding her arms over her chest in a no-bullshit manner. "It's time to go shopping. You promised."

Lyric hisses under her breath. "Can't I listen in?"

Viola belts out a no-way in hell laugh. "Not on your life, babe.

This is my one chance to buy you baby stuff. Plus, I think Eden needs the time alone with the guys. I'm hauling all of them to Hawaii despite their deadline, so the sooner they get moving, the better."

"Fine," she grumbles, pushing herself awkwardly out of her chair. "Let's go shopping. Yay. Rah." She punctuates her cheer with a snarky eye roll. "But I reserve the right to first listen." She points a finger at Viola first and then me.

"Whatever you say."

The door shuts behind them and I swivel in my chair, eyeing each of the guys in turn. My nerves start to pick back up in tandem with my increased heartbeats. All eyes fall on me. All eyes except Henry's. He's been sitting at the far end of the table, either staring at his phone or staring out the window in boredom. It makes me want to throw something at his head.

After we called that truce in the car, we drove the rest of the way to my building in total silence. I mean, he was playing music, but it was like I wasn't even in the car with him.

It seems Henry's idea of a truce is to ignore my existence. Isn't that what he said?

And while I know that shouldn't bother me, it does.

Henry may want to fuck me, but he doesn't want *me*. He doesn't care what makes me tick. He doesn't care where my heart and passions lie. He. Doesn't. Care.

Remember that. You heard it here first, folks.

To Henry, I will never be anything more than his best friend's little sister and that's nowhere near good enough for me. I deserve to be worshiped for me. I deserve to come first. Something I've never been to any guy before.

Not Chad, and certainly not Henry.

Maybe Henry's right with ignoring me. Whenever we're in the same space, we're reactive. An accelerant on an open flame. We're explosive and not in a good way. All combustible heat with nothing of substance left after the fire burns off.

He said it plain as day the other night, nothing will ever happen between us.

I clear my throat and pull myself away from Henry, realizing a little too late I was watching him for a little too long. I cross my legs under the table, mentally get my shit together, and find Jasper's green eyes since he's the lead singer.

"Okay. Tell me about this album you wrote. Is there an underlying theme to it? Do particular tracks feed off others? Walk me through your vision for this."

Jasper looks to Gus and for a couple of seconds they have a silent conversation with just their eyes. They do this a lot, always freaking have, so I don't rush them. I may have only been twelve when Keith left to come out here, but I've visited him plenty since then. I all but followed these boys around from the time I was little on. I used to sit in and watch them jam whenever I could get away with it.

I know them.

I know their sound. I know how they operate.

So much better than they even realize.

"Keith and I have messed around with some of the tunes for a couple of the tracts," Gus states as he shifts his focus over to Keith. "We have... what? Three done?"

Keith tosses his clasped hands behind his head as he rocks back in his chair. "Yeah. Three, I think. We're behind if we want this done in a couple of months."

"Then that's where we should start," I announce because this is now my show, not theirs. "Let's get you guys going with some instruments. All of you together. Other than in concert, I haven't seen you play in a while and I think I need to. I need to see if how you figure each other out is the same way you used to. Once we get the music going for these songs we can start laying them down. I think it will be easier to do this part first, here in the main studio, instead of trying to make something happen when you're on vacation on your minds aren't as focused."

"We can do that," Jasper agrees as we all start to stand up and gather our things.

"Perfect. I have studio five reserved for the day and I believe your instruments are already there?"

"Marco made sure of that when we got here this morning."

I return Keith's smile. "Awesome. I'm really excited to hear your new stuff."

Keith, Jasper, and Gus all head for the door, talking animatedly about random ideas they already have going for some of the songs Jasper has written, when I feel fingers brush along my exposed neck. My head whips around to find Henry directly behind me, staring at the tattoo on the back of my neck.

"I didn't notice this before," he notes softly, reaching out and caressing the nape of my neck again. Chills dance across my skin that I know he doesn't miss for an instant.

"I haven't worn my hair up in a while," I manage on a breathy whisper.

Way to play it cool, Eden. I sound like one of those women in porn films ready to ask the cable man to install something inside her, and all he's doing is touching my neck.

His fingers trail up, following from the treble clef at my nape to each subsequent note I have floating up to my hairline. I shudder, turning away from him and closing my eyes to try and hide my reaction to his touch. His stupid touch that should not undo every ounce of resolve I just constructed where he's concerned.

"Does that tickle?" the bastard asks. "You're trembling."

My teeth saw into my bottom lip before I fix my poker face and turn back to him. "No. Your touch just makes me cringe."

He smirks as his eyes play all along my neck, all over my tattoo, the side of my face, like he's memorizing every goddamn detail. Every inch of blushing flesh and ink. He leans in, breathing the word, "Liar," directly into my ear.

I shudder, appalled at my involuntary response. My teeth find my lip once more, biting so hard I'm shocked I'm not drawing blood.

Desperate to quell this... damn him. This fucking *fire* I feel whenever I'm around him.

"I'd ask if you were copying me but there is no way you could have seen it or known. I got it done about four months ago."

"Huh?" I spin around and reflexively drop my gaze to watch as Henry lifts up the side of his gray T-shirt, revealing a hint of drool-worthy toned abs and a perfectly cut V that angles into his jeans.

Holy mother-of-pearl, that's a sight that could never grow old. My fingers itch to touch him. To glide along each ridge. Each valley. Each perfect indent. And once I'm done with that, my tongue is desperate to get in on the action.

"What do you think?"

"Huh?" Yeah, I just repeated that brilliant question. Only I added a super awesome blush into the mix. Just to make my drooling even more obvious and humiliating.

"This." He grins knowingly, pointing to the region my eyes are already glued to.

"Oh. Um..." Starting right at the hemline of his jeans is a gorgeous tattoo. A black trouble clef with various music notes dancing up along his flank, stopping just short of his armpit.

Some of the notes are different but other than that, the tattoo is almost identical to mine, just on a much larger scale. A small, bemused laugh flees my lips. My hand extends out, needing to touch his the way he touched mine. And I think I might mean that in more ways than just his tattoo. I drop my hand immediately.

"I got mine about four months ago too. Does yours accompany any song in particular?"

"No," he says, dropping his shirt back down. Pity.

"Mine either."

Silently, with his eyes locked on mine, he roughly yanks the elastic from my hair. I emit a surprised squeak as a zap of pain burns my scalp. My hair tumbles down around my shoulders but before I can ask him what the hell he's doing, he starts massaging my smarting scalp where he pulled.

My eyes close only to reopen just as quickly, not wanting to miss a second of the way he's staring at me. I need to look away. He's just so intense.

I almost snort out loud at that.

Let's be real here, I needed to look away about five minutes ago.

Instead, all I do is stare back with stunned, wide-eyed amazement as he slowly removes his hands from my hair and tucks my elastic into his pocket. His gaze drops to my neck in the direction of my tattoo that is now covered and then back up to my eyes. He inches forward, looking as though he's about to say something when Keith pops his head back into the room.

"You two coming?" he questions, his eyes hard on Henry who has straightened back up, creating a world cold indifference between us.

"Yeah," Henry replies, blowing right past me as if I was never here to begin with. As if he didn't just toy with skin and steal my elastic after ripping it from my hair.

What the hell was *that?*

He slaps Keith on the shoulder as the two of them start talking about a particular song. I stand here frazzled, needing an extra second. My teeth sink into my bottom lip, a meager attempt at trying to subdue my holy-shit-that-just-actually-happened smile. My mind whirls as my body buzzes with a strange kinetic energy.

All I know is Henry ripping my elastic from my hair and keeping it in his pocket feels like some strange form of foreplay. Like yet another promise he's challenging me with. Only this time I made a promise to myself I intend to keep. No matter what.

NINE

EDEN

"Why are you standing?" Henry asks as he sits in one of the insanely comfortable recliners they have in here. The damn things even massage you.

I ignore him as I press the button for the microphone on the soundboard. "Keith, that progression is too fast. I love the intensity level, but you're a half-beat ahead of Gus and I like Gus's rhythm better with this part of the song. Start again, okay?"

Keith gives me a nod, throwing his hand with his drumstick in it into the air in acknowledgment.

I turn off the mic and while Gus and Keith try working out the exact tempo the song should be, I twist from side to side until I finally feel the pop in my spine that releases the tension that's been mounting there over the last two weeks we've been at this nonstop.

And by nonstop, I mean fucking nonstop.

I'm talking twelve, sometimes fourteen-hour days.

"Back bothering you?" Henry quips because he can be a dick like that. "You should try one of these recliners. They're amazing. I've been sitting in this one for what... ten minutes? My back is now perfectly knot-free while you're the definition of tense and miserable. At least that's how you look."

"Shut up, Henry." I hit the mic again. "Yes. That's it. I love this," I tell the guys. Thank god because I swear I'm a hot buttered biscuit from collapsing to the floor and calling it quits.

Jasper isn't even here right now. He went home to have dinner with Viola and the girls. I told him not to bother coming back. We leave tomorrow bright and early anyway.

Speaking of I still need to finish packing. And possibly consume something other than coffee because just the tiny thought bubble of that hot buttered biscuit is making my stomach growl.

When was the last time I had anything to eat?

"I heard that."

"*Shut up, Henry!* Jesus. You and your freaking mouth. It's either silent as a nun in church or louder than a drunk at a football game. Aren't you supposed to be in there with them working this out?"

He is. And he was. But as he said, he came out here about ten minutes ago complaining about his back hurting and then took to the recliner with a smug bastard smile while I stand because the thought of sitting back down in that chair makes me want to weep.

"Eden, can I give you a piece of advice?"

"No."

"Learn when to call it. Gus and Keith will keep plowing away at this until you tell them to stop. But I think it's clear we've all hit the point of diminishing returns. Especially when we leave tomorrow and it's now well past dinnertime."

Dammit. He's right. I hate that he's right.

I hit the mic, interrupting Gus and Keith mid-playing. "Guys, it's getting late and I think we're all fried. I'm also starving like a lioness in heat. Let's call it a night."

"Thank Christ," Keith groans. "Maia has been texting me every five minutes asking when I'm bringing home dinner."

And now I feel like shit. I've been keeping a pregnant woman—a woman who is having twins she found out yesterday—from food.

That's close to grounds for losing potential godmother status of my future nieces or nephews. "Why didn't you say something sooner?" I moan as they step out of the booth. "Poor Maia must be starving."

"Like you're not," Henry deadpans, and I ignore him. Because that's what we do. Ignore each other. It's been working quite nicely until he decided to today was the day to start pestering me again.

Keith tosses his big, heavy, *sweaty* arm over my shoulder as he drags me away from the mixing board toward the door. "She's fine, Ede. Relax. Have you seen yourself? You're a hot mess of a woman right now. About a half-beat from going postal and taking down a Taco Bell."

"Har, har." I sigh, sagging a little into him because it's true. I'm beyond wound up and stressed with this gig. I want this album to be perfect. I want to do this job perfectly. So yeah, hot mess is probably as accurate as it gets for me right now. I don't even remember if I shampooed my hair in the shower this morning, that's how preoccupied my mind is.

And tomorrow we leave for Hawaii and between sun, fun, wives, fiancées, and kids, I have to imagine dragging these guys into the studio the resort is allowing us to set up in one of their conference rooms will be nearly impossible. This album has to be done in a little more than two months and if I can't deliver on that...

"I just need a good night's sleep." And maybe a huge glass of wine and a hot bath before it. And food. Lord have mercy on my stomach, it's an empty wasteland of churning acid with nothing to digest but the lining of my gut.

We say our goodnights in the garage as we each get into our respective cars. I take a moment to check my messages, something I haven't done all day, and after I go through the few I have, I text Jess to let her know I'm on my way home. She's been dating Bartender Ben pretty steadily since that night in the club, but their hours could not be any more different, so I wonder what she's up to tonight. I'd like to spend some time with her, maybe watch a movie or something before I leave for three weeks for this trip.

Setting my phone down, I press the button to start my car. Only it doesn't start. It makes some strange grating sound instead. Sort of like metal grinding against metal. The check engine light flashes, but that's it. Nothing else is lighting up.

"No. Not now. Not today," I yell desperately as I try again, only to get the same result. "You've got to be kidding me. You're a new freaking car. Ugh!" I cry out, slamming my hand repeatedly against the steering wheel and falling dejectedly against the seat. "Mother-fluffer this sucks some serious balls."

I'm tired, hungry—I think I mentioned all this already—but now it feels infinitely worse. To the point where tears are a legit possibility.

I pick up my phone, staring at it as I debate calling Keith, who can't be too far away since we all left together. I quickly discount that when I think of Maia waiting on him to deliver their dinner and decide on AAA instead, already knowing it will take at least a solid hour for them to arrive.

Just as I'm about to google the number, my phone rings in my hand. Chad. I move to hit ignore when something sparks in my head. Swiping my finger across the screen, I answer, "Did you sabotage my car?"

"Huh? Your car? Why would I ever sabotage your car?" He sounds as shocked and flustered as I am. "Where are you?"

"I'm at work."

"Then I guess that settles it. I don't even know where you work since you've been avoiding me for two months now."

"You know where I work, Chad."

"I don't actually. I could assume it's for the same label as your brother's. But at the time you broke up with me, you were still enter-taining other offers than the one Lyric made you. Even if I did know, I would never do anything to intentionally hurt you," he quickly adds. "Though I will say whatever got you to pick up the phone for me, I'm instantly grateful for."

I blow out a silent breath. Of course, he didn't sabotage my car.

Chad Mason isn't that clever. Or skilled. The guy has been driving a new luxury car every two years since I met him and the one time he accidentally left the inner light on and the battery died, he freaked, having no clue what to do. One of his frat brothers had to jump his car for him.

"Okay. Thanks for clearing that up. I'm hanging up on you now."

"No, babe, wait! Please don't hang up. I'm so happy to hear your voice. Where are you? If your car is dead, I can come get you. Help you."

It's tempting for about zero point two seconds. And during those zero point two seconds, the passenger side door of my car opens, and Henry gets in, his eyes meeting mine with concern. I don't think I've ever been this happy to see him before in my life, and coming from me, that's saying a lot.

"I don't need a ride, Chad, and I definitely I don't need you to come and get me. I need to go." I disconnect the call as I hear him urgently call out my name.

"Car trouble?"

My eyebrows pinch in. "How did you know?"

"I heard your car when you tried to start it. It sounded like someone was bashing your engine with a tire iron."

I wince at the imagery because that's exactly how it sounded. Not good. "I thought you had left."

He shakes his head as he stares at me, something passing over his features that I don't understand. "Come on." He unbuckles my seat belt for me, picking up my phone and dropping it back into my purse.

"What about my car?" I push out.

"You don't need it for the next few weeks. It's safe here in the garage. I'll arrange for someone to come and take a look at it and deliver it either to a shop or back to your place while we're gone. For now, I'll take you home."

I blink at him, a little stunned. "You don't mind?"

He laughs. "Oh, I mind. But what am I going to do? Leave you here all alone in an abandoned parking garage to wait for a tow?"

"You know what? Forget it. I'll just Uber home."

He grins at me, reaching over and tucking a piece of my long bangs behind my ear. It's such a simple gesture and yet so intimate, especially as we sit close, alone in my car. "I thought you broke up with the boyfriend."

I stare Henry down, my mind reeling in too many directions to count. Is he kidding me right now? "Chad? I did."

"Then why were you talking to him on the phone?"

As if the bastard can hear his name being called, my phone rings from my purse. I don't so much as flinch or move for my phone, but Henry does. He retrieves it from my purse, holding it up and wiggling it back and forth tauntingly. "Oh look. It's him again. Do you want to answer it?" He offers me my phone and I shake my head no, gnawing on my bottom lip. He shrugs indifferently as he answers it for me. "Hello?"

"Holy shit," I half-laugh, half-murmur under my breath. "You didn't."

"This is Henry Gauthier. Who's this?"

Another laugh escapes, this one louder and mixed in with a squeal. I cover my mouth with my hands to try and stifle the sound as I twist to face Henry, who is smiling equally as broad as I am.

"Chad Mason. Yeah, no, that doesn't ring any bells."

Now I snort into my hands, tossing my head back as I die.

"You're looking for Eden?" He finds my eye, winking at me. "Well, she's with me. And tomorrow we're headed to Hawaii for three weeks together." Silence ensues as Henry listens and with the silence, I catch the bark of Chad who does not sound happy. "No, you can't speak to her. Listen, man, I have no idea what happened between you and Eden, and I seriously don't care. All I know is that she's obviously done with you if she's here with me. Get used to it and get over it." He hits end on the call and drops the device back into my purse.

My mouth hangs unhinged behind my hands. "Wow. I'm just... wow."

"I didn't lie. You're technically in the car with me, and tomorrow we go to Hawaii for three weeks. I fail to see the issue. He did, but that's really not my concern right now." His eyes hold mine and my hands drop to my lap. "I'm wondering how you feel about it."

"You could have told him I was knocked up with your love child and we were on our way to Vegas to make it Facebook official. I seriously would not care."

"No?" he challenges.

"No."

"Didn't you two just break up?"

I shrug. "A week before I moved out here."

"And you're over him already?" he asks dubiously.

"No. Not entirely. But that doesn't mean I want him back or in my life either."

"Want to tell me why that is when this guy sounds extremely determined. Maia told me about the present he dropped at your door."

"Dammit, Maia," I hiss under my breath. Why the hell would she go and tell Henry that? She knows about my history with him. About my adolescent fantasy and the sex and all the subsequent shit that I'm now living through. "Did she tell you anything else?"

"No. Just that. And she didn't tell Keith. Only me, she said."

My eyebrows scrunch in at that. That's kinda weird for her to tell Henry and not Keith or anyone else, isn't it? "He cheated," I state simply. Henry's face instantly transforms into one of murderous rage and I hold my hand up, stopping the rant I see forming in his head. "Keith doesn't know about that either, okay? You can't tell him, or he'll kill Chad."

"Am I supposed to care if that happens? Fuckstick's lucky I didn't know that before I picked up the phone. Why are you defending the prick?"

"Because in fairness to Chad, I'm not entirely sure he meant to cheat."

"Explain," he grits out through clenched teeth.

"He was plastered at a party. A sorority sister of mine was obsessed with him, went into my room, stole a dress of mine and then sucked him off. I walked in while she was doing it. His head was back and hers was down and the second I entered the room he looked like he couldn't comprehend how I was in two places at once." *He also looked guilty as fuck.* "He swore to me that was the case. That he thought Marni was me." Though she claimed otherwise. Adamantly, in fact.

"I'm confused. If that was the case, why end it?"

Because I don't know if I believe that. Marni and I don't look much alike. Plus, there's the other part. The one I don't like to talk about.

"Can you just take me home?" I ask instead of answering him.

He glares at me, shaking his head, unwilling to let it go.

"No, Eden. Because you were with this guy for two years. Believe me, I know all about it. Two years that..." He stops abruptly, turning to face the front windshield. His fists clench, matching the tension mounting in his jaw. "You looked like a homecoming queen the last I saw you three years ago and then you showed up right after ending it with Chad looking completely different. Not better or worse, just a hell of a lot different. So no, we're not going anywhere until I get some answers."

I reach out and grasp Henry's jaw, dragging the reluctant thing back in my direction. He pushes my hand away and I sigh. "I'm tired, Henry. And hungry as a pack of wolves. And stressed out beyond measure. I really don't want—"

"I don't give a fuck what you want. I need you to tell me."

Fantastic. "Fine. Drive me home and I promise I'll explain everything along the way."

TEN

EDEN

"What are you doing? I thought you said you'd take me home," I grouse as we head in the opposite direction of my apartment.

"And I thought you said you were as hungry as a pack of wolves. Well, that makes two of us. You worked us all day without much of a break."

"I didn't agree to go out to dinner with you."

Henry laughs at my appalled face. "We're getting takeout. It hardly qualifies as dinner. Hell, I don't even hit up this place with the dates I care nothing about. So, relax."

"You just compared me to one of your dates and you want me to relax?"

Henry rolls his eyes as he turns into a roadside taco bodega of sorts. "That's what you're upset about? Not the fact that I said that I treat the dates I don't even care about better?"

"No. I'm upset about the fact that you brought me here when you don't take any of your dates here. Including the ones, you don't care about. Which means you like this place and don't typically share it with anyone. I can't believe you brought me somewhere special on our first non-date. How could you do this to me, Henry?"

I toss him a satisfied grin as I hop out of the car, inhaling the spicy scent of peppers and cooking beef as is wafts through the air. Yum. This place is little more than a roadside shack but judging by the foot traffic coming and going and the crowded picnic tables, a good one. We're also close to the beach if the half-naked surfers carrying their boards and the faint hint of brine in the air is anything to go by.

Damn. I think I'm in love. With the tacos, not Henry, of course.

"This is my dream," I murmur wistfully. "I've always wanted to own a place like this. Only I'd have picnic tables with blue and purple umbrellas and flowers lining the walkways. I'd cute it up a bit." I take another deep inhale. "Eden's Roadside Tacos in Paradise."

"Huh?"

I grin like a madwoman. "That's what I'd call my roadside taco haven. One day, right? Dreams for the future and all that?"

"Go see if you can snag us a place to eat while I order."

I pivot on the toes of my flats and stare up into his death-of-me green eyes. "Yes, sir." I'm still smiling stupidly. It can't be helped. We're talking roadside tacos after all. That's like my personal form of crack, and I think Henry knows this. I wasn't even joking about my dream to own something like this one day.

"What do you want?"

"Whatever you're having. Now that I know you don't take your dates here; I know anything you order will be amazing." I grin cheekily up at him, rocking back on my heels. He mutters something under his breath as he stalks off in the direction of the stand to order our dinner. "You're cute when you're trying to impress me."

He flips me off from behind, and I laugh under my breath. Riling Henry up is simply too much fun. I spin around just in time to catch a couple finishing up at one of the smaller picnic tables and make a beeline for it, snagging it before someone else has the chance.

I sit down, lowering my shades as the last remnants of daylight flitter across the summer sky, heading for the Pacific not too far in the distance. I slip out my phone, not surprised to find it full of messages and missed calls from Chad.

Henry can play it all he wants, but I know exactly who he is, and I'm not worried about him.

I frown at that. Because yes, Chad knows who Henry is because Chad knows all about my brother. And no, Chad shouldn't be worried about Henry because nothing will ever happen with Henry. But Chad doesn't know I spent my youth rocking a schoolgirl crush on Henry with the dedication of a doctoral student about to present their dissertation.

I miss you.

I love you.

I didn't mean to cheat on you. I'd never do that. Ever. You're the only woman I want. Forever.

Don't fall for someone else.

I swear, you're who I want.

I almost snort aloud at that last one. Because both he and I know that's not true. Because if it were... things might be different. Maybe. Honestly, at this point, I don't know anymore. How can you go from thinking you're so in love with someone to questioning everything within a couple of months? I don't... miss him the way I thought I would.

The way I felt I should.

Maybe it's my anger and resentment that's clouding things where he's concerned.

I was devastated when I walked into that room and found Marni on her knees and heard Chad's groans of pleasure. I was wrecked when I discovered my friend betrayed me and my boyfriend broke my heart. I cried like I've never cried before. Dodged him until the day I moved and then ever since. Every attempt he made to reach me, I thwarted.

But in leaving Chad, I feel like I finally realize and appreciate who I am. And I like this version so much better than the lost girl I was when I was with him.

Five minutes later Henry drops down holding two huge white to-go boxes and two black plastic cups with lids and straws. "What are those?"

"Margaritas."

"They have margaritas here?" I practically scream. "Holy Toledo, you just became my hero." I bark out a laugh. "Ha, that rhymes."

I grab one of the plastic cups and take a long pull as I open the white box Henry slides to me, practically orgasming from the smell. I lift the first taco and go in for the kill. Crunchy, spicy perfection hits my tongue in an explosion of heat and flavor only to be quickly cooled by the sour cream and the guacamole, and yes, orgasm. Right here.

"God, that's so good my toes are curling." I wipe my mouth on my napkin only to find Henry watching me. "What?"

"Nothing."

"Okay. Nothing. That's why you're staring at me like..." I tilt my head, trying to bait him because I honestly don't know what he's staring at me like. The man can be an unreadable fortress when he wants. At least with me. He's typically not this surly with the guys. And never ever with their better halves. Especially Maia. The two of them are thick as thieves.

He rubs absently at the tiny hint of a smirk on his lips and then goes about digging into his own food. "I believe you owe me an explanation," he announces as he swallows down his food with a sip of his margarita.

Ugh. I was hoping he'd have forgotten by now.

"Why do you care?"

"Because if there's a quarterback out there in need of castration, I'd like to know about it before we leave for Hawaii and I lose precious time."

"You sound like Keith."

"That's sorta the point."

"I don't like it when you sound like Keith. One big brother is plenty. Two is superfluous. And annoying if we're speaking candidly.

Plus, I happen to know you don't look at me like a little sister." I bat my eyelashes at him as I slurp down another sip.

"You're stalling," he mutters dryly, unimpressed.

I deflate a little, twisting on the bench seat and turning in the direction of the ocean so I can take in some of the breeze as it kicks up my hair and blankets me in its gentle caress.

"You're right. I did look like the homecoming queen. Because I was her. Every bit of it. Chad was homecoming king, and we were that couple. Perfect. The one everyone envied. Only..."

"Only what?"

"Only that never felt like me." I abandon the waning sun and the delightful breeze in favor of my tacos before they get cold and this really turns into a pity party.

"What do you mean?" he asks around a mouthful of food.

"I mean, I hate heels, Henry. And skintight mini dresses in pretty pastels. And when my hair is long, it's impossibly thick and heavy and requires so much time and effort to style. And it's brown, dude. Do I strike you as the type of chick who likes brown hair?"

"Is that meant to be rhetorical since your hair is purple?"

"Maybe? I just never felt like that girl. That perfect queen. I had to try so hard to be her. To be everything everyone expected me to be. Because that's exactly the type of woman Chad wanted on his arm, and since I loved him, I thought that's who I had to be. The one time I tried to dye the ends of my hair pink—pink, not even a hard color— he freaked and demanded I dye it back. He liked the bellybutton ring because it's easily hidden, and a lot of girls have it, and he tolerated my nose ring because it's a tiny diamond stud, but when I got my nipples pierced—"

"You have your nipples pierced?"

I cock an eyebrow at him. "I sure do."

"Shit," he groans, throwing his head back and closing his eyes for a second. "I wish you hadn't told me that."

"Why? That turn you on, Henry? You into piercings?"

"Shut up, Eden."

"Wanna see them? I'll give you a private show right here."

"No. I most definitely don't want to see them." Only the fire simmering in his hooded eyes is telling a completely different story. "Go on. About Chad, I mean."

"You just looked at my boobs."

"Christ, Eden. I did not. Finish your fucking story so I can take you home already."

"Is that an invitation?"

He growls, something low and deep and insanely sexy under his breath. "I swear to God, if you don't finish—"

I couldn't stop my laugh if I wanted to. "It's like shooting fish in a barrel with you. So easily wound up when it comes to me."

He murmurs something that sounds an awful lot like you have no idea but quickly covers it up by glaring at me as he finishes off his taco and swallows it down with his margarita. "Chad?" he reminds me.

"There's nothing left to say. I have tattoos and piercings and unnaturally colored hair. He wanted me to be one way and I wanted to be another. I walked in on him getting a BJ from my friend, freaked out, broke up with him, and then realized I never want to conform to someone else's ideal of who I should be again. You've asked me more than once what's happened to me and that's the answer. Chad didn't care who I was on the inside as long as I fit the mold of the woman he wanted me to be on the outside. My wants and desires were secondary to his. My dreams of being a producer were a hobby, not a career like football. He says he loves me and wants me back, but the truth is, he loves the perfect sorority girl I left behind."

"Then it's his loss, Eden."

I snort, rolling my eyes. "Yeah, I know. Thanks dad."

"No. I mean it." He pauses, his eyes flittering around my face before a slow, easy smile spreads across his. "You have no idea how beautiful you are, do you?"

I blink, utterly gobsmacked by his declaration. By the earnest intensity in his eyes.

"Now, here, sitting across from me, the woman I'm looking at is everything any guy would be lucky to have. You are strong and independent. Rebellious and wild. Hard working and determined. Smart and funny. You are absolutely beautiful, Eden, and any guy who prefers a cookie-cutter mindless Barbie to this" —he waves his hand up and down in my direction— "is a goddamn fool."

My heart stops dead in my chest before it springs back to life, beating off rhythm as I absorb his words. Memorize them syllable by syllable. Stick them into their own private box in my brain, knowing I'll take them out later and repeat them over and over again. Analyze them from every possible angle.

Even when I know I shouldn't.

"You mean that." It's a statement. Because holy shit, he does.

Even as he tries to ruin it by saying, "Whatever. Don't get carried away in that crazy head of yours. I was just trying to make you feel better. You looked all broken up."

Liar, liar, pants on fire, Henry Gauthier. "I think you've got a hate-crush on me, Henry."

He blusters out an exasperated breath. But I think that anger and frustration is more directed at himself. Henry seems to have very little control where I'm concerned. He's a sweater with a loose thread, and all I want to do is pull that thread and watch him unravel.

God, imagine that. What would that be like?

"Grow up, Eden. You read too much into thing where there is nothing to read into."

He's not wrong on that, so I don't argue. But for real, find me a woman who doesn't. "Tell me I'm wrong then."

"You ready to go? I'm exhausted and I still have to finish packing." He balls up the rest of his to-go wrappers and stuffs them into his now empty box before tossing the whole thing in the trash. He does the same with mine though I never answered his question.

Henry grabs my hand, hauling me out of my seat and dragging me over to his Escalade. But before he opens the door for me, he presses me against the warm metal, bracketing me in with his hands on either side of my head, getting right up in my face.

"There is no hate and there is no crush. There is no emotion or feeling about you, Eden Dawson. There can't be. Your brother has me that absolutely fucking crystal goddamn clear to me. Don't let shit that has no business being there get confused in that pretty head of yours. I'm no better than the Chads out there. I fuck women, maybe date them for a bit, but I don't get serious with them. Ever. I don't care about them beyond their bodies, and I sure as hell don't give a damn about their dreams or who they are on the inside. Your brother knows this about me all too well. So get over your adolescent fantasy of me, Eden. It's never gonna happen, baby."

With that he pushes off, casually strolling around the car and hopping in the driver's side with a cool, casual indifference that leaves me reeling.

And for the first time in all the years I've known him, a question enters my mind. A question he's already directly asked me. *What happened to you?* It has to be something. Because now that he says he doesn't get serious and he doesn't care about the women he fucks, I know it's true. But it's so much more than that. So much more than just about me.

Keith has intimated about this before, but even he was clueless as to why Henry is the way he is when it comes to women. It's not just a 'I love my bachelor life' thing. It's an actual thing. A mission state- ment printed boldly across his chest to fend off any would-be ladies who would dare try to gain access to his heart.

The one thing I do know for sure is that this Ferris wheel we seem locked on is making me dizzy. Up and down. Slow and fast. It's a toxic loop I can't seem to get off of. One moment I'm steadfast in my resolve to hate him and keep my distance, the next I can't resist riling him up. Hell, I can't resist *him*.

Devastating, idiotic, ill-placed? You bet.

This man has always held a piece of me. A piece I don't know how to retrieve, even when I'm desperate to.

And that's the most dangerous thing of all.

ELEVEN

HENRY

Sleep came in fits and stuttered, restless attempts. My mind was hopelessly stuck on her. *Her*.

At first, like everything else with her, I tried to fight it. Then, around one a.m., I decided maybe if I isolate what it is exactly about her that I find so irresistible, I'd be able to put it behind me and get over it already.

The problem is, I can't pinpoint it.

It's not just one thing.

I don't do this. Think about women beyond my fleeting encounters with them. I've never even been tempted before. But for three years this woman has lingered and now that she's in my life, it's only gotten worse.

One night. One interlude with someone who I thought was a stranger.

Only... the second I walked into that club and saw her; it was like being hit by a truck. There is just something about her that drew me in. That sped up my heart rate. That made me walk across the room simply because I needed to be closer.

It makes as little sense to me now as it did then.

If only I had recognized her none of this would have happened. But I didn't.

Now look at the mess I'm in. A mess with no resolution as far as I can see, which means I'm back to ignoring her. That worked well the first two weeks we were in the studio. Until I reached the point where it no longer did, but that's done. It was like getting a fix. And after hearing what actually happened to her with Chad? Yeah. I can make it through three weeks in Hawaii. I can make it through recording the rest of the album without touching her.

Then, with any luck, I won't have to see her again for at least another three years.

A sharp tug on my shirt snaps me out of my reverie, forcing my gaze down. Adalyn Diamond is staring up at me with her bright green eyes and adorable upturned nose. "Move please," she says in that high-pitched little girl voice of hers.

"Hey sweet darling," I greet her with a smile, but it takes me a second to catch what she said. It's only now that I realize I'm standing in the doorway to the bedroom on our plane, blocking her access. How did I get here? And why was I staring at the bed while thinking of Eden? Well, that's not good. "You want to get in the bedroom?"

"I have to go potty," she explains, and the trouble in her eyes tells me I need to move my ass quickly out of the way.

"Oh. Right. Sorry, kiddo."

I slide to my right and watch as she scurries into the bedroom, yanking down her little purple leggings as she goes. Her adorable tushy makes a brief appearance as she hops the rest of the way into the small bathroom.

"She'll only use this bathroom on the plane now," Jasper clarifies, coming to stand beside me. He waves for me to follow him into the bedroom. "She's getting so particular with things. Like, she'll only use certain bathrooms in the house. And she'll only sit in one chair at the kitchen table. She can only use a purple towel after the bath or swimming in the pool. Things like that."

We hover near the bathroom door, casually keeping an eye on

Adalyn without watching her directly. "How will she do in kinder-garten with that, do you think?"

Jasper quickly meets my eyes, the worry in his more than evident. "I'm not sure. We had a PPT for her with the entire special education department at her school. They've done an IEP and it sounds like she's going to be getting all the services she'll need in addition to having para support."

I clap a hand to his shoulder, squeezing gently. A small burst of turbulence hits the plane and we each press into the doorframe, smiling as Adalyn squeals out a, "Whoa, bumpy ride."

"I'm sure she'll have everything she needs and more."

"She will," he agrees. "She'll have everything she needs and then a lot more. Vi and I have made sure of it. It's just..."

"What?"

"She's my girl."

My lungs empty at that, because yeah, she's his girl. And she's our girl. Six years ago when we found out Karina, Adalyn's birth mother, was pregnant, that Jasper, our best friend, was going to be a father, none of us knew how to handle that. We were living the rock star dream. Parties and women and booze. We could buy whatever we wanted. Go wherever we wanted.

It was freedom and then months later, Adalyn was born, and all our lives changed. Karina was an absentee mother. Ditched out six months after Adalyn was born. And the three of us, Gus, Keith, and I did what we could to pick up the slack. It was easier for Gus and Keith than it was for me. Gus is Adalyn's uncle and Keith helped raised his five younger sisters.

Then there was me.

The man with no siblings or cousins or experience. The man with no real family except the one I created with these guys. So, I jumped in full steam ahead. Didn't think twice. And then Adalyn was diagnosed with ASD and our world changed yet again.

"Ady is my goddess in the sunrise. I would never change the fairest hair on her head. But sometimes being her dad is like running a triathlon without training. Every muscle hurts. My inner fortitude weeps for relief. And just when I think I've reached the finished line; I realize the race is just getting started." He sighs, his eyes now on his girl. "Still, knowing all that I know now, I'd still run the race. Training or not. She's worth a thousand sore muscles and aching bones."

"We all would," I tell him unequivocally, looking at our little lady. "She's our heart, Jas. No matter what, she'll be okay because she has the right people on her side. Always."

Adalyn does her thing and pulls up her pants, going to the sink and stepping up on the stool we have for her so she can wash her hands. "She won't let me flush while she's in here. It's too loud."

"I can take her back out. Wanna watch some Mickey with me, kiddo?" I ask, catching her reflection in the mirror. "Cora's napping on mommy right now, so it would be just you and me. It's been too long since I've gotten alone time with my favorite big girl."

"Mickey Mouse," she states firmly with a gleam to her eye, which is Adalyn's way of saying hell yes.

"We're lucky," Jasper muses, and his tone and words catch me so off guard I look up at him, my eyebrows pinched. "We've been doing this for ten years, Henry. And maybe I'm just turning into a p-u-s-s-y now that Ady is getting to this stage and Cora is two and Vi is talking about another kid. But yeah... lucky is all I feel lately. We're still topping charts and as successful, if not more so, than ever. But with all that we've accomplished in this business, it's never changed us. We're still us and we're still brothers. A family that will always have each other's backs."

I swallow thickly at that, hit by the same surge of guilt I've been flirting with for two weeks. Hell, for three fucking years. My gaze drops to the floor.

"Is this the heavy talk portion of our in-flight entertainment?"

He chuckles, rubbing a hand over the back of his neck. "Yeah. Maybe." He punches my shoulder. "You gotta be a d-i-c-k about it?"

"That's been my thing lately."

"No, it's not. You're just playing the bad guy when you don't need to."

I push out a breath. Maybe. I don't know. My mind is a chaotic, jumbled mess and I hate it. I'm not that guy. I'm the guy who was never like this while all these other bastards were.

"I know I pushed this quick-snap album. I know I demanded it getting finished on the ASAP. And I know you've all been there for me throughout. I also know this vacation was forced on you, and I'm sorry for that. Have you thought about what you're going to do during this year off?"

No. I haven't. Not really anyway. It's impossible to think about if I'm being honest. I've been nothing without this band. Since I was fourteen and we started jamming together, this band, these guys have been my life. Their children. Their women. Their lives have been mine.

And thank fuck for that, right?

It's been my guiding, my motherfucking surviving, force all these years.

So yeah, I'm not so excited for this year off. But I'll do what I always do, adapt. Survive. Make it through. At the end of the day, it's me and me alone. No. Backtrack that. I have them. I always knew I had them and that hasn't changed.

But a year off feels like a death sentence to me. Instead of giving him a real answer, I just hitch up a shoulder, blowing it off.

"Eden's pretty great," he continues, and a strangled laugh flees my lips before I can stop it. Fucking Jasper. "I think she can do great things with this album."

"Uh huh."

He smirks. "Does Keith know you watch her?"

Bastard. I should have known. I don't reply.

"I know a thing or two about lost causes and wanting someone you shouldn't."

"It's not the same thing, brother." That's a promise he can hold on to.

He studies me closely. Intently. "Maybe not. Just be careful, okay?"

I shake my head. "Nothing is happening there. I made a promise, but more than that I'm not—"

"I know what you think you're not. I also know what you don't tell anyone."

Now it's his turn to squeeze my shoulder and I finally man up and meet his steadfast gaze. My heart is pounding in my chest because even though he might think he knows; I know for a fact he doesn't know everything. Add to that, I have no desire to clue him in or talk about any of it.

"I get it, man," he continues. "And I'm not judging shit. But I will tell you this, she's there with you. For whatever that's worth to you, she watches you too."

He slaps my shoulder and then goes into the bathroom to help Ady wipe her hands dry. I can't do this. I can't think like that. Let his words create a wormhole in my brain. I am the way I am and even if I weren't, Keith's warning was pretty damn clear.

Stay the fuck away from his sister.

"You ready little lady?" I ask as Ady jumps off the stool and bunny-hops over to me, taking my outstretched hand. She's warm and soft and small and precious and my heart tugs in my chest as if to remind me it's there. This girl. This baby girl is our grounding force. The reason we're still 'us' as Jasper put it. Baby Cora hasn't hurt either. She's another star in our sky. But it's different with Ady. When Jasper had Ady, it was just him and just us.

No Maia or Naomi or even Viola in sight. It was a group of rough and tumble rock stars with this perfect baby to care for.

"You wanna watch Minnie's Martian Tea Party?"

Yup. I know all the Mickey Mouse Club House episodes. We all do.

"No," she says, shaking her head and skipping out ahead of me, her reddish-brown hair bouncing in her wake. "Minnie's pajama party."

"You got it," I promise, leading her to the TV Keith and I typically play video games on. The flight to Hawaii is about six hours. Private plane or no, it's long.

Keith catches what I'm doing with Ady and shuts off the game he's playing with Gus, switching it automatically to our streaming video. "Which one we watching?"

"Minnie's pajama party."

Gus peels out a laugh. "Sweet thing, we watched that two nights ago together."

Adalyn stares blankly at him. Waiting. Expectant. Not even cracking so much as a smile.

"Damn." Gus sighs, running a hand over his head. "She's so much like Jas it freaks me out sometimes." He bends down and gives Ady a kiss on her cheek, nuzzling his nose against hers. "Alright baby girl, Keith's got you covered."

"Putting it on right now for you, little darlin'," Keith tells hers. "You can watch Minnie with Henry."

Keith meets my eye as he goes about setting up Ady's video. "Can my twins both be boys? That too much to ask?"

"You want someone like you or me near girls like Ady?"

He hisses out a fake curse under his breath, staring down at our girl.

"This parenting stuff... Maia being pregnant. What if I'm not a great dad?"

I nearly laugh at that. "You mean because you'll be even better than great?"

That's not even sarcasm.

I grab the remote from his hand and the little girl from the floor, and I sack out on the couch, tucking her small body on top of mine. She digs in instantly. Her cheek meets my chest, her arms down by her sides. The TV flows with the opening credits that she sings along to. Ady settles in. I do the same. And for the first half of the show, I resist the pull.

That pull!

The one I perpetually feel when she's in my presence.

I adjust my position, listening as Ady's breathing evens out and she coasts into a blissful slumber on me—the sweetest fucking thing ever. But that pull. It's strong. And unrelenting. And *determined*.

I adjust a little more, rolling my neck and peeking over my shoulder. And instantly find Eden staring at me. Like she was waiting for me all along. Like she knew it was only a matter of time before I had to look at her.

My hand protectively covers Ady's back, holding her so close. My armor. My protection. My humanity.

But I still stare at Eden.

Her hair is different than it was last night. Blue. It's a light blue now, which makes the darker blue of her eyes seem impossibly bright. Almost like they're glowing. Her hair is the color of the sky outside the airplane window. She's stunning and I don't resist in this moment. I don't hold off the way I should. Instead, I continue to stare at her as she's staring at me, her expression as indecipherable as I'm hoping mine is.

I think about Jasper's words.

And Keith's.

I don't want to be another bad man in your story, is what my eyes tell her. The truth is I don't know how to be anything but. I'd give my life for the women on this plane. The women who belong to my friends, but... I don't want what they have. I don't want to be in love.

Totally. Completely. Unconditionally.

Still Eden doesn't look away.

She got my message. Of that I'm positive. I watched her flinch.

Look away, dammit. Just fucking look away. Get over it already.

She grins at me instead and my chest tightens the way it always does when she does that.

That smile slays it all. Defenses crumble. Rationales fray at the seams. Lies I tell myself laugh obstinately.

This woman. This motherfucking woman. She will be my downfall. Mark my words. You can count on it.

TWELVE

HENRY

When I heard we were coming to Hawaii, I didn't expect this. Maybe I should have. Okay, I likely should have, considering who was running the show. The women. Let me amend that... the woman who values comfort, their kids, and privacy.

"Everyone has their own private beachfront house or cabana or whatever they call them. I honestly can't remember," Viola says as our caravan of SUVs pulls up to the gates of what can only be described as exclusive Hawaiian paradise. "Jas, the girls, and I are staying in the main building because the thought of being beachfront with Adalyn gives me premature gray hairs. But the rest of you have your own space. Your own concierges. They will see to anything you need including special meals, spa treatments, hikes, rentals, whatever the hell. This is all a lot of luxury for me, but if we wanted exclusive, safe, room, and a recording studio, this is what we get."

"Yeah, babe," Gus grouses playfully, a smile spread across his face. "This shit sucks. I mean, how am I supposed to function with my own beachfront whatever they're called and a concierge."

Vi flips him off since Ady and Cora are in the other SUV per

Ady's request. "Gus Daniel Diamond, do not test me today. I am a woman on the fucking edge."

Jasper leans over and kisses Vi on the corner of her mouth, taking her hand and intertwining their fingers. "Everyone is going to love this," he tells her. "It's paradise, baby. And our family will be more than safe."

She pushes out a breath, her eyes glistening over. "I know. I'm just. I want everything to be perfect for everyone but now I'm all..."

Gus squeezes her other hand, calling her attention back over to him. "I'm sorry. I shouldn't have pushed," he says.

"What?" I ask. "What did I miss?"

Vi meets my eyes. "Ady tried to break out of the house to get to the pool the other night. She set one of the kitchen chairs in front of the back doors, climbed up, and unlatched all the latches. Then she opened the door. Thankfully the alarm went off. But if we had been a minute too late..." She trails, not needing to finish.

"Damn," I hiss out. "But you got to her. Nothing happened."

"Right," Naomi agrees. "You have a metal gate surrounding the pool she would have needed to get through. And a baby fence beyond that. And an alarm on the pool cover plus cameras," she reminds her, angling forward and propping her elbows on her knees so their faces are close across the small divide of the bench seats. "Ady wouldn't have been able to get close."

Vi nods on a heavy, grim swallow. "I know. It's just..."

She doesn't have to follow that up and we fall silent until the doors of the SUV are opened for us and we're being welcomed by an army of staff with lays in hand. The other SUV pulls up right behind ours and Keith, Maia, and Eden climb out. Keith is holding Adalyn's hand as she stands beside him, and Maia is holding Cora in her arms.

The manager of the resort goes over the details of the place. All the dining options, the spa, golf, hiking, rentals for any water sports, everything. We're also informed our personal concierges can take care of everything for us. I guess this is what you call the luxury treatment since we have our own exclusive beach, pool, bar, and concierge lounge.

Then we're placed in golf carts and driven along the gorgeous fauna-lined pathways to our waterfront suites, as he called them. And because the universe obviously hates my guts at this moment, I'm stuck beside Eden. I guess this is what happens when you're the only two singles amongst all the couples.

"I guess so," she agrees, and awesome, I'm starting to muse aloud.

"Do we have a schedule for recording?" I ask, getting us back to business since that's the only reason she's here with us.

"I figured after settling in, I'd go check out the event space they've given us use of. All our equipment is already being brought over there, so it'll just be a matter of setting it up. So... I don't know. Maybe tomorrow we'll start in? I figure half days five days a week. Eight to one and then the rest of the time people can do what they want."

"Sounds reasonable."

"We'll see how productive we are. If we're not getting enough done, I'll adjust accordingly."

"I'm glad you're taking this seriously."

A torrent of angry air flees her lungs. Arms folded, menacing glare in position, she's gearing up to lay into me when her phone rings. She checks it quickly only to decline the call, silencing it.

"Chad?" I ask, chuckling, already knowing by her expression that it is. "The guy is determined, I'll say that much for him. How long before he wins you back over?" I don't mean for my voice to sound the way it does. Hard. Bitter. *Jealous.* I meant to sound teasing and cruel. She's nowhere close to mine and yet I'm pissed off he still calls her as much as he does. That she hasn't set firmer limits with him.

But most of all, I'm pissed that I care.

That I have this sort of reaction to a stupid phone call and a stupid boy.

"I told you last night, that's not going to happen."

"Yeah," I snap, because clearly, I haven't gotten control of my resentment yet. "But obviously Chad doesn't know that."

She juts her elbow into my side hard enough to piss me off more. "He should. I've told him enough times. But Chad Mason doesn't stop until he gets what he wants or grows bored chasing. Eventually the latter will happen."

I shake my head, already knowing there is no growing bored with her. He'll keep wearing her down until he succeeds. Until she's his again.

Women like it when we pay attention to them. They like to make us chase. My mother told me that pearl enough times for it to sink in and if her words weren't enough, I saw it firsthand. It's why I've never done either with any woman.

You have with Eden, my brain oh so unhelpfully chimes in.

Unfortunately, it's true and it stops now.

I look away only to realize we're slowing down at the two last suites—that are really more like small houses—on the strip. The houses aren't side by side. But they're not far apart either. In fact, from this angle, these two appear to share a beach and a small pool. "These are the joined family suites," the driver tells us, practically reading my mind. "They're the most secluded on the resort, meant for larger family gatherings. I apologize," he continues, reading the horror on my face for what it is. "These were the last two suites available. Mrs. Diamond said it should be okay. That you'd barely be here anyway and that since you're both single, would like the most privacy."

"Right," Eden says, her voice a bit dumbstruck.

"Yeah," I add, not much help beyond that. I wonder if Keith knows about this arrangement. Something tells me he doesn't and when he finds out, he'll be pissed. And I'll get the warning again.

Eden and I both turn to face each other at the same time, thinking the exact same thing, shit.

"It'll be fine. I mean, it's not like we're sharing a house. Just the pool and the beach."

"Yeah," I say again because obviously, I'm slaying this language thing. Then I shake myself, laughing lightly. "It's fine. For real. Vi was right that we'll hardly be in our houses. We'll be doing a hundred other things than being here. And it's not like anything is going to happen. Separate places, as you said."

I have no idea why I felt the need to clarify that nothing will happen, but it drags a small smirk from her. Eden's eyes dance about my face as she gathers her purse, pulling the strap onto her shoulder. "They why do you look scared, Henry?"

She winks at me, hopping out of the golf cart.

"Because I am, Eden," I whisper under my breath when I'm positive she can't hear me.

I climb out too, noticing a guy standing in front of the house that is set to be mine. His name is Francis, but everyone calls him Frank. He's native to Hawaii and has been working for this resort as a personal concierge and butler for fifteen years. I catch Eden heading into her house behind her concierge, not so much as paying me a parting glance and I follow her lead, heading into my own behind Frank who is going over everything in the suite I need to know.

There's a huge master suite with a walk-in closet and a marble bathroom that rivals the one I have at home. Frank sets my luggage down, telling me he'll unpack for me and make sure everything is in order. Then he leads me out into the main part of the house that has another full bathroom, a large top-of-the-line fully equipped kitchen —already stocked with food and drinks, but he's happy to add whatever else I'd like—a dining room, a living room with a huge flatscreen and a small office.

Then he leads me out onto the porch and I'm instantly slammed with the view. Gentle waves lap against the pristine shore not even fifty yards out. Palm trees sway in the soft breeze, the scent of flowers perfuming the air. It's paradise, pure and simple, and I can't find it in me to begrudge a second of it. Despite my reluctance for coming, my dick's anger at the woman in the house next door, this might actually turn into everything I never knew I needed.

A break.

I thank Frank, who leaves me here as he attends to my suitcases and whatever else he's up to. The large hammock on the side of the porch is tempting as hell, but the lure of the sand beneath my bare feet is stronger. Stepping out of my shoes, I head in that direction, veering to the right to get a better glimpse of the pool Eden and I share. It's not huge, but it's big enough with a row of umbrella-covered loungers lining it and a hot tub I hadn't noticed before.

Warm water glides through my fingers as I bend down to test it.

"How the hell are we supposed to get any work done with a setup and view like this?" Eden asks, coming out of her house and joining me on the opposite side of the pool.

Her face tilts up in the direction of the sun, closing her eyes. She's wearing a simple white tank top that rides up her smooth, toned stomach as she raises her arms out wide like she's offering herself to the sun as a sacrifice, and cut-off jean shorts that hit her upper thighs. And damn, those thighs. Long, slender, shapely... perfect.

"You're staring at me," she declares. "I can feel your eyes. They're burning into me hotter than the sun."

"Tough shit. Maybe you should wear more clothing and I wouldn't stare."

A smile spreads across her face and I fight a losing battle with my own.

"Pretty badass words for a man drooling a puddle on the ground."

"Just admiring the view, Dragonfly."

"Being attracted to me is the pits, isn't it?"

I laugh, rubbing a hand along my jaw and turning back to the view of the ocean. "You really have this whole scenario in your head, don't you? Who said I'm attracted to you?" I don't make it longer than a minute before I turn back to her.

"You just did when you admitted you were admiring the view of me. But if that weren't enough, I already knew you are, so you don't have to pretend otherwise. You get hard whenever I walk in the room." Her chin drops and she swivels to face me, defiantly crossing her arms over her chest. "Deny it. I dare you."

"Why does it matter what my dick does?"

She smirks, her eyes gleaming. "It's okay. I like the view of you too. Kinda the same with poisonous snakes, right? They're pretty and alluring, but you'd have to be a fucking idiot to get too close. Especially when they've already bitten you once."

"You don't have to worry about me coming too close. Even if we both know you like the way I bite."

She emits a breathy laugh, dropping her hands to her waist. "But not the poison that comes after."

I can't say anything to that, so I stay quiet. Thinking. Wondering if fucking her hard against that palm tree over there would get her out of my system once and for all. The way it always has with women I've been attracted to. That didn't happen the first time and all I can come up with is the way it ended. Troubled. Almost unfinished because I had hurt her, and I wanted to make it right. So maybe that good, hard fuck is just the ticket to be done with her once and for all.

"Don't worry, Henry. My mind is too full with the task ahead to even be thinking about you."

"Stressed a little, Dragonfly? Worried you no longer have what it takes?"

A flush rises up her cheeks and her eyes narrow in on me. "You know that's wicked rude, right?"

"Just calling it like I see it. Am I wrong?"

Her ire along with her body deflates like a popped balloon. "I'm stressed. More than stressed. I'm an overflowing bucket of anxiety. I'm worried as hell I don't have what it takes to not only complete this album on the timeline Jasper gave, but also that it won't be nearly as good as the ones Lyric has done for you guys in the past. But self-doubt doesn't sit well with me, so I'm trying to work my way through it."

"I'm not worried about you, Eden. I not only heard what you did for Cyber's Law, I've seen you in action these last two weeks. You'll do just fine. Besides that, we're not exactly new to this game. If we thought you were bullshit, we'd have ended this already. Timeline be damned."

"Is that a compliment or did I just stroke out and am now hallucinating?"

I laugh, because this woman's mouth... "I can take it back."

"Noooo," she rushes. "Don't do that. I'll never survive it if you say something harsh right now." She runs her hands through her hair, lifting the heavy strands up and piling them on top of her head.

"You should wear your hair up more."

Her eyes flash in my direction and I instantly regret my words.

"Why? You like the way I look when I do?"

Yes. I get to see your tattoo that matches mine. It's why I yanked that elastic from your hair so I wouldn't have to look at it.

"I'll see you at dinner," I tell her instead of answering, turning around and walking away before I do something stupid. Like bite her again.

THIRTEEN

EDEN

Dinner is taking forever. It's all of us. Ten people stuffed into the private dining area of the Asian fusion place located on the hotel grounds. Let's start this off by saying Asian fusion is not my favorite. I get it, okay. I do. Adalyn does not eat dairy and she does not eat gluten, so Asian fusion is right up her alley.

I don't begrudge that.

I'm just not in the mood for it either and my tolerance level was already at like a five out of ten before I even stepped foot in the restaurant. For starters, I'm tired. Time change notwithstanding, I haven't had a lot of sleep the last few nights coupled with a long plane ride today and all the stress on my mind, and yeah. I'm exhausted.

Add to that freaking Chad calling like a man obsessed. He spoke to Jess, who was trying to do me a solid by confirming that I am in fact in Hawaii, and that yes, Henry is with me. Then there's Henry. What he said to me by the pool? I shouldn't be thinking about any of it but of course I'm thinking about all of it.

Speaking of... he's another thing that makes this dinner suck.

Angry and surly with me and nothing but smiles and charming

fun with everyone else. The mercurial bastard is giving me whiplash, and I'm just so over it. Especially when he throws me looks—like he's doing right now—almost like he can't help himself. Like his brain is on its own mental timer. Ping, time to look at Eden with a glare that makes her panties wet. Check.

By the time we reach dessert, I'm so peopled out it isn't even funny.

I just want to chill out for a bit, attempt to mentally unwind, but no matter what I do, or what I try, nothing is working. I'm a hot ball of mess. Which leads me to this...

My mind is going places.

Getting ideas.

Forming plans it has no business formulating. But I need to break this tension, this stress, this fucking heartbreak hangover somehow. And the only way I can think to break it is—

"Will you be my maid of honor?"

Maia, bless her heart, has been doing all the heavy lifting with me tonight. Chatting away about this and wait... did she just ask me to be her maid of honor?

"It's stupid, right?" she continues despite my stunned silence. I turn to her, dragging my pathetic ass away from Henry, something I should have done like a hundred times before now.

"You're serious? Me?" I point to my chest just to confirm.

"Look. I get it. You've known me like two months and I'm marrying your brother. It's weird. But that's kinda my life, so I'm trying to roll with it. People are already judging the hell out of this." She waggles a finger between her and Keith. "It's in magazines and everything, so it must be true," she states, rolling her eyes derisively. "'I'm the opportunistic gold digger who got herself knocked up and forced Keith to marry me.'" She puts air quotes around the words. "Anyway, people are nasty and judgmental and you're not. You've never been. It's going to be a tiny ceremony. Just us" —she waves her hand around the table— "and your family. I thought of asking Vi or

Naomi first but you're going to be my sister. And I really do love you. So..." She trails off, blushing.

"I'm honored. And floored. And hell yes—" I hold up my hand, stopping myself. "Wait, do I have to wear some hideous bridesmaid dress in some crazy pastel like mint green?"

"Is mint green considered a pastel?"

"Humor me."

She laughs, leaning back against her seat. "No. You can wear whatever you want. I for real don't care. By the time we do this thing I'll be large with not one but two children and the idea of fitting into a white dress gives me hives. But your brother is super traditional and wants his ring on my finger before these kids come out. So that's how it's gonna be."

Yeah, I can see that about Keith.

"Well, I'm in. Till death do us part."

A smile explodes across her face and she reaches out, wrapping me up in a bear hug. "Thank you, Eden," she whispers to me. "And because you're doing me this huge solid, I'm going to do one in return for you." She holds me tighter as I try to pull away. "Henry has been staring at you with a fire in his eyes that has only one way of extinguishing it. And going by the fire in yours when you look at him, I'm thinking you need it too."

I laugh, despite myself. "My brother will cut a bitch. And then some balls."

"No, he won't. Well, okay, I take that back. He might. He did tell Henry not to touch you and I think he was serious on that. But more for your protection than anything else and I don't think you need protection from Henry the way Keith believes you do. And since nothing has happened yet, I'm not lying by not telling him anything. So don't tell me anything. Unless you really need to talk to someone and then I'm putting it in the girl vault and by definition, you can't break that. Even for husbands and baby daddies to be. It's practically written in the scripture."

Wow. That strangely makes so much sense.

"You do realize I already have more on my mind than I can handle with this album, right?"

She finally releases me, staring at me with a glint in her eyes that makes me want to squirm.

"I do. I think some extra stress-relieving activities might help with that."

"Are you suggesting I have some sort of an illicit affair with him?"

She nods her head yes while firmly saying, "No. I would never, ever suggest such a thing. I'm simply saying, we're in paradise for three weeks. It's beautiful and romantic, and wow, I mean, just sexy, right? The sun, the heat, the ocean." She shrugs, picking up her sparkling water and taking a sip. "Three weeks and then we're back home. Back to our reality. Never again will we have an opportunity like this."

I think I'm impersonating a goldfish right now.

"Did she say yes?" Keith cuts in, dropping his hand to Maia's slightly rounded tummy the way he always does whenever she's near. Whoever the hell called this woman an opportunistic gold digger seriously does not have eyes. Talk about cutting a bitch. They're lucky I haven't come across them.

"She said yes." Maia beams. "But I promised her she can wear whatever she wants."

Keith groans. "Not back to that again."

"Yes, back to that again," she snaps. "I will not resemble an orca at my wedding, Keith."

The two of them continue to go at it since that's what they do when they're not being sickeningly adorable. But Maia's freaking non-suggestion is hitting me like a bullet to the head. My brains are splattered about and I'm not sure I want to pick them back up and become smart again. Hadn't I just been thinking the same thing she refused to say?

No. I can't do it. It's madness and my heart has already been put through a paper shredder where he's concerned. And then again two months ago with Chad.

I just need to get out here and decompress a bit.

"I'm calling it a night," I declare, standing up and finishing off the last of my margarita, which really does not mesh well with Asian fusion in case you were wondering. "I'm totally wiped. The studio is all set up and I will see you clowns tomorrow morning at eight."

And with that, I make my rounds, kissing everyone on the top of the head or on the cheek, depending on who it is, bypassing Henry altogether, and then head out, choosing to take the eight-minute walk back to my house instead of climbing into one of the waiting chauffeured golf carts.

No one follows me and it's a relief as much as it's a disappointment. I think about what Maia said and I actually laugh out loud. Likely because my stupid brain was like ten steps ahead of her. But for what? What would I hope to gain? Some orgasms?

Sounds fun, but at what cost?

Entering the house, I immediately go into the bedroom.

But nothing feels right. My body is shifty, and my skin is itchy, and I just... "I can swim," I announce to the bathing suit sitting out on my bed. I had taken it out earlier, thinking maybe I'd jump in the pool or the ocean, and then I got caught up trying to get the studio together. But now, now I'm thinking a quick swim in the pool, not the ocean since I'm not an idiot, seems like just the thing to work this out of me.

This crap eating at me is what my great-grandma Celia would have affectionately referred to as shpilkes. Like you're literally crawling out of your skin and the idea of stabbing something repeatedly with a sharp object isn't off-putting. I need to nip this in the bud now if I'm going to be on my A-game tomorrow.

"This is how close to the edge I am."

Because why did I agree to this? This album? This timeline? This band? And why do I have assholes still trying to peck at the festering remains of my heart as it lays scattered on the side of the road? I change quickly into my bikini.

Laps? No. That's so something Keith would do. Instead, I grab the unopened bottle of tequila they stocked for me—like they knew I would need it or something—and head outside.

The air is mild, calm almost, lacking the breeze I was enjoying earlier in the day. But it's warm and pleasant and the pool is a glowing blue oasis of come swim in me. Yanking the cork from the bottle, I take a few swigs, realizing this is hitting a new low and not caring all that much.

At first, I just sit in the lounger, staring out at what I know to be the ocean though I can hardly make it out in the darkness. I think about all that I have to do over these next few weeks. The plan I have in place. And I stand up just as quickly as I sat down, taking another drink. I know I've been thrown into the lion's den headfirst, expected to make it out alive with nothing but my cunning to fight with.

Sink or swim.

That's what Lyric said and even though she called me a shark, thinking of the studio I created today and knowing all that we have to get through, I feel like a minnow. Tomorrow I will be spot on my work because I have no choice in the matter, but for tonight, I just want to zone out.

Warm water laps at my chest as I enter the deep end. My head dunks back, wetting my hair and I suck in a deep breath, butterflying my arms on the edge of the pool before I sink down, dropping to the bottom, my eyes still closed. Just as I begin to float back up, a turbulent rush of water slams into me, pushing me sideways. My eyes burst open, immediately locating another body in the water.

I scowl, my face breaching the surface.

"Really?" I yell at him, splashing water in his direction. "I mean, for real?"

"What?" he barks back, brushing the wet strands of his blond hair back from his face. "I didn't know you were in here." Drops of water trail down his face, neck, and upper chest and fuck him. Just fuck him for looking so hot right now. For making me jealous of the water that gets to touch him every place I wish I could.

For getting under my skin the way only he seems to be able to do.

I curse under my breath, swimming back to the edge of the pool, and picking up the bottle of tequila. I take a large swig, wiping my mouth with the back of my hand. If I'm doing it, I might as well do it right. Henry swims up beside me, stealing the bottle from my hand and doing the same. He sets it down on the ledge and for a few moments, we just stare at each other.

Me watching his eyes, how they darken. How water drags a lazy path from his hair, across his cut-from-stone face. How he licks his lips when he discovers that's where I'm staring.

Him starting low, gliding up my exposed belly. The triangle of my bikini, clinging to the swell of my breasts and nipples—barbells included. The hollow at the base of my throat and up to my lips.

Us moving toward each other at the same time, no sound other than the rippling of the waves on the shore and the thrum of my heartbeat through my ears.

"What are you doing?" he rasps, his hand coming through the water and landing on my hip.

"Thinking things I shouldn't. What are you doing?"

"Touching things I shouldn't. We should stop."

We should. He's right. I was just thinking a whole slew of things about him and how this is a really bad idea. He's as dangerous for me as they come, but I just... I'm tired of fighting this too. I hate him and I want him, and I'm consumed by him. He's eclipsing my thoughts and the things I should be focused on.

"I don't want to stop," I tell him honestly.

He swallows impossibly hard. So hard I hear it over all that blood and all those waves.

"I don't want to either."

"I hate men. I hate you. I know I said I wasn't hating you anymore, but I lied. I hate how much I want you when you're the last man on the planet I should want. You're bad for me, Henry."

He grins, inching in even closer. So close that he bends down, his tongue swiping from my clavicle up to my ear. I shudder and his grip on my hip tightens. He rights himself, staring into my eyes.

"I hate women. I hate what you do to me. The way you control and manipulate all these different pieces of me when I swore I'd never let any woman do that. I fucking hate how much I want you when you're the last woman on the planet I should want. You're not just bad for me, Eden. You're a poison I'm terrified there is no antidote to."

I agree with that. I feel exactly the same way.

"There is nothing right about it," he continues. "I am all wrong for you in every imaginable way. But that doesn't stop me from wanting you the way I have *never* wanted anyone else."

My hand captures the back of his neck, hauling his face to mine, and slamming my lips to his with enough force that my teeth smash into my lip and I catch the faint metallic taste of blood. He growls, fisting my hair and forcefully ripping me back. I whimper at the zing of pain and slap his face with a resonating *smack* that tears through the air.

He doesn't jar. He just stares at me, burning me alive with his eyes alone.

"You stopping this?"

He stares, silently warring.

"Do whatever the hell you want with me," I tell him with a bitter laugh. "Just stay the fuck out of my heart."

His lips come back down on mine, opening me up for him instantly, taking no prisoners as he plunders every inch of my mouth. This is it. The moment. There is no going back now. And he knows it too.

FOURTEEN

HENRY

Fuck. I can't do this. I force Eden back off me, spinning us in the water and slamming her into the wall of the pool. I'm too violent. Too chaotic. I stare down into her fiery blue eyes and lose my goddamn mind with how she looks right now. Consumed by lust. Out of control. Drunk on me.

Part of me wants her to slap me again. Partially because it turns me on, but the larger part is hoping it will smack—literally—some sense into me. I made a promise, only right now, looking at her, I can't fully remember what it was.

She hikes her body up the wall of the pool and wraps her legs around my waist, grinding down and then up against me. And Christ. That's everything right there. Her body against mine. The feel of her heat seeping into me.

This woman. This fucking woman...

Never have I craved a look, a touch, a smile, a thought. Tell me all your evils, Eden, because I already know mine are worse, darker. I can slay yours in two seconds without breaking a sweat. That's what this girl does to me. She rattles my mind and shakes me up in ways I don't want to be shaken.

"This won't happen again," I promise her. "Walk away, Eden. You deserve a hell of a lot more than what I can give you."

She laughs. Actually laughs. "Why would I do that when all I want you for is this?" She grinds into me again, hitting my cock so perfectly I have to swallow my groan. "You think I'm looking for another relationship after what I've been through? After I already know how fucked up you are?" She smirks when I try to pull away, holding me tight with her legs. "Yeah, Henry. I know. No one says something like that to a woman unless they're as fucked up as it gets. You're all outwardly charming. A good guy at your core. But it's your in-between parts that are the mess I want nothing to do with."

I'm floored. No one sees this about me. No one. Well, maybe Jasper, but he's Jasper, so it doesn't count. But Eden, how on Earth does Eden read me so well when I do everything I can to ensure no one does?

"Eden—"

A piece of me breaks.

But when her mouth presses gently to mine, her arms snaking around my shoulders, something else feels like it's falling into place. It knocks the wind from my lungs, awful and uncomfortable, but immovable all the same.

"Shut up, Henry," she breathes into me. "Just shut up. Stop talking and fuck me already. Fuck me so good I don't care about tomorrow. Fuck me so good, I no longer think. That's what I need from you, and I swear to God if you don't deliver—"

Her words get stifled as my mouth attacks hers. I've been fighting this attraction for too long. Trying to be the good guy. Trying to be the best friend who keeps his promises. Trying to be an asshole or ignoring her when nothing else seems to work.

And she's here, wanting me regardless.

Needing me as much as I need her.

With a grip on her ass, I thrust her against me as my lips takes over. My tongue invades her mouth, swirling with hers. She tastes like tequila and forbidden fruit and paradise. Eden. Aptly named for the wonder she evokes and a temptation impossible to fight.

Water sloshes around us as we go at each other. Frantic and far too crazed. Her mouth attacks the side of my neck as mine heads for her chest. I shift her ass into the pool wall, freeing my hands to rip the top of her bikini off. Small, perky breasts bounce into my hands, her pink nipples tight and needy with silver barbells strung through them.

She has no idea what a vision she is.

How she takes my breath away.

So perfect, I can't stop my mouth from clamping onto her right nipple, my teeth biting down around her piercing and pulling.

"Oh, holy hell," she yells, loud, her hands rip at the hair at the back of my head. But I don't cool it. I punish her because since I laid eyes on her three years ago, I've been nothing but punished.

She doesn't know. She has no clue.

No one gets in. No one gets to me.

Except her.

I've wanted her for so long I find myself saying, "Eden," just to make sure it's real.

And because that infuriates me like nothing else, I take it out on her tits. Biting and nipping and gripping and marking every inch of them. Her entire tit practically fits in my mouth, and yes, fucking yes, there is nothing better than that. Her head falls back as she cries out louder than before, undulating those hips and causing pool water to slosh about like a hurricane.

I need her naked and I need it now.

With a final flick of her nipple ring, I haul her up and out of the water, loving how she shivers, erupting in goose bumps as the cool night air hits her wet skin. I slam her ass down on the edge of the pool, spreading her legs wide open, and then untying the strings on the sides of her bottoms. It falls quickly away, and I ignore her yelps, my eyes feasting on her hot, pink pussy a second before my mouth can no longer be denied. My tongue hits her opening, stabbing inside without preamble, doing this as much for her as I am for myself.

This isn't gentle.

I don't want gentle, and I know for a fact she doesn't either.

My top lip hits her clit as my tongue starts to fuck her rabidly.

"Oh. Hell. Yes." A loud moan. "I said goddamn. Goddamn. Goddamn."

I chuckle into her, slowing my pace. "Did you just quote Pulp Fiction while I'm eating you out?" Looking up, I catch her eye.

She belts out a laugh, her grip in my hair tightening. "I did. And if I liked you at all, I might like you more for picking up on that. But since I don't..." She pushes my face back into her heat and that something inside me that fell into place before goes *thunk*. Kinda hard. So hard now, I'm the one shivering.

It's like a knife stabbing me in all the wrong places, and I have to make her come now. Now!

I up my ante, biting on her clit and tweaking her nipples, twisting the barbell from side to side. Then I slip two curved fingers inside her, pumping while making sure I hit her spot every damn time. That motion does it. She starts to go crazy on me. Pushing her pussy into my face and panting to God and Jesus and Hell and Heaven and I think even Moses gets thrown in there. It's a holy trinity of sex and lust, and I'll take it.

I'll run away with it.

"I am going to punish your pussy with a slow fuck if you don't come on me now. I'm getting tired of waiting."

She smacks the side of my face and I growl into her, my cock jerking. But this girl, this wild, sexy, monster of a girl... she comes. Hard. My lips and chin are covered in her as she rides my face, my fingers, and tongue refusing to relent for a second until I know she's absolutely spent.

She sags back, her arms trembling under the weight of supporting her upper body.

"I wish you had done that three years ago," she heaves on a hot breath.

I'm so thankful I didn't. If I had tasted her back then I'd really have been done for. As it is, I already know when I'm done with her it will take me months to get over the way she tastes.

Eden scoots back as I move to get out of the pool, hoisting myself up and landing with a wet slap of my feet. I take a swig of the tequila, handing it to her to do the same. It's diversionary. I'm trying to think. Not so easy when my dick is so hard it could cut granite. Not even the chill of the air on my wet body is doing anything to stop it. I can't bring her to my bed. She'll sleep there if I do that because I won't want her to leave. The thought of morning sex will drive that.

So, no.

Too dangerous.

That's a habit in the making and we need lines. It's the only way I can force myself to make this just tonight. I need all the lines with her even if the thought of crossing them—

"Are you clean?" she asks, and I blink, coming back, watching her as she strolls, gloriously naked, over to the lounger. She's having the same thoughts as me. Thank god.

"Yes. I've been tested since the last time I was with a woman. I don't have it with me, Eden. The results are on my phone back inside. I can either run and get it or you can trust me with that. I'll show you everything tomorrow if you want, but I don't have any condoms out here. I wasn't expecting this to happen."

"I trust you," she declares. "Despite you being you, I know you'd never intentionally do something to hurt me."

No. I wouldn't. That doesn't mean I won't though.

"What about you?" I ask, redirecting my thoughts.

"I'm clean. I got tested after I found Chad with Marni. I can show you too. I also have an IUD."

Perfect.

"We can't sleep in the same bed together tonight."

"Agreed," she exclaims with a smirk. "You seem like the clingy type. I like my space when I sleep. If I want morning sex, I'll have it with myself."

I grin. That *thunk* shifts again. Like dynamite. Dangerous and explosive, taunting in all the wrong ways. I tamp it down before it can do something stupid like grow into something else.

"I want you to ride me. I want your tits in my face when you do."

"I think this chair will be perfect for that," she says, patting one of the loungers.

I drag water away from my face, slicking my hair back. Eden stares at me with a hunger that matches my own as her eyes trail over my arms, chest, and abs.

I don't waste time; I just pull down my trunks and get my ass on the lounger. The sooner I fuck her, the sooner she'll be gone.

Her eyes find my cock, hard, standing at attention, begging for her, and her jaw drops. She blinks a time or two and then pulls herself together and walks boldly over to me. There is no lack of confidence with Eden. I mean, why should there be? If I were granted access to heaven and God said create your perfect woman, it would be her.

Nutty ass hair and all. It keeps things interesting.

"Come here," I demand, grabbing her hips and helping straddle me. She adjusts herself, dragging her hands up through her hair and piling it on top of her head. "Fuck," I hiss between my teeth as I take her in from this angle. "I wish you weren't so beautiful."

My hands cup her breasts, toying with those piercings I cannot get enough of.

The things I want to do to these.

Having her above me. Her skin against my skin. It's too much. I almost can't take it. *Mine.* No. I quickly shake that off. Not mine. Just for tonight.

She slips up and then back down on me, angling my cock so it can fill her up. Lower, inch by inch, she sinks down deeper. The sensation, the control, it frazzles my mind. I want to thrust up. I want to take over and destroy her the way she's destroying me.

But I can't.

It's the look in her eyes that's forcing me to hold my position. The way the pleasure surges through her, reddening her cheeks and chest. The way her lips part and she breathes out only to have a moan tag on at the end.

Eden lifts all the way up, my cock nearly slipping out completely before she slams all the way down. Spots dance behind my eyes as I throw my head back on a loud growl. "Fuck, Eden. You're so tight."

My eyes flash open to find her chin pointed to the sky. I reach up, grabbing her breasts, massaging them as she adjusts to my size. Little by little, her body relaxes. Her chin drops and my lips capture hers as she starts to grind and rock. Greedy hands clasp her hips, need has me thrusting up and up and up. She throws her head back, bouncing her body up and down to a rhythm that has both of us breathless and beyond repair.

My dick can't get deep enough. There is no place I do not want to touch this girl. Warm. Wet. Paradise. "So good." My hands are everywhere. Hers too as what started off slow and testing turns almost frenzied.

And I swear, being inside of a woman has never felt like this does. "This. Uh. Oh."

That's as far as she gets, her body rocking, grinding, bouncing, undulating, testing, taking. She doesn't stop and she doesn't slow, and I just take, take, take her as hard as I can. I want to hurt her for making me feel this good. For letting this thing between us get this far. For making me never want to stop. I'm already planning all the dirty ways she'll like it when I know, *I know*, I can't have her again. If I do, I'll never want to stop.

Eden. My Eden.

She's fucking me like a pro. Like a woman who knows how to pleasure herself and has no shame in it. Nothing—and I do mean nothing—has ever turned me on more. I hold her hips and tuck in for the ride of my life. Lips capture her breasts, my teeth scraping up to her neck where I latch on, feasting on her.

"That's right, Dragonfly. Squeeze my cock just like that." She moans as she does it again. "Tell me, Eden. Tell me how good it feels having my cock buried inside you." I smack her ass when she doesn't answer, adjusting myself so I have more control as I take over. My hips piston up, my grip on her bruising and unrelenting. Hating her the way she's hating me. "Tell me," I demand.

"No," she whimpers as I smack her ass again, this time harder. "Because I already wish you didn't feel this good inside me."

I pull back and meet her eyes, cupping her jaw. She bites down on the pad of my thumb until a zap of pain sears through me. My lips come down over hers, my tongue stabbing into her mouth in rhythm with my thrusts. I need to be closer. I need to be deeper. I need more of her whether she wants that or not. I'm dripping and groaning and desperate—so desperate—to flip her over and fuck her into oblivion. So I do. I grab her ass and drop her back down onto the chair, my cock never leaving her body.

Then I pound.

My eyes on hers, hers searching mine. Our foreheads meet and I fuck her and fuck her and fuck her so good. So hard. So thoroughly. Filled with a rage that has its own color and taste. My hips don't stop. Hers meet mine in synchrony. My cock seeks her magic spot. One hand on her face, the other pulling hard on her nipple.

"Henry," she rasps, and I just about blow my load at the sound of my name on her lips.

Her fingers wrap themselves in the back of my hair as she presses our foreheads harder together, holding me to her as she trembles and whimpers. Getting close. Closer...

And then she detonates.

A scream pierces the air, her head twisting to the side, eyes closed because it's impossible for her to keep them open. That doesn't stop me from watching her.

She comes all over me, a warm wet gush of fucking heaven that rips a howl from me, her name an expletive. I keep thrusting, not wanting this to end. This feeling. Damn, this feeling is everything I never knew sex could be.

She sags down, her eyes heavy and her smile sated as I slow my motion.

Beautiful.

How is it possible she's this beautiful?

I could do this. I could get lost in this. I could pretend. I could live inside of her.

And I'd be happy.

For the first time in my life, I'd be truly happy.

I'd have it all. I'd know what that feels like.

And then I'd watch helplessly as it's ripped away. The way it always is. Then what would I be? I'd be less than zero. Nothing lasts forever. I've heard and seen that enough times in my life to know it's true.

Which is why I pull out of her. It's why I get up and grab my trunks, tugging them on. Grimacing at how cold and wet they are. I hand her her bikini, helping her up and off the lounger, making sure she's steady on her feet and then turning away as she silently dresses. Ignoring the way I know she's looking at me.

I can't say any of the things I'm dying to say to her. It's not fair. I told her it was tonight and that's it. She asked me to stay the fuck out of her heart and I'm trying. Even if it makes me the asshole. The bad guy.

I'm doing this for you, Eden. For both of us.

I walk back to my house without a backward glance or even a word of goodnight. And never in my life have I been so horrified with myself while simultaneously feeling so complete.

FIFTEEN

EDEN

Notes flow through my head, my mind desperate to catch each one. I'd say nothing else is breaching my consciousness, but that would be a lie. That said, I'm doing everything I can possibly do *not* to think about him and all that transpired between us last night. Especially when my mind needs to be occupied by other things. Like this music I'm listening to.

Yes, this music is all I should be focused on.

Last night did accomplish one thing I was after. It took the stress I was feeling and zapped it out of my body. For ten glorious hours, I was right as rain. I slept. I woke with a smile of anticipation. Then we entered the studio and all that Zen I had been rocking went to hell in a handbasket.

But no more about that. Or him.

I'm sitting on a chaise that's about ten feet from where the waves are breaking on the shore. There's a mostly eaten Cobb salad and a half empty margarita on the small table beside me. And the sun. The glorious sun is shining down on my SPF 50 lathered body, warming me through and through.

I mean, it's workcation, right? No sense in not indulging in all this place has to offer me while I work.

But this song. It's the one we finished up this morning in the studio. Day one was a success. Tomorrow we will start a new song, so I have to make sure this one is perfect before we can do that, or I'll find myself buried too deep by the end of this.

Movement on my left has my eyes popping open. Naomi is heading my way, dropping her surfboard into the sand and grabbing the towel from the chaise on the other side of the table that's dividing us.

"Hey," she says, wringing out her nearly black hair and wrapping herself up in her towel. "Sorry. I didn't mean to interrupt you."

If the fact that my brother is a world-famous rock star and I get to work for Lyric Rose and with Cyber's Law isn't a big enough trip, the fact that I am quasi friends with Naomi Kent is. Chick is a superstar, and I would be lying if I said I didn't worship her. Growing up, my walls were plastered with her posters—something Keith likes to tease me about in front of her. I am not an easy fangirl, but every time she talks to me, I swear, I forget how to form coherent sentences.

"You didn't," I tell her, pausing the track. "I'm just listening to what we did this morning. Making sure it's perfect."

"I love that you guys are doing this here. Gus said you're not messing around either. That you worked their assess off all morning."

A surge of pride swells through my chest at that.

"Would you mind?" I ask with a hopeful, yet hesitant tone, wiggling my phone in her direction.

"You want me to listen? Sure. Of course. I'd love to."

Yeah, Naomi is also the sweetest thing on the planet. Her and Viola both. Hard not to love these women when they are legit the coolest, most easy-going peeps.

"Thank you. I think at this point I've listened to it too much, you know? I can't tell if the tempo's too fast or if I've officially just gone insane."

"I get that. Sometimes you need to take a step back because

you're too close to your work. I doubt it's too fast, but I'm happy to tell you my opinion." She eyes my food and then her head whips around and she finds a passing waiter, ordering the same thing I was having. Turning back to me, she shrugs, smiling ruefully. "I don't start fertility treatments until we get home. It may be my last chance for a drink for a while."

I snort out. "You don't have to justify it to me. I'm right there with you." I hold up my drink, giving it a little shake and taking a long sip.

"Thank god for that." She laughs, settling down onto her chaise. Rolling onto her side so she can face me, she says, "Okay, cue it up."

I play the song for her, watching her face as she listens while I chew on my lip like a college student waiting for their final grade from their professor. The song ends and she opens her bright blue eyes, a soft smile on her lips. "I think it's perfect, Eden. Any slower will be too slow for the vibe they have going. Really. Don't overthink it and definitely don't touch it. It's awesome. I love the way you have the acoustic and the electric in there. It adds such a nice texture."

"Yeah?"

She nods emphatically. "Definitely. It's seriously good. Trust me, I've been doing this a long time with a lot of different producers along the way. You have real talent, Eden. Lyric and Jasper aren't wrong with that. Trust their judgment, but more importantly, trust your own."

I stare at her, trying to tamp down that giddy feeling in my chest. "You know it's taking all my restraint not to leap over this table and hug the hell out of you, and I'm not usually a hugger."

"I'm not usually a hugger either, but I wouldn't have stopped you." She winks at me. "I like the idea of them getting this album going and done, and I love the idea of Gus taking some time off to be with me while we go through this bullshit. I hate that we have to do it, but it is what it is. Having one less stressor over our heads is exactly what we need."

Yikes. No extra pressure or anything.

"I swear, Naomi, I will do absolutely everything I can to make this album go as quickly and smoothly as possible. I want it to be perfect, but I know you all have a lot going on in your personal lives and the last thing I would ever want to do is add something else for you to worry about onto that."

Just then her food and drink are delivered, and she raises her drink to me. "I'll toast to that." We clink glasses and each take a sip, falling quiet as the sounds of the ocean soothe us into quiet introspection only to be pierced by the ear-splitting sound of a two-year-old crying and a mother trying to calm her down.

Naomi and I both look over our shoulders to find Viola holding baby Cora, who is two, but I think will always be called baby until another child comes into the fold. Vi is walking in our direction, bouncing Cora on her hip while Cora tucks her head in her mommy's chest.

"Hey," Naomi says, standing up. "What's wrong?"

"She was running—because this girl is always freaking running— and she tripped and fell. She's fine. No scratches or anything. But you wouldn't know that to hear her cry." Vi giggles, rubbing Cora's back.

"Can I try?" I ask, standing up and walking toward the small blonde thing clinging to her mama like a baby Koala.

"Sure," Vi exclaims, a bit surprised. I may be the youngest kid in my crew, but for some reason I've always been good with kids.

"Hey Cora?" I ask softly, walking slowly up beside her and getting close to her face. "Do you wanna come play at the pool with me?"

Cora's crying goes from a wail to a gentle cry, her body still doing that hiccupping thing that happens after a good cry, but she's starting to calm down. Her head swivels against Vi's chest and her green eyes meet mine.

I reach out with grabby fingers and an calm smile. "Come on, babe. Let's go make a mess in the water."

She sucks in a shaky breath and then looks up at her mom who smiles and nods encouragingly. "It's okay. You can go with Auntie Eden. I think Daddy and Ady are still at the pool too."

Cora stares at her mom for another half-beat before launching herself into my arms. This girl does not mess around. She is all movement. "I got her. Go have a margarita with Naomi," I tell Vi as I readjust Cora in my arms.

Vi laughs. "Bless you. I think I will."

I laugh as Cora and I head up the path toward the large private pool area specifically for the band.

"Alright Cora. Let's get real here. I'm thinking a cannonball into the pool. You with me?" She stares up at me with a goofy grin. All teeth and sunshine with this one. "You look nothing like your daddy."

"Nope," Jasper says. "She's all Viola." Jasper is camped out on a lounger with a sleeping Adalyn on his chest. He points at Ady with a smirk. "This one is all me. This girl hasn't napped in years but give her a solid day of sunshine and water and she's like a baby again. Same thing on the plane. Vi will kill me for this because she'll likely have trouble sleeping tonight, but I don't get many of these moments anymore with her, so I'll take it. Now this bundle of trouble on the other hand." He points to his other girl in my arms. "Thank you for helping out with her. She stopped going down for naps like a week before we came out here. I think Vi is going a bit nuts with that. Especially when I'm working all these hours."

"This one?" I gesture to the bundle in my arms. "Trouble, you say?" I look at her with an adoring smile. "Nah. You're easy street, right, kid?"

Cora giggles as I tickle her belly. "No. I wanna swim."

"And swim we shall."

"Uh uh," Gus says, coming up and literally stealing Cora from my arms. "Niece time. Back off, little Dawson. This one's mine."

He wraps Cora up and then without hesitation runs full speed to the pool and jumps in. I squeal out in alarm but Gus bursts from the water two seconds later, Cora raised high up in his arms, and nothing but smiles and delighted giggles. I don't think her face even touched the water.

"He does that to piss me off because he knows it works. That crap drives me absolutely bullshit."

"Um. I think I just peed my pants."

I watch Gus toss Cora up in the air and catch her, her peals of laughter pulling a smile of my own. That is until my gaze crosses the pool, finding Keith and Maia standing with their backs to me in the water and Henry sitting on the edge, dangling his feet in.

Staring straight at me.

He's shirtless, only wearing swim trunks like he was last night, and instantly I'm assaulted with all the visions I refused to allow myself to indulge in all day. The roughness of his touch. His face between my thighs. His mouth devouring my breasts. Me above him. Him above me. The way he stared into my eyes.

There was nothing sweet or gentle about the way he took me. It was as close to a hate fuck as you can get. But hell...

I foolishly thought if I spent one night with him, I would be able to put it behind me. That maybe we were just unfinished business and once we had each other, this... *heat* between us would die.

But looking at him right now, with his clenched jaw, intense green eyes focused straight on me, carved pecs, and washboard abs, all I can think about is how foolish I was to ever imagine I could fuck Henry Gauthier out of my system.

My body wants his. Insanely so. My skin ignites with this fire at just the sight of him. This burning. This insatiable need that's so tormenting it makes me ache in places I didn't know it was possible to ache. I want him and I hate myself for it. He will break my heart if I let him get too close and he's already too close.

The turbulence in his eyes matches my own and I can't do this...

I can't look at him and pretend I don't want to tear him apart and crawl inside of his broken pieces and glue him back together as mine.

I watch as he talks to Keith and Maia, but his gaze never deviates from mine. He licks his lips, his eyes dropping to mine, and my breath stutters in my chest as my nipples tighten.

Those lips. That tongue.

I practically moan.

My heart thunders in my chest, blood rushing through my ears.

No.

Just no.

I can't let this happen again.

I was with a man for two years who claimed to love me, but who didn't truly know me. And the man who seems to truly know me, will never love me. Never have I felt more alive with someone as I did last night. It's an addicting tonic I want to drown myself in. I wasn't wrong about Henry's poison. It's insidious. Ensnaring.

I have to stop it now.

Without a word, I pivot on the balls of my feet and flee the pool area. Taking one path and then another through the lush grounds, I force one foot in front of the other without noticing or caring where I'm headed. Finally, I stop, needing to catch my breath. I lean against a large palm that shades me from the sun and close my eyes.

Only...

I'm not alone.

SIXTEEN

EDEN

Long fingers splay out across my hip, right above my bikini bottoms. I feel his body heat behind me. The scent of him infiltrates my nose, heading straight for my core, bypassing my better sense altogether. Henry is enticing in a way no man should ever be.

An angry expletive forms on my tongue, but as his hand travels up my bare skin it gets lodged in the back of my throat.

What is he doing?

He grasps my ribcage, his thumb on my shoulder blade, his fingers hitting the underwire of my bra-like bikini top. I don't have a lot of boobage by nature, but this suit takes what little I have and hikes my girls up to the sky. Most importantly, it hides my nipple rings. While I typically wouldn't care enough to hide them with friends, when I'm around my brother, his friends, and their children, I do.

Henry's lips press into the crook of my shoulder and for what feels like forever he just stands there breathing into me, touching me without copping a feel, and staying silent. It doesn't matter. I feel bare with him. Raw and exposed but turned on as hell.

"What are you doing?"

His only response is to thrust forward, his large erection planting itself against my ass. He cups my breast, and I whimper like the wanton fool he makes me. I grit my teeth, hardening my stare even as I look out at nothing.

"I hate you, Henry. I hate how you make me feel. How you think you're hot shit and can take me however you want me. I hate that I don't have the strength to stop you despite my bold inner expletives and proud, tough girl bullshit. You make me weak in all the ways I want to be strong."

"I'd never take away your strength, Eden. Your strength is one of the things that turns me on most about you."

Fuck.

My eyes close and my head tilts back, meeting his shoulder. His lips, his tongue, his goddamn teeth rip at my skin. I will have marks on my neck and shoulder. I have to imagine that's his intention.

"I need rules," I manage as his other hand wraps around me, toying with the hem of my bottoms. My eyes open and I stare out at the palms as I try to regain control of my thoughts.

I feel his smirk. "Rules?"

"Yes, Henry. Rules. Because if you intend to fuck me as I think you're about to, I need rules. Especially when I have a hunch this won't be the last time it happens. I need rules that keep you out of my heart as I previously instructed."

That grin. That stupid, perfect, seductive grin...

"I can do rules."

Oh good. At least one of us can. That's a help, considering I'm already plotting loopholes in my own plan.

"It stops the second we get stateside."

"Absolutely," he agrees.

"Your dick doesn't go near or even entertain another female until this is over."

He laughs at that. Like my request is ridiculous. "Not a problem."

"You leave right when we're done. No sleepovers."

"Same goes for you. You seem like the clingy type," he says as he bites his way up my neck, echoing my words to him from last night. "I like my space when I sleep."

"Jesus, Henry. What are we doing?"

"What I can no longer deny," he rasps, and my eyes close in defeat. "I tried, Eden. I tried all damn day. The same way I've been trying for weeks now. But I want you. I want you hard and rough and kinky and sweet and dirty and slow. I want you all the ways possible, and the only way I can see myself not wanting you like that is to take you all those ways."

That should make sense, but I'm not stupid and neither is he. I've read enough romances to know how that particular plan goes.

Only he and I are different, aren't we?

We're both freaking messes. I just got out of a two-year relationship. And though Henry was my first love, this could also be considered rebound and frankly, it's just too freaking soon for me. Plus, he's Keith's BFF. Bandmate. And he's a disaster of a man. I mean, come on.

So that's where we are: I won't let myself get hurt again and he is the epitome of damaged goods. We are the definition of a fling. Emotions need not apply.

"Just sex, Henry."

"Just sex, Eden."

Okay. I can do that. I can do just sex. I mean, I never have before other than with him, but how hard can that be? He screwed me ten ways to Sunday last night and it's not like I fell in love with him as a result. If anything, it made me hate him more.

"I want to fuck you so hard you have trouble sitting tomorrow when we're in the studio," he growls, biting my earlobe. "I want to watch your body shift and move, trying to find a more comfortable position because every inch of you is sore from the way my cock takes you."

And that's it. If I had any piece of resistance left—which let's face it, I obviously didn't—it's gone now.

My hand wants to raise in the air, my mouth wants to scream,

"Sign me up!" But it won't and it doesn't because I'm not that crazy. But damn... my body squirms. Hungry for all his naughty promises.

His fingers dip into the cup of my bikini, finding my nipple and pulling on the barbell. Like a slave to his touch, I moan on command, arching into him. I need contact. I need friction. I need something— I'm not even picky at this point, fingers, cock, toy—inside of me right now.

"I love these," he hums in my ear, tweaking the barbell again, making my eyes roll back in my head. "One of these days I'm going to have you suck my cock and instead of coming down your throat, I'm going to come all over your gorgeous tits. All over these pierced nipples."

Um... "Can we do that now?"

He chuckles in my ear, likely because I was starting to turn around and my voice was just a notch above desperate. "Later. Tonight, maybe if you're a good girl."

Good girl. Why is everything he's saying hot when I feel like it shouldn't be?

His other hand, the one not taking my nipples on a pleasure cruise, dips into my bottoms and finds me absolutely soaked. He toys with my clit, strumming it the way he strums his bass and I just about lose my mind. At this rate, it won't take me long. Voices in the distance reach the outer edge of my consciousness, but before I can react or even start to care, Henry moves us deeper into the thick bed of vegetation, hiding us from anyone who might pass.

Henry works my clit faster, adjusting his position so he can slip two fingers inside me as the voices grow louder. I attempt to fight him, fight the building orgasm that's already sparkling to life deep within my core, but he is undeterred. "You think they'll hear you," he rumbles in my ear. "Hear your breathy moans and cries of pleasure? Think you'll get caught with my fingers in your pussy and toying with your nipple?"

"Oh god. Henry. I..."

I tremble, my legs shaking so badly I'm worried my knees will give out at any moment.

"I should take my cock out. Shove it in your tight little pussy right when they walk past us."

Holy hell. I'm dying right now. "Please," I beg, not knowing if I want him to stop or do everything he just said. The threat of getting caught and people watching us is a delicious sort of treat I never knew I was into.

"You're so close, Eden. You're dripping all over my hand. Clamping around my fingers. You're so fucking beautiful when you come. Did I tell you that yet?"

Oh god.

"Are you ready, baby? Are you ready for my cock?"

"Yes. Yes. *Yes!*" I start to yell, only to have his hand abandon my nipple and cover my mouth. Tight. Practically cutting off my air supply which only seems to heighten the orgasm that slams through me like a freight train. I have no control over myself. Over my body. I'm all sensation. All fluttery warm, explosive sensation. I have no idea if the people passed us or not. If they heard us or even saw us. Hell, they could be watching us now for all I know.

Truth, I don't care in this moment.

Because just as my body starts to come down from what is very likely one of the biggest orgasms of my life, my bottoms are ripped down my legs and Henry thrusts inside me all the way to the hilt in one motion. Ripples of pleasure skyrocket through my body and I can't tell if that one thrust just made me come again or if I never stopped after the first one.

His hand abandons my mouth, wrapping around my neck and squeezing as he pushes me up against a palm tree, growling at me to hold on tight. That's when he starts to fuck me. Loud, wet slaps of skin against skin coupled with his heavy grunts in my ear are all I can hear. My eyes are closed, my hands scraping along the rough bark of the tree as I do just what he told me to do.

I hold on.

I hold on so I don't collapse. I hold on so I don't smash my head into the tree. I hold on because he told me to, and this man now owns my body. It's his. I never want it back. I just want this.

With one hand on my throat, restricting my breath just enough, and his other gripping my hip, he pounds into me. Over and over and over again, he fucks me. Each thrust I swear is harder than the one before it.

He turns my head and suddenly his lips are all over mine. His tongue thrusting into my mouth. "They're going to hear you," he tells me, and I moan though it comes out weak and raspy between his hand on my throat and his tongue in my mouth.

With that, he bends me forward, dragging my ass back and taking me from this new angle. It's deeper like this somehow and all I can do is hold on for the ride he's giving me. His stance widens to accommodate his powerful thrusts. I'm teetering on the edge. Desperate to come and just as desperate to stave this off so it doesn't end.

But the game-changer happens when he presses in on my clit only to pinch it between two fingers. This time I don't come. I shatter. Every cell in my being is on fire with a pleasure unlike anything else. My mind splinters, lost in a euphoria I pray doesn't end. Black spots dance along the periphery of my vision though clear almost immediately as Henry releases my neck. A sharp intake of air forces itself into my lungs, only to be expelled on one final resonating moan.

Henry emits a feral growl behind me, cursing under his breath as he slows his thrusts, emptying inside me. I start to sag, my hands falling away from the tree, and I go down only to have a strong arm wrap around my waist and haul me back up. He shifts me, spinning me around and drawing me into his chest that smells like sweat, sunshine, and Henry.

His fingers stroke along my hair from root to end as he holds me tight, letting me catch my breath and use him for support.

"You okay?" he whispers softly into me, kissing the top of my head, my temple, my cheek. "I didn't hurt you, did I? Cut off your breathing too much?"

I'm not sure I can speak yet, so I just shake my head into him.

He continues to hold me and slowly consciousness begins to filter back in.

"Did anyone see us?"

"No. As hot as that notion is, no one gets to see you like that but me."

My eyes open and I blink a few times, thinking about his words and trying not to at the same time. He squeezes me tighter, holding me closer. His heartbeat pounds through his hard chest against my ear and this, this right here, it's heaven. Being held by him like this after he just did the dirtiest things to me is the most perfect balm.

A balm I could get lost in along with the man delivering it.

Which is why I pull back, resting my chin on his sternum and looking up to meet his eyes.

He stares down at me with an indecipherable expression, cupping my cheek and running his thumb over it the way I've noticed he likes to.

"We should get you cleaned up and then get back. People are going to start to wonder where we are."

I nod, swallowing hard at that.

"Do me a favor?"

"Okay," I whisper.

"I'll do my best to stay out of your heart. But you have to promise you won't fall in love with me."

I blink at him, a little stunned by his words. I thought he was going to say something like don't tell your brother this happened or keep your mouth shut or I don't even know what. Just not *that*. His other hand comes up until he's cradling my face in both hands, staring straight into my eyes.

"Don't fall in love with me, Eden, because I can never love you back."

Holy hell. What did I just do?

SEVENTEEN

EDEN

"I did something epically stupid," I tell Jess, my arm covering my eyes as I lay on my bed in the predawn hours. Shockingly, I fell asleep okay. But then around four am I woke up in a panic. I checked my cell phone. I checked my freaking keys locked away in my purse that's stored in the safe in the closet. My email. The song we had finished recording yesterday.

Everything.

But even as I was going through all that, I knew what woke me up that way. I knew why I was freaking the hell out. It's the same thing that had me playing it cool all yesterday afternoon while completely avoiding Henry.

"With the album? I thought you said that was going well."

"It's going really well. Awesome, in fact. I mean, yesterday we finished the song we had been working on in LA and today we're set to start something new. Oh, and in a not so unexpected twist, did you miss the part where I said I did something epically stupid?"

"What do you mean by *epically* stupid?" she smarts, clearly not taking this as seriously as she should.

I pinch my eyes shut behind my arm. I take a deep breath. "I might have slept with Henry. Twice."

"*Might have?*"

"Um. Well. Yeah. I did."

She starts laughing into the phone. Hysterically. To the point where I have to pull the phone away because the sound is hurting my eardrums. She does this for about three minutes, no joke. "That was fast. I had the over under on a week into the trip. Not day one. Must be all that Hawaiian air."

"Har. Har."

"Tell me everything," she demands. "Give me all the details. How was it? Better than the first time?"

"Jess," I whine. "I screwed up. And it was a mistake. For so many freaking reasons."

"Okay," she says, finally getting into business mode. "Lay it on me."

So I do. I launch into everything that's happened since I got here and Henry and I started our wham, bam, thank you ma'am sessions. Everything. Including all the promises and warnings we've made. Right down to the... "*Don't fall in love with me, Eden, because I can never love you back.*"

"Damn. That's actually what he said?"

"Yup." That's all the energy I've got left. Just getting that entire story out was taxing enough. Plus, it's only something like six in the morning.

"Um. Okay then. Wow. I have like fifty thousand questions with that. What did you do after he said that?"

I throw my arm over my head, my fist smacking down into an overly plush pillow. "I think I said something along the lines of no problem Broken Joe and did the hundred-yard dash faster than an Olympic gold medalist. Then I proceeded to avoid him for the rest of the night."

"You did all that minus calling him Broken Joe, right?"

I roll my eyes though I'm the only one here. I have no idea why

I'm taking his words this hard. I don't want to fall back in love with him. I don't want a relationship with him. And I already knew he was a mental disaster. So this reaction? Yeah, I have no answers.

"Obviously."

"But you just told me you agreed to sex with no strings. To vacation sex only. That you don't *want* him for anything beyond that."

"All true."

"Let me see if I've got this straight then. You don't want anything beyond sex with him and he doesn't want anything else but sex with you. You both agreed to keep feelings off the table so you're freaking out why exactly?"

You didn't hear the way he said it.

"Because what if I can't keep feelings off the table?" I whisper the words, my greatest fear when it comes to Henry vocalized. A man I was obsessed with for so much of my life, I hardly remember a time when I wasn't.

"It doesn't sound like you have a choice."

"Thanks," I grumble.

"Okay. Listen. Truth, after everything you've been through with Chad, I think you're entitled to some safe, no-strings fun. Henry is telling you point blank it won't go anywhere. That it has a real and finite expiration date. So stop thinking so much about it. Stop reading into it. Take his words for exactly what they are. A warning to heed. In fact, you should continue to hate him. That way, you won't fall in love with him and he won't fall in love with you and you will both have really amazing sex in between."

My jaw unhinges itself as I stare dumbly up at the ceiling fan. I think about everything she just said. Can I do that? It certainly can't hurt to try. And she's right. I could use this kind of thing. As long as I keep myself in lockdown, I should be fine. I can hate fuck Henry for a few weeks and walk away when it's over because I won't have a choice.

"Why aren't you becoming a therapist instead of a lawyer?"

"Because I like solving peoples' problems, not talking about them."

She has a point.

"Okay. I'll think about it."

"Right on. I gotta get back to class. Good luck today in the studio. You've got this."

After we hang up, I lay here a while longer, thinking. I wasn't lying when I said I didn't want a relationship right now. I also wasn't lying when I said I know Henry is about as fucked up as a guy can be.

Because he is.

I mean, who says something like that and actually means it?

In truth, I never thought about it before we got here.

I hadn't seen it when I was younger. Hadn't noticed anything in particular, and no one talked about it. Like ever. No one discussed the fact that Henry, from practically as far back as I can remember, either slept at our house or Gus's and Jasper's. No one talked about how he spent every major holiday with us or them. Still does, as a matter of fact.

The one time—and I'm not even exaggerating here—I heard my parents talk about it was when my mother told my father that Henry's dad worked long hours and his mother traveled a lot for her job.

Only... that doesn't really make a whole lot of sense, now does it? I used to see his dad about town. His mom, practically never.

Henry worked at my dad's auto repair shop for money, and he was a staple in our home. That was just how it was. That's likely why my infatuation with him started early and hung on tight.

But what was he hiding? Why was he living at his friends' houses and not with his family? Why is he the consummate loner, swearing off love at all costs?

I honestly don't know, and I decide to let it drop as I get myself up and ready for work.

The nice thing about these houses is that they're stacked with food and drinks. Coffee. They even have the fancy gourmet stuff and an espresso maker. I make myself a huge to-go coffee and toss in two shots of espresso because today, like yesterday and tomorrow, is no joke.

"Eden Dawson, you're my hero," Gus says in a slightly creepy voice as I enter the studio to find everyone here except Henry.

"Thanks Cameron. I always wanted to be as cool as Ferris Bueller."

Gus tosses his large arm over my shoulder, shaking me slightly as he drags me along beside him. "This setup is sick. I mean it. You really outdid yourself. It has everything we're going to need."

I beam at that. Gus is known for being loquacious and generous with his praise, but I can also tell he means it. After my romp in the wilderness, I didn't go back to the pool or the beach. Instead, I came here and redid some things. Moved some pieces around. Recreated the makeshift sound booth. We may be in an event room, but I've made it ours as best I can.

"I'm like UPS, I deliver all day, kid."

He laughs, taking my hand and spinning me in a circle before tucking me back in under his arm. "It's great. While Naomi surfs and chills with her besties and nieces, I get to work on music. I wasn't sure this would all work, but looking at this space and all we got done yesterday, you have made me a believer."

"I for one am glad we have this going," Keith states, dropping a kiss on my forehead right at my hairline. "While I'm all for beaches, sunshine, and relaxing, three weeks of nothing but that is too much."

"There is a lot more to Hawaii than that," I tell him. "Have you seen all the cool hiking places around here? Not to mention we can rent a catamaran, go whale watching, check out an active volcano, tons of stuff."

"Oh boy. Here she goes." Keith grins indulgently. "I was wondering how long it would take you to become a travel brochure." I flip him off. "Maia has already signed us up for a snorkeling thing next week sometime if you want to join us."

"Um. Hell yeah, I do. Count me in."

Just then the door opens, and Henry comes waltzing in, his usual warm smile for his bandmates present. He gives both Jasper and Keith a fist pound, though I don't miss the way his gaze drops slightly when he does it with Keith. He does the same with Gus, only offering me a curt nod I don't bother returning because that's how we roll.

Love hate, hate love. Extra helping of the hate.

Now sex. Hot sex. Hot, sweaty sex. And incredible kisses. God, the kisses...

I clear my throat, bitch smacking myself away from Henry and his wonder mouth and penis.

"Alright," I start, disentangling myself from Gus and clapping my hands together to get everyone's attention. "Did you guys all get the schedule I emailed this morning?" I get a series of grunts for that. "Any questions or issues with it? I know we talked it over briefly yesterday, but I figured having an outline planned is easier."

"I think it's smart to map out the songs we're going to be working on," Jasper says, picking up his acoustic and strumming a little, tuning and tweaking as he does. "Five hours, five days a week should give us a really solid base. Plus, what we already worked on the last few weeks."

"I'm definitely good with it," Keith agrees, bending down and whispering in my ear, "You did really good, Ede. We're all really excited to keep this going."

I wrap my arm around his middle, giving my favorite bear a bear hug.

He pats my back and heads straight for his drums and the others fall in line, getting set with their own instruments.

Henry's fingers coast across my ass as he passes me, and I suck in a deep rush of air. I can feel my cheeks heating and I quickly look around only to find no one is paying us any attention. "Morning, Dragonfly. You're looking especially beautiful this morning." His eyes scour my entire body and when they finally reach mine a roguish smirk quirks up the corner of his lips. He gives me a wink and then schools his features before going to join everyone else.

How on Earth am I going to make it through the rest of the morning without combusting if he keeps looking at me like that while saying things like that?

I clear my throat and head for my mixing table or what is commonly referred to as a soundboard. It was impossible to bring an entire one with me here. Instead, I brought a small version of one, two laptops, and an effects mixer. So far, this seems to give me the sound quality I want. That's probably what I'm most nervous about.

I know these guys can deliver an album in their sleep.

But if it's anything short of the perfection they're known for, that will fall on me.

"Today I thought we'd work on the music for 'Sweet Serenade'. That work for you?"

"Huh. I'm not sure I remember which one that is," Gus mutters dryly, though there is a glimmer in eyes that means trouble is coming. "Can you sing it for us?"

I blanch, my head whipping up to find him. "Come again?"

"That's what she said," Henry quips.

Keith reaches out, smacking him in the back of the head and then pointing at me. "Dude. Sister."

"Dude. Chill."

Oh boy. "Um. No. I can't sing it," I state firmly, hoping to redirect Henry and Keith. "Isn't that like Jasper's job or something?"

Jasper shakes his head. "I don't remember the lyrics. I've written so many over the years."

I fold my arms over my chest, glaring at them. "I'm not falling for your bullshit, boys. You forget, I've dealt with you my whole life. No initiations." I point at each one in turn. "I'm onto you. That time has long since passed."

Jasper smirks, clearly not letting it go. "Hum it for us then? Let's hear how you envision the song going."

Keith who has been fighting a smile fails miserably when a small chuckle pops out. Gus is already practically in stitches because the man has no willpower.

"Ha, ha, douchebags. Very funny. I know what you're doing. You all know I can't sing a note to save my life."

"But you used to sing The Cure so well. Oh, and The Cars. You used to sing the hell out of The Cars."

I flip Henry off. Then each one of them as they laugh harder at my expense. Gus strums The Cars, "You Might Think" and I spin around in a circle, my hands going to the top of my head, unable to hide my reaction. Because I used to rock out hard to that song, dancing around the garage and begging them to let me join the band. Not my best moment, but considering I was seven, I have no shame.

"So thrilled you boys remember that." I can only shake my head, biting into my lip to stop my own amusement while feigning—and failing—annoyance.

"I think it's burned into our minds, Ede. No offense doll, but you're much better behind the booth than you are in front of it if you get my meaning."

"I do." I squint at my brother. The only man on the planet allowed to call me Ede though Gus gets away with it too sometimes because, well, he's Gus. "So how about we start working on the damn song already."

They finally relent—not that I'm giving them a choice. Eden teasing hour is over and then we get started. That might happen after I threaten to pump a siren sound through their headphones. It never quite reaches that point.

They play through what they envision for the instrumentals to the song, jamming and laughing, but also taking this seriously. They know the time crunch we're under. They know what this means for their band and for Jasper and Adalyn.

For all of them really. With the exception of Henry, they all have reasons to finish this album quickly and take some much-needed time off.

These aren't the same guys playing shows, hitting up clubs, and sleeping around that I saw even three years ago. Now their focus has shifted to being about something much larger than just themselves and their music. They're not what you think of when you imagine rock stars, that's for sure. They don't do groupies. They don't do drugs. They don't do flashy.

But I think I like this version of them better.

Still sexy and bad ass and all fucking hot male, but with uncompromised hearts that makes any girl who looks closely enough swoon.

In under four hours, I'm splitting them up so they can begin to lay down their preliminary part individually. The instrumentals are still rough. I know this. But I want to hear it compiled so we can see what needs adjusting. It's how it's typically done, and I won't take any shortcuts with this.

Jasper goes first because it's easiest for him to lay down the lyrics first even if it's simply with his acoustic to guide him. Then Gus, because he's backup guitar and vocals. Then Keith on drums, and last, Henry with his bass.

By this point, it's after noon and I let everyone else go.

The truth is, they don't really need to linger for this. But that doesn't mean Keith is happy about it either. I see the infinitesimal scowl on his lips that he's trying to hide. The way his eyes shift to Henry, then over to me, and then back again as he quietly assesses the situation.

Only, there is nothing to assess other than us working.

He doesn't know our truth and in reality, he's not really owed an explanation. I am a woman. My sex life is my own. My secrets are mine to share or not. I owe Keith nothing when it comes to that, and though the world might disagree with me on this, I don't think Henry does either.

I have Henry in the booth, his bass in hand that he's playing around with, and the music piped through his headphones. He's listening to it first, his eyes closed, and my attention is on my tablet. Not Keith. Or Henry, for that matter.

"Catch you later?" Keith asks, a note of hesitation lingering in his voice.

"Yeah," I call over my shoulder, refusing to look up or acknowledge what he's doing. "I'm going to work on this for a while, but I'll probably meet you all at the beach or the pool or something."

Henry opens his eyes, the song finished, and he says, "I'm ready. Let's go."

I throw Keith a wave and get back to work, not even listening for the sound of the door though I know he takes the hint and leaves.

I cue up the song and set everything up on my end and watch as Henry plays. Each artist addresses their instrument differently. Has a different approach to the sound they attempting to coax from it. The bass is often times a complementary instrument, but not the way Henry plays it. He plays it like it's the most important thing you'll hear in the entire song, imparting Wild Minds with a deep, soulful resonance that you feel in the marrow of your bones. Jasper's lyrics and voice give you chills, but Henry's bass amplifies them to the next level.

Undeniably, there is nothing sexier than watching someone play music. It's why there are groupies and obsessed fans and the 'Rockstar' mystique. But it goes deeper than money, bad boy mentality, and sex appeal. You just need to look closely enough. When done right, it's a converging of the senses. It's passion and mayhem. A visceral experience.

That's what gets us.

That's what calls to us.

Henry plays through the song three times, and by the end of the final note, I have a mostly completed song ready for me to listen to and make notes on. All done in record time I might add because damn, that shit never works out like this. Typically, a new song can take days to weeks to lay down. This is pretty damn close to ready for me to layer.

It puts a huge smile on my face. Day two is another success.

While I don't anticipate them all going like this, and I know we have a long three weeks ahead of us, I'll take whatever victories I can get.

Henry's smiling too as he comes out of the booth, grabbing Gus's electric as he does. "Two down, only what? Twelve more to go?"

"Dick," I mutter, some of my shine fading. "Thanks for the reminder."

"It's what I'm here for." He plays the intro to Guns N' Roses "Sweet Child of Mine" only to slowly transition to Led Zeppelin's "Over the Hills and Far Away". He pulls them both off flawlessly, though those are some of the most complex guitar arrangements of all time.

For a few minutes, I watch in awe.

"If you can play guitar like that why aren't you lead with Jasper instead of Gus?"

Henry laughs as if the answer should be obvious. Maybe it is, Jasper and Gus are twins after all, but damn. Henry can shred in a way I never realized before.

"This is just how it went. Jas and Gus have been playing guitar and singing together since before I even met them. Keith has always been drums and if I wanted in, I needed to play something useful. I love the bass though, so don't go all feeling sorry for me. I'm not a front man. Never wanted to be."

"You guys used to play for hours and hours in our garage. I remember my mom would bring dinner out there to you boys before she left for her night shifts at the hospital. My dad would have to cut the power sometimes to get you to stop and go home."

Henry's smile dies a little, his head tilting down as he works on Eruption by Van Halen. "I hated having to go home," he finally says halfway through the solo. "Twilight was my least favorite time of day. I would have done anything to make those hours stretch out forever. Playing was my one and only escape."

My insides twist but I don't dare move or breathe.

"Escape from what?" I find myself asking even though I know I shouldn't.

"Keith is probably waiting on us," he says instead of answering, and I curse myself for my curiosity. He was opening up to me and that's not something Henry does. With anyone as far as I know.

"Probably," I concede on a heavy sigh. I don't know what I'm doing trying with him. It's an ill-fated attempt at best. "I think I'll head over to the pool. Order myself a burger and a Diet Coke and listen to what you guys just put together."

He grins, pulling the guitar up and over his head. He cuts the space between us by half, and I rock back on my heels, needing to regain some of the distance he just swallowed up.

With his eyes holding mine hostage, he bends down until he's hovering over me. His lips skirt my cheek, his hot breath against my neck below my ear. "Did you bring a bikini to change into and torture me with?"

"Yes," I breathe out, my eyes closing as his lips capture my earlobe, sucking gently on it.

"Mmmm... good. Only I'm not going to chase you this time. I'm not going to touch you. I'm just going to watch you. Knowing how much you like it when I do. Knowing how wet it will make you. How desperate. And tonight, you won't run from me my little dragonfly. You'll come looking for me because you won't be able to hold off any longer."

EIGHTEEN

HENRY

The soft crackle of the firepit fills the air. A perfect juxtaposition to our heavy laughter. Flames dance out into the night, casting just enough of a glow and the right amount of heat for this to be perfect. Especially after the heavy meal we all consumed like we've been starved in the desert for the last forty years.

We're sipping on expensive wine, lounging back in our chairs, and when I envisioned this vacation, this is the sort of moment I was hoping for. All of us sitting around and relaxing while teasing each other the way we always do.

"I still can't believe you ate bugs," Vi says to Jasper, her face scrunched up in disgust.

"We were in a market in Thailand," he replies evenly. "It was offered to us by our guide, and I didn't want to be rude."

That's when Gus, Keith, and I burst out laughing.

"What?" Vi asks, not getting the joke.

Jasper groans, leaning back in his seat as he tosses his hands behind his head.

"We told our guide to do that," I explain. "When we were in China eating at a restaurant, none of us had any idea what we were supposed to order. Our person there took the liberty of ordering for us. We all got the same main dish except Jasper."

Vi snorts out, glancing over to Jasper and then back to me. "What did you guys eat?"

"Toad."

"Oh god," all the women groan in unison.

Naomi makes a gagging sound in the back of her throat. "Did it taste like chicken?" she asks with an amused yet sickly smile.

"Yep," Gus tells her. "Oddly enough, it did. Except it had weird, tiny bones."

Naomi gags again.

"We didn't find out until after we ate it and Jas was cracking up," Keith clarifies "So we decided payback's all fair in brotherhood and food. He ate fried grasshoppers and scorpions. Good sport since the rest of us wouldn't."

"Scorpions?" Naomi hisses. "I hear they give you nosebleeds."

Jasper shrugs, taking a sip of his wine. "Only if you eat more than one."

"That's freaking horrible," Maia exclaims in outrage, turning to Keith. "I take it back. I no longer want to travel the world with you fools. You guys are brutal to each other."

"No joke," Viola agrees as she begins to tell her about the time we tried to get her to eat dirt. In our defense, we were twelve-year-old boys.

Eden has been quiet for most of the night. Most of the day actually. We wrapped up our fourth day in the studio this morning though today we made very little progress, same with yesterday, and if I had to guess, I'd say that's what's eating at her now. I know she's stressed with this album. With how it's coming along.

I'm also learning when Eden Dawson gets stressed out she shuts down and turns inward.

A bit too quiet.

I didn't touch her all day. Not once. She seemed like she needed space and I took that little gift and ran with it.

The sex has been nonstop. All over the place. Every chance we get. Earth-shattering, mind-blowing, epic, no contest, best sex of my life, sex. My days have become centered around her. The woman weaseling her way under my skin. I watch her. I think of things to go and talk to her about. I pick fights because when we fight, we fuck like twin tornados converging. We create chaos and leave beautiful destruction in our wake.

All I can think about is the next time I can be with her.

It's a problem.

One I'm starting to have trouble controlling. Like right now. Because my hand, this fucking beast with a mind and directive of its own when it comes to its dragonfly, is slipping under the table so it can find the smooth, creamy flesh of her thigh.

And when it does, Eden does a delightful little jolt. Her body goes rigid as if she's not sure how to react to my touch when we're surrounded by all these people. By her brother. But no one can see, and I can no longer resist. My thumb strokes her leg, my fingers lightly tickling her inner thigh but that's all I do and when she realizes I'm not about to try anything scandalous—I'm not that fucking twisted of a bastard—she relaxes for the first time all night and finally smiles, enjoying my touch.

Maia puffs out a breath and then an exaggerated shudder at Viola's story. Cora is fast asleep on her chest and Maia appears to be in heaven with it. Adalyn is tucked into her favorite aunt, Naomi. She's awake, but barely, enjoying soothing back and arm tickles she always tends to pry out of Naomi.

"I love you, Keith, but I think I would murder you in your sleep if you ever tried to pull something like that with me," Maia asserts and all of us, including Keith, chuckle under our breath because we can actually see Maia doing that. She may threaten, but I wouldn't put it past her to act either.

"We were just kids, babe. And whenever we travel overseas next, I promise, no funny business with you. Forget you, Marco would likely kill us all if we tried. You wouldn't even have to threaten."

"True story," Maia agrees with a laugh.

"I liked the hell out of Asia," Keith maintains, changing the subject back to our travels. "But every time we ate outside of the hotel or a specially arranged restaurant, it was like Russian roulette."

"Yes," I assent. "Big time. But the people were incredible, and the cities were for real the coolest I've seen. I think Japan was my favorite stop in Asia."

"Definitely," Jas and Gus say together.

"Where is your favorite place you've been in the world?" Maia questions, shifting a little so she's comfortable but Cora doesn't wake.

"Paris," Vi and Jasper blurt in unison, only to look at each other and smile. That's where Jasper told Viola he loved her for the first time. Where they finally came clean about their relationship to the rest of us who already knew because they couldn't hide their attraction for shit.

"Australia for me," Naomi chimes in. "The surfing is out of this world."

"Ireland is mine," Gus announces. "Pubs. Food. People."

"I think I like Rome the best. The food. The wine. The city."

Keith laughs. "Yeah, Henry, but I think the real reason for that is because it's where you met your soulmate and love of your life."

Beside me Eden grows stiffer than a board, shifting a bit almost as if she's trying to shake my hand from her body. Not happening, sweetheart. I grip her thigh before continuing to caress it.

"Christ. Remember that?" Gus reminisces on a laugh. "That woman was relentless."

"Yep. Stalked me all over the city. Even found her way into my hotel suite."

"For real?" Eden finally asks, her head swiveling in my direction as her eyes reluctantly meet mine. Finally, I want to shout. Instead I take a few seconds to drink her in. She looks so pretty tonight. Hair down, blowing in the gentle breeze. Long, red, gauzy dress revealing the perfect amount of cleavage through the dip of the halter neckline.

I smile. Is she jealous? "Oh yeah. We had to have security escort her out and I still changed rooms because the chick had been naked in my bed. She also stole a shirt of mine and I swear was wearing my cologne."

"And Rome is still your favorite city?" Maia smarts incredulously.

"That only happened our first time there. The other few times we've been since were awesome."

"I think it's time to get this little one to bed," Naomi announces, talking about Adalyn who is finally passed out.

"Same with this one," Maia agrees, kissing the top of Cora's blonde head.

"Might as well call it a night for all of us," Jas says. "We need to get going in the studio tomorrow."

I can practically hear Eden swallow at that. Feel her deflate. And without a word, she stands up, gives everyone a small wave and heads out. Just like that. The woman is a ball of nerves and endless tension.

The rest of us say goodnight and within a minute or two, I'm jogging to catch up to Eden who can't be too far ahead of me. She never takes the offered golf carts, always choosing to walk instead, and quickly I find her gliding along the pathway like a siren in the night. She hears me coming, knowing it's me because she slows her stroll without stopping or turning over her shoulder to see who's approaching. My arm wraps around her waist and I tug her into me, brushing her hair away from her neck and inhaling deeply.

I shouldn't be touching her out here, even though Keith is likely already in bed with Maia. Still, I can't deny that part of the thrill is sneaking around under everyone's nose. It makes it dirty. Hot. Illicit. But more than that, she is worth the risk of getting caught. Yet another thing I can't wrap my mind around.

"Do I smell like the fire?" she asks softly.

"No. You smell like flowers and vanilla."

"I'm using the body lotion they have here. I forgot mine at home."

"But you didn't forget your perfume. I can still smell some of that too."

"You like my perfume."

I grin into her statement. "Is that why you brought it with you?"

"No."

Liar. My grin grows into a smile as I suck on her neck.

"How many women have you been with?"

Oh boy. That's a loaded question. "More than a few and less than you think," is the only way I can answer that. The truth is, I have no clue how many women I've slept with over the years. I never kept a tally and early on in this, when the women started coming at us from all sides, I didn't think twice about sleeping with them. But in the last few years, all that's slowed down. It just doesn't hold the same appeal it once did.

Now it's tired and empty and kinda boring. One woman bleeds into the next. No thrill. No chase. It's a release and most times not even a great one at that.

"You don't want to know how many men I've slept with?"

"No," I tell her firmly because I don't. The idea of other men touching her makes me irrationally angry. "Why do you ask anyway?"

"Just curious. Listening to you guys tonight talk of your travels. The women stalking you. Knowing how long you've been at this game. The way you approached me that night in the club three years ago."

Ah. I see. "The second I laid eyes on you, Eden, I couldn't look away. I approached you because I had to talk to you. Had to touch you. Hell, just had to get a closer look."

She twists in my arms to face me, walking backwards. "Has that ever happened before?"

I swallow, knowing I shouldn't answer her with the truth, but incapable of saying anything else. "No. It's never happened before. Or since."

No smile. No reaction. Thank fuck for that.

"I need to burn off some of the stress from this album. Wanna go for a swim?"

I dive in and take her lips with mine. My tongue thrusts into her mouth, claiming it for my own like a triumphant warrior. "Yes."

She takes my hand, swivels back around, and tugs me along until we're behind our houses, bypassing the pool and heading for the dark and desolate beach.

"Here?"

"Afraid of the ocean at night?" she smarts.

Um. Maybe a little, yeah. But then she starts to untie the knot of her dress at the back of her neck. And in one stunning swoosh, it collapses to a pool at her feet, leaving her in a red strapless bra and tinier than tiny red panties.

"You're still dressed, Henry."

Uh huh. "Henry isn't here right now. Please leave a message and he'll call you back when he remembers how to think."

Eden laughs, tilting her head back and taking in the now tiny sliver of a moon since it was full the other night. "Come swim with me, Henry."

"Night swimming," I start singing REM to her as I remove my shirt and shorts, sliding out of my man flops because only chicks wear flip-flops.

"I love that song."

"I'll keep singing it to you then."

I saunter over to her, my hands hitting the tops of her bare shoulders and slowly swooping down and around to unclasp her bra. I sing the words into her ear and against her skin in between kisses. Eden shudders and shakes, her back rising and falling in quick succession along with her breathing.

Her panties hit the sand and I continue kissing her lower, lower, over the perfect swell of her ass and down to the backs of her knees that buckle a little at the touch of my lips. I spin her around and from my knees, I stare up into her blue eyes, darkened by shadows and night.

Thunk.

Yup. Thanks for the reminder, I know. I feel it almost every damn time I look at her. Only this time it hits just a bit harder than the last.

My nose dips in, inhaling her arousal, my tongue swiping out for a taste because I have to. Her taste. Nothing should turn me on as much as this woman does. Her fingers thread through my hair, her lips parted to accommodate her pants.

"You stopped singing."

She's right. I did. I start singing into her as I lick. The vibrations against her clit drive her up higher, her grip tightening, and I don't stop until she comes so hard her body gives out and I catch her, cradling her against my chest so she doesn't fall. She can't fall, and even though it's beyond tempting in moments like this, I won't let it happen.

For either of us.

I drop her to the smooth sand, my hands clutching hers, her eyes locked on mine, and I take her. Sinking in deep. No end in sight. Our bodies caressed by moonlight, sand, water, and fire become one in ways I know better than to allow them to. Soft words are spoken in a language I'm terrified to learn.

Erotic cries get lost in the night air. A colorless vacuum of pleasure that drives me from one heartbeat to another, one mess to the next. Only she and I exist here in the dark. Tainted and damaged. But I can't find it in me to trade it for anything else. There is nothing better than this. I know. I've tried and tasted them all. None compare.

My lips meet hers, my arms a fortress around her naked body as we both attempt to control our ragged breathing. "Night swimming," I finish against her lips and she smiles dreamily into mine.

"I think that's my new favorite REM song ever."

I grin airily, picking her up and carrying her to the water, ready to dunk us both before I take her body again. "I bet I can find some other songs to make your favorite."

"Do you take requests?"

"From you? No."

She laughs, smacking my shoulder but kissing me senseless before I can absorb the sting of it.

"Tell you what, Dragonfly. I'll start singing to you and at the end of the night, you can tell me which one is your favorite."

"I already know they'll all be my favorites. They always are with you."

Her words crater inside me. They were light. They were playful. But they hit me with an unexpended weight and force. They scare the absolute shit out of me. Because for that reason alone, I should stop this.

Only with moments like these, those thoughts die before they form. Just another night. Just a touch longer. What harm can it cause?

NINETEEN

HENRY

The wind whips across my face and through my hair. Dirt and sand splatter against me, pelting my goggles and stinging the exposed skin of my neck and arms. This has never been my thing. Nor Jasper's. We're more chill out over a couple of beers and watch the game guys. But Keith and Gus live for this shit.

The adrenaline rush.

No matter how busy our schedules are or how exhausted we might be, they always seem to plan something that puts all of our lives in danger and drag us eagerly toward it.

I kick up some speed on my ATV, the ocean a blue blur on my right, the forest a green boundary on my left, as I get myself up and over a sand dune only to break quickly on the other side, sand shooting from my tires in all directions, so I don't crash into Keith who is closer than I anticipated. I catch his head falling back in a bellowing laugh and he points a finger at me, loving this way too much and knowing I don't.

"That wasn't cool, fucker," I yell at him, my voice getting caught in the breeze.

He grins like a sadistic devil, revving his ATV up so he can fly over the next dune, spinning around and doing tricks before he comes to a stop at the top. I follow him up and over, Gus and Jasper already there, standing beside their ATVs with their helmets and goggles off, laughing and shooting the shit. We woke up just a little after dawn and made our way out here. Considering what little sleep I've had lately between recording and a blue-haired siren, I'm particularly dragging ass today.

Braking the ATV, I power it down, handing it over to the guy running this show for us along with my helmet and goggles. Rough grains of dirt and sand meet my hand as I wipe at my face. The sun is beaming down on us, the waves crashing against the rocky shore below and I join my friends who are taking a moment to appreciate it.

"That was fun as hell." Keith slaps my back, squeezing my shoulder and giving me a small shake. A smile of pure contentment perks up his face while causing mine to frown. What am I doing? Why am I risking this? Not just my friendship, but this life, these guys, our band.

I look over at him, the words on my tongue, but I can't force them out. I feel like a coward. Like a real man would own up to the shit he's involved in with his best friend's little sister. And no matter how much fun I'm having, despite how much I don't want to, I need to stop sleeping with Eden. It's the only way I won't break her heart and lose everything at the same time.

I've spent a week tracking her movements.

Thinking about her. Obsessing over her. Dreaming of her.

Staring at her while being grateful for the invention of reflective sunglasses so no one is privy to my creeping except her. She knows. I can tell. Even when she tries to play it off. Even when she holds off as long as she can only to knock on my door close to eleven at night and sneak out around three.

No sleepovers.

Just sex.

Just crazy hot, dirty, kinky as shit sex. Eden likes it rough, and she likes to play. So that's what we've been doing. Every goddamn chance we get. But all that has to stop. My best friend. Her brother. Yes. I have to end it.

I need to tell her. I need to tell her today.

"Next time I say we go parasailing," Gus suggests.

All three of us turn in his direction with 'are you kidding me' glares. "So I can have some high school punk making shit for money lock me into a harness that will chafe my balls for two hours," I mutter dryly. "No thanks."

"Can't be all bad. Look." Gus points out in the distance at a boat tugging along with two people attached to a parachute, suspended high up in the air.

"Yeah, I'm gonna have to agree with Henry on this one," Keith says. "That doesn't look like fun. We could try hang gliding."

Jasper chuckles under his breath. "Forget the chafing harness, my wife would cut my balls off if I ever told her I was doing that."

"Remember when we went skydiving in New Zealand and Keith nearly died," I remark, laughing lightly under my breath.

"Oh shit," Gus cackles, his head dropping forward, his hands clutching his stomach. "I totally forgot about that. What were you doing, man?"

"Being an asshole," Keith says smiling though he's not laughing the way we are. "I thought because I had already been once I was a pro. Newsflash: I wasn't."

"You were headed for that mountain until the guide came and redirected you right before you pulled your shoot," I grunt through my laugher.

"It wasn't funny, dick."

I laugh harder. We all do except him.

"Yeah, it was," Jasper shoots out, practically doubled over, all of us at the point where we can no longer control it. "It really was. But only because you were so pissed when we landed. Like the guide by saving your life took all the fun out of it."

"Yeah, yeah. Ha fucking ha. Enough already. Let's head back. I'm starving and it's getting late."

***

Hours later, I'm walking along the path back to my house, my eyes heavy and muscles sore. We got back, showered so we were no longer caked from head to toe in dirt, and then met up at one of the bars Jas had rented out. We proceeded to scarf down an overabundance of bar food like we'd never have the chance to eat again. Then we sipped on expensive bourbon and relaxed, taking it easy and shooting the shit the way we used to do before life got so complicated.

I don't remember the last time I had this much fun. The last time things felt so easy and relaxed. The last time it was genuinely just the four of us without any of the added pressure that rules our lives on a daily basis. I'm not even talking about the women or the kids. They're the time that keeps my friends' clocks ticking.

It's the pressure of everything else.

The music. The business. The tours. The money. The fame clawing at our skin.

This was none of that. This was us. Unfiltered.

We say goodnight to Gus and Jasper who head off in the other direction, leaving me and Keith alone as we meander toward our houses. For most of the day, I was able to push away everything that's rattling my mind, but now it seems to be coming back with a vengeance.

"Today was a good day," Keith announces beside me.

"It was," I agree quietly as we pass the event space we're using as a studio, feeling more and more like shit than I have all week. Deciding to end things with Eden is the right call. The only call. So why does just the thought of doing that make breath quicken and my chest tighten?

Almost as if reading my thoughts, Keith says, "I hope Eden was able to relax today. She's been working herself ragged and when I was texting with Maia earlier, she said she hasn't seen her much today."

"Maybe she just decided to stay close to her house?"

"Maybe," he muses, though his tone is unsettled. "Still, I'm going to check on her before I head to bed."

"Go for it. I'm gonna grab my bass from the studio and then pass the fuck out. I'll see you tomorrow for snorkeling."

I give him a fist pump and slip out my key card, using it to enter the dark building. I want my bass before we get back to work on Monday. There's something I want to mess around with. Something that's been playing through my head that I think will work better for the next song we're set to work on than what I already have for it.

The automatic lights flicker on as I'm hit with a blast of air conditioning from the overhead vent. My bass is tucked against the far wall on a stand, exactly where I left it, but I only make it four steps in that direction before I freeze mid-stride.

Eden is in front of the mixer, her head bowed with her headphones on, but she hasn't moved, and she isn't making a sound. I would wonder if she's asleep, but given her position, there is no way. Does she know I'm in here?

"Eden?" I call out. She doesn't respond and I cross the room with heavy steps, hoping she'll hear me and look up. The last thing I want to do is scare her. "Eden," I bark, this time louder and she jolts upright, twisting in my direction while simultaneously removing the cans from her ears in a quick flustered motion.

"Holy bananas foster, you scared me." She breathes out harshly, practically panting, a hand to her chest as if she's trying to slow her heart.

"What are you doing in here this late?"

She gives me a sheepish smile, twisting back to the board as I drop down onto an office chair, rolling closer until I'm right beside her.

"I just wanted to get some more work done on the album. What time is it anyway?"

"Around ten."

She puffs out an exhausted sigh.

"How long have you been here? And why were you sitting in the dark?"

She emits a self-conscious laugh, running her hands over her face before going back to the mixer in front of her. "About six hours, I think. I didn't realize they had turned off. I had my eyes closed as I was listening."

"Six hours? Eden, Jesus. Today is supposed to be your day off. You need a break."

A growl slips past her lips. "I can't take a break." She practically throws her headphones across the soundboard. "Not when every-thing sounds wrong."

"What do you mean sounds wrong?"

She makes a huffing sound but otherwise ignores my question. And now that I really take her in. Her hair is on top of her head in a messy ponytail, but half of it has fallen out, hanging limply around her face and neck. She has no makeup on to cover the purple stains beneath her eyes. The dress she's wearing is wrinkled like mad. She's a mess. Stressed past the breaking point and working herself into exhaustion.

"When was the last time you ate anything?"

She shrugs, going to put her cans back on and no. This has to stop.

I put my hand on them, lowering them back to her board as I twist in my chair to face her head-on. "Okay, tell me what the problem is and let me see if I can help."

She peeks over at me, gnawing on her bottom lip. "This is my job, Henry. My responsibility to—"

"Quit being so stubborn," I interject. "Do you think Lyric does this all on her own and never gets any help? No. She brings Ethan in all the time to listen to something or get his opinion. Or even one of the other producers. Music is a collaboration and that includes all facets of it. You've been going at this too long, Dragonfly. You're too close to it at this point. So take those fucking headphones off and pump it through the speakers so I can hear."

With the flick of a button and tapping something into the computer she has set up, music from the last song we worked on fills the empty space. Eden sags back into her seat, looking beaten down, defeated, but also resigned. She wants this to be perfect. But she's young and too new at this to understand that doesn't mean she has to make it so all on her own.

I listen to the entire song, watching her as I do. Her eyes are closed, worn out, sure, but also straining to hear just what it is about this song that's bothering her. She wouldn't be at this so long if it wasn't something.

Reaching over, I swipe some of her hair from her face, tucking it behind her ear. As the song comes to a close, I lean in, take a deep inhale of her fragrance, and whisper, "Tell me what you don't like about it."

"I don't even know," she whispers back, her voice dejected. "That's the problem."

"Do you want to know what I think?"

"No."

I bark out a laugh, poking her in the ribs and finally, *finally*, getting her to crack a smile.

"Keith's drums are too heavy," I tell her, watching her expression, suddenly only inches away from her when I'm not even sure how I got this close in the first place. "They're overpowering the bridge and the second chorus."

She throws me a sideways look, going back to that lip with her teeth again. "You think that's it?"

"I do. It's a fast song with a good strong beat and I think that's what makes it take off. Keith's drums need to be solid on it and maybe that's where you're struggling. But them being that way shouldn't eclipse the other sounds and in those two parts, they are."

Her head falls to the side, meeting my shoulder, and I wrap my arms around her, holding her up so she doesn't slide off her chair and fall. I kiss her forehead, running my fingers through her hair. Tugging the elastic out of it, I massage her scalp, listening and grinning as she hums in pleasure with that.

"Thank you," she says, her hot breath fanning across my neck. "I think you're right. I think that's it."

I bend in a little more and kiss her lips. Even though I shouldn't. Even though I just told myself I was ending this with her. But now, when she's like this, isn't the right time for that talk so what's the harm in tasting her. Just this once. Just this last time.

Just one more time.

And with that thought lurking in my brain, on their own volition, my arms squeeze her tighter, not wanting to let her go, afraid she'll slip away before I'm ready to let her.

All too soon she sits up, making the adjustments I suggested and then we listen to it again. Only this time I lift her up off her chair and set her on my lap, forcing her to eat the other half of my burger I couldn't finish at dinner and was planning on munching on tomorrow.

"What kind of guy doesn't finish his burger?" she murmurs around a mouthful of food, popping my cold fries into her mouth.

"The kind who had already eaten his weight in buffalo wings, potato skins, mozzarella cheese sticks, and fish cakes."

She smirks, devouring another bite, and I lean in, licking the side of her lips because there's a speck of ketchup there. "Thank you for your help. I know I suck at asking for it, but I really appreciate it."

"You can't do this alone," I tell her, sounding firm. "I mean it. If you don't want our help, ask Naomi. She'd be perfect actually."

"I did the other day, but that song was in better shape than this one."

"Well, I'm sure she'd be more than happy to help you whenever you need it. But seriously, you need to take breaks. You need to give yourself time and space away from this or you'll burn out worse than you are."

"This is my first solo album and it just so happens to be not only for Wild Minds but for my brother."

I shift her until she's tighter against me, loving how she feels in my arms and hating myself all over again for that. "I get that you're under a lot of stress with this one and we didn't make it any easier with the travel and the time constraint. But you're doing a great job. You're keeping us motivated and knowing when to push and when to pull back. You're an excellent producer, baby. Now you just have to learn the hard part and that's how to find balance."

"I like it when you compliment me." She gives me a side-eye, finishing off the food and closing up the box. "It's how I know you mean it. You don't tend to say things you don't mean, do you?"

"I try not to. I've been lied to a lot in my life. It's not a favor I want to return."

Except that's exactly what I'm doing now. I'm lying to my best friend. I'm fucking his sister like it's the best job I've ever had because it is and I'm keeping that from him. Nothing has ever made me feel worse. I stare down into Eden's tired blue eyes and I know what I have to do for everyone's sake.

"Come on. Let's get you to bed."

I take her hand, helping her off my lap and leading her out of here, back into the soft, muted night. It's just us out here, so I don't let go of her hand. I allow myself to have this. To enjoy it, knowing tomorrow it will be gone. Right thing to do or not, the idea of not touching Eden again turns my legs into lead, making each step toward our houses and tomorrow that much harder.

I walk her past my door and over to hers, stopping when we reach it. "I'm not coming in tonight," I tell her, turning her and cupping her face in my hand, running my thumb along her smooth skin. "You need sleep and truth be told, so do I."

She nods like she agrees though I catch a small flicker of disappointment in her eyes. We still haven't spent the night together. Not in the week or so we've been doing this. But if I sleep with her tonight, even if it's just to hold her, I'll never be able to let her go. That will be it for me. I know it. I'll want to keep her when keeping a woman is not part of the fabric of my being or my life.

I can't love her, I remind myself. That's not who I am or what I do. And that won't change, no matter how great the temptation.

"Good night, Dragonfly." I lean in, pressing my lips to hers, my hand on her face, the other clenching her hip. A wave of sadness sweeps over me, turning my simple kiss just a touch more desperate. I deepen our connection, sweeping my tongue with hers while taking as much of her as I can. Knowing this is likely our last kiss. Our last real moment together.

TWENTY

HENRY

I'm not gonna lie, this is probably one of the coolest things I've ever been talked into in my life. While Jasper and Vi took the girls to the aquarium, the rest of us are geeked out with goggles, snorkels, and fins, swimming our way through one of the bays by our resort. As far as the eye can see is deep blue water and tan coral. And fish. There are fish everywhere, as you'd expect, but I didn't expect there to be so many. And I didn't expect to see so many different varieties.

In front of us are Naomi and Gus who swim directly behind our guide followed by Keith and Maia and lagging up the rear are me and Eden. We're paired up for safety purposes though being in the bay we're pretty well protected from any predators.

We've been instructed not to touch the coral or any of the sea life, just to keep swimming and enjoy the show.

So that's what I've been doing.

Enjoying the show. The fish, yeah. But I've mostly been watching Eden.

I sat up for way too long last night thinking about everything with her. My exhausted mind overthinking and overworking. I want the next two weeks with her. But will I be able to stop when every time I have her I only seem to want more?

If we keep this up, it's only a matter of time before Keith finds out and when he does... I don't know. I don't know what I'll say. Or more importantly, what he'll do. But on top of all that, I can't keep lying to my best friend. It's eating a hole in me.

Being with Eden has been fucking heaven. And hell. Both in equal measures.

She is perfect.

Too perfect and the rational part of me knows what I'm doing is stupid and reckless. That I could end up hurting her worse than I did the first go-around. That despite her promises and us sticking to our rules, she could fall for me.

Which is why it's done. Over. My plan is to tell her tonight.

A sharp tug on my arm snaps me out of my reverie and I turn to find Eden practically vibrating with excitement. She frantically points over to her right and when I glance in the direction of her hysteria, I find a sea turtle swimming alongside us, no more than ten feet away.

I smile into my tube, expelling air, and give her a thumbs up. She keeps yanking on me, urging us to swim just a touch closer without scaring it. I follow her lead only to have something moving behind Eden catch my eye.

For a half second, I can't make sense of what I'm seeing. It's short, fat, and globular with long clearish-white endless tentacles that glide and sway and dance as the creature undulates through the water. It's horrifyingly beautiful. Almost mesmerizing as it terrorizes my senses.

We were warned about the box jellyfish. About how they come out at this point after the full moon. About how deadly their venom is. But we were also informed that they don't come into the bay.

Hardly ever, the guide said. That in all her years of doing this, she's only encountered two, and she's been doing this a long time.

Which is why for longer than I should be, I'm frozen, staring in disbelief until I feel Eden's hand on my arm again. Like a rocket my reflexes ignite, shifting into gear along with a not so healthy dose of panic and adrenaline. Because this jellyfish is getting closer and closer to Eden. And Eden has no idea it's there because she's completely focused on the sea turtle.

Before I can even start to process what I'm doing, I kick at the thing, hoping to use the rush of water from my flipper to propel it in the other direction without getting myself stung. I have no idea if it worked or not because I grab Eden, wrapping my arm around her body and hauling her against me.

She begins to fight me, unsure what I'm doing, but considering we're completely under water and it's a natural fucking response, she hits at me, trying to break free.

Only that jellyfish is still there. I didn't alter its course in the slightest, and it's close to Eden's flapping legs. Fucking inches now and this thing will sting her.

And if it stings her, she could die.

It's that easy.

Using my strength to overpower Eden, I grip her with all my might, tucking her into my body and away from the venomous creature. I swim as hard and as fast as I can with only one hand and the movements of my kicking feet.

All the while battling a determined Eden.

I can't even yell at her or warn her. With instinct as my only compass, I race us forward. My second thought beyond Eden is Maia. Maia who is pregnant. I have to get them out of the water. All of them. Now. My heart thrashes around in my chest, my lungs burning from the need to breathe, but I just don't have time.

Eden is still fighting at me though, scratching my neck and arms, and I realize I'm holding her under, forcing her to hold her breath too long. Pushing her up, her face breaks the surface, but I have no idea where that jellyfish is. No clue how close it is. Just as quickly, I yank her back down into my chest, meeting her wide, terrified eyes with a steadfast determination in mine that she instantly reads.

She nods her head and I hold her close, unwilling to let her go even as I race to grab Keith. My hand meets his flipper first and I yank on it with all my might. His head whips around and I point urgently to the others and then to the shore. He needs to get Maia out. He needs to get Naomi and Gus out.

But I need to get Eden out right now.

Air forces itself into my lungs the second my face breaks through and I watch as Eden does the same. "What is it?" she cries, coughing and sputtering from holding her breath. "What happened?"

All I can do is shake my head as I direct us along the rocky bottom in the direction of the shore. I catch Keith doing the same with Maia and beyond them is Gus, Naomi, and our guide, all wearing matching startled, dumbfounded expressions.

"Henry!" Eden yells, but the moment my feet find purchase and it's shallow enough I can walk with my head above water, I kick off my stupid fucking flippers and lift her up into my chest. Cradled against me, I hold her as high up out of the water as I can manage while walking us to the shore. Something sharp slices up the instep of my foot, forcing a grunt from me, but I don't stop or slow down.

I have to get her out. That's all I can think about. I have to get her out.

"Henry, put me down," she demands as we reach the sand, the waves now barely tickling at my feet.

"Shut up, Eden. Just shut the fuck up until I know you're safe."

Something about my harsh growl or the way I hold her tighter against me has her doing just that. She stops fighting and lets me carry her until we're a solid twenty feet from the water and then I collapse down into the sound, breathing hard, scared out of my goddamn mind, but filled with such a strong swell of relief, I shudder with it.

I adjust Eden on my lap, removing her goggles and snorkel from her face and tossing them off to the side. Then I look her over. Every inch I can touch and see, I examine. It didn't touch her. I know it didn't. She'd be dead or close to it by this point if it had.

But god. If that thing had come any closer to her...

"Eden," Keith yells, running up to us. "What happened? Is she okay?"

"I'm fine," Eden calls over her shoulder before turning back to me and meeting my eyes. "I'm fine," she whispers this time for me.

I know she is, but someone needs to clue my racing heart into that.

Keith drops into the sand beside me, trying to grab Eden off my lap but no way motherfucker. That shit is not happening, and I narrow my grip, glaring at my best friend. I need a minute to get my head on straight and the only thing that will make that happen is the woman sitting on my lap in my arms.

"Henry," Keith snaps, getting right up in my face. "What the fuck is going on?"

"Box jellyfish," I finally manage, taking in a deep breath and trying to clear my head. "There was a huge fucking jellyfish, man. It was not even a half foot from touching Eden."

Eden stills in my arms and everyone falls silent. I didn't even know they were speaking until they stopped but suddenly the silence is deafening. Keith falls back on his haunches, running his hands over his face and through his hair.

"Are you sure?" the guide asks. "Absolutely positive you saw a box jellyfish?"

"Yes," I snarl. "I'm absolutely fucking positive that's what I saw. There is no mistaking something like that. Whether it was the kind you mentioned specifically or not, I don't know. But it was big."

The woman curses under her breath and pulls out a phone, making a call and telling whoever is on the other line that they need to shut down the bay immediately. Luckily, it's a pretty rocky area with a lot of coral so you don't get many casual swimmers and we had rented out the area this morning so we wouldn't be bothered.

"Maia? Naomi?" I ask.

I feel a hand on the top of my head. Maia. "We're good, Henry. We're all good thanks to you."

I swallow thickly, part of me ready to collapse at that. Thank Jesus they all got out of the water.

"You're bleeding," Naomi states. "Your foot, Henry. You've got a cut on the bottom of your foot."

I don't give a shit about my foot.

But someone else does as my foot is suddenly doused in something cold that stings and then it's wrapped in what I assume to be a bandage. "It's not bad. Just a piece of coral that I removed. You need to wash it out though, but the bandage should hold you until we get back to the resort," Maia tells me.

"Does it hurt?" Naomi continues, and I shake my head, staring down at Eden who is staring back up at me. That's all I've been doing since I sat down. Staring at her. Holding her against me.

"Well, I think I need a drink and I don't even drink," Maia continues. "Maybe some pancakes instead. Definitely a nap."

"Yes," Naomi agrees. "To all of that. I'm not sure my blood pressure will ever be the same."

"Let's go get you those pancakes, sweet darlin'," Keith says. "I sure as shit could go for that nap. A jellyfish." He grabs hold of Maia, his hand cupping his babies growing in her belly. "We're not doing this crap again." He growls, dropping his face to her neck. "You're by my side or on land at all times. My heart can't take it. My heart just can't take it."

No. For Keith, I imagine it can't. He's already lost someone in a way no one ever should.

"You ready to get up yet, brother? Get the hell out of here?" Gus questions, dropping a hand to my shoulder, trying to jostle me out of my panic-induced stupor.

"Yes." With my hands on her hips, I help Eden to stand and then I get myself up and out of the sand, dusting myself off.

"Is your foot okay?" Eden asks me. "Can you walk on it?"

"I'm fine. My foot is fine."

It's everything else that doesn't feel like it is.

On numb legs, I trail slowly after everyone as we shuffle in a daze back in the direction of the resort that is only half a mile down the beach from here.

"Could you imagine if Ady had been in that water?" Gus asks and I shudder again, just thinking about that. Ady who loves to swim like a fish. Ady who if she were big enough to snorkel would have been all over that.

"You can't go there," Naomi states. "You just can't. It was a freak thing. The lady even said so."

Did she? I didn't even hear her.

"You good?" Eden whispers, drawing in closer to my side so I can hear her.

"Yeah. No. I don't know." I turn to catch her eye. "You didn't see that thing, Eden. It was there and long and so close to you, baby. It was like the bastard knew you were there and was gunning for you. All I could think about was that I had to get you out of the water."

She heaves a deep sigh, grasps my hand, squeezing my fingers.

Stoically, the six of us make it back to the resort, each of us heading toward our respective houses without even having say so. I think we all need a shower and nap and to get our collective shits together.

Eden murmurs something about seeing me later at dinner when I grab her hand. Her head comes up, her pretty blue eyes questioning. Instead of answering her, I drag her into my house, not letting go of her hand until we're in the palatial master bath and I'm turning on the shower to hot. I check the temperature and then return to Eden who is watching me with caution.

But all I keep thinking is I could have lost her out there.

She's never seen me like this before. No one has because I'm not sure I've ever been like this. It takes an awful lot for me to get riled up. For me to lose my cool. For me to take anything seriously other than music and my friends.

If you're not serious about anything than nothing can touch you. Nothing can hurt you.

I don't let that happen.

I've suffered enough heartache and pain at the hands of others, and I decided a long time ago, that was enough. That I would never again put myself in that position with someone.

I don't like being this guy.

This unnerved guy. I like being the other one. The easy-going one. The one who doesn't get fucking scared of losing someone they care about. Someone I have no business caring about. I promised her I wouldn't. That I couldn't.

I remove Eden's bikini string by string. It drifts to the ground and then I remove my own swim trunks, the bandage on my foot, and take her by the hand into the shower.

I feel her hand on my chest, her eyes beckoning me. But I can't. If I do, I'll be lost, and I can't be lost. I'll be out of control, and I can't be out of control. Not again. Not ever. Instead, I grab the shampoo, pour some into my hands and mechanically rub it into her hair, lathering it up before guiding her under one of the sprayers to wash it out.

I do the same with the conditioner and then I go at her body, making sure every perfect inch of her is clean. Is okay.

Once I'm positive she is, I get going on myself, turning my back to her. Finally breathing. But still not thinking all that much.

Except this is Eden. She doesn't take my shit lying down. She wraps her arms around me, her hands pressing into my chest as she steps into me, holding me from behind.

My eyes cinch shut, my hands balling up into fists in my hair.

I want to tell her to stop. To let me go. To get the fuck out of places she has no right to be. But I can't do any of that. Her touch that shouldn't be everything suddenly is.

She doesn't even know what she's doing to me. This is just how she rolls. The fact that she's remained silent for this long is a miracle, so maybe she does in fact know what she's doing.

Is she reading me or just lost in her own headspace?

A strangled laugh nearly escapes my throat. She's reading me.

She already reads me too well. Always has. And I don't like that either. I don't like the way she's affecting me. Dismantling me.

Shaking up every piece of the foundation I've built and force myself to stand on.

"Your heart is racing."

I nod because I know it is.

She pushes me until I'm under the sprayer and fully rinsed off. Once the shower is off and we're both wrapped in towels, Eden word-lessly bandages my foot that really only needs a simple Band-Aid, and then pours us each a shot of tequila. And once those are down our throats, we go to bed. Together. In the middle of the afternoon. Me holding her and her holding me and within seconds she drifts off. Right before I do the same, I realize I'm breaking a rule with her.

I'm sleeping with her.

First I broke a promise, now a rule.

What will I break next when it comes to Eden Dawson?

TWENTY-ONE

HENRY

When I wake up, it's dark and for a moment I'm disoriented. My eyes fix on the alarm clock on the nightstand shining twelve-thirty in bright green. And in the space where a body should be, it's empty.

She left. She snuck out.

I can't tell if I'm relieved by that or not.

Rolling onto my back, I heave a sigh. There is no way I'll be able to fall back to sleep now. A clatter followed by a low curse coming from the kitchen catches my attention and before I can stop it, I'm smiling. Guess she didn't run out after all.

Getting up, I pad barefoot out into the main area of the house. Eden is wearing one of my t-shirts and a pair of my track shorts rolled at the waist about a million times. They're still about fifteen sizes too big for her. She's standing in the dark in front of the stove, sautéing something that smells out of this world good. Like mushrooms, peppers, and onions. I watch as she adds bacon to another pan while drinking something that doesn't look like wine from a wine glass.

She hasn't heard me yet.

And for that, I'm grateful.

Because just the sight of her in my clothes, cooking breakfast at midnight after sleeping in my arms for hours makes it nearly impossible to breathe. Like my lungs forgot how to expand and contrast and my heart is desperately trying to smack some sense into them by racing like a banshee.

I was going to end things early with her. Call us quits once and for all. That was my plan, but after yesterday... after seeing her like this now...

Eden is dancing around, bopping her head to and fro. It's only now that I catch the AirPods in her ears, which explains why she hasn't heard me. She continues to cook with a skill I didn't know she possessed, humming and singing terribly off key to what I believe is a Sonic Youth song. She sprinkles some chopped herbs over whatever she's making, and a fresh wave of deliciousness hits the air right before she pours a scrambled egg mixture over the entire thing.

A smile spears my lips as she does some crazy dance move only to freeze as she catches me standing here idling in the corner. She belts out a blood-curdling scream, dropping the thankfully now empty bowl that had the eggs in it as her hands fly up to her chest. The bowl makes a loud clanging noise and a few drops of egg go flying onto the floor.

"Did I scare you?" I deadpan as she removes her AirPods from her ears and sets them on the counter.

"You absolute motherfucker." She smacks at me as I get closer, bending down to retrieve the forgotten bowl. "I cannot believe you did that. Warn a girl before you sneak up on her in the freaking dark in the freaking middle of the night." She smacks me again as I set the bowl down and then grab some paper towels to wipe up the mess she made. "Don't you know anything about women? You're lucky I didn't hurl the bowl at your head. Or even better, the frying pan with the bacon."

"Ouch," I quip, grinning at her. "I guess I should be grateful you didn't have a knife in your hands then either. I'll remember that for next time. Sorry." I drop a kiss to her cheek. "I didn't mean to scare you like that. You were just so adorable dancing around I couldn't help but watch."

"Good thing I wasn't singing," she retorts on a deep breath like she's trying to get her heart back under control. I know the feeling.

"You were actually. Both humming and singing."

She pauses mid-stir of the egg concoction, meeting my eyes and gnawing on her lip as an adorable blush hits her cheeks. "I didn't realize I was."

"Don't worry. I don't have it on video."

She rolls her eyes at me, returning to the pan and sprinkling everything with cheese. "I hope you don't mind that I stayed and am using your kitchen. I woke up hungry and didn't want to just leave because that felt weird, but now I'm wondering if I should have just left—"

I silence her with a kiss on her lips. "I'm glad you stayed. Are you making enough for two? It smells incredible and I'm starving."

She laughs, pulling away to check the pans. "Clearly you haven't looked at all the food I'm making. This is enough to feed all you boys and then some. Vi really had them stock your fridge. I hope you like omelets."

"Yup. Vi told them all of my favorites. I was talking with the guys yesterday morning on the way to the snorkeling trip from hell and we decided to chip in and get Vi something really special as a thank you for setting this all up for us."

Eden glances up as she shifts the eggs around in the pan, before taking the whole thing and putting it into a pre-heated oven. "That's insanely thoughtful of you guys."

I chuckle under my breath, leaning against the opposite counter, watching her work. "Don't look so shocked."

"I'm not. I just really love that you guys thought to do that. I think that will mean so much to her. Do you know what you're going to get her?"

I shake my head, reaching out to snag a piece of bacon from the pan only to get my hand smacked away. "No. But Gus said he'd talk to Naomi and Keith said he'd talk to Maia to see if they have any suggestions. I told them I'd ask Jas. I have no idea what to buy a woman. Especially a woman like Viola who isn't into material things and quite honestly could buy anything she did want."

"Then make it personal," Eden replies, turning her back to me so she can finish cooking the breakfast that smells so amazing my stomach grumbles. "Like you said, she isn't into anything material. Girl walks around in the same Docs she's had since you were teens. But she loves her people with all her heart."

"If it were Naomi, we'd buy her a surfboard or some cool music shit. If it were Maia, we'd buy her a computer or something tech because she's really starting to get into all that more now that she's running all of our social media and is starting college this fall. But Vi? Yeah, I'm kinda at a loss."

"I'll think on it too. I'm sure there is something that she'll go crazy over." Eden lifts her glass, taking a sip before setting it back down and tending to the bacon and checking on our omelet.

"What are you drinking?"

"Water." She laughs the word. "Ever hear of it?"

"Wasn't sure if it was tequila."

"Nope. Good old-fashioned water. I can get you some if you'd like. They have the good stuff here." She throws a wink at me over her shoulder. With a twist of a dial, she turns off the stove and the oven and goes about making up two plates loaded with bacon and a cheesy, bubbling omelet. I grab the plates from her before she has the chance and walk them into the family room. It's pitch black over here. The dim light above the stove barely providing any ambient light to lead the way, but I manage to set everything down on the coffee table without dropping any of it.

"Why are we eating in here?" she asks, joining me with another glass of water, I assume for me, and some napkins and silverware.

I flip on the gas fireplace though it's not cold out, and then drop to the floor, sitting with my back against the sofa and the coffee table right in front of me. Eden does the same, both of us staring at the hissing and flickering flames for a second before wordlessly digging in. The eggs are buttery and soft, the veggies cooked to perfection, and the herbs and cheese add just the right amount of flavor. The bacon is greasy and crispy, exactly the way I like it.

"This is delicious." I can't keep the awe out of my voice.

"Mmhm. I love to cook," she says around a mouthful of food. "I wasn't joking about Eden's Roadside Tacos in Paradise being another dream of mine. I'd love to do something like that one day. My current kitchen isn't all that conducive to the kind of meals I wish I could whip up. In the sorority house, I was the resident chef. I used to make all kinds of spreads. And since we were the 'football house'"—she puts air quotes around the words—"because all our boyfriends were on the team, I used to have to make a lot of food."

"What would you make?"

"God. Tons of things. Different kinds of pizzas, Mexican—my favorite as you know—chili, stews, game time food, including home-made buffalo wings and mozzarella sticks. If you've never had them made from fresh mozzarella, I'll make them for you one day and your life will never be the same."

I chuckle under my breath. "That a fact?"

"I would never lie about something as important as homemade fried mozzarella. Anyway, I just liked cooking and being in the kitchen meant it was quiet since not a lot of the party ever came in there. Chad used to make sure of it. He wasn't much of a cook, but he was a good helper and since he never drank during season, we'd hide out together."

Just listening to all the things she did with Chad brings a stab of jealousy to my gut.

She pauses here, tilting her head and glancing quickly in my direction. "Is that weird for me to talk about?"

"No," I force myself to say. "He was part of your life and I'm your... well, not quite your friend, but if you want to talk about him, I'll listen."

"I didn't even realize I was talking about him. Whenever I think about my life in college, I think about it with Chad. It's like the first two years of my time there didn't exist. I had no identity until I was Chad Mason's girl." The disdain in her voice is unmistakable. But I think most of that is directed at herself. "Then again, I was pretty heartsick over some douche I met in a club and had a fling with."

Fuck. A laugh escapes my lungs and I nearly choke on the bacon I was in the process of swallowing. "Thanks for that."

"Any time." She smirks, batting her eyelashes at me as she forks some eggs into her mouth.

"Well, now you answer to no man. Now you're you, Eden. Doing your thing and experiencing your life through your own eyes with your own goals to direct you and your own voice to lead your way."

She twists to look at me, her eyes wide as they flitter around my face. They drop to my lips quickly, almost as if she's thinking about kissing me before they find mine again. They shine with some unnamed emotion. Something that makes my insides quicken and my breath catch.

"You really believe that?"

"You're a force of nature, Dragonfly. Any man worthy of you and lucky enough to win you will know stifling that power would be the biggest crime of all." I clear my throat and go back to my food, though suddenly it tastes bitter beyond belief as I say, "One day you'll find the right guy for you."

"Maybe," she whispers, her voice suddenly hoarse. "What about you, Henry?"

"I don't think I'll ever find the right guy for me. Not really my thing."

She snorts out a laugh. "Come on. You know what I mean."

Honestly, I'm not sure I do. Is she asking if I'll ever find the right person or if I'm the right person for her? Instead, I force myself to swallow more fucking eggs that feel like lead as they go down and change the subject. "College always looked and sounded like fun."

She laughs lightly, going with the flow as Eden does. "Sorta like traveling the world and going from one after-party to the next?"

"Yeah," I muse, smiling. "Sorta like that, I guess. I never regretted not going to college. It didn't seem necessary for what we wanted to do. The other guys had all applied as a backup. Keith was going to go for football, as you know. Me, I never applied."

"How come?"

I shrug, looking away from her back to the fire and then down at my now mostly empty plate. I open my mouth to say something banal when the truth starts tumbling out instead. "I was lost back then. All I had was my music and my guys. If that didn't work out, I had no idea what I was going to do with my life. I had no backup plan."

I shift some of the food around my plate. I've never admitted that aloud to anyone. Not sure I ever thought it through as clearly as that before either.

"I get that," Eden reveals, surprising me enough that my head jerks back up. Now she's the one staring at the fire while I watch, enraptured as soft orange flames dance across her smooth porcelain skin. "I was pretty lost too. For such a long time. I had music, right? Same as you. But no one got the music I liked. No one really understood that side of me, and the only one who would have was already grown and gone by the time I really came into it."

"Keith?"

She nods. Then looks over at me. "You too."

I never saw her. Never looked. She was a child with a crush I had no idea what to do with. Six years can be a large age gap at the wrong age. This woman before me is something so very different from that.

"I was the youngest and my family was busy because that's life, so I was alone a lot, unsure who I was supposed to be and how I was supposed to fit in when I never felt like I did. I went to college because that's what you do if you have nothing else to go on. Only I continued to be the girl I thought I had to be. The one you met at the club those years ago."

I reach out, toying with a strand of her blue hair, so light it's almost colorless against the darkness of the room and the light of the fire. "Why did you feel you had to be her?"

She turns to meet my eyes. "I don't know exactly. I think I was still unsure of who I was and because of that, I just conformed to look and be like everyone else. People liked her, so it was easy to keep that up until it wasn't." Her eyes glimmer in the light as they search mine. "Why were you so lost that all you thought you had were the guys and music?"

And once more, like she injected truth serum into our food, I find myself saying words I never imagined I would with another living soul. "Because that's all I had. I had no family. No love or support from anyone. No money. All I *had* was my music and my friends."

Eden smiles softly, pushing the table away from us and climbing onto my lap, straddling my thighs. Her hands run through my hair and my head tilts back so I can continue to look at her.

"But now you have the world, Henry Gauthier. Money. Fame. Your friends. Women throwing themselves at you." She leans down and kisses my lips. Once. Twice. Three times before pulling back. "Why do you still seem so lost and lonely?"

Because I am, I nearly say, only this time, the truth doesn't leak out. It gets lodged in my throat. Staring up into her eyes, into her soft yet seductive smile, I suddenly don't feel so lost or lonely. Suddenly I feel found and complete. Satisfied almost, which is strange and a bit ill-fitting. Like a suit a size too big, I'm not sure I'll ever be able to grow into but hope I will all the same.

Cupping the back of her head, I draw her lips down to mine.

And the moment they meet, the moment our tongues touch, that now familiar *thunk* pulverizes my insides with a brutal pounding. This isn't a shift or a feeling. This is an onslaught.

But instead of being afraid of it, I almost welcome its pain.

I never felt alive until Eden Dawson walked into my life and destroyed it. Here, with her in my arms, I'm terrified to admit that this feels like how it was always meant to be. Even if the truth remains.

"I can't keep you, Eden." But I'm not sure I can let you go now either.

TWENTY-TWO

EDEN

Oddly enough, I slept like a baby after Henry and I fell back to sleep somewhere close to dawn. We spent the next few hours after we ate with him inside of me and I gave myself the pep talk. The one where I convinced myself that I was getting *exactly* what I needed and wanted.

I don't want a relationship. I only want sex. My emotions are not involved. Henry is not the right guy for me.

Even if I knew I was lying.

Whatever happened in that water, it seemed to change something in him. The problem with that change is that I can't tell if it's for the better or not. He was scared and held me and washed me and took care of me. He may very well have saved my freaking life because I looked up those damn jellyfish and those fuckers don't mess around.

They're venomous as hell, killing quickly and efficiently.

But despite those confessions he made about being lost and alone, it also felt like another part of him broke. And in breaking, he shut down along with it. I felt it. I saw it. I heard it when he said he can't keep me. I tried not to think about it. I tried to push it all away...

Whatever, it didn't keep me up.

I didn't allow it to. Trying to figure Henry Gauthier out is a slippery slope into a vacuous minefield otherwise known as the feeling zone. It is a place I cannot allow myself to go. He promised not to love me. That he *can't* love me. Enough said.

I need to take care of me and protect my heart.

That is rule number freaking one with this.

Which is why shortly after Henry passed out and dawn was breaking through the horizon, I slipped out and came back to my place to sleep alone. See, I'm being smart. I'm sticking to the rules. Thank all miserable fuck we don't have work today because the guys all texted last night that they want to take today off. I'm not upset about it. I'm exhausted.

I think yesterday rattled all of us a bit and we need the mental breather.

Coffee in my hand and a yawn on my lips, I twist to crack out the kink in my back. Just as I'm taking my first sip, the back door of the house bursts open and Henry storms in.

Probably should have locked that when I came in this morning.

Intense green eyes narrow in on me causing my heart to instantly speed up.

He's dressed in jeans, a plain white shirt—Lord help me, why is that so damn sexy—and a freaking devilish smirk. He crosses the room and stops right in front of me.

So close I try to step back, only to bang into the counter behind me. His scent hits me like a two-by-four and I blindly inhale a little deeper. My neck cranes to meet his eyes, blinking at him while I attempt to acclimate to whatever the hell it is he's doing.

He steals the large mug from my hand, takes a sip of my sacred coffee, and then sets it down on the counter beside me.

"Hey—" I start to object, only to have his lips snuff out any protest I had. Strong hands rake through my hair, cupping the back of my head and holding me just so. His mouth fuses with mine, stealing my breath and my sanity in a soul-crushing kiss that makes my naked toes curl against the marble floor.

In a beat, he grabs my ass, lifting me up and placing me on the counter. Spreading my legs, he moves between them and deepens the kiss to a whole new level. This isn't frenzied or angry. This isn't unbridled passion or desperate. This is slow. Sensual. Tamed.

It's so damn erotic I hardly realize when my arms cling to his shoulder blades, hungry for him to be as close to me as possible. I want to feel him everywhere.

He makes out with me, for I don't even know how long. Hands in safe territory only as they drag feather-light caresses up my bare arms, over my neck, through my hair, before tickling my jaw and cheekbones.

It's everything I never knew kissing could be.

Simple and magical and done for the sake of tasting and being close.

"What are you doing?"

"Saying good morning," he answers breezily. Like that's a thing we do when it isn't, and it shouldn't be.

"I think it might technically be the afternoon now."

"Saying good afternoon, then. You snuck out on me again."

"Yup."

He chuckles, his thumb dragging over my bottom lip, his eyes following the motion.

"I know we're not sleeping together, but I liked you in my bed anyway."

A terrible yearning creeps over me, one that starts low in my belly but spreads rapidly through me. I wrap my legs around his waist, trying to reconnect our bodies and screw this feeling away. I whimper into his mouth when he denies me. Almost angry and feral, I hate what he's doing to me. How this all feels.

He laughs, his hand coming down and cupping my pussy through the material of my silky shorts. "This what you want, Dragonfly?"

"Yes," I hum because it's a currency I can work with. This kissing stuff, all this talking and sharing meaningful words, not so much.

I feel his smile against me, his thumb trailing down my slit teasingly. I bite his lip and he punishes me with a kiss that has my body arching back, the occiput of my head meeting the upper cabinet.

"Patience," he whispers while smoothing his hand up my inner thigh. Sliding my shorts and panties to the side, he runs one long finger from my opening to my clit where he takes the moisture he collected and circles it. "This what you need?"

"Yes," I say again, only this time I pant it as he continues playing with me, all the while his mouth feasts on mine.

"I didn't come here for this. It was just supposed to be the kissing, but now I want you to suck my cock, so you better come first."

Oh, god.

Shut up, Henry. Stop saying everything perfect.

Two fingers enter me, pumping in and out, the wet sound of my arousal so lude it drives me farther faster. "I want to eat you," he snarls as he starts thrusting into me harder, deeper, his thumb working my clit in the most obscenely incredible way. "I'd eat you so good right here in this kitchen, on this counter, and then once you came on my tongue, I'd pick you up and take you to the bed and do it all over again. I'd make you scream until you can't take anymore and beg me to stop."

"Fuck," I groan. "Fuck, fuck, fuck."

"You like this," he growls into me, biting at my neck and the top of my breasts as they peek out over my tank top. "You like it when I tell you all the filthy things I want to do to you?"

"Yes. Yes. Holy shit, don't stop."

He laughs into me, his tongue diving into my cleavage.

"Eden, a name so pure for such a dirty fucking girl. Even after you suck me, I'm going to be hard all day thinking about you like this. Your thighs clinging to me. Your wet pussy, dripping for me. I'm going to make you crawl to me, Eden. I'm going to make you take my cock in your mouth and then I'm going to fuck you while you're still on all fours."

He goes faster, slipping a third finger in and pressing down hard on my clit, almost to the point of pain, and I lose it. Fall apart at the seams as never-ending waves of pleasure crash over me, consuming me. Henry doesn't stop until I sag, my body shaking and shuddering with aftershocks.

No one has ever fingered me like that.

Then again, I'm learning Henry is capable of a lot of things I've never experienced before. I was the bad girl trapped in the good girl's body. The one who never asked for it or instructed on how I wanted it.

This is an awakening.

A dawn breaking and I plan on using Henry to fulfill every raunchy fantasy I've ever had.

Henry's fingers slide out of me as he simultaneously rights my body on the countertop. I feel a hand cup my face, and I open my eyes when I feel wet fingers drag across my lower lip. I open instantly, sucking myself off each of his.

"You really are the most gorgeous woman I've ever seen, Eden Dawson. I'm a lucky bastard you let me touch you." Gentle kisses grace the tip of my nose, followed by my forehead. He smiles softly at me, his eyes glittering as they take me in. His thumb sweeps my cheek tenderly and my insides quake. Hard.

Don't fall in love with me, Eden, because I can never love you back.

Those were his words, my freaking mantra, but as I stare into his eyes, into that blissful smile, all remnants of his dirty words and our dirty deeds slipping away, something goes *thunk*. Hard. It doesn't take a genius to figure out it's my heart settling in to a place it's never been before. A new shudder thunders through me. One that has nothing to do with the orgasm I just had. My throat swells with emotion, and if he weren't right in front of me, I'd be tempted to cry.

Shit.

How could I have let this happened?

Dumb question, right? This is Henry. It wasn't a matter of how, it was a matter of when.

I wonder how long it will take me to get over him this time. All that leaving before dawn and sleeping here and ignoring how much I fucking like him obviously didn't work. He just ruined me in two seconds flat. One look. One goddamn kiss. A few simple words. And now, now I am his. Irrevocably. Painfully.

Tragically.

Don't fall in love with me, Eden, because I can never love you back.

Yeah. That one really sucks. I don't seem to care enough to stop this though.

I swallow past that lump in my throat, pushing the bitch down.

I shove him back, hopping off the counter and dropping to my knees as he said he wanted. That blissful smile grows devious and dark as he backs up a few more steps. He wants me to crawl to him and though it feels like it should be degrading as hell, it's also making me wet all over again.

Maybe it's the hunger and need in his eyes doing it, but I will crawl to this man and blow his fucking mind while I blow his cock. My hands meet the cool marble floor and I start to crawl to him, ignoring the discomfort in my knees as I do.

He hisses out a slew of curses under his breath, his eyes feasting on every inch of me. The sound of metal jingling stirs my eyes away from his, down to his belt. He undoes the latch and then the swoosh of leather through the belt loops of his jeans zaps through the air like a current of electricity.

"On your knees, Eden. Eyes on me."

I gulp and do as he commands.

"If you want me to stop at any point, hold your hand up, fingers spread in that signal."

"W-what?" I ask in a stunned, yet husky voice.

"I'm going to tie your wrists behind your back with my belt and

I'm going to fuck your mouth. You won't be able to stop or push me away. So if it gets to be too much, hold your hand up and I will stop."

Oh Jesus.

Henry binds my forearms and wrists with his belt, testing the resistance and instructs I do the same. Then he makes sure I can still move my hands and that he can see them. But I'm not going anywhere until he lets me. "Do you know how hot you look like this? With your tits pushing forward and your arms restrained? You're a vision. An erotic fairy tale."

I lick my lips, more than ready.

Henry pulls down the top of my tank top and bra, exposing my breasts to him. Bending down, he takes one nipple in his mouth, sucking hard on it as he takes his cock out of his pants and slowly begins to stroke himself. I'm so turned on I'm leaking onto my thighs.

"Ready?" he asks, tickling his fingers along my jaw.

"Yes."

"Open for me, Eden, and remember what I said about your hand."

He can say whatever he wants, but there is no way I'm stopping. I want this too much. I want to take him in my mouth and down my throat and I want to watch as he comes apart. As I own his pleasure because up until this point, he's owned all of mine.

Henry's long and thick and perfect, but did I mention he's long and thick? It's a challenge to take him in as deeply as I want, and I have to talk myself into relaxing my jaw and throat while breathing through my nose.

He's patient with me at first, but once he senses I'm there, he unleashes himself in my mouth. He thrusts into me, his hands in my hair and his eyes that of a fire-breathing dragon locked on mine. He grunts and growls, praises me while he takes without restraint.

Saliva pools in my mouth and drips down my chin. Tears stream down my face. But I don't stop sucking him. I work him as best I can, trying to gain some control over this. My tongue flicks at him, toying with his crown and licking the precum that's leaking from it. Flattening my tongue, I massage his veiny shaft. He hits the back of my throat and I swallow, causing a low, feral moan to rip from his lungs.

That's it, Henry. Lose your mind.

"Eden," he bellows. "Hold up your hand, baby."

Baby. That's like the third time he's called me that. No fucking way am I holding up my hand. My eyes tell him so and that's when he does in fact lose his mind. He pumps into me and I suck him with everything I have until he pulls out and comes all over my tits as a deep, guttural groan flees his lungs.

When he's done, panting and cursing, he bends down and kisses me like I'm his reason for breathing. "Christ, you're perfect. Don't move," he instructs, and I practically laugh at that. I'm on my knees with my arms bound. Where the hell am I going?

A minute later he returns with a warm washcloth and goes about cleaning me up. Then he helps me to stand and unties me.

"You okay?" he asks, checking my arms and wrists. They're a little red and there are a few marks where I must have pulled against the restraint.

"I'm fine. It doesn't hurt."

"You sure? I can get you cream or something." His expression is filled with concern as he rubs gently at my abrasions that are already starting to fade. "You should have put your hand up. I went too far with you."

"I liked it, Henry. It was hot as hell. I would have stopped it if I wanted to." I tilt my head, studying him. "Why are you being nice to me today?"

He chuckles like I'm just the funniest person ever. I'm not, so I have no idea what he's playing at. "Eden, I just tied you up with my belt and ruthlessly fucked your mouth. I'd hardly call that nice."

True. But still, there is something different about him. There's a lightness to his eyes this morning. The green's a little clearer and I don't get it. Harsh Henry I can manage. This guy is making me think and wonder. "Forget I said anything."

He stares at me for several heartbeats, trying to read my expression. "I thought we had gotten over that. Found a mutual understanding. Believe it or not, dick isn't my default setting."

I know it's not. It's his coping mechanism.

"If you want me to be an ass, I can take you in yours."

"Now there's an idea."

His hands hit his hips as he spins in a circle, huffing and puffing and already growing hard once again. "Eden—"

"I was thinking of going for a hike today, so maybe later with the ass thing? I can't imagine taking your sizable dick in my virgin ass will make hiking after an easy task," I say, teasing him just as a knock comes at my door. My eyes burst open wide as do Henry's. "Who is it?" I call out.

"It's Keith. Open up."

Oh boy.

TWENTY-THREE

EDEN

Henry's eyes flash around, taking in our appearance. My boobs are back in my bra and tank, and the redness on my arms is pretty much gone. Henry redoes his belt, kisses my cheek, and then goes over and sits on the couch, flipping on the television and making himself comfortable. I half expected him to run out the back door, but he doesn't.

I'm not sure if I like this or not.

Swinging open the door, I assumed I'd find Keith with Maia, but he's alone. "Hey," I say brightly, my voice a touch higher than necessary. I silently clear it and get myself under control. "What are you doing here?"

I totally feel like a teenager whose father just walked into her room while her boyfriend hides under her bed. Only Henry isn't my boyfriend and he's not hiding.

"Can't a brother drop in on his little sister?"

"Um. Not without an appointment or at the very least calling first."

Keith snickers. "Thought I'd drop in and see how you're doing today. I stopped by Henry's house first, only he wasn't there."

And yup, there is accusation in his tone. I try not to blush. I truly do, but I think the bastard is leaking out anyway, so I spin around just in case, giving Keith my back. "You're in luck. He's here watching my TV and bothering me, same as you."

"He's here?"

"Yes, asshole. I'm here. Come in and watch Sports Center with me."

Keith plows past me, and I close my eyes, trying to rein in my thundering heart. But then I hear, "S'up brother." My eyes snap open and catch Keith doing a fist pound with Henry, plopping onto the sofa beside him and getting comfortable.

Well, that's unexpected.

But maybe it shouldn't be? I mean, Keith really has no reason to suspect anything is going on. I shut the door and return to the kitchen area, grabbing my now cold coffee and putting it in the sink. "You guys want anything?" I ask. "Or, you know, you can go now since you both decided to check up on me and can plainly see I'm fine."

Smooth, Eden. Way to play it cool, girl.

I mentally roll my eyes at myself and judging by the smirk Henry quickly tosses me, I'm not selling it.

I grab a water from the fridge, downing half of it and then wiping my mouth with the back of my hand. If they're going to watch TV, I'm not going to stand around and watch them do it.

"Well, this has been a bundle of laughs and good times and all, but I'm going to go for a hike. I'll catch you losers on the flip side. Lock up when you leave."

"You're going for a hike?" Keith questions.

"Yes. I'm a bit beached out today, as you can imagine."

"You're not going alone, are you?"

Folding my arms over my chest, I give my brother my most derisive glare. "You do realize I'm a grown woman who has been hiking all by her big girl self for a long time now, right?"

"Yeah, except you don't know the area. You don't know the

wildlife. It's dangerous to go hiking by yourself, even when you do know all that."

"Ugh. Come on, Keith. Just stop."

"He's right, actually," Henry unhelpfully chimes in. "You shouldn't go alone. It's not safe."

I flip them both off, but I'm not getting anywhere as they glare at me. Great. "You're welcome to join me."

Keith adamantly shakes his head. "Not on your life. I hate hiking."

I know. That's why I asked him.

"Oh well. Can't say I didn't try. Bye now." I give them wiggly fingers and go to grab the backpack I already have packed and ready to go.

"Henry can go with you," Keith offers nonchalantly.

"He can what?" Henry and I snap at the same time. I spin back around on the balls of my feet, ready to do murder.

Keith stares at Henry, the two of them having some kind of nonverbal standoff. Henry shakes his head. Keith nods his. I've seen Jasper and Gus do this crap before, never with these two.

"You can go with her," Keith almost demands though his tone is relaxed. "I trust you. You'll keep her safe and since Eden is too stubborn not to go, I'd feel better if you went with her."

"Did I suffer hypoxia yesterday in the water, or did I drink LSD-infused coffee this morning?"

Keith laughs like it's just so funny. "I'm serious, man. You like hiking and that shit. What else were you going to do today?"

"Um..." Only Henry has no response beyond that because he's just too incredulous. "Not that. I doubt Eden would want me to tag along anyway."

"Bullshit. Eden would love the hell out of it."

"I would?"

They ignore me completely.

"You're serious?" Henry pushes.

"Absolutely." With that, Keith stands up and slaps Henry on the shoulder. "Thanks, man. I owe you one. Both for yesterday and today."

Keith crosses the living room and wraps me up in a hug. "Glad you're okay. I was worried out of my skull about you." He kisses the top of my head and then heads for the door. "Have fun on your hike. If such a thing is possible." He snickers. "Try not to get eaten alive by bugs."

That's why Keith hates hiking. The bugs. We all went camping once when we were kids, and he was nearly eaten alive by bugs. He came home covered in Calamine lotion and swore never to hike or camp again. Wimp.

The door shuts with a resounding click and then it's just me and Henry again, staring blankly at one another.

"Why does this feel like a setup?"

I point at him because it totally does. "Yeah. Like a trap. Like he'll have us followed by cameras only instead of being on some cool National Geographic Survivor Hawaiian-style show, we'll be on some smutty celebrities getting it on in the wild rag."

"Huh?"

I wave him away. It made sense in my mind. "You really don't have to come with me."

He laughs, standing up and shutting off the television. "Actually, I do. Not only did your brother ask me to do him a solid, but I agree that it's not safe to go hiking alone."

"Great," I grumble, knowing there is no way I'm going to be able to talk him out of joining me. I unzip my backpack, already opening cabinets and loading it up with more food and water. "You're carrying this pack then because now it's heavier than I want to deal with."

"Whatever you say, weakling."

"I'm not weak." I show off my right bicep that he proceeds to squish. "Ow. That hurt."

"You're lucky weakness in females turns me on." I smack at him and he grins, kissing me soundly on the lips. "I'm going to change. I'll be right back and if you dare try to sneak out again, Eden Dawson, I will spank you till your ass is red and it won't be the erotic sort of spanking either."

"Yes, daddy."

"That does nothing for me other than creep me out."

I laugh. That's why I said it.

***

Ten minutes later we're driving up the bumpy path in a resort Jeep we borrowed, following the directions my concierge gave me. The warm breeze whips all around us as I grip on to the oh-shit bar so I don't go flying out the doorless side. It's a perfect cloudless day and to say I'm excited for this hike is an understatement. There is apparently a really cool natural waterfall not too far away and it's a good trail leading there, but first you have to drive to the landing point.

"I take it Keith has no idea you and I have been at it like kinky rabbits or he never would have asked you to come with me."

Henry turns the Jeep sharply to avoid a huge rock on the road, but I don't miss the grimace before he does. "I don't like lying to my best friend."

"Do you want to stop?"

His head whips back in my direction, his eyes searching mine. "Do you?"

I shake my head. "No. I don't." It's that simple and that complicated.

He turns back to the road and is quiet for a very long beat. Finally, he sighs and says, "Neither do I. And since we both agreed it's just for now, just while we're here..."

"Yeah," I agree, ignoring the sting those words bring. "If it's just for now and won't go anywhere, there is nothing to say. Besides, I'm a grown woman and my brother is not my keeper. I'm allowed to do whatever the hell I want. Frankly, it's none of his business."

"Except he told me point blank not to touch you."

I didn't know he told him straight up like that. Which also makes the fact that he pushed Henry to come with me today weird.

"And now he's trusting me to look after you. To keep you safe and make sure you don't get hurt."

I roll my eyes at that. Like I'm not fully capable of doing that myself? Why are men so freaking ignorant when it comes to all us women are capable of? "Since when does having a vagina make me incapable of taking care of myself?"

"That's not what this is, and you know it. But you're deflecting here. Us screwing around is me breaking a promise to your brother." He runs an agitated hand through his blond hair. "Jesus. I'm a real piece of shit. He's my lifelong best friend and I'm screwing his sister when he asked me not to."

That hasn't stopped you for the last week, I want to say but am smart enough to keep my mouth shut. I promise not to love you, Henry. Except my body is savagely crying out, I promise to love you. It's a mess of a situation if ever there was one.

"Keith was out of line to put that on you in the first place. It's not his call to make. He never consulted me on his lovers, temporary or otherwise. I get he's trying to look out for me, but I'm not a child anymore. The days where he can make demands over my life have long since passed. Henry, the truth is, why would we tell him? What would that accomplish other than starting an unnecessary fight. What happens between us is exactly that. Between us. It legitimately doesn't involve anyone else."

He stares straight ahead, driving us on the rocky terrain while mulling my words over. Whether he needs the rationalization or not, he finally nods in acceptance. But then he reaches out and squeezes my hand, resting on my lap.

It's brief, over just as quickly as it happened, but it's like a shot straight to my heart. Because it's his way of saying we're doing this. His way of saying we're in this together and it's our secret. I shouldn't feel such a thrill from it, but I do, and I know it won't go away.

The real bitch of this scenario is, much like Henry who broke a promise to Keith, I broke my promise to him. *Don't fall in love with me, Eden.* Oops. Too late. Sucks for you, Henry. Well, more for me than him. Truth, I'm not sure I ever fell out of love with him.

And because of that, I want this time with him. Even though it will rip me apart when it's over. I survived a broken heart at his hands before, I can do it again. Better to have loved, right? Maybe.

Truth, I can't think of the pain right now when I'm busy riding the high.

"Here," I say, practically jumping up and down in my seat as I point to the side of the road where there is a small gravel turn-off and a sign with the trail's name. "Park here. This is this perfect."

Henry glances over at me for a quick flash but does as he's told. Then he looks up the mountain we're now parked in front of. "How is this perfect?"

I point at the mountain because it should be obvious.

"*This* is what we're hiking? A fucking mountain?"

"Well, yeah. What did you think we'd be hiking?"

Henry's wide, incredulous eyes slowly swivel in my direction. Then he takes me in from head to booted toe. "You're serious with this shit?"

I mash my lips together to contain my smile. "Yep. Pretty damn serious. And you agreed to go. Now you know why Keith was all worried. And why he didn't warn you ahead of time. I like hiking. I like camping. I don't fuck around with either. Despite my current LA digs, weird penchant for all things dark, and current shade of blue hair, I like the outdoors. One day when I'm able, I plan on purchasing a ranch at the base of a mountain so I can wrangle cattle by day and climb mountains by night."

"Another dream of yours?" Henry blinks at me more times than I can count. "You're not serious?"

Why does he keep asking me that question?

"Not fully. I'm not sure I'm a wrangling cattle type of girl. That just seems wrong to me. But I'm not joking about the hiking and camping stuff."

More blinking. Back to the mountain for a very long beat. Then back to me. I'm tempted to tell him we're not actually climbing the mountain, just taking the trail that leads around it, but his horrified expression is too much fun right now. I don't even care if that makes me a bitch.

"This is very likely a volcano given where we are."

"Yes. But a very dormant one. There are no active volcanos on this island." I frown. "I know. I was disappointed by that too. It's why I'm hoping to hop on over to another island to see if we can find a live one. But that's for another day."

"Um. Eden?"

"Yes, Henry," I purr. He's not amused.

"I'm wearing, a T-shirt, shorts, and fucking Chucks."

I know he is. Chucks are quite possibly the worst shoes for hiking since they are flat-soled with zero grip. But what was I going to say when he showed up like this? I doubt he has hiking boots like I do. He's here. With me. Too late to back out now. And in truth, I don't think this trail is going to be all that challenging.

"Since we're talking about our wardrobes, have I mentioned that the only thing I'm wearing under my tank top and shorts is a barely-there bikini?"

"Eden—"

"Come on. I've got you, princess." I hoist myself up and over the gearshift to kiss his cheek. Then I climb out of the Jeep before he decides to turn this puppy around in record time.

"This better be worth it," he grumbles under his breath.

Oh, it will be for what I've got planned for it.

TWENTY-FOUR

HENRY

The problem with Eden is that from the moment I saw her in the club three years ago, I wanted her more than anything. I had to have her in a way I had never wanted to have any woman. And since then, that hasn't changed. And in the weeks we've been here, instead of that desire fading the way I had hoped, it's grown. A persistent beast who will never be sated.

The days tick faster and faster and with each one, the panic that sits in my gut swells.

I don't want Hawaii to end. I don't want to go back to life before her. I'm a piece of shit who not only broke a promise but is blatantly lying by omission to his best friend.

And I have no idea what to do about any of it. Nothing that makes sense. Especially when everything else about my life is unchanged. I'm not right for Eden. Even if I'm starting to think I want to be.

Like right now. This has to be about me. Right? I mean, why else would she be standing on the beach naked, her back to me, facing the water like she's about to become one with it. Naked. Did I mention that already? Because yeah, her adorable pert ass is practically calling out to me, begging for my attention that I'm only too happy to give.

Rain pours from the heavens in tropical storm fashion. Lightning flashes across the sky along with a rumble of thunder in the distance two seconds behind. It's not over us. This I know. But still, you can feel the electricity in the air. It only seems to ramp up my nerves more as Eden takes another step into the water.

Water and fucking electricity.

Is she fucking kidding me with that?

"Eden," I yell out, cupping my hand around my mouth, hoping the sound of my voice reaches her. But nope. Or if it does, she ignores it completely. It started raining overnight. Eden's body, heavy with sleep, was tucked against mine as I lay awake, thinking about things I shouldn't while listening to the rain on the roof.

We recorded all morning and then separately retreated to our suites due to the weather. Adalyn was having trouble. Or so Vi's text indicated. Gus bailed early too, wanting to be with Naomi, and Keith couldn't resist either, feeling like he was given a free pass.

I walked back here with Eden, hoping our afternoon would be spent alone on the couch, naked in my bed, or sleeping on the hammock with the rain surrounding us only for her to take off. Take off and strip down. Strip down and walk to the ocean's edge.

Her arms fly out around her, her face tilted up at the sky as she allows the rain to pelt her in angry torrents. Another rumble of thunder and my heart instantly picks up the pace, feeding off the energy in the air in the worst possible of ways.

"Eden," I try again only to be ignored. Again.

Goddamn her.

Ripping my shirt over my head, my sneakers hit the porch floor next, followed by my socks. I can't stand here and watch as she gets electrocuted. Fucking twenty-two-year-olds. She thinks everything is an adventure. And now I sound like the man who raised me. I would laugh if I didn't hate how that thought feels in my head. Like a punch to the soft tissue.

Rain slaps across my head, chest, and back, instantly soaking me as I march out into the storm, passing the pool and narrowing in on the beach beyond. My shorts weigh me down, heavy with water, and I undo the button and zipper as I go, letting them fall and not giving a fuck if they're ruined or not. "Eden!"

Her position is unchanged. Like a sacrificial goddess offering herself to the heavens above and despite my unease, she is a sight to behold unlike any other.

"Do you feel it, Henry?" she calls out to me, righting her body and twisting her head over her shoulder to find me. She heard me all along. She knew I was coming for her. "Earth." She points to the sand beneath her feet. "Water." Her hands, palm side up, meet the rain as it falls. "Fire." A bolt of lightning, as if on cue, hits the sky. "Air." Thunder cracks so loud I jump in place, the wind howling angrily as it blows past us. "I've never done this. Stood naked in a storm to meet it head-on."

"What are you doing?"

She laughs, reaching out for my hand, urging me to take it. "Living. I don't live enough. I worry too much." Her eyes glimmer as she licks the rainwater from her lips. "Sorta like you."

"This is crazy," I yell, even though I'm right beside her. It's too loud out here. Too turbulent. "And dangerous. Come on."

She spins in place and pins me with a stare I can't ignore. And if I thought my heart was racing before... I was wrong. "You watched me all morning," she challenges.

I did.

"Why do you do that?"

To make sure you're real.

When I see her, I can feel her. When I can't, I'm afraid I've lost her. It's like my mother without being about my mother. Even when my mother was there, she wasn't. Eden is different though somehow. Because when she ignores me, I feel the intention behind it. It's a challenge for her to remain impervious to us. Ignorant of me. My mother just didn't give a fuck and maybe that's why I watch her.

"Because I have to. I have no control over it anyway."

She smiles. She likes that answer because Eden is doing something she should not be doing. Something she promised she wouldn't. She's falling for me.

More thunder rolls and I suddenly find myself feeding off the energy instead of being afraid of it. Still, I'm not stupid and I haul her into me, pulling her away from the water's edge. Her wet, naked body presses to mine.

"Do you remember the waterfall?" she asks, breathing heavily into my ear.

I smile despite myself. "You mean the one I fucked you behind?" It wasn't the type of waterfall you see in movies. There was no cave behind the falls. Just sharp rocks. Still, we tried it out and I took her there, sitting her on a stone and devouring her body inch by inch. That waterfall is the reason she's talked me into hiking with her twice since then.

Somehow in the last week, it's become more about the way I crave her and less about the way I need to take her. I blame the ocean. I blame the jellyfish. I blame it all, including her. I didn't know it was possible to think this much about one person. To be this worried and consumed. It's awful and for that reason alone, for the last week I've been trying—again—to talk myself into cutting this thing between us short.

And yet here I am. Following her out into the storm. Desperate to be near her despite the imminent peril.

"Feel the excitement, Henry. It's magic."

"This isn't magic. This is dangerous," I snarl, losing my patience fast.

"There might be reward in the risk."

I've never found any. Then again, I'm not sure how many risks I've taken other than being with her. Mostly I just go along for the ride. She's breaking me open, and I need to find a way to stop it.

Cupping rain in her hands and dumping it on my head, rivers run down my face as I stare into her bright blue eyes. Riled and entranced with the fury of nature surrounding us. With the woman trying to coax a playful reaction from me. A smile. A laugh. "Are you living a little yet?" she questions, her eyes casting about my face.

I growl. "Is that what you call this? You're fucking crazy."

"Maybe."

Without a word, I scoop her up into my arms, tucking her cold, naked body against mine, and storm back to the house. She doesn't protest. She wanted me to chase after her, and I did. She wanted me to rescue her, and now it's done. We've got less than a week left here, and I don't want to waste what little time we have left with playing games.

I reach the back porch of my house, trudge up the steps, and practically throw her down on the hammock. Her tits bounce with impact, the hammock swinging wildly to and fro. Without a word I climb on top of her, making sure I don't capsize us both, and take her wrists in my hands.

Her breaths come out in quick pants, her chest rising and falling with the effort. Her molten eyes hold mine as I lift her arms over her head and weave her hands and wrists in between the knotted diamond-shaped rope of the hammock until they're so twisted and bound she'll never escape.

"If you try to free yourself, I stop."

Without another word, I spread her legs and slip two fingers inside her. Her back arches, her head along with it as a moan flees her lips.

"You drive me crazy, Dragonfly. I love it as much as I can't stand it."

My lips dive down, feasting on her cold, wet lips that taste like the rain we were just in. I bite down on her bottom lip, dragging it between my teeth as my fingers keep up a relentless pace, thrusting in and out of her without touching her clit. She loves it, but I know her enough to know she wants, *needs* more.

"You push me past my every comfort zone," I breathe into her, my lips layered against hers. "You make it so that no matter what I do, no matter how hard I try, I can't get enough of you. Why do you do that?" I demand, throwing her words back at her.

I drag myself away from her lips, down her body, putting my mouth where my fingers are. Her arms jerk, her hands twisting in the ropes, unable to grasp my hair the way I know she likes to do when I go down on her. But I don't care. I'm furious.

She made me worry about her. Again.

She made me desperate for her. Again.

She made it so I can't get enough of her. Always.

She's made me fucking care so much about her when I swore I'd never care about anyone.

"Henry," she cries, the hammock swinging dangerously now as she fights the bindings, her body writhing as I continue to lick her, my tongue thrusting in and out. My fingers toying with her clit. A crack of thunder eclipses the sound of her orgasm as it shakes and tears through her without mercy. And before she can catch her breath, I'm inside of her, losing my mind at the feel of her. Why does every damn time have to be like this? Like the first time. So good. So perfect. So... right.

Doesn't she understand? Doesn't she get it? I made that promise to her for a reason.

But the deeper inside her I go. The more times I have her. That promise grows farther and farther from my mind, and all I'm left with is her. Is this smart, sexy, wild, vulnerable woman I want to wrap up and keep safe while doing dirty, dirty things to.

Eden's body shudders beneath mine, her thighs shaking so hard they have trouble holding onto me as she comes apart on me for the second time. I follow her over the edge, breathing impossibly hard as my mind gallops in a million different directions.

I collapse onto her, instantly loosening the bindings on her wrist and rolling us so she's lying on top of me, her head against my racing heart. And for the longest time, the two of us just gently sway while I massage her wrists, listening to the storm rage just steps away, the air thick and damp.

"I don't want to go home," she whispers, and my body instantly fills with regret. She doesn't want us to end, and neither do I. But what is the alternative? To be with her? I just can't do it. I just...

"We don't have a choice." I'm telling her that as much as I'm telling myself.

"We do," she states clearly. "We could live like this forever and not ever have to go home."

"I can't do that, Eden. It's not who I am. It's not who I ever wanted to be." The thought of truly giving myself over to her...

"Why? Tell me why."

I sigh. I know exactly what she's asking, and she deserves a truth I've never given anyone. "I don't talk about it. And it's not because I'm stuck in the past or because it's so tragic I can't handle it or anything. My shit isn't like Keith's. It's just shit, okay. It's happened to dozens of other kids out there and it doesn't make me special or unique. It's personal shit and I don't talk about it because I just never have."

Eden falls silent as she watches the storm. I hate this. I hate the reason we're out here. I hate the silence and the questions and the demands. All over one woman. This isn't some fairy tale bullshit where only one woman will fit into my glass slipper or whatever. This is a girl I'm strung out on and need to find a way over.

"What did you mean when you said you have no interest in ever falling in love? That you can't. If you want me to understand this thing with you, then I want to know what happened to make that your reality."

I sigh again, angling down to kiss the top of her wet head, and then I fall back, staring up at the wood-plank ceiling of the porch, intertwining my legs with hers. "I've never told anyone. Not the guys. No one."

"I know."

"It's ugly."

"I figured."

"I'm not going to tell you everything. I'm just not."

"Okay," she says, her voice growing distant.

"I'm not going into details either."

"Fine."

I puff out a breath, my chest tight as I think about what I'm willing to say and what I'm not. There is a hell of a lot more on the back end of this than there is on the front and I don't even know where to begin.

"My dad wasn't really my dad," I start, my eyes closing as visions I wish would die instead spring to life behind my eyes. "He was my mom's boyfriend, only I didn't know that until I was fourteen or so because I had lived with him my entire life. He was obsessed with my mom. And she didn't give two shits about him except for the fact that he was obsessed with her. That she liked. A whole lot. So much so that she kept him going." I swallow hard, my head spinning as a cold sweat breaks out on my forehead despite the miserable humidity. "Even though she had a completely separate family. A real family. A husband and two other children. She had me first. Kept me with her boyfriend while she flittered in and out because she was mostly with them."

Eden stiffens against me, her body going rigid even as she places one of her hands over my heart, dropping a kiss beside it.

"He was a lovesick idiot. He gave her all his money. Bought her anything she wanted, whether he could afford it or not. Waited by the door for her to return and drop him the smallest bit of attention and affection before just as quickly leaving his pathetic ass behind once again. Leaving me behind along with him. She owned him. And every time she would leave him, things got worse and worse. I was just there. A place to store her fatherless kid she didn't give two shits about without child services getting involved."

The drinking. The words he would say and the things he would do.

I scrunch my eyes shut tighter, willing the images, the sounds, words, and smells from my mind.

"Anyway, eventually her husband found out about him and me, and that was the last we saw of her."

Just like that, she was gone. No goodbye. No, I'm sorry, Henry. Just gone. Like I never existed to her to begin with. She never even returned my phone calls or texts, and fuck knows I sent plenty of both her way.

Things got really great from there. So fucking great I have scars as reminders in case I try to forget. As if reading my mind, her finger trails along the three-inch white depressed tissue in my side from when he took a knife and slashed at me in a drunken rage. Lucky for me, it wasn't deep. Superficial and I was able to take care of it myself without anyone knowing about it.

That was my last day living there. The day I made the promise to myself. I would never fall in love with anyone. I would never give anyone that sort of power over me again. And I would never end up like *him*.

"Do you know who your real dad is?" she asks softly after a very long, silent few moments. She has tears in her voice, and I lean in and kiss the top of her head, my fingers trailing up and down the smooth skin of her nude back.

"No. No clue. I don't even know if she knew."

"And your mom? Where is she now?"

"Still with her other family, I guess."

"Does she know about you, Henry? Do your half-siblings?"

I wince at the way she says that. Like they're a part of me. They're not, and they never will be. "If they do, thankfully they haven't cared enough to get in touch with me. I didn't tell you this so you'd feel bad for me. I told you this so you'd know that it's just not how I'm built. But if I were ever going to be with anyone, it would be you. Please know that. You're perfect. It's me who isn't."

"You lied to me." Her hand tightens on my chest. "You said that wasn't a big thing. That it was just shit and happens to dozens of other kids. You lied. That's a very big thing, Henry. What you went through is awful and I'm mad at you for never telling anyone. For never talking to Keith or even my parents. You went back home and endured that when you didn't have to."

"It wasn't something I wanted anyone to know, and the last thing I ever desired from your perfect family or my amazing best friends, who took me in when I needed it without question, was to see pity. There were a lot of things I endured, Eden. That would have broken me for good."

"I know there is more since you told me there was." She shifts in closer to me, trailing kisses up my chest and along my neck. "You're also stupid."

"What?" I burst out, my voice coming out in a strained half-laugh.

"Stupid. For thinking your friends wouldn't understand or get you and that they'd pity you. For thinking you're alone when you're not. For believing love is toxic and only ends with pain. You're wrong about all of it. One bad apple doesn't mean the whole bushel is rotten. Look at your friends. At all the love you're surrounded in now. I've only had bad experiences with love myself, but I know enough to know just how wrong you are." She perks her head up, forcing my gaze to meet hers. "You're wrong about love, Henry," she tells me adamantly. "I only wish you'd let me prove it to you."

TWENTY-FIVE

HENRY

"All I'm saying is I don't want him to do it."

I stare at Maia and shake my head, dismayed, watching as she licks a huge ice cream cone filled with vanilla frozen yogurt.

"Maia, give me a break. It's your birthday. You're turning twenty-one. It's a big deal."

"Only if you drink, which I don't, pregnant or otherwise."

"He loves you. We love you. We want to celebrate you."

"You wanna celebrate me, Henry. Feed me. It's like I have parasitic aliens living inside me. They control everything. Did Keith have to be right about twins? It's like the bastard knew he'd do this to me when he knocked me up." She points to her adorable tiny round belly that's peeking out between her bikini top and bottoms. "Look at this thing. It's growing bigger by the freaking second and so are my boobs. Do you know how much that sucks, by the way?"

"Um. No. Nor do I want to know."

Maia rolls her eyes at me because she's gonna tell me anyway, whether I want to hear about her boobs or not. "I started out with double Ds. Big, full ones at that. Cute and upright if we're talking dynamics, which given their size was like a blessing from Jesus."

"Please stop," I beg.

"Now I have to buy specialty bras *and* bathing suits because they don't sell my goddamn size at Victoria's Secret if you get what I'm saying. And they're heavier, Henry. They're so heavy and full and sensitive—"

"Maia, for the love of your pal Jesus, can we not talk about your tits? I'm honestly begging here."

She smirks knowingly. "Oh, that's right. You prefer the perfect little perky ones. The ones attached to the blue-haired goddess otherwise known as my future sister-in-law. Yeah, I'd like her tits a whole hell of a lot more than mine right now."

"I have no idea what you're talking about."

"I saw you dancing with her," she tells me, trying to keep up with the dripping vanilla as it takes over her cone in record time, licking the sticky vanilla residue from her fingers as she goes.

"What? When?"

"Last night," she states casually. "I was going to pee and on my way back inside the bar everyone was drinking in, I took a minute to watch the ocean roll in. I saw you. You were off to the side behind the bar and your white shirt caught my eye. I saw you with Eden. You were all over each other, Henry. You were staring into each other's eyes. You were touching her, and she was touching you. But best yet, you were smiling at her in a way I've never seen you smile at anyone. And that look in your eyes? It's the way Keith looks at me right before he tells me he loves me."

Well, damn. I don't even know what to say to that. Instead I sigh, taking a sip of my coffee.

"So now that I know, will you tell me all about it?"

"No." I glance over at her, smirking as vanilla starts to drip. "You better eat that quick, babe. It's about to melt everywhere."

"I know," she says, licking at it furiously. "I'm working on it here. I'll lick, you talk."

"That sounds dirty."

She laughs. "It does, but it isn't. Drink your freaking coffee that

I'm no longer drinking thanks to this pregnancy and tell me your shit, Henry. All of it."

So I do. I explain everything that's been going on over the nearly three weeks we've been here. And in that time, Maia finishes her cone, wipes her hands, and scoots in closer to me like I need the comfort of a good friend, which maybe I do.

"You're never going to be able to keep that promise to her. No way in hell."

I scoff indignantly. "And how would you know that?"

She leans over the arm of her chaise and drops her head onto my shoulder. "I know this because you're the male version of me and I'm the female version of you. When we confide in each other, it's like talking to ourselves. Our brain just works the same way."

It's true, and because of that, I smile like crazy. "You're more stubborn than I am."

She laughs, nudging into me. "That's such a lie. We're both equally as stubborn."

I kiss the top of her head, scooting closer to the edge of the chair so she has an easier time resting on me. There is that old cliché that men and women can never be friends because sex will ultimately always get in the way. Well, Maia is gorgeous. She is tall and voluptuous and blonde, and my dick has never noticed her. Not once. Even when we first met, and I was teasing her about dating her. That's all it was. Teasing. And an easy way to get a rise out of Keith.

"All I'm saying is I know you and you're going to break that promise. Same as the one you broke with Keith."

"Thanks," I deadpan.

"Any time. But you need to tell her you want to continue seeing her when we go back home. Ending it in three days is madness and stupid and just plain wrong. Promise you'll do that, Henry."

"You're not going to let this go, are you?"

She snorts. "Why on Earth would I do that? You're happy. *She* makes you happy. No way in hell I'm letting that go."

"Dammit. I knew I should have sat next to Jasper and Gus."

Maia laughs. "I didn't give you the choice."

She didn't. She started screaming my name like a hyena, waving me over. She's lucky I love her as much as I do. I don't suffer this shit for just anyone. "Can't we just sit here and enjoy the sun and not talk about anything serious. We've got, what, three more days of this vacation?"

She scoffs, righting herself and leaning back in her seat, tossing an arm behind her head as she glares at me. "Yeah. Then we go back to warm and sunny California. Real freaking hardship for all of us. I'm not joking on this Henry."

"Maia. Please. Just stop. Can't we talk about normal stuff? Or nothing at all would even be better."

"That's not really how I operate. And I know you know that. When do you plan on telling Keith you're in love with is sister?"

I groan. Loud. My head falls back as I stare up at the cloudless sky while rubbing my agitated hands over my face. "Will you quit it. I mean it, you can't know about this Maia. Pretend you never saw or heard anything."

"No way. I'm a woman on a mission here. You watch her obsessively. Smile whenever she walks into a room. Light up like a boy on Christmas morning whenever she smiles or laughs. And if you think I'm the only one who has noticed, you're dumber than you look. I didn't need to see it with my own eyes or listen to you to have it confirmed. It's outrageously obvious."

"I don't do any of that." Do I?

"You do. And then some. It's plain as day, my friend. You're in love with Eden Dawson."

"Thanks," I grumble. "Always setting it straight for me."

"That's what friends do, but women notice these things. And Jasper because he's weird like that for a guy. But if you think you and the fair maiden over there are incognito and haven't been a topic of conversation between me and the other ladies, you're delusional. It's time you face the facts where Eden is concerned."

Awesome. That's freaking awesome.

"I'm not in love with her, Maia. It's just some fun. It'll be over in a few days when we return."

And suddenly I feel sick. The spot between my heart and stomach squeezes like a vise, and it's getting harder to breathe. Three days. That's it. Then it's over.

I should be relieved.

Instead, I'm terrified.

I already know I'm in way deeper than I want to be—should be— with her. I haven't thought much about our time limit over the last couple of weeks. But now...

"Uh huh," Maia mocks, not buying it for a second. "That's why all the color just drained from your face and you look like you're about to throw up."

She can tease me all she wants but it's true. I'm not in love with Eden. I can't be. It's just not possible. Is it? No. I mentally shake myself. That's not what this sick, panicky feeling is.

Right?

"Would it be the worst thing in the world if you were?"

"Yes," I answer automatically, because it would be. No two ways about it.

I don't want love. Because when you love someone, when you give them that part of yourself, they have a power over you unlike anything else. They can annihilate you with a single word. Rip you apart without a care or a backward glance.

Love maims. It terrorizes. It destroys.

A flash of blue catches my eye and I watch as Eden laughs, splashing in the pool with Ady and Cora. My chest tightens in an entirely different way. Eden with her smiles. Eden with her laugh. With her teasing banter. With her perfect touches and the way she listens to me. The way she gets me. The way she fills in all my gaps and missing pieces and makes me... whole. I trust her with myself in a way I've never done with anyone else. I've told her things I've never told anyone else. My past. My history. She knows it all, every fucked-up detail. She would never betray that. She would never use it against me.

Because Eden Dawson loves me. At least I'm pretty positive she does.

Shit. What the hell am I going to do with that?

"Maybe it wouldn't be the worst thing in the world," I mutter under my breath, unsure if I'm telling Maia or myself. "She's pretty great, right?"

"The best. And she deserves the best. That's you, in case you missed that."

She deserves me. Does that mean I'm deserving of her?

I look back to Maia, sliding my shades up on top of my head so I can meet her dark eyes. "I have to tell Keith."

"You do. But maybe it won't be as bad as you think it will be?" She shrugs, gnawing on her lip because she's as nervous about that as I am.

Ever since the jellyfish incident, Keith has been encouraging me to stick by Eden's side whenever she decides she wants to do something crazy. Go for long hikes in the middle of nowhere? Definitely, Henry loves that shit. Go visit an active volcano? Sure, Henry, you go with her. Parasail? Yep, Henry's your man, even though I distinctly remember the conversation when I said I was not.

I can't say no because Keith is asking me to watch Eden and I can't say no because I'm legitimately worried about Eden and all her hair-brained stunts and I have to be there to make sure she's okay. Still, Keith being all Henry-Eden is a complete one-eighty from when he specifically directed me to stay away from his sister.

When I press, he says, I know you'll look out for her. He has no idea I'm doing a hell of a lot more than that. Since we arrived on this island, hell—way before that even—I have felt nothing but guilt when I look at my best friend. I have been fucking his sister every chance I get, doing it completely under his nose and behind his back. The ramifications of such a betrayal are gutting and far-reaching.

I could very likely lose my best friend.

I could potentially dismantle our band.

I could lose everything I hold as vital in my life.

But I'm starting to believe Eden might be worth the risk and the resulting fight.

I glance across the pool area, thankful for my reflective shades as I lower them back down. It takes me two seconds to locate Eden—for the fiftieth time in the last ten minutes—still in the pool, splashing around with Adalyn, Cora, and now Viola.

Yeah. She just might be worth it. I smile like a stupid bastard as I watch her. As I do nothing to hide it. "I'm in big fucking trouble."

"Yep."

I chuckle, suddenly not so afraid of that. Maybe Eden was right? One bad apple, not the bushel? Maybe *he* and my mother were the exceptions and not the rule? Maybe.

"Help Keith throw you a birthday party."

"You're a dick."

"Never claimed otherwise, honey. Still, I'll take your crap all day long and twice on Sunday if it gets you to agree to the party."

"If you love her, he won't be mad. That's all I'm saying. He won't be mad. He'll be *happy*. For both of you. That's all he wants, you know."

I do some kind of snort-chuckle thing under my breath. "You're a fucking liar, but I love you." Then hop off this stupid chaise that is leaving an imprint in my back from the wet towel I've been lying on. I kiss Maia's cheek, ignoring her scowl and pointed stare, and take the path back to my house.

We leave on Sunday, and today is Thursday. We worked all morning and thus far have completed eight of the fourteen songs we set out to record including the two before we left for Hawaii. At this rate, we will have no problem meeting that September one deadline and then Eden is gone. Poof. A figment of my imagination.

I will have no reason to see her.

No reason to interact with her.

No reason to drag her into my bed and keep her there, unwilling to let her go or sneak out. The thought of this ending has me scrambling. Thinking. Undoing a lifetime of fuckedupness in order to coerce myself into doing something entirely new. Something I swore I would never do.

Plan a future with someone.

I need to tell her. And I need to tell her brother too.

"Hey," Eden says, running barefoot to catch up to me. She's wearing only a bikini. I know because I looked even when I tried to force myself not to. "Maia said you had something you wanted to talk to me about."

A bark of a laugh slips past my lungs. Maia. That snake.

"Come here." I toss my arm over her shoulder, drawing her sweet little body against mine.

Eden glances nervously over her shoulder, back in the direction of the pool, making sure no one is watching us. "What are you doing?"

"Walking with you. Let's go hammock."

"I don't know if hammock can be used as a verb."

"Improvise with me."

Eden chortles. The sound tugging a laugh of my own. "That's all I do with you, Henry. I improvise."

"Then this shouldn't be much different. Besides, I did want to talk to you," I tell her, my voice suddenly shaky and nervous at what I have to say.

She lets out a short, choppy breath, almost as if she's gearing up for the worst. Especially when she says, "I was going to go for a run. I need a run. It's been, what, a couple of days since I did that."

"Eden," I start, my tone turning serious. Twisting her in my arms so my hands clasp her waist, I stare into her eyes with a steadfast determination. "We really do need to talk, don't you think?"

She gulps and steps back, extricating herself from me. Her eyes glisten with emotion before she quickly gets it under control. "I think I want to go for a run, Henry. Can we talk later? I'm not ready to do that now."

Oh. Huh.

I wasn't expecting that. And I have no idea what to do. Do I just blurt out that I want to continue what we're doing? That I want to possibly entertain us being something more? That I want to tell Keith the truth because not telling him is eating me alive? I have no idea what to do with this type of thing. I'm a man in uncharted waters.

"I guess if you need to go for your run, go for your run. But I really want to talk to you, Eden. About us. About Keith."

Blue owl eyes blink rapidly at me before she takes another step back. "Later, Henry. Okay? Later. I can't do this yet. I'm not ready."

She gulps and turns away, running at breakneck speed toward her house. I'm so stunned that by the time I decide I want to stop her and tell her anyway because I think she's reading this wrong, she's already in her house, slamming the door shut behind her.

Well, that didn't go as expected.

I puff out a breath, rutting my hands through my hair as I stare at her now closed door, thinking about what my next move should be. She said she's not ready. That she wants to go for her run.

Okay. I'll let her have her run. And then I'm going to tell her everything. Including something I can no longer deny... I think I've fallen for her.

TWENTY-SIX

EDEN

My feet pound the pavement, an annoying layer of sand already wedged between my socks and my sneakers. But I can't slow down. I can't stop. I just keep pushing on. Hoping to outrun my thoughts and my heart and my stupid I-told-you-so voice that's running through my head on repeat like a sad seventies 8-track.

In case you're wondering, it goes something like this...

Henry's going to end this. He's going to tell you it was fun and now it's done.

I could see it in his eyes. The uneasiness. The dread. The nerves he's never had a day in his life before today. Damn him. He doesn't have to do that. We don't have to talk about it. I don't want to fucking talk about it.

Because I don't want it to end.

I have to tell him that.

If I don't, I'll always regret I never took the risk. I know all about his hang-ups with love and relationships. I know why he says he can't love me. And in truth, if his past were my past, I might feel the same way. So I get it. I'm just unwilling to accept it.

Henry has feelings for me. I know he does. They may not be as deeply rooted as mine, but there is potential there. What we have is too good to let go of without a fight.

If he still says he doesn't want me then, well, at least I tried and gave it my all. It'll hurt. It'll hurt like hell, but no matter what, I won't allow it to break me. I can't. That is my promise to myself. One I fully intend to keep.

With a newfound determination in my steps, I find my way back to my house. I need a shower something fierce before I can go and talk to him. But just as I reach my door, I come to a skidding halt, staring incredulously at the man sitting on the ground leaning against it.

"What are you doing here?"

Chad stands up slowly, his eyes starting with my sneakers and rising with him, taking in every inch of my bare legs, running shorts, bare stomach, sports bra, all the way up to my eyes. Then he smiles like the heavens just parted after a storm, showering me in endless sunshine.

He takes a hesitant step toward me, his hands outstretched, and before I know what the hell is happening, he's wrapping me up in a hug like I've never felt from him before. The fact that I'm dripping sweat doesn't even seem to register as he clutches me to him, his face in my neck, his breathing ragged.

"God, Eden. You have no fucking clue how much I've missed the sight of you."

My eyes slam shut, and I try to work through how to react to this. Do I hug him back? No. that doesn't feel right. Do I push him away? That doesn't feel right either. But standing here immobile is awkward and weird, so I give him a few more seconds and slowly extricate myself from him.

His hands come up, cupping my face as his eyes search mine. There's something in them. Something I don't like, and it instantly has my heart thrumming faster than it already was. I was with this man for two years. I know his expressions inside and out.

My lungs empty. "What is it? What's going on?"

He licks his lips and reaches down, taking my hand. "Can we go inside? Preferably somewhere with air conditioning. I need to talk to you about something."

I try to swallow, but my mouth is bone dry. All I can manage is a nod. I lead him into my house, the door shutting behind him, and I immediately go for the kitchen, grabbing a bottle of water from the fridge and downing it.

Chad is looking all around, taking everything in before joining me in the kitchen. He takes the bottle from my hand and sets it on the counter. He stares at me, and I'm just about losing my goddamn mind with all manner of horrors. "What Chad? Just tell me."

"Sweetheart, I'm so sorry to be the one to tell you this, but Jess's parents were in a car accident last night."

I start shaking my head violently, my whole body trembling. "No, Chad."

"They swerved to avoid hitting an animal in the road and ended up going over an embankment into the river near your hometown. They didn't survive the accident."

My legs give out from beneath me and I start to fall, only to have Chad catch me and lift me into his arms. He walks us over to the sofa and sets me down just as the first of the sobs rip from my lungs. I've known Jess my entire life. We grew up together. Her parents are like second parents to me and vice versa.

Only my parents moved out of Alabama years ago when Keith bought them a place closer to our sister Beth and they retired. I doubt they even know.

"Jess?" I finally manage, my arms clinging to him as I cry endless tears into his shirt.

Chad holds me close, whispering empty words of comfort in my ear. "I was there when she got the call. It was just around ten p.m. California time. I put her on a plane and promised I'd come and get you."

I shake my head. "Why were you there with her?"

He chuckles, but there is no humor in it. "I was hoping you were back. Hoping to see you. You blocked me and she wouldn't tell me where you were, and I was desperate."

Jesus. "Chad—"

"Not now, Eden. Not now. Not when you're this distraught. I told Jess I'd take you to her in Alabama and that's what I intend to do. I have my family's private plane here waiting. Jess needs you and I know you need her."

He's right. This isn't the time to go another round. I'm glad he's here. I'm glad he was with Jess and got her on a plane. I'm glad he came for me and is taking me to her. But that doesn't change anything between us. I'm not in love with Chad anymore. If we're going based on feelings here, what I felt for him doesn't even compare to what I feel for Henry.

Henry.

Keith.

I need to tell them I'm going. I need to pack. Another sob flees my lungs. I can't believe this. I can't believe they're gone. I want Henry to comfort me. To come with me. But I can't ask that of him. I don't even know what's going to happen between us.

Pulling back, I wipe at my face and stand. My knees buckle instantly, but I catch myself, forcing my body to move and not to think. Compartmentalize, I demand, and it works. Sorta. The tears don't stop. Not for a second.

They're a river of anguish.

How could something like this have happened? So random. So freak. So wrong.

Jess. I need to get to her now.

She has no one else. A younger sister, but that's it. I'm her family. God, what she must be going through? I can't imagine. I'm devastated and they're not even my parents.

"I'm going to shower and pack," I tell Chad. "I have to let the guys know I'm going to be leaving and that I'm not sure when I'll return." I don't know why I'm telling him all this other than talking through a plan helps. Again, sorta. It's diversionary but I'll take it.

"I'll wait here for you. The plane will go whenever we get there, so do whatever it is you need to do."

I look down into his eyes, at his face. Eyes and a face I did love. I gave Chad everything, even things I shouldn't have. That was on me, not him. I have no idea what really happened with Marni, but I no longer feel bitter or angry about it. I almost feel grateful. What would have happened otherwise? I wouldn't have left him. I wouldn't have become the woman I am now.

I wouldn't have been with Henry.

I give him a slim nod and leave him in the living room. Entering my bedroom, I shut and lock the door behind me. I pull everything out of the drawers and closet, including the suitcase, and check my phone. Something I haven't done all day and now feel horrible about.

Sure enough, there are missed calls from Jess.

I call her back and thankfully she picks up right away.

"Hi," she croaks into the phone only to break down into tears. I do the same, sitting on the end of the bed and for a few minutes, that's all we do. We cry with each other in silence. There is nothing I can say that will make this better. All I can do is be here for her. Let her know she's got me no matter what.

"I'm coming. Chad is here and I'll be there as soon as that plane can get me to you."

"Okay. Eden—"

"I know. I know. Where's Tess?" Tess is her younger sister.

"School. She didn't come home this summer. She stayed up in Vermont with her friends. She's trying to catch a flight home now."

"Can I do anything before I get on the plane?"

"No. I just need you here. I can't deal with this alone."

My eyes cinch shut and on a shaky breath I say, "You're not alone, Jess. I'll be there soon."

We disconnect the call and then I start packing everything up, throwing it all into my suitcases. Then I strip down and walk into the bathroom to shower. I ache all over and none of it is from the run. I have to get to my friend, but part of me is terrified about what happens if I leave before I get a chance to talk to Henry. I'll lose him too. I just know it.

TWENTY-SEVEN

HENRY

It's been a goddamn hour and a half and I'm going insane. I've paced the house. Walked the beach. Strummed a bit on my bass. But I can't take it any longer. I'm restless with this. The need to make her mine. To give this thing between us a real shot.

I have to talk to her, and I need to do it now whether she's ready for it or not.

Sneakers slap against the hard ground before I even realize I've left my house. My feet carry me, my focus so single-minded I don't even realize I'm pounding on her door. I hear rustling as she approaches from the other side.

"Eden, it's me. Open up, baby. We need to talk." Silence. Then some kind of sound I can't distinguish. I pound again. "Come on, Dragonfly. No more running. I can't stand it when you run from me."

The door flies open and any relief I felt at that dies instantly along with my smile. My lungs empty as I come face to face with a tall, half-naked man. Chad. I know it's him, even though I've never met the fucker. He's in Eden's house. Without his shirt on. With the button of his shorts undone.

He folds his arms over his chest, leaning against the doorjamb, glaring at me.

"Can I help you, Henry? I think you must have the wrong house."

"Where is Eden?"

He smirks. "In the shower, waiting for me."

Bullshit. Just fucking bullshit. "Eden," I call out like a fool.

He chuckles under his breath. "Don't believe me. Give a listen."

But I don't have to. His words were barely out of his mouth when I caught the sound of the shower running. The high-pitched keen of water running through pipes. It's faint, but there is no mistaking that's what it is. Eden is in the shower and Chad is answering the door half-naked.

What the hell is happening? Eden wouldn't do this. She wouldn't cheat.

Only, it's not cheating, is it? We're not together. We've been temporary all along. I told her I can't love her because I have zero fucking trust when it comes to women and love.

I've seen it firsthand.

Lived through the worst of their crimes.

And now, almost as if my insides are mocking me, my mind is screaming that I was right all along. That I should have never let this go so far. Except I did and now look.

"I'm gonna spell this out for you, Henry," Chad drawls as he stands up to his full height and tries to glare down at me. Too bad I've got about an inch on the prick. "Eden is mine. She always has been. She told me she still loves me and is ready to give us another chance. Whatever separated us before, is long since forgiven. Obviously." He smirks, glancing down quickly at his undone button. "Whatever bullshit you two had is over. Stay the fuck away from her or I promise, I'll ruin your life."

With that, I laugh. Too late, pal, I wanna say. Or maybe that was her who already did that to me. The one person I was starting to care about more than anyone else. I gave her that power, knowing better the entire time, and look what she did with it.

"We're leaving this island the second *we* get out of the shower. She's done with your album. She's done with you. Now fuck off."

He goes to slam the door in my face, but I thrust my hand against it, stopping it. I step forward, crowding him, and the douche flinches. I look him up and down, sizing him up, knowing I could kill him with my bare hands without breaking a sweat. Rich pretty boy has probably never thrown down in his life.

I didn't grow up the same way.

Now I smirk because I can be a mean, vindictive son of a bitch when I want to be. I learned from the master, after all.

"Eden told me all about you, Chad. All about what a miserable, boring fuck you were. How you never understood the things she wanted. All her beautiful, kinky fantasies that *I* fulfilled. Never tied her up, did you? Never talked dirty to her either, huh?" I grin when I catch the flash in his eyes. "Did you even know how much she likes that? Maybe I should give you some pointers? Tell you all the sordid details of the way I pleasured her body. She couldn't get enough of it."

Fury dances across his face, some of his cocky bravado crumbling before my eyes. "Right." He scoffs. "That's why I'm in here and you're out there."

I give a careless shrug, though his words burn me to the marrow of my bones. "You'll never fully understand her and because of that, she'll never truly be yours."

Nor will she ever be mine.

That thought has my heart bottoming out into my feet and I can no longer keep pretenses going. I want to punch his face in. Watch him bleed the way I'm bleeding. Make him hurt the way I'm hurting. But what's the point in that? It won't change the reality. He's in there and I'm out here. She ran from me straight into his arms

Eden...

I didn't think this was possible from her, but I was wrong. The visual of a half-naked Chad and the sound of the shower running is pretty goddamn telling.

Everything inside me deflates and I take a step back, then another, and spin on my heels walking away. I don't hear him if he says anything else. All I hear is the door shutting behind him. Is the latch on the lock clicking into place.

Is the end of me and Eden.

Motherfucker!

I tear into my house, slamming the door behind me, but it's not enough to stop this... feeling. This fucking powerless, out-of-control toxin that's leaching my insides. I fucking swore I'd never feel like this again and now look. "Fuck!" I bellow, smashing my fist into the wall and delighting in the satisfying *crunch* that subsequently follows.

I don't even know if it was my fist or the wall that made that sound, but I don't care either way.

Ripping the cork from the glass bottle, I take a large swig of tequila. For a moment I'm tempted to hurl the bottle against the wall and watch it smash. It tastes like Eden. Because tequila is what we both like to drink. But it's that thought that has me gripping it tighter, taking another long pull. Blood drips from my hand, my eyes following the drops as they splatter one by one on the white marble floor.

What am I doing?

Losing my mind over her like this?

No. I won't be him. I've shut myself down before. Locked away things I'd just assume never think of again. I take another swig and set the bottle down, grabbing a cloth from the cabinet and wrapping my hand up tight. It doesn't hurt enough to numb me to everything else. I guess that's what the alcohol is for.

With another gulp down my throat, I head to the door. I have to get out of here. Clear my head. My fucking bed smells like her. The panties I wouldn't let her put back on this morning when she left to get changed are still there as well. I took her savagely and sweetly and every way in between all over this house. She's here. In every corner. I don't even have to close my eyes to picture it. To picture her. My game-changer. Or so I thought.

No. She was. She is.

Eden wouldn't do this. She told me time and time again that she was done with Chad. She even blocked his number so he would stop calling and texting. She was in the shower. Did she even know he was there? Jesus.

Tugging the front door open, I nearly plow straight into the woman standing on the other side with her fist raised in the air as though she was about to knock. Eden's hair is wet from the shower, her face is void of any makeup, her blue eyes bloodshot and red-rimmed. The moment our eyes meet, tears begin to well up, one slipping almost instantly down her cheek.

The urge to grab her, haul her into my chest, and make this all better nearly consumes me.

If that bastard hurt her...

But as my gaze trails past her, I lock on to a smug-looking Chad sitting patiently in the waiting golf cart along with all of Eden's things. She really is leaving with him. He wasn't lying.

"Henry," Eden starts, her voice stricken with grief. I shift back to her, neutralizing my features as I continue to stare just past her. "Chad told me you stopped by. Did he tell you I'm leaving?"

Is she fucking kidding me right now? Why is she even here? To watch me fall? To witness my devastation? To cry a few tears so she doesn't seem like the bad one in all this? Or is she trying to do the right thing by ending it so I don't have to? She has no idea of the feelings I have for her and right now, I'm grateful for that. Her knowing and still leaving with him would be like a knife to the gut.

"Yes," I say, my tone as flat as my affect. "He told me everything."

She puffs out a relieved breath and I think another piece of me dies right here.

"Good. That's good. I didn't think I'd be able to say the words." She sucks in a deep breath, staring tentatively up at me through her lashes. "I'm sure you understand why I have to leave with Chad. I still can't believe all this happened like this. So unexpectedly. But Henry, I wanted to talk to you before I go. I know we both have things we wanted to say—"

I cut her off. "We don't. I think we've already talked enough about this over the last few weeks. We had our fling, but now it's over." I shrug apathetically. "You're leaving with Chad and then we're back home. What else is there to say?"

Eden jerks back at my harsh words and sharp tone, but quickly composes herself despite the tears that just don't seem to be stopping. "A lot. There's a lot to say. It doesn't have to end like this. That's not what I want—"

"I don't give a shit what you want," I yell before quickly reining myself back. "You don't want it to end like this? What, with us pretending it never happened? With us going back to hating or ignoring each other? There is no other way for us, Eden. How did you think this would go? That we'd be friends? That I'd be cool watching your life from the sidelines?" I point in Chad's direction, but I'm not sure she even sees it. Her face is in her hands and she's crying.

Stop crying. I can't fucking take you crying.

But did she truly believe we could be *friends* after this? That I would just sit quietly and smile while she runs off with Chad and gets her fairy tale happily ever after while I'm stuck with nothing but heartache? I can't do it. Fuck that, I *won't* do it.

I love this woman and she's breaking my heart.

Doesn't she see it? Doesn't she get that at all?

I thought she got me, I thought she felt the same way back. I was ready to risk everything. To change everything. Everything about myself and my life... *for her.*

And then Chad blows in declaring his love and peppering her with bullshit flowery prose and I'm instantly pushed aside. Just like that. In the blink of a goddamn eye. She was in my bed this morning. Now she's with him. I don't think I've ever hated anyone as much as I hate her and coming from me, that's saying some serious shit.

If I'm to survive this and come out the way I was before her, I need to forget her. I need to shove all things Eden Dawson away and pretend like they never happened. Can't she understand that?

"I didn't think it would end like this," she murmurs into her hands before dropping them back down at her sides. She glares up at me with fiery indignation. Right there with you, sweetheart. "Well, Henry, it seems you have gotten exactly what you wanted. You're right, we are done. I truly hope sticking by your bullshit rules and promises brings you nothing but happiness."

With that, she spins around and climbs into the golf cart beside Chad. Chad who immediately puts his arm around her, tucking her head on his shoulder. Comforting her. I have no idea if he heard our conversation or not, but the visual of him with his arm around her makes me see nothing but red.

They drive off, her blue hair whipping behind her, and my fucking heart leaps out of my chest, chasing after her. Good. Let the fucker run. Let it leave my body for good. I have no more use for it anyway.

TWENTY-EIGHT

HENRY

If heartache and country music go hand in hand, then what kind of fucked up universe have I entered? After Eden drove off into the sunset with her douchebag, I couldn't go back in that house. Instead, I wandered forever only to find myself here at some random bar in the resort watching crap baseball on television and listening to some depressing as shit Rascal Flatts song that makes me want to rip my ears out of my goddamn skull.

Add to that, this...

"America Fortress is gorgeous. Like OMG gorgeous. How come you didn't date her longer?" That's the bartender asking me this question as she stares at her phone, going through image after image from Google or IG or wherever of me over the years with random women. It's all being done in a very this-is-your-life-Henry-Gauthier-see-how-lonely-and-empty-it-is way. She's been up my ass about my dating life since I sat down ten minutes ago. Plus, there are tourists idling around the bar, trying to not so obviously take pictures of me when they're being nothing but obvious about it.

"Can you please change the music?" Before I go postal,

massacring your customers, and the next photo they take of me is my mugshot?

"What? You want us to put on Wild Minds?" She laughs and I raise an exasperated eyebrow at that. "No. I'm sorry, I can't. Managements' rules." She gives me a sweet, placating smile, but I'm not buying that for a second. "So yeah, America Fortress? What happened there?"

She was a vapid narcissist I only went out to dinner with once and slept with once because she was more concerned about how she looked in bed than actually having sex. She was boring, brainless, and exactly like every other woman I've been with. Except Eden. Because if I wasn't touching Eden then I was listening to her talk and asking her questions to keep her talking and thinking about her nonstop.

The shitty thing about this is I can't tell if I fucked up or not.

She created the rules. I was the one who broke them. I was the one who broke my promise to her. I fell in love. It just never occurred to me that I was alone in that. The way she ended it was shitty. Beyond shitty. But I told Eden it was never going to happen, and she deserves happiness. Maybe that's why she did it? I never told her the truth, so she never knew.

The bartender taps her too-long fingernail on the counter and I realize she's waiting for a response from me.

"It just didn't work out," I go with. Why am I still sitting here? Why haven't I gotten up and left? Or better yet, taken a bottle with me.

"Oh, and then you were with that model?" She holds her phone out for me to see a picture of myself walking into a restaurant with a tall blonde holding my hand. "Heidi something or another?"

"Yeah." Because I don't remember her last name and until she said it, I didn't remember her first name either. I shake my head, staring down at my shot glass. If I didn't know for sure it would be all over TMZ, I'd take her phone and smash it. It's moments like these that I hate the celebrity that comes with my job. It's why Viola rented out half the resort for just us. So we'd have privacy and not have to deal with any of this crap.

The half of the resort I'm not currently sitting in.

"Actually, they were never together," a voice says, and I turn to find Jasper coming out of nowhere, dropping down beside me. He slaps a hand on my shoulder, giving me a squeeze and a shake, and I sigh. I should have known this would happen.

"Nope," Gus continues, taking the seat on the other side of Jasper. "They weren't. You never really dated any of those ladies. Did you, Hank?"

I glare over at my two best friends who are staring at me with strange unreadable smiles. My forehead creases, but I find myself shaking my head. "Um. No. I didn't." I give them a what the hell look, shaking my head again.

"Now that we've cleared up his public love life, how about all of you go over to that bar over there?" Keith stands on the other side of me, pointing clear across the resort in the direction of what I can only assume is another bar. "All your drinks and food are on us. We've already set everything up."

And just like that, all the lingerers scurry off in the direction of free booze and food, snapping one last pic of us as they go.

"You too, doll," Keith repeats for the bartender.

"But. Um."

"We've already cleared it with your boss. They'd like you to go to the other bar and help out with all the new customers they suddenly find themselves flush with."

She gnaws on her lip, studying each of the guys with their charming smiles and then huffs out a disappointed breath. "Can I have a quick selfie first?"

The guys all exchange looks and then rise up on their seats, crowding over me and smiling into her camera. She skips off with an exuberant smile as she types God only knows what into her phone.

"And suddenly there were four again," Jasper announces as he hops off his chair and moves around the bar to the other side. He takes in his new setting with an amused smirk.

"You boys just saved the lives of all those tourists," I declare.

Keith laughs. "We would have helped you cover up the bodies. Brothers for life, right?"

I stare down at my hands. "Keith—"

"I've always wanted to be on this side of the bar," Jasper quickly interrupts. "What can I get you?"

Keith laughs. "Bahama Mama."

"You already got yourself one of those," Gus quips.

"True. How about just a bottle of Jack then? Old school style. Like when we were just starting out and shit."

"Because that's not how you drink now?" Jasper deadpans as he reaches over and grabs the bottle, setting it down in front of Keith. "Easiest fucking gig I've ever had. Who's next? I can go all night."

"Does your wife know you give it up so easy?" Gus drawls.

"Yes. She does. Who do you think I go all night long with?"

I stare around at my friends. At Keith who is still smiling at me as he rips the shot pourer thingy out of the top of the bottle. "How did you know where to find me?"

"You mean other than the fact that Marco already called us because your image and videos aren't all over Instagram and TikTok?" Keith asks.

"Seriously? That fast? I've only been here for like ten minutes."

"They tagged you," Gus states. "Marco has alerts for that kind of thing."

"Jesus," I hiss, scrubbing my hands over my face and through my hair. "Sorry. I wasn't thinking when I sat down here. I should have stayed on our side of the resort."

"But then we'd be missing out on our boys' night of drinking. Remember the trans woman who sucked your dick in... where was it, New Orleans?" I turn to glare at Gus because he went there. Three years ago and they'll never let it go.

"She was hot," is my only reply, but I'm suddenly smiling despite myself.

"She was," he agrees. "Maybe you should look her up now. Maybe she's had the last of her surgeries and is in need of a good man."

"No thanks," I tell him.

"In that case." Gus points to an expensive bottle of bourbon. "That's the one right there, Jas. Grab that pretty lady and two glasses and get your ass back on this side. Oh, and while you're at it, drop that Gran Patron Platinum for Hank here. If we're drinking to heartache, we need to do it up right."

I freeze, my eyes growing wide. The dead organ in my chest gives a startled, sickly jolt.

"What?" Jas jests, setting the bottle in front of me and then the other in front of Gus like we own this bar. "Did you think we didn't know?" He chuckles at my bewildered expression, jogging back around the bar and taking the seat beside Gus.

I pivot to Keith, who is staring at me. Seems to have been this entire time. His eyes search my face and I've never felt worse in my life than I do in this moment. "You knew too." It's a statement, not a question, but he nods anyway. "For how long?"

"Since the night before the jellyfish."

Well, shit. That was two weeks ago. I look back down at my hands. "Keith—"

"I went looking for Eden that night, remember? I couldn't find her, and I was tracking back to her house when I saw you holding her hand and as you two walked. I followed you and then watched as you kissed her sweetly goodnight and left. I was going to confront you about it. Kick your ass all the way to Fiji for being a lying, piece of shit, backstabbing friend."

I flinch at his accurate description and force myself to meet his gaze head-on. I deserve this and then some.

"But then I saw you with her that day on the beach. How you got her out of the water. How you held her and made sure she was okay.

The look of pure abject terror on your face pulled me up short. I thought, shit, Henry's in love with my sister. And Henry's never been in love with anyone. Swore to us whenever we tried or pushed that no matter what, love was the last thing he ever wanted."

"It was. It is."

Keith smirks like he knows better. "Nah, man. I watched you protect her. You looked at me like if I tried to take her from you, you'd kill me where I stood, fighting heaven and hell if you had to. And the way she clung to you, looked at you... I thought, maybe they're right for each other after all."

I laugh bitterly at that. He has no clue how wrong he is. "That's why you kept pushing me together with her?"

He nods like he did a service to mankind.

"You should have beat the shit out of me instead. Would have been a hell of a lot better than this. Did you know she's gone now? Left about an hour ago?"

"Yes. We know all about it."

Fuck this. I lift my bottle and take a big gulp, wiping my mouth with the back of my hand. I stand up, shoving my stool back. It makes a horrible grating sound against the hardscape, punctuating my point. "Then why the fuck haven't you killed me yet?"

"Honestly, the better question is, why aren't you with her?" Jasper asks.

"Are you fucking joking?" I seethe at him. "What did you want me to do?" Furious, I stab my finger into the air in the direction of the front of the resort where she left.

"How about go with her?" Keith barks, suddenly growing angry the way I was hoping he would. "I assumed you were still here, drinking like an asshole because you were going to finally tell me the truth about you and Eden and you needed a little liquid courage to do it. I thought you were finally over your bullshit about never wanting to fall in love and were going to tell me you were leaving to join her. But that's not what this is, is it? What the hell is going on, Henry? You let her go alone with no intention of following?"

"Alone?" I bellow. "What the hell are you talking about, man? She's with him. With Chad." I stab the air two more times.

"With Chad?" Gus stares dumbfounded. "She didn't mention that in our group text. Just that Jess's parents died, and she was flying to Alabama to be with her."

I blink as my mind swims from the tequila and adrenaline. What did he just say? Suddenly I feel like I'm drowning with no source of air. "*Jess's parents died?* What? When?"

"Last night. Car accident."

I stare at Gus, though I'm a half-second from throwing up. That's why Chad was there. He came to get her. That's why she left with him.

No. It was more than that.

He was practically naked when he answered the door. She was already in the shower. He put his arms around her. She let him comfort her.

"What did you do, Henry?" Keith roars, snapping me back by giving me a shove. "You let her walk away with him, didn't you? You fucking idiot. I bet you didn't even fight for her. Anything to not have to feel. Did you hurt her?"

I glare at him. "Yes. Intentionally."

His fist flies out, slamming straight into my cheek. I stagger back, stumbling as I practically fall over only to have Gus catch me, righting my body and holding me back with a strong arm as if I'm going to retaliate. I'm not. I said that for him to hit me. White-hot fire erupts across my face and my mouth pools with blood. I spit it on the ground, not bothering to wipe my mouth clean.

Keith curses under his breath, agitated beyond measure as he paces back and forth, Jasper standing guard, same as Gus.

"Goddamn you, Henry. Why did you have to do this?" He spins around, glaring at me with fury blazing in his eyes. "I didn't want to hit you. After all you've been through, I never wanted to hit you. Why did you have to push me?" he growls, pointing at me. "Why did you have to hurt her? You and your goddamn bullshit you think we don't know about. That's it, isn't it? That's why you did this? That's why you pushed her away?"

I stare at him, floored. Did Eden tell them? She's the only one who knows.

"That's right. We know," he spits, though his stance softens along with his expression, growing pensive and sad. "We know all about how your dad used to hurt you. How your mom was never around much because she was always working and never did anything to stop him." He sighs, running his hands over his face, through his hair, and clasping them at the back of his neck. "When are you going to stop letting what they did impact the man you are now? You're a good man, Henry. You fucking are. You're my best friend and I love you. We all do, but sometimes you're so fucking stubborn. You let the best thing to ever happen to you walk away because you're stupid and scared."

I step into Keith, getting right up in his face. Gus is behind me, ready to take action, but he knows I won't hit Keith. "You think you know my shit so well... you're wrong." I push my fist into his chest. Not hitting him, provoking him. "My dad didn't hit me." I watch as shock flashes across his narrowed features. "He would have had to have been my dad first. He wasn't. He was her boyfriend. The lovesick piece of shit she left me with who was too weak and pathetic to ever say no to her. And you wanna know the real reason why she wasn't there? She had another family."

Keith sucks in a rush of air, his eyes searching my face before he glances over at Gus and Jasper, who are suddenly so quiet you could hear a goddamn pin drop out here.

"And when her *husband* found out about me and the boyfriend, she bailed. Just like that. She chose them. She left without even a backward glance, and the man I was living with, the one with zero connection to me at that point, found me to be the perfect outlet for all his pain, rage, and sick, deranged heartache. You have no idea the things he did to me. The things he said. The man he became. *She* did that to him. *To me.* She lied and manipulated and used and left."

I push my fist into his chest again, hoping, praying, he'll hit me again and finally end this.

"That's why I never wanted this. Any of it. And look at me…" I wave a hand up and down my body, "I was right. About all of it. Because Chad shows up and she goes right back to him. I saw it with my own eyes. I was simply the fool who fell for her anyway, knowing it would end like this, but naively hoping I was wrong. I don't want to turn into *him*! But guess what, Keith? I'm in love with your sister. I fucking am. So I guess you all got what you wanted from me in the end."

"Henry…"

I shove Keith away. He backs up a step, but doesn't go far, his eyes holding tight onto mine. He's not going to hit me again. I can see it in his eyes. They're filled with pity. All of theirs are and I just can't with that. It's why I never told them. That look right there.

"Whatever. It doesn't matter. It's over. She's with Chad and I…"

Said things to hurt her. I blow out a breath as realization crashes down on me with the force of a tsunami. She was crying when she knocked on my door because of Jess's parents. She was leaving because of that and she thought I knew. She thought Chad had told me when he didn't, and now she believes I was pushing her away after her best friend's parents died.

Fuck.

My insides twist, revolting.

What did I do? Fuck, what did I do?

She said she wanted to talk and I…

I spin around, not sure where to go or what to do, only knowing that I can't be here anymore. Only, I don't make it far. Maia is standing in front of me with a very pissed-off scowl aimed right at me.

TWENTY-NINE

EDEN

When Whitney Houston belts it, you should always listen. Except for now. Because it's absolutely ridiculous. I'm staring at Chad, listening to, "I Will Always Love You," being piped through the speakers of the plane and to say I'm not amused is an understatement.

"You're for real with this?"

"What?" he asks, feigning ignorance. The smirk isn't doing much to sell it.

Ugh.

I roll my eyes at him and fall back onto the love seat I've been sitting on, my stupid phone still clutched in my hand even though it's off. Henry isn't calling me, nor do I want him to, and yet I can't let go of the damn thing either.

I had sent a message, a very professional one at that, to our group chat informing the guys that I would be missing the rest of the trip and likely a few days in the studio due to the loss of Jess's parents. All of them, with the exception of Henry, replied sending condolences and telling me to take as much time as I need.

Then I texted Viola to thank her for an incredible trip.

Naomi followed and I told her how much I enjoyed getting to know her and that I hope to spend more time with her in the future.

Maia was last because by the time I got to her, I was a sobbing, blubbering mess of a woman. She had encouraged me without encouraging me to try things out with Henry. And while I've tried to regret that and regret the weeks he and I spent together, I can't. I knew this was the eventual outcome. I had told myself I was prepared, but are you ever truly prepared to have your heart broken?

I don't think so.

Me: **I had to leave. But you should know I took your advice with Henry. It didn't work out so well though.**

I sent her a sad face emoji with a tear drop coming from its eye and a broken heart emoji. Then our conversation went something like this.

Maia: **What happened? Where are you? I talked to Henry earlier and he was going to talk to you and then come clean to Keith.**

Me: **My friend's parents died, and Chad came to get me. I'm about to get on a plane for Alabama. But Henry and I did talk. And it went something along the lines of, our fling is done and now we can go home and pretend like it never happened.**

Maia: **WTF?! No. I'll kill him for that. Wait. Are you with Chad again? Why did he come for you?**

Me: **Absolutely not. Chad flew out here to pick me up and I made it clear to him already that it wasn't going to happen. I'm crazy, but I fell hard for the stupid rock star.**

Maia: **Something is wrong, Eden. This is not what Henry and I talked about at all. He was going to tell you he wanted more with you too.**

At that point, I paused, reading her words about a dozen times over because that just didn't make any sense to me.

Me: **Well, clearly, he changed his mind**.

I left it at that and turned off my phone. Henry is no longer my focus or concern. Jess is. I will return to LA when I can, and if they still want me, I will finish the album. I will be a professional and nothing more.

Whether what Maia is saying is true or not, I'm done anyway. I can't keep doing this to myself where Henry is concerned. Where any man is concerned. I deserve better and it's time I take it.

Past or no past, he should have treated me with respect. He didn't. He spoke to me like I was nothing. Less than nothing. Meaningless.

"You know I didn't know Marni was Marni, right? I mean, I've told you this a million times, but I'm not sure if you ever believed me or not."

That's because I'm not sure if I believed him or not.

"It doesn't matter, Chad."

I don't want to be or sound ungrateful to him. He flew all the way out to Hawaii in a private plane to pick me up and take me to my friend. I'm insanely grateful to him. But that doesn't mean I want to get back together with him. Being in love with another man aside, Chad never wanted this version of me. He may say he no longer cares about any of that, he just wants me, but how can that be true?

Regardless, I need to be alone for a while. I haven't been on my own in years. Hell, probably my entire life because if I wasn't obsessed with Henry Gauthier, I was heartbroken by him and if I wasn't heartbroken by him, I was with Chad.

Chad lowers himself to the floor of the plane, scooting across the small divide between our seats on his knees. He removes the phone from my hand, setting it down on the small table and then cups my face, getting so close and with so much intensity that I lay here frozen.

"You're really done with me, aren't you?"

"I'm sorry."

He sits back for a second, thinking while he stares at me.

"Do you love him?" he asks softly, his eyes searching mine.

I swallow thickly and nod, unable to form the words.

"I know about him," he continues. "About how you always wanted him. I know you hooked up with him one night before you and I ever happened, and he broke your heart. I know you used to look him up online a lot."

"How?"

"I heard you and Jess talking about it a few times when you didn't think I was able to hear."

Oh.

"Did he love you back?"

I freeze, thinking about that. My heart hurts so bad at that question, I can hardly push out a breath. Then I shake my head because it's all I can manage as pain slices through me.

A tear leaks out of the corner of my eye and I puff out a strangled breath. "I don't know. I thought, maybe, but then he just..." I trail off, still unsure about everything.

Don't fall in love with me, Eden, because I can never love you back.

Chad sits back on haunches, staring at me with something in his expression that makes me sit up a little, staring at him as an uneasiness creeps over me. "I might have done something, Eden."

"What?" And when Chad doesn't follow that up, I sit up straight, tucking my knees up to my chest, suddenly beyond nervous. "What did you do, Chad?"

"I love you. That's why I've been doing everything I've been doing these last few months. I hate not being with you. We had such a good thing, Eden. Such a good thing." He inhales a sharp breath, exhaling as he says, "I fucked up with Marni, okay. I admit that. I fucked up. I was drunk as hell, and at first, I thought she was you and I didn't figure it out until a few seconds before you walked in the room. I started to pull away but then Marni grabbed me, trying to keep me there and then you walked in. I was scared to tell you because I thought I would lose you and never get you back, but I think it's too late anyway. I lost you no matter what. Didn't I?"

"I'm sorry," I repeat, my voice hoarse. "You're a great guy, Chad. That was never in question to me. A lot of what went wrong with us was my fault. I hid a lot of who I am. The things I want. The person I feel comfortable being. You liked me a certain way and I tried to be her. I really did. I was just never really good at it."

He glances up at the ceiling of the plane, his hands going to his thighs. "I like your hair long and brown. I like your skin free of ink. I'm not really into the piercings. Maybe that makes me boring, but I can't help that." His eyes drop, meeting mine. "I love *you* though. I do, and if you're willing to give me another chance, I'll never say another word about any of that."

"Neither of us should have to settle for what we don't want. We're not right for each other, Chad. We had a great go of it. We're just not meant to be."

He nods his head, sad, but also resigned. He knows I'm right. I loved Chad. It just wasn't the right kind of love for it to last.

Dark eyes hold mine as he says, "Henry came to the door when you were in the shower. I opened it without my shirt on and my shorts unbuttoned. I told him you were mine and we were back together. He wasn't happy about it, Eden. Actually, he was pretty pissed. He tried to rile me up and then he told me that I don't understand you and because of that, you'll never truly be mine. I also never told him about Jess's parents. I let him believe I came to get you and you were leaving to be with me."

I suck in a breath, falling back against the cushioned leather seat, my head going along with me as I close my eyes. Wow. "I really wish you hadn't done that." A humorless laugh empties from my lungs as I drop my chin to look at him once more. "Jesus, Chad. I can't fucking believe you did that. How could you?" I practically scream the words at him, ready to smack him and strangle him. "You knew how I felt about him, and you did that? Do you have any idea what you've done?"

"Yes. And I'm sorry. I truly am, Eden. I shouldn't have interfered. I just thought... if he wasn't in the picture anymore... if I had a second chance to prove myself to you..."

"Well, it's all fucked now, so save your apology for someone who gives a shit."

Christ. Henry thought I was leaving with Chad. That I was back together with him.

I think about that. I replay Henry's parting words in my head. Just how cruel he was.

Don't fall in love with me, Eden, because I can never love you back.

Henry was looking for an easy out and he took it. He didn't ask me what was up. He didn't demand answers from me. He didn't fight. Not even a little. I came to his door with tears in my eyes and on my face and he was callous, demonstrative, and utterly indifferent to me.

I know he suffered brutally at the hands of his mother and her boyfriend. I know he has no faith or trust in love. I know this. But he also knows me. He should have trusted in me. He knew how I felt about him, even if I never told him. I'm positive on that.

No, he was always planning to end it. That's what he was going to do before I ran off on him and went for my run. I saw it in his eyes. He just punctuated it by being a prick because he was angry about Chad being there.

But the outcome was always going to be the same.

I can't keep chasing after a man who does not want love in his life. I want too many things from mine to tolerate that bullshit.

"Do you hate me now?"

Do I? No. He was fighting for me, for us, and I know that. I see that. Doesn't make it right, but I know why he did it.

"I'm seriously pissed at you, Chad. Like epically pissed. But I'm glad you told me the truth. And I'm grateful you came to get me so I can go be with Jess."

Chad leans in and places a soft kiss to my lips. A goodbye kiss.

"I'll always be there for you, Eden. In whatever capacity you'll allow me. And again, I'm so sorry you're hurting like this and for whatever part I played in that."

I reach out and clasp his hand, squeezing it because I believe him, and I want him to know it's the same for me. Even if I still want to ring his neck.

AFTER A QUICK STOP in LA to refuel and to let Chad off the plane, I continue on. Chad insisted I stay on the plane instead of trying to navigate a commercial flight. He said Jess needed me, and by the time I land, rent a car, and drive the couple hours to the town I grew up in, it's so late I don't even know what day it is anymore. The only time I turned on my phone was to text Jess that I landed and was on my way.

That was it.

I didn't check to see if I had missed texts. I didn't check to see if I had missed calls or voicemails. I don't want to know either way. I'm raw and devastated and so fucking *sad* I can hardly stand to be in my own skin.

Driving didn't help. I was able to nap on the plane some, but driving, listening to music is not helping me. I want to drive to the house he grew up in with that man and kill him. Or at least scream in his face and hurt him. I'd love to find his mother too and give her a real piece of my mind.

So much of my life in this town was spent pining away over Henry. Idolizing him. Following him around. Only instead of growing out of my infatuation the way most little girls do, my infatuation grew into a love I'm not sure I'll ever be able to get over.

I miss him.

And I absolutely fucking hate that I do.

I don't want to love him anymore.

That doesn't stop me from crying the entire drive and by the time I pull into the motel Jess is staying in because it's too painful to stay at her parents' house, I'm such a fucking wreck I can hardly put one foot in front of the other.

She opens the door after the first knock, her blonde hair in wild disarray, her face puffy with grief. The moment she sees me her eyes instantly start watering and before I know from anything else, I enter the room, drop my bags, shut the door, and hug my friend.

"I've got you," I tell her. "I'm here and we'll get through this together." All of it, I think.

THIRTY

HENRY

"Here," Maia snaps, shoving her phone in my face. "Read this."

A scowl purses my lips, the burning on my jaw and the sting in my cheek from where Keith hit me morphing into a throb I gladly welcome. I stare at Maia's phone like it's the anti-Christ. I don't need to read how badly I fucked up. I don't need to read how I didn't trust her, and I didn't talk to her, and I didn't listen.

Still, I take her phone and force myself to read what I can only assume will be a straight shot to the heart.

Eden: **I had to leave. But you should know I took your advice with Henry. It didn't work out so well though.** Sad, crying face emoji and a broken heart emoji. Awesome.

Maia: **What happened? Where are you? I talked to Henry earlier and he was going to talk to you and then come clean to Keith.**

Me: **My friend's parents died, and Chad came to get me. I'm about to get on a plane for Alabama. But Henry and I did talk. And it went something along the lines of,** our fling is done and now we can go home and pretend like it never happened.

Maia: **WTF?! No. I'll kill him for that. Wait. Are you with Chad again? Why did he come for you?**

Me: **Absolutely not. Chad flew out here to pick me up and I made it clear to him already that it wasn't going to happen. I'm crazy, but I fell hard for the stupid rock star.**

I suck in a sharp rush of air, reading and rereading that last line over and over, my heart about to explode and my brain calling me every synonym for asshole under the sun.

Maia: **Something is wrong, Eden. This is not what Henry and I talked about at all. He was going to tell you he wanted more with you too.**

Eden: **Well, clearly, he changed his mind.**

Eden fell for me. Not just fell for me but fell hard. Like I did with her. And now she thinks I changed my mind. That I don't love her the way I fucking love her. The way I never wanted to love anyone but now it's too goddamn late. I'm stuck in this so I can either face it and try to scavenge some happiness out of it and pray she doesn't eviscerate me down the road or walk away now.

I already know I can't walk away from her. Not if she truly wants me the way I want her, so I guess that settles that.

My hand trembles and my body quakes as I look up into Maia's dark eyes. I hand her her phone and without a word I storm off, heading in the direction of the beach. I can't be around any of them right now. First, I call Eden's phone, already knowing it'll be off since she's on the plane. Still, the second her sweet voice hits my ears in her pre-recorded greeting, I sag with disappointment. I get the beep and then I freeze, my voice lodging in my throat.

What the hell am I going to say to her?

"Eden... I'm... shit. I'm sorry. I need to say this to your face dammit and you're already on the plane and I... I was wrong, okay? I was so very wrong. I saw what I thought I saw and he... it doesn't matter. I should have talked to you and I didn't because I was furious and bitter and so goddamn—"

A loud beep sounds in my ear noting the end of my allotted time.

"Heartsick," I say, finishing my sentence.

I go to text her, but I can't tell her the things I want to tell her like this. I pace a circle before I set off back to the beach, typing as I go.

I'm sorry. Send. **I love you.** Delete. **I can't picture my life without you, and I fucked up.** Delete. **I never meant to fall for you the way I did and now that you're gone, everything feels wrong. I need you back like I need air to breathe because when you left, you took my fucking heart with you and now I'm dead.** I stare at that, my finger hovering over the blue up arrow to send the message. But god, how unfair is that to do to her after the things I just said. After the fact that she's mourning the loss of her best friend's parents—people she's known her entire life.

I delete everything once more, staring at the blank text box. I'm not the poet like Jasper. I'm not the whimsical creative one like Gus, and I don't have the heart that Keith does. All I had was her. A firework breaking through and lighting up my dark sky with all her color.

I never wanted to be *him*. Sick with a love that had no antidote.

Necrotic and decaying from the inside out. But now there is no turning this off. It's Eden.

My feet hit the sand, the granules crunching under my weight and slipping between my toes until I reach the cool water as it glides up to meet me. I stare out at the vast ocean beyond me without seeing any of it. No. Instead I picture her. Her face as she told me she hoped I'd be happy with all my bullshit rules and promises.

I'm not. I've never felt so tortured and helpless.

For the first time in my life, I understand *him*. Not the things he did. That I'll never understand or come to grips with. He can die a thousand painful deaths for what he did to me.

But this feeling? Yeah, that I can get.

Only... I don't regret falling for Eden. And I sure as hell wouldn't change it.

I back up a few paces and drop down into the sand, hiking my knees up and raking my fingers over the finely ground rocks.

"Men are so freaking stupid," Maia grouses from behind me only to join me in the sand a second later. I pause my ranking to glare at her. "What, Henry? Don't look at me like that. You are."

"I know. But you telling me things I already know isn't going to help."

"You're looking for guidance?" She laughs out. "I was a virgin who crashed into a rock star, moved in with him after only knowing him a few short hours, was crazy enough to fall in love with him, and then get knocked up with his kids. Not one, but two."

"You'd do it all again."

"Every second of it. Love is weird, Henry. What can I tell you? It makes us do rash, foolish things we wouldn't otherwise do. It makes us say crazy-ass things we wouldn't otherwise say. It drives our emotions all over the place. Humans are capable of twenty-seven emotions, and for better or worse, love makes us feel each and every one of them."

I fall back, tucking my arm behind my head, the fading sun coating my face until I have to squint up at the blue sky. Again, Maia joins me, the two of us just breathing in and out for a few minutes.

"I have to get her back."

"You will."

I'm not so sure about that, but I'll die trying.

"She's gonna make me work for it."

Maia laughs. "That's our job. It's your job not to give up. You should be good at that. We're survivors, you and me. And while the people we're busy surviving tried to make us feel weak and inadequate and like we'd never amount to anything, we did anyway."

"Sucks for them. Party on us."

"Exactly." She reaches over and hits me in the stomach. Hard.

I emit a grunt that quickly turns into a laugh. "What was that for?"

"For Eden. It's a girl thing. How are you gonna get her back?"

"I don't know. What do you suggest?"

"I suggest you think about who Eden is and what's important to her. What makes her tick? What are the things she loves? What are the things you love about her?"

But as she says the words, a smirk curls up my face for the first time all afternoon as a devilish plan forms in my brain. Yeah. I know exactly what I'm going to do. I just hope it works.

THIRTY-ONE

EDEN

"Your phone is ringing," Jess declares as we make our way through LA morning rush hour traffic to the studio.

"I hear it."

"But you're not going to answer it," she states flatly, already knowing I'm not. Henry called and texted a few times the first few days I was gone and then that was it. Nothing since then until right now. I didn't pick up any of his calls. None of them. Nor have I returned his texts.

Truth, I don't really care that he's sorry. It's a nice sentiment and everything, but the words too little too late keep popping into my mind. What does he expect? That he can tell me he's sorry for being a world-class dick, and I'll just get over it? Welcome him back with open arms and a smile on my face?

It's been ten days. Ten miserable days of me crying and sad and hating him and missing him. The man ruined me and then he went and ruined me again and now look. Now I'm this girl and I hate being this girl.

The broken one who knew better and did it anyway.

"Can I pick up? Give him a piece of my mind?"

I snicker. "Sure. Go for it."

She doesn't pick up the phone and after another ring, the call dies. No voice message, though I didn't expect one. He only left one saying he was sorry about Jess's parents and that he was sorry for the way he acted that day. That was it. His texts said pretty much the same.

Dick.

"You know he paid for the funeral, right? All the expenses."

I do know that. It was insanely generous of him because Jess's parents weren't wealthy. They were as hard working as hard working gets and between them helping Jess through college and now her sister, there wasn't much left. And what was left, Jess wanted her sister to have so she wouldn't have to worry so much through college.

Henry paid for everything for my friend.

He also sent the plane for us to fly home in. Keith told me that it was all Henry's idea to do that, and when I saw the plane arrive, a nervous jolt of butterflies hit me that he was going to be on board waiting for me. But he wasn't.

Such a relief, right? Ugh!

My plan is to thank him for both helping Jess and sending the plane when I see him this morning at work. I spoke to Lyric and Jasper while I was away and they both agreed that with progress we made while in Hawaii, the week plus I took off to be with Jess and help her lay her parents to rest and settle their affairs won't derail the expected completion date of the album.

The band still wants me, is what Jasper told me, and though part of me was tempted to have them find another producer, I can't do that. This is my work. My career. My name on the line. I don't want anyone else finishing what I've already started.

Even if it means I have to deal with Henry Gauthier.

Jess pulls up to the curb in front of Turn Records and for a moment I just stare out the window, nerves I had been working to keep under check suddenly running rampant through me. I don't want to see him. I don't want to hear his apology. I just want to be done with him and move on.

"You'll be okay?"

I rhythmically tap my fingers on the buckle of the seat belt, still staring out the window before I turn back to her. "Will you?"

She gives me a tragic half-smile. Right. Stupid question. How okay can a person be after they lose their parents? "I'm going to see Ben. He says we're going to spend the day having fun."

Ben the bartender is a good guy. I didn't expect it would still be on at this point, but he flew in for the funeral and stayed for an extra day before he had to get back for work and classes.

"Use protection," I muse, and she smacks my shoulder, but smiles, laughing lightly and that was obviously the point.

"You're sure your car is still here?"

No. I have no clue, but I'm going to assume it is. In truth, I forgot all about my car having trouble before we left for Hawaii. Henry said he'd have it taken care of it and with everything else going on, it slipped my mind completely. Yet another thing I have to ask him about.

"If not, I'll get a ride home with Keith." I lean in and kiss her cheek. "I love you."

"You too. Stay strong. Fight the power and all that shit."

"On it. Bitches hear me roar." I smirk, giving her a wink that belies my confidence level and then get out of the car. Business mode activated, enter the building, brandishing my badge to the security guy, Gerald, and then heading up to the studio floor. I've got a song to produce today. An album to complete.

And no motherfucker is going to stop me.

Beyonce's "Run the World" flows through my head and I let it hype me up. By the time the elevator stops, I'm practically Rocky before he went after the Russian dude who killed his boy, Apollo Creed. I'm ready to fight this thing fifteen rounds and take the man down.

That all sounds good in my head, but my heart is calling me a punk-ass liar as I open the door and nearly puke all over the pristine carpet seeing the guys already here.

All of them.

"'Morning boys."

Keith crosses the room in two large strides and wraps me up in one of his epic bear hugs and all that bravado I built up jumps off the platform and onto the tracks in a tragic leap like it's Anna Karenina. My eyes burn with tears I refuse to shed, and I have to swallow so many times I'm shocked Keith isn't checking to see if I'm choking.

"I'm so sorry about Jess's parents. Did she get my flowers? All the food I sent?"

I love my brother.

"She did. And she says thank you."

"It wasn't enough, but I wasn't allowed to do more. Someone else made sure of that," he whispers into my ear and it doesn't take all my brain cells to figure out who he's talking about. Henry is Keith's best friend, and I would never want him to pick sides or favorites. I never wanted to cause a rift, and I'm relieved there doesn't seem to be one.

That would not only destroy Henry, but Keith as well.

I plant a kiss on Keith's cheek because words suck right now and then I pull away, squaring my shoulders and forcing a smile I don't even remotely feel. "Thank you all for giving me time to be with my friend," I say, meeting everyone's eyes including Henry's, because I am trying to show him nothing gets to me including him, but they hit me like a bolt of lightning.

I thought I was prepared.

I thought I could be impervious.

I was wrong.

Green eyes pierce into me like a sword, cutting straight through my armor without even breaking a sweat. He's staring at me and for a flicker of a beat, everything and everyone else fades away and there is nothing left but us. He takes a bold step forward and I manage to shake my head, stopping him in his tracks. His eyes feast on me, scouring every inch, his expression pained like me stopping him from coming to me actually, physically hurts him.

Welcome to the club, buddy.

I clear my throat, lick my suddenly dry lips, and look away, back to the others.

"I'm back now and I'm ready to finish this album. Thank you for being so patient while I was away and for believing in my vision enough to stick with me. It truly means so much to me. We have six more songs and a month to get them done in. Should be cake."

"Pie, babe," Gus says. "We southern boys like our pie." He gives me that charming smile he's perfected and then picks up his electric guitar, looking directly at his brother. "Wanna jam out some tunes? My wife starts fertility treatments today. To say I have enough pent-up nerves in me that need to be expelled is an understatement."

"I hope your kids look like Naomi," I quip and watch as Gus's lips twitch.

"Me too."

I laugh and because we actually have three songs that are completely bare of instrumentals, I tell Gus and the guys that they can go jam for an hour as long as it's productive and they pick a song from this album to work on.

Henry doesn't follow them into the booth.

Henry sits on one of the loungers the way he did what feels like forever ago while I sit at the soundboard twisting knobs and pushing dials with a bit more gusto than necessary, doing my best to ignore him. It's not easy. I know he's staring at me. I can feel his eyes burning into me, making the back of my neck hot and the hairs stand at attention.

"You went back to purple." He reaches out and for one awful second, I think he's going to touch me before he thinks better of it and lets his hand drop to his knee. "I can't decide which I like better on you. The blue or the purple. Maybe black would be pretty too. Make your skin glow and your eyes pop."

I hold in a breath, willing my heart to slow and for him to follow the others into the booth. I don't respond because not only is there nothing to say to that, I have my headphones on and am listening to the guys. I didn't pump the music through the room for this reason.

I don't want to talk to him.

"How's Jess doing?" he continues amidst my silence.

"She's as well as can be expected," I finally reply, if only to get this part over with. "Thank you for taking care of all the arrangements. And for sending the plane for us." I glance over my shoulder for a half-beat before turning back to the mixer, my heart now hammering so hard I'm positive he can hear it. "That really meant a lot to her."

"Just to her?"

Shut up, Henry. Don't fucking do this.

I let out some noncommittal humming sound and return to ignoring him, adjusting the mixer to the sound of Gus's guitar.

"Do you want to know why your brother hasn't killed me?"

"I don't care." This time I reply instantly because this isn't happening. I'm glad Keith didn't kill him and I'm sure he has his reasons and I'm fine with that. I don't need to know the inner workings of men, their relationships, and this band. I only care about the work they create, and I produce.

"Dragonfly, I have so much—"

"Don't," I snap, ripping the headphones from my ears and chucking them on the soundboard. I spin in my chair to face him because I guess we're doing this after all. "Don't call me dragonfly. Don't even call me Eden. I am nothing to you. Remember? I was a fling that's over so now we can go back to hating or ignoring each other. That's what I'm trying to do! If you had half a heart in there, you would stop trying to mess with mine and let me do it."

His gaze locks on mine as he takes a deep breath, his nostrils flaring. He inhales another, this was slower, and then he just stares at me. Like he has a million things he wants to say and is torn. He leans forward, his hand reaching out, attempting to draw into my space. The scent of his cologne hits me with such potency, I have to sit back, crossing my arms and legs as if that will somehow protect me.

He licks his lips and holds my eyes, shifting to the edge of the chair so he can be that much closer to me as he says, "I've wanted to talk to you so badly. But I didn't want to do it over the phone or by text, and I couldn't just show up while you and your friend were dealing with that sort of grief. It wouldn't have been right to do that for my own selfish reasons." His eyes bounce to the ground as he collects his thoughts before they jump back up, searching my face and capturing my gaze in earnest. "I'm sorry. I'm so sorry. I didn't mean anything I said to you that day. I was angry and I misread the situation. You weren't just a fling. And I could never hate or ignore you."

"Well, that makes one of us here."

He pushes out a breath, intertwining his fingers and dropping his hands between his parted thighs as he inches in even closer. "So that's it then? You won't even listen to me?"

I actually laugh at that. It's awkward and strangled, but yeah. I want to ask what difference does it make, but I'm terrified of the answer either way. I don't want him to tell me he just doesn't want me, his best friend's little sister, to hate him. And I don't want him to tell me he's sorry and wants another chance.

Because either way, he's not going to love me the way I want to be loved. He's told me that enough and it's finally time I listen. This was a wake-up call I shouldn't have needed in the first place. He's damaged. He's broken. He doesn't want love. And I'm done trying to fix his pieces and force my heart into his. It's futile. He's sorry. I can see that. He didn't mean to be as cruel as he was. Awesome.

But it doesn't. Change. Shit.

Twisting back to the soundboard, I pick up my headphones and set them back on over my ears. "Thank you for the apology. I appreciate that. But we had always planned to end our whatever you want to call it. You just expedited the process. So it's done, and now we can both move on separately."

"Eden—"

"I'm trying to work, Henry. It would be nice if you did the same."

I watch from the corner of my eye as Henry slowly rises, taking a small step until he's directly beside me. Then behind me, hovering above me and staring down with the full measure of his weight and heat pressing into me. My hands tremble as I tweak a sound that doesn't need tweaking on the effects processor.

Deft fingers sweep my hair back as his hot breath fans my neck and I start, jerking forward into the table. My heart skips a beat, and my breath hitches as he moves the can to the side so he can speak directly into my ear. "For the record, this isn't over. It wasn't going to be over in Hawaii or when we came back here, and it sure as hell isn't over now. I'm not done with you, Eden. I never will be."

He replaces the can over my ear and walks off, entering the sound booth, but it's too late. The damage is done. I felt that promise everywhere and nothing I do can stop it.

THIRTY-TWO

HENRY

"You jerk," Eden yells just as something cold and wet hits the back of my head and neck, dripping down into my T-shirt.

Spinning around, my eyes are wide with shock as I take in the fuming vixen before me, my gaze landing on the now empty water bottle in her hand. I pull my phone away from my ear, thankfully having just finished the call I needed to make and slip it into the back pocket of my jeans. My hand touches the back of my head, collecting some of the moisture and then surveying it, making sure it is just water and not something else she was storing in that thing.

"What did I do now, Dragonfly?"

I can't keep the mirth from my voice or the smirk from my lips despite the discomfort of the water sliding down my back. Her fists are balled at her side, the plastic of the water bottle crinkling beneath her ninja grip. Her expression brings new meaning to the phrase if looks could kill and never have I wanted to kiss a woman so badly in my life as I do right now.

"You told me you were going to get my car fixed. That you'd take care of it."

Tilting my head, I take two steps in her direction, reaching up with the back collar of my shirt to wipe away the water she doused me in. Her gaze drops, snagging on the hint of my abs as they sink into my jeans from beneath the hem of my raised shirt, and I inwardly allow my smirk to grow into a cocky smile. I quirk an eyebrow, letting my shirt drop and she looks away, the color rising in her cheeks.

Still...

"Is it not working? I had a guy come and look at it. He jumped your car, drove it around for half an hour, and then parked it back in your spot."

"Why didn't you have him drive it to my place? I thought that's what you said you'd do."

"Because I don't just give out people's addresses and to get into your parking spot at your building, you need to use the fob. With that, he could have gone straight up to your apartment or anyone else's."

"Oh."

I chuckle. "Sorry for drenching me in water?"

She grins smugly, rocking back on heels. "Not even a little."

"I can live with that. Have you forgiven me yet? If you have, I'm going to kiss the hell out of you."

Her jaw drops and she takes a step back. "Don't even think about it, mister."

"Is now a good time to tell you that I'm not only sorry for what I said, but that I'm crazy about you?"

"Henry. Don't—"

"I have to, Eden." I take a step, cutting the distance between us by half. My voice climbs with my desperation for her to hear me, all playfulness gone. "I have to tell you because I need you to know. I'm fucking insanely, over the top, crazy about you. The ten days you were gone were entirely too long. I couldn't stand not being with you. Not touching you and looking at you and listening to you and teasing you. I want you back. I want us to try again. For real this time. No time limits. No restrictions. You and me. A relationship."

She shakes her head, gnawing on her lip. Her eyes are growing glassy, her breathing ragged. "Don't do this me," she whispers. "I've been hurt enough. It's done. I need it to be done. I need to move on once and for all."

"I can't let you do that."

She takes another step back and I know she's two seconds from running. Only her car is dead again and I won't leave her here in a parking lot to wait on a freaking jump. Or worse, for her brother to come back and decide today is the day he's done being patient with my ass and kills me when he sees how hurt Eden is. I think that's the one reason he didn't kill me last time. I promised to make this right with her, and that's what I intend to do.

But the steely determination in her eyes tells me something else.

It tells me she really is done with me.

I clear my throat, scrubbing my hands over my face, trying to think through the panic that thought elicits. "The battery in your car must have died again. The car has been sitting here for a month now. Maybe it needs to be replaced. Do you want me to try jumping it? I have cables. Or if it's something else, I can take a look. I did used to work in your dad's shop if you remember."

"I don't want your help. I should never have taken it in the first place. I'll do what I should have done the first time and call AAA."

"Except I'm here," I quickly add just as she turns to flee. "And it's rush hour in LA, which means AAA isn't getting to you any time soon."

"I seem to remember a similar conversation the last time this happened."

Amusement tilts my lips up into a smile impossible to fight as I walk up to her, her back now facing me but she hasn't moved. And she hasn't run. My eyes wash over her, following the dark ink of her tattoo with her hair up all the way down to her narrow waist and adorable ass. God, it's been way too long since I've held this woman in my arms.

"Good," I say, softening my voice, wanting to reach out and touch her but refraining. "Then you know it's futile to fight me." I dip in, inhaling the fragrance of her skin. "Let me take you home. It's late and it's been a long day. I'll get your car taken care of for you tomorrow. I promise."

She pushes out a sigh. A sigh is good. A sigh isn't yelling.

I spin her around, holding onto her shoulder and dipping so I can meet her eyes head-on. "Hungry? I'm starving. Wanna go to Eden's Roadside Tacos in Paradise with me?"

No laugh. No smile. No light in her pretty blue eyes. "I just want to go home."

Eden is angry and heartbroken. And no words I can come up with will fix that. I saw it that day in Hawaii.

I officially broke her heart one too many times. My words are meaningless. My apologies insignificant. She's as done with me as I told her I was done with her.

"There's something I want to show you," I plead, dropping my hands to her narrow hips.

She tries to shake me off. "Stop, okay? Just stop."

Fuck. Just fuck. What did I do to this girl?

I have to believe I can fix this. That I can change her heart and mind. The cruelest form of torture is not knowing what you have until it's gone. Thanks. Lesson learned. I had perfect, everything I could ever need, and I not only let it slip away, I pushed it with both hands.

Desperate men do desperate things and before I know what I'm doing, I wrap my arm around her waist and haul her against me, holding her so tight, even as she tries to fight me.

"Give me a chance to make it up to you," I murmur into her, kissing the crook of her neck. "Please, Eden. I'll never hurt you again. I promise."

"Your promises mean nothing to me. You break them the moment it suits your purpose."

She's right. She's absolutely right. My promises are meaningless. I swallow hard, my eyes closing as I gear up to say the words I've never said to another human. "I love you."

She goes rigid in my arms, shoving herself back from me. "If that were true then you would have trusted me, Henry. You would have known I would never have done something like that to you with Chad."

"I *did* know that." I reach out and cup her face, forcing her gaze up to mine and holding on. "I fought everything I was seeing and when you came to knock on my door, I was headed back over to your place to find out what the hell was going on. But then you were standing there, and Chad was waiting for you, and all your bags were packed, and suddenly, it felt like everything Chad had said was true. I was a dick. I know I was a dick. I said and did everything wrong. Please Eden, give me a chance to make it up to you," I repeat.

She heaves a heavy breath; her face drops to the cement ground. "Can you just take me home? I just want to go home and not talk about this anymore tonight."

Tonight.

She just said tonight.

Which means there's an opening. It means she's not done, and I still have some skin in this game. Hope blooms low in my gut, bubbling up through me like a geyser. Without a word, I reach out and take her hand in mine, leading her to my car. I open the passenger side for her and help her up.

Then I slam the door shut and run around to the other side. I won't push it. Tonight is not the night for that. But maybe tomorrow or the day after or the week or month after. It doesn't matter how long it takes because she didn't say never.

She just said not tonight.

I start the SUV up and instantly Eden turns up the music playing through the Bluetooth. "Sonic Youth? You're listening to Sonic Youth?" she rasps out incredulously, staring back and forth between me and the sound system like we're both lying to her.

"Yep." I'm listening to Sonic Youth because she listens to Sonic

Youth. Because in the three weeks we were in Hawaii, she was always listening to music, and if she wasn't, she was humming it horribly off key. Much like her, it grew on me despite my resistance.

"This is my absolute favorite of theirs."

I nod because I already knew that even though she never told me. She always bopped her head to this one the hardest.

"It's like three songs in one with the segues into a slower middle section and alternative vocals. It's so goddamn brilliant and the instrumentals are just..." She sighs. "They're so out of this world and different, and this song is why I wanted to produce music."

That I didn't know.

"You can do that, you know. Get creative. Push artists past their comfort zones into making someone just a little different than anyone has done before. That's the beauty and art of music, Dragonfly. It evolves. Jasper would love the hell out of that too. He's always looking for new ways to express his poetry."

"You think he would do something like that on 'Surrender to Me'?"

I think about the lyrics on that one. It's not Jas's usual style of writing. It's a rougher, slightly angrier course of words. I have no idea why he wrote it. Only Jasper does, and often when we ask him what the meaning behind something is, he just smirks at us. He's a secretive guy who lives in his head and dies in his heart, and that's just how he rolls.

I'm starting to understand that more and more the longer I spend with this cute honey on my right.

"I think Jasper would absolutely be open to exploring whatever your creativity can come up with, and the rest of us have no fear at this point. Sure, we want to be the Rolling Stones and touring into our sixties, but at this point in our careers, we're not trying to make a name. We're playing for the music and the love of it."

"Huh," she muses, tapping rhythmically on her knee before turning to me, shifting in her seat and staring into the side of my face. "I still hate you."

"I know."

"Don't think me talking to you means anything different."

I hit the blinker and bang a left, heading in the direction of her apartment, slowed by traffic but not in any hurry either. "This is how we do things. We pretend to hate when really we can't resist."

"I'm trying to resist you, Henry, and if you gave two shits, you'd let me do that up proper. I don't want to love you. I don't want to like you or forgive you. I've loved two men in my life, and both have hurt me beyond words. But this last one takes the prize. The pulsing lump of clay inside my chest has up and quit."

I shake my head, reaching my hand over to grab hers and since she lets me hold it, I know her last statement isn't at all true. She's just scared, and I get that. She doesn't trust me, and I get that even more. I've given her no reason to think I'm in this with her for the long haul. But I will. I just have to show her.

Only not tonight.

"Did you know I've just officially changed my profession?"

"What?" she bursts out in a half-laugh.

I glance at her, nodding with a huge goofy grin on my face that cannot be contained. "I'm a doctor now, Eden. And I will resuscitate the hell out of that lump of clay in your chest. Just you wait."

"That's corny."

"Men in love are always corny. How do you think we get the girl in the first place and win her back after we fuck up?"

THIRTY-THREE

EDEN

"Can I walk you up?" Henry asks and I stare at the front of my building, not wanting to get out but knowing I absolutely need to.

"No."

He sighs. "Eden, you were an epiphany. Love was never anything beautiful or desired. It was ugly and tragic and soul-crushing. I wanted my mother to love me because she was my mom and that's what kids do. Then the guy who I thought was my dad wasn't and while I watched his soul die, he brought me down with his every last breath. This is *not* what I wanted. But now it's everything I need to survive because living without you sucks in ways I never imagined living without someone could." He grasps my hand, and I can't look at him. Tears annoyingly cling to my lashes and I'm so teared out I never want to cry again. I won't give them the attention they crave, and I force them away.

His words are everything when they should be nothing.

But that's all you are, Henry Gauthier. Words. And I've had enough of your words to fill a lifetime. How quickly do those turn given the mood and the shift in the wind? Still, the fact that he's saying this, thinking this, after all he's been through? No. Stop it. Bad,

Eden. If I give into this now, what happens the next time something goes wrong? I can't do this with him again.

"Can I pick you up for work tomorrow? Maybe broker a dinner date after? I want to take you somewhere, Eden."

No. *No!* "I don't believe in third chances."

"Really? That's so strange because those are the best kinds. The ones where the dude pulls out all the stops."

"Henry—"

He cuts me off. "Just shut up, Eden. Your brain is like a funhouse and right now it's stuck, high on the warped images that don't reflect the real deal. I get it. It's my fault for making it that way. But I am a man who hates love but loves you enough not to give a fuck. I don't tell people I love them. I don't fall in love. I did both with you. You get me on that?"

I do actually, and that's why I'm feeling like a sheep on her way to the slaughter. Lots of words. So many words. So many perfect words. It's like falling for the dark side when you know all along it only leads to sinister shit. He said the three words I always dreamed he would.

Three words he swore he never would.

So is it for real, or is it that he just wants back what we had and doesn't like me pissed at him? And how long before he tries to take them back when he gets spooked by all that comes with loving me?

"I don't trust you." I leave it at that.

Without another word, I hop out of his Escalade and slam the door shut behind me. He doesn't come after me, and I'm grateful for that. I need space. I can't think when he's around because all my heart wants to do is believe him. Is get lost in him. I've done it before so many times that it's become rote. Fucking muscle memory.

No more.

I don't look back. I just get up to my apartment and lock my door, sagging against it. "Jess?" I call out.

"Yeah," she yells back. "Be right out. I'm just changing."

Relief hits me like a warm hug at the fact that she's here and will keep me from doing stupid crap. That dark side, man. It's a tempting bastard.

Just as I push off the door to go get myself a glass of water, the buzzer for our apartment sounds. I jump about ten feet in the air, spinning around like my ass has been lit on fire, and press the intercom button. "I said not tonight, Henry," I clip into the small square box hovering beside the door.

"Um." A voice comes through that is most certainly not Henry's. "I have a delivery for Eden Dawson?"

Oops.

"Sorry. Thought you were someone else. Let me buzz you in." I press the button until I hear the two clicks of the front doors to the building and then I release it, clinging against the door while I gnaw on my lip.

"What was that?" Jess asks, coming out, her hair is wet and she's in her pjs.

"The door. Apparently, I have a delivery." I stare at her with troubled eyes. Deliveries have never been anything good. Hell, I still have the box Chad gave me that I have to return to him.

"A delivery, huh? And here I was hoping you had the foresight to order pizza."

I point at her. "That would have been smart. And totally something I should have done except my car that was still in the garage didn't start. Something about the battery."

Jess frowns just as there is a knock on our door.

"You want me to do the honors?" she asks, trying to hide her smirk.

Ugh! My shoulders hunch forward like a scolded child's but I unlock the door, opening it up to find a delivery guy. "Are you Eden? I was told I couldn't hand this to anyone other than Eden."

"That's me," I say warily, only the guy misses my unease completely as he smiles excitedly, reaching out and handing me the large non-descript brown to-go bag.

"That's great. So cool about your name. Enjoy."

"Um. Thanks?" comes out like a question as I reach out to take the bag that's heavier than I expected.

"Have a good night."

And then he's gone. I shut the door, locking it as I peek over at Jess. "Should I open it?"

She laughs, snatching it from my hand and walking it into the kitchen, setting it down on the counter. "Yes. It smells like food."

It does. Like spicy food. Like really good spicy food.

"I think it's from that place. That roadside taco place you took me." Jess starts pulling out multiple boxes of food only to freeze with her hand on one of the white boxes, her eyebrows pinching in with confusion and disbelief as she squints to read the sticker on the box. Then she bursts out laughing. "Oh my motherfucking god, dude. Your man."

"What?"

She's still laughing, shaking her head like she just can't get over it. "Come and see for yourself."

"It's from Henry?"

She gives me a mocking look. Of course, it's from Henry. No one else would even know or go to this trouble to get me delivery from that taco place that I'm pretty positive doesn't even do delivery.

"What, did he leave a note or something?" A weird tingle of excitement prickles my skin and the back of my neck as I cross the apartment and lift one of the boxes. "Eden's Roadside Tacos in Paradise," I read, my jaw unhinging. "He had stickers made and had them put them on the boxes?"

Jess shrugs as she pulls out two margaritas in plastic cups that are set in a drink holder and then we look at the massive buffet of food that could easily feed six people. "Looks that way. It's adorably sweet that he knows this about you and went to the trouble to make it happen. Also, are we expecting company because there must be one of everything here on that menu."

Jess pops the top on one of the boxes, checks it out, and then reaches in, lifting a taco out. She takes a bite, groaning and moaning as she chews. "God, these are so damn good," she exclaims around a mouthful of food. "I know we're hating on all things Henry Gauthier right now, but man, I'm so glad he's in love with you and trying to win you back if this is how he does it."

I pause, a taco poised in my hand as I look at my friend. "I didn't tell you Henry told me he loves me. And I also didn't tell you he's trying to win me back."

She snorts as she takes a sip of her margarita. "Right. Because guys have freaking stickers made with the name of hypothetical dream restaurants and have it delivered when they're not in love and/or trying to win a girl back?" She snorts again. "Please. That's just stupid talk."

I stare at the taco in my hand then down at the simple white sticker with the black script lettering all except for Eden's which is in light blue. Like my hair was when we were in Hawaii.

"I don't know if I can forgive him, Jess. I don't trust him with my heart. What if I give him another chance and he breaks it again? I'm barely holding on as it is. It's been ten miserable days without him. I miss him. But that will fade, right? When this album is done and I don't have to see him anymore, I'll get over him."

She eyes me while she takes a sip of her drink and I know the words about to leave her mouth before she even utters them. "You mean like you did the last time?"

Yup. Knew it.

"I might not have gotten over him the last time, but I moved on. And that's what I intend to do again." I dig into my taco because you can't waste this food. It's just too good to consider such a crime.

"Except last time he broke your heart, he wasn't trying to win it back."

***

Shutting off the light in the bathroom, I pad barefoot into my room, crawling into bed and under the covers, pulling them up to my chin. I breathe out, staring sightlessly up at the ceiling. I don't want to think about him but it's impossible to think about anything else. Only, instead of Hawaii, as I have been all week, my mind is trapped on today. On the words he said and the way he looked at me with such a fierce, fiery determination.

But also like he loves me.

That look isn't even new on him. I saw it in Hawaii as the days grew, and it's why I was ready to put my heart at risk and tell him I wanted more. But I also wasn't lying to Jess. My heart doesn't trust him. And what kind of life or love or relationship can be built when that's its foundation?

Pushing out a sigh, I roll onto my side, finding my alarm clock. It's bright blue light telling me it's a little after ten. I need to get to sleep so I can be on my game tomorrow in the studio. Where I'll have to see him again.

Another sigh flees my lips, this one a touch more hopeless just as my phone chimes with a text. I'm tempted not to check it. Because if it's him, I'll be pissed and if it's not him, I'll be even more pissed. But then it chimes again, indicating a second text, and I know it's futile to resist.

Reaching over, I pick it up, removing the charger from it and rolling onto my back with it in my hand.

Henry: **Did you get the tacos? How were they?**

Henry: **I had them send you one of everything on the menu. You hadn't had a chance to try everything from there yet.**

I debate. I deliberate. I growl and sigh and debate some more. In the end, he wins. He always does with me and that only enrages me further.

Me: **Yes. I got the tacos. They were delicious. Thank you.**

There. Simple. Straightforward. No room for more.

Only this is Henry, and he doesn't follow the rules.

Henry: **What did you think of the logo on the box? Is**

that the way you had always envisioned it looking? If not, we can change it. Make it anything you want.

Me: **It was cute. Thank you for the thoughtful gesture. I'll see you tomorrow.**

Now stop texting me.

Henry: **Can I call you? I want to hear your voice.**

My eyes slam shut. Dammit, Henry. Just stop.

Me: **No.**

Henry: **Do you remember that day on the hammock? When I told you if it were ever going to be anyone, it would be you? It's you, Eden. That day you left, I was going to tell you I wanted more with you. I was going to tell you that no matter what, I couldn't let you go when we got back to LA. That I wanted to tell Keith that you were mine and I didn't care what he had to say about it.**

Tears roll down my face, one quickly followed by the other until the strands of my hair and the fabric of my pillow catch them.

Me: **Please stop. I can't do this with you again.**

Henry: **I can't stop. I'm fighting for you, Eden Dawson. Push me away. Shrug me off. Hate me. It doesn't matter. I'm fighting for you. The way I should have done in Hawaii. Get some sleep, Dragonfly. But this isn't over. Not by a long shot.**

THIRTY-FOUR

EDEN

The totally annoying thing about loving someone you hate is that even though you hate them, you still love them. It's been two weeks. Two weeks of Henry, who is everywhere and makes sure I know it too. Two weeks of producing this album that is now going slower than it was even when we were in Hawaii. It's like they're trying to drag it out.

Jasper, for all his rushed impatience to get this thing done by September first is now all, maybe we should tweak this. Or maybe we should add on an extra song I wrote overnight. Or I'm not so sure about this note in particular—the freaking note was perfect—hey Gus, can we play around with this?

I wanted to be done with this album yesterday because that would mean I would officially be done with Henry. But no.

Add to that the way he looks at me. All the damn time. The way he sends or brings me things he thinks I'd like, or that made him think of me. Cue the songs and special locally made tequila and dragonfly pendant with blue and purple jewels on it—I think he had this one made though he denied it when he put it on my neck without asking.

The randomly sent tacos with Eden's Roadside Tacos in Paradise stickers on the boxes.

The late-night texts...

The ones I can't resist and hate myself for.

The ones that say I miss you and I'm thinking about you and I'm sorry and I love you and I need you and I crave the feel of your skin and the smell of your hair. Those goddamn texts.

But for real, what's a girl supposed to do when she's in love with a guy she hates?

Especially when a lot of that hate has faded and all that's left is the... love.

"No. I don't think the song should have that fast a rhythm," Jasper says, admonishing Gus. "I think this is more of a ballad."

Oh my fucking god. Is he motherfucking kidding me with this?! "Jas," I cut in, hitting the mic button on the mixer with a bit more oomph than necessary because I seriously think he's losing his ever-loving mind. "What we already have down for this song is perfect. I promise you; it is. If you'd like to call in other producers to corroborate, I'm cool with that. But please, trust me when I tell you, this is *not* a ballad."

He stares through the glass pane at me with a smile I can't discern because this is Jasper Diamond we're talking about here. "You really think so? You don't think it might work better slower?"

NO! "I just don't hear it that way in my head. But if you have a different vision..." *Please keep it to yourself and figure it out for the next album.*

His grin widens, his hand running through his reddish-brown hair. "I think we should at least entertain the option and see what we think in the end."

Wanna know what I think in the end? I think I'm a dangerous second from ripping this room apart, setting it on fire, and storming out like the diva I have no right to be.

Instead, I force a smile I'm sure he sees right through and say, "It's your song."

And my funeral.

"You know, if you just gave forgave me and gave us a second chance, all this misery would end."

"What?" I spin in my chair to face Henry because whenever he's not in the booth, he's right beside me in one of those recliners, invading my space and my mind and my sanity. He also smells really good today. Like epically good. And he's wearing a green T-shirt that accentuates the green in his eyes. His hair is just a touch longer on top too. Just looking at him fills me with a rush of heat in places I seriously do not need to be hot so I typically don't look at him. Only this time he caught me off-guard with that statement and now I'm looking and now I'm in trouble.

Henry smirks the smirk that makes him look like a mischievous bad boy and my heart lurches in my chest. "I'm just saying that it's nice to have friends on your side who want to see you happy for a change."

I think steam might be exploding from my ears. "You mean to tell me they're intentionally dragging this out as a ploy to get us together?"

Henry chuckles at my enraged and incredulous expression, running a hand through his hair but when he does that, something on the underside of his left arm, tucked along his triceps catches my eye. I narrow in on it, inching closer because there is no way I'm seeing what I'm seeing.

"What is that?" I point only for him to quickly drop his arm when he realizes I saw his tattoo. His tattoo that was not there in Hawaii. "Is that a…" I hesitate, my mouth suddenly dryer than the desert, and I force a swallow, looking up into his eyes. "Did you get a dragonfly tattoo?"

His eyes rove over my face, filled with uncertainty. "I might have," he hedges.

"Why would you do that?" I want to scream, only it comes out as a hoarse whisper. My heart pounds in my chest as tears burn the backs of my eyes. It was beautiful. The wings were shaded in blue and purple, the bottom of its tail slightly curved.

Holding my gaze, Henry slides off the chair and onto his knees, inching along until he's right against me. Strong hands cup my face while holding me gently. He smiles, his eyes glittering as they stare into mine from inches away. "Why would I do that? Get a dragonfly tattoo when the nickname I've given you is dragonfly?" His thumbs brush my cheek. "Because I love you, Eden. My dragonfly. Because even if I never win you back, I still need you with me. Forever."

Thunk.

My chest is squeezing so tight I can hardly breathe. "I... um..."

His eyes drop to my lips and he leans in with intent just as my phone rings from my purse, startling me back.

"Don't answer it," he commands.

I shake my head and in doing so, shake him off. He falls back onto his haunches, his hands slapping against his thighs in frustration. "I have to. It's probably Jess letting me know she's here." I stand quickly, ripping my phone from my purse. "In fact, it's late." I swipe to answer the phone and tell Jess that I'll be right down. Then I frantically press the button for the mic and tell the guys we're done for the day and that we'll pick it back up again tomorrow. Then I bolt out of the room as fast as I can, ignoring Henry and the way he calls out to me.

I just... I need to think for a second and I can't think with him saying those words and staring into my eyes like that. Like he means absolutely everything he's saying.

Dammit!

The elevator opens on the ground level and I immediately race for the glass doors at the front of the building, finding Jess's car idling right in front.

"Are you okay?" she asks just as I slam the door shut behind me and buckle up.

"No. Just go."

She hits the signal, checking for oncoming cars before pulling out onto the street. "Do you want to talk about it?"

I shake my head.

"Are you sure your car is ready to be picked up?"

This time a shrug. They said it would be. Evidently it was some connection problem with the battery, so even though we replaced the battery, the car died again, and I had it towed to an auto repair shop to be fixed once and for all.

"Okay, I'll take you to the shop."

Leaning my head back, I close my eyes, trying to calm my warring thoughts. If he had kissed me, that would have been it. I know it. I barely held on with his hands on my face. "I don't know what to do," I admit.

"What do you want to do?"

"I want to love him, Jess. I want to love him and not be scared to."

"Don't you think that by this point if he wasn't seriously in love with you, as he says he is, that he would have given up?" My eyes snap open in her direction and she throws a hand up. "Just playing devil's advocate here."

"Do you think I'm being ridiculous?"

"No. I think he genuinely hurt you and you have every right to not only make him work for it to prove to you that he's serious, but every right to take this slow and think it through so you know you're making the right choice. Everything with Henry has been blindly jumping in. I'm just saying that I think he's the real deal this time."

I blow out a silent breath, closing my eyes once more as I think about that. "I think I just need a sign. Something... just something so I'll know for sure."

"Well, I think I have one. A sign that is."

My eyes flash open, my brows knitting. "Huh?"

"Don't be mad, okay? I owed him for my parents' funeral. Not that he was collecting or anything. He simply asked for my help to get you here, and if I didn't believe he was for real, I wouldn't have done it."

"What are you talking about?"

She smirks, pulling into a parking lot. "The sign you needed."

She juts her chin in the direction of whatever is beyond the wind-shield. "Here's your sign."

I turn and look only to have my lungs immediately empty, my hand flying up to my mouth to stifle the sob that mixes in. "Is this for real?"

I feel her hand squeeze mine. "Only one way to find out."

Unclicking my belt, I climb out of the car on numb legs, my entire body shaking. I manage two steps before I stop, unable to go any further. Henry is standing by himself about five feet away, but closely behind him is everyone. Jasper, Viola, and their two girls. Maia and Keith. Gus and Naomi. All giving me the same hopeful smile Henry is.

Yikes, how long were we driving around for without my noticing?

He takes a step forward, his shoulders broad and his head high as he gazes at me while I take everything in. Picnic tables with alter-nating blue and purple umbrellas. The fence wall is now lined with pots of brightly colored flowers. Just like I told him I wanted. But the sign. Yes, there is one of those, and when I get the irony behind it, I hiccup out a laugh.

"I thought it was just stickers."

Henry shakes his head, taking another step. "I was hoping you were going to ask, but you never did. You told me one of your dreams was to own a roadside taco stand called Eden's Roadside Tacos in Paradise. Now you do."

"But... what about the people who owned it before?"

"I bought them out and believe me, they were only too happy to sell for the price I gave them. Plus, they weren't too far from wanting to retire anyway. But the food, the recipes, all of it is theirs and I promised I would never break that tradition. Especially since I know that's the last thing you would want. They promised to teach you everything if you ever wanted to learn."

If I ever wanted to learn? Is he kidding me? Of course, I do. My mind is already going wild with the possibilities of all the things I could create.

"You bought me a roadside taco stand?" I still can't believe he did this for me.

"I did. It's all yours." That hesitant smile explodes across his face. "I wanted to make all your dreams come true and since you're already a music producer, this was the only one I could come up with."

Jesus. Is he for real?

"But this can be the start. There are plenty of celebrities who own restaurants. Could be something fun we do together. If that's what you want, we can make it all happen."

"Henry—"

He cuts me off, taking two large steps until he's right in front of me. So close but still not touching. "Eden, this isn't something fleeting. This is real. My whole life, baby, nothing has made me happy other than my friends and my music. Until you came along and showed me all that I've been missing. You showed me that love doesn't have to hurt or be ugly and cruel. That when it's the right kind of love, it's worth taking all the risks for. Please. Give me a chance to show that this time everything is different. *I* am different and I will never hurt you again. My life isn't a life without you by my side."

A bubble of laughter flees my lungs. Well, I asked for a sign, didn't I?

Without a word, I launch myself at him, my sudden unexpected move forcing him to take a step back as he reflexively grabs on to me, holding me against him. Wrapping my arms around his neck and my legs around his waist, I kiss him. He growls into me, adjusting me as he cocks his head and sweeps his tongue against mine.

"Ewww, gross," Keith yells, amusement in his voice. "If you want me here, then quit shoving your tongue into my sister's mouth. There is only so much a brother can take."

I laugh, feeling the tilt of Henry's mouth against mine. "You and Maia were worse," he calls back, though his eyes are on mine.

"Still are," Gus grouses. "But you do know there are small children here, so you might want to let go of her butt."

"Can we eat now?" Jasper asks. "I know we had to wait to see how this would all turn out, but we're starving."

"Yes. Go eat," Henry yells out before softening his voice so only I can hear him. "I need to kiss my woman some more." Without so much as a backward glance, Henry walks me, still in his arms, to one of the picnic tables, sitting us down and having me straddle his thighs. "Grab us something, would ya?" he hollers before diving back into my mouth. His hands sweep through my hair, cupping the back of my head and holding me against him. "Missed you," he murmurs into me, kissing me with an insatiable hunger that makes my toes curl and my body hum.

"I still can't believe you did this."

"I did it before we even left Hawaii. It was already in motion the morning after you left."

"Henry—"

"Whether you were going to be mine again or not, I wanted you to have this. I love you."

My forehead drops to his, the tips of our noses kissing. "I love you too."

"Thank fuck." He sags with relief, pressing my chest tighter against his.

"Thank you for doing this. For not giving up. For fighting. For making all my dreams come true."

"Dragonfly, for our life to come, I'll never give up. I'll always fight for you. And I'll always make your dreams come true. Always."

EPILOGUE
HENRY

Two and a Half Years Later

"EDEN," someone yells. "Eden, pause for a picture. Henry, you too."

Blinding flashes of light assault us, coming from all directions.

Eden smirks at me, her blue eyes dancing the way they have been all night. With so much happiness it's radiating from her. She's glowing. So radiant, so goddamn beautiful she takes my breath away. As she always has.

Tonight was a big night. For her. For us as a band. For everything.

One hand hits my chest, the hand with my ring on it, the other holding her Grammy. I wrap my arm around her waist and hoist up on my own statue, leaning in and kissing my girl on the cheek because I don't think I could be prouder of her if I tried.

More flashes of light as they take our pictures, calling out question after question.

This isn't Eden's first Grammy. She won her first for our album she produced when we were in Hawaii. Jasper, for all his bullshit about slowing down and taking time off, did that for about eight months. Then he got itchy and wanted to go back into the studio.

He had also been writing like a madman.

Adalyn having taken to school better than anyone expected helped. Now she's in second grade and none of us can believe the progress she's made. She has support. Speech, occupational therapy, a para, and other special education teachers. But she's reading. She's writing stories. She's keeping up with her math and everything else.

She's kicking ass and taking names, just the way we knew she would.

She's also singing and writing music. Like her father.

"So when's the big day?" a woman who's face is stuck behind the lens of her camera asks. "You've all been very tight lipped. Can't you give us something?"

Eden just smiles, gazing up at me with a mischievous glint. "What do you think? Should we tell the world when we're getting married?" She bites into her glossy lip and I know exactly what she's thinking.

"Tonight," I say back to the press. "Tonight's the big night." I wink at them, laughing as they give us a series of annoyed boos and scowls. They've been hounding us for months for a date, since Eden was spotted with a large diamond on her finger. "Have a good night everyone." We both wave and head out, rounding the corner, and spotting the two large SUVs waiting for us. "You ready?"

"I'm ready."

"I love you."

"I love you too. I'm so glad we're doing it like this. It's absolutely perfect."

I lean in and press my lips to the corner of her mouth, our security escorting us back along the red carpet and away from the theater. We're immediately flanked by Jasper, Viola, Gus, Naomi, Keith, Maia, Lyric, and Jameson.

"Well, that was a fun night," Lyric states, her smile huge as she rubs her pregnant belly, about four months out from delivering their second child. "Turn Records and their artists scored fifteen Grammys tonight. Now this to finish it off." She looks over to Jameson. "Yeah. Tonight's a good night."

"The best," he agrees. "And it's only just getting started."

All of us climb into the waiting SUVs and then we're off, speeding out into the night. My hand hasn't left Eden's. My eyes either. My girl is stunning in her purple gown that hugs and accentuates every perfect curve. Her now black hair is piled up on top of her head, revealing the tattoo on the back of her neck.

My favorite tattoo on her.

I lean in, unable to resist, my teeth grazing her diamond studded earlobe. "I can't wait to get this off you."

She shudders, her hand squeezing mine. Twisting in her seat, her nose glides along mine. "Have I told you how hot you look in this tux?" Her lips capture mine, but they don't linger. Not yet. That will come later. She wipes her thumb along my bottom lip, removing the smear of her cherry gloss. My teeth jut out, capturing her thumb and nibbling on the pad.

"Okay. That's enough you two," Maia playfully chimes in. Tonight she's the one wearing white. A sparkling white gown loaded with sequins.

"Yeah. No kissing the bride before she says I do," Keith growls. "And definitely no talking about how you want to undress my baby sister."

I snicker. "Then maybe you should have gone in the other car."

He flips me off, but he's smiling. We all are.

We're not doing this the traditional way. That's not really our style. I wasn't lying when I told the paparazzi we're getting married tonight. It was actually Viola's genius plan. We couldn't come up with a date that would stay a secret. We wanted our wedding to be small. Just family and close friends. But Jas and Viola tried that as did Gus and Naomi. Even Keith and Maia. All of their weddings were crashed by a barrage of press.

But now all the press are focused on the Grammys. On all the after parties.

Not on us.

Certainly not on our wedding that no one knows about.

Ten minutes later we pull up in front of Eden's, her taco and tequila restaurant. This is her second restaurant in addition to Eden's Roadside Tacos in Paradise. The girl can't stop. She can't get enough. She is relentless when it comes to her passions and there is absolutely nothing sexier.

Stepping out of the car, I help her down, Keith doing the same with Maia, and then we head in, the other SUV having beaten us here. The restaurant is decked out with blue and purple sparkling lights, all the tables and chairs that typically take up the main part of the restaurant are pushed back and off to the side for later when we eat.

Eden's parents are the first to greet us, her mom kissing my cheek before taking her hand, and ushering her away from me. "I'll see you soon," she says to me.

"See you soon."

You'd think I'd be nervous about this. About all of this. But everything with Eden has been natural. From the moment she jumped into my arms, there was no going back for us. It was full steam ahead without so much as a backward glance. No more second guessing. No more hesitation or fear. Just us. Just love.

Keith grips my shoulder, tugging me back to the room. He's holding his son, Xavier. His other son, Griffith hanging on Maia who is talking with Viola who is pregnant with hers and Jasper's third daughter, and Naomi who is holding one of her own twins, Parklyn.

Gus and Jasper are watching as Adalyn, Cora, and Gus's other daughter Taylor dance and twirl about the open room.

Jasper's parents are off to the side, talking to Lyric, Jameson, Ethan, and Lyric's parents. Marco must be with Eden since he's the one officiating this crazy thing we're calling a wedding.

"Are you ready for this brother?"

Brother. That's exactly what Keith's about to become. Not just in our fraternal band sense. But in marriage. I have a family now. A real connection that means more to me than anything.

"I've been ready."

"Are you sure you want to leave tonight? I mean, it's a long motherfluffing flight to Fiji."

I grin. "Worried about our plane?"

He scrunches up his nose. "Just saying I wouldn't mind you not making it your honeymoon suite. Especially considering it's where my kids nap when we fly on it."

I laugh. I can't help it. "I thought we were buying a bigger plane before this summer?"

We are. More kids. Bigger family. Especially since this summer, we're all going on tour. It's a split show. Naomi and Wild Minds. Adalyn will be on summer break. The other kids are still too young for that to matter, but since none of us are leaving anyone behind anymore, this is how it has to go.

"Yeah. But." He groans, burying his head into Xavier who squirms and whines. He doesn't like to be still. Much like his father, he likes to move. Keith puts him down and he runs off to join his friends. His cousins, I guess since that's what we call them. Keith turns on me. "Fine. I won't give you the speech. Just don't knock up my sister tonight, okay? She's still too young?"

"How old is Maia again?"

"Dude—"

"I'm kidding. Eden and I have no plans on getting pregnant tonight." But if I have my way, it will be soon. The second she gives me the green light, it's on. I want this. I want all the babies with her.

Marco steps out from the back room, his dark eyes meeting mine. "Showtime, folks. Take your places."

"I still can't believe you allowed Marco to talk to you into marrying you," Jasper says, coming to stand beside me as I move to the front of the room where the alter, if you can actually call it that, is located.

"I don't think they had a choice," Gus tells him.

"No. They didn't," Marco snaps, raising a pointed eyebrow at all of us. "Besides, ask Keith, I did a fantastic job at his wedding, right?"

"I think you cried more than Maia did."

"Whatever. I won't cry tonight—" his words cut off, turning into a gasp instead just as the simple strings of a guitar begin to trickle through the air curtesy of Gabriel Rose, Lyric's father. "Oh my god. Look at her."

The three of us spin in place and the moment my eyes meet Eden's, all the way on the other side of the room, my breath catches and suddenly I'm the one choked up. "Holy hell, she's stunning."

And mine.

I knew it that first night I saw her. I might not have known who she was that night, but I knew she was someone special. Someone I had to know. And now she's about to be my wife. My other half. My partner. My family. Till death do us part.

All of us.

THE END

Thank you so very much for taking the time to read Promise to Love You. I sincerely hope you enjoyed Henry and Eden's story. If you haven't read the entire Wild Love series, you can start with Lyric and Jameson's second chance, friends to lovers story, Reckless to Love You. If you like more of the enemies to lovers vibe, check out Jasper's and Viola's forbidden romance, Love to Hate Her.

Keep reading for an excerpt of my HOT billionaire, office romance The Edge of Temptation.

You can also sign up for my newsletter so you never miss a release, sale, or any of my exclusive content!

THE EDGE OF TEMPTATION

Halle

"No," I reply emphatically, hoping my tone is stronger than my disposition. "I'm not doing it. Absolutely not. Just no." I point my finger for emphasis, but I don't think the gesture is getting me anywhere. Rina just stares at me, the tip of her finger gliding along the lip of her martini glass.

"You're smiling. If you don't want to do this, then why are you smiling?"

I sigh. She's right. I am smiling. But only because it's so ridiculous. In all the years she's known me, I've never hit on a total stranger. I don't think I'd have any idea how to even do that. And honestly, I'm just not in the right frame of mind to put in the effort. "It's funny, that's all." I shrug, playing it off. It's really not funny. The word terrifying comes closer. "But my answer is still no."

"It's been, what?" Margot chimes in, her gaze flicking between Rina, Aria, and me like she's actually trying to figure this out. She's not. I know where she's going with this and it's fucking rhetorical. "A month?"

See? I told you.

"You broke up with Matt a month ago. And you can't play it off like you're all upset over it, because we know you're not."

"Who says I'm not upset?" I furrow my eyebrows, feigning incredulous, but I can't quite meet their eyes. "I was with him for two years."

But she's right. I'm not upset about Matt. I just don't have the desire to hit on some random dude at some random bar in the South End of Boston.

"Two *useless* years," Rina persists with a roll of her blue eyes before taking a sip of her appletini. She sets her glass down, leaning her small frame back in her chair as she crosses her arms over her chest and purses her lips like she's pissed off on my behalf. "The guy was a freaking asshole."

"And a criminal," Aria adds, tipping back her fancy glass and finishing off the last of her dirty martini, complete with olive. She chews on it slowly, quirking a pointed eyebrow at me. "The cock-sucker repeatedly ignored you so he could defraud people."

"All true." I can't even deny it. My ex was a black-hat hacker. And while that might sound all hot and sexy in a mysterious, dangerous way, it isn't. The piece of shit stole credit card numbers, and not only used them for himself but sold them on the dark web. He was also one of those hacktivists who got his rocks off by working with other degenerate assholes to try and bring down various compa-nies and websites.

In my defense, I didn't know what he was up to until the FBI came into my place of work, hauled me downtown, and interviewed me for hours. I was so embarrassed, I could hardly show my face at work again. Not only that, but everyone was talking about me. Either with pity or suspicion in their eyes, like I was a criminal right along with him.

Matt had a regular job as a red-team specialist—legit hackers who are paid by companies to go in and try to penetrate their systems. I assumed all that time he spent on his computer at night was him working hard to get ahead. At least that was his perpetual excuse when challenged.

Nothing makes you feel more naïve than discovering the man you had been engaged to is actually a criminal who was stealing from people. And committing said thefts while living with you.

I looked up one of the people the FBI had mentioned in relation to Matt's criminal activities. The woman had a weird name that stuck out to me for some reason, and when I found her, I learned she was a widow with three grandchildren, a son in the military, and was a recently retired nurse. It made me sick to my stomach. Still does when I think about it.

I told the FBI everything I knew, which was nothing. I explained that I had ended things with Matt three days prior to them arresting him. Pure coincidence. I was fed up with the monotony of our relationship. Of being engaged and never discussing or planning our wedding. Of living with someone I never saw because he was always locked away in his office, too preoccupied with his computer to pay me even an ounce of attention. But really, deep down, I knew I wasn't in love with him anymore.

I didn't even shed a tear over our breakup. In fact, I was more relieved than anything. I knew I had dodged a bullet getting out when I did.

And then the FBI showed up.

"I ended it with him. *Before* I knew he was a total and complete loser," I tack on, feeling more defensive about the situation than I care to admit. Shifting my weight on my uncomfortable wooden chair, I cross my legs at the knee and stare sightlessly out into the bar.

"And we applaud you for that," Rina says, nudging Margot and then Aria in the shoulders, forcing them to concur. "It was the absolute right thing to do. But you've been miserable and mopey and very . . ."

"Anti-men," Margot finishes for her, tossing back her lemon drop shot with disturbing exuberance. I think that's number three for her already, which means it could be a long night. Margot has yet to learn the art of moderation.

"Right." Aria nods exaggeratedly at Margot like she just hit the nail on the head, tossing her messy dark curls over her shoulders before twisting them up into something that resembles a bun. "Anti-men. I'm not saying you need to date anyone here. You don't even have to go home with them. Just let them buy you a drink. Have a normal conversation with a normal guy."

I scoff. "And you think I'll find one of those in here?" I splay my arms out wide, waving them around. All these men look like players. They're in groups with other men, smacking at each other and pointing at the various women who walk in. They're clearly rating them. And if a woman just so happens to pass by, they blatantly turn and stare at her ass.

This is a hookup bar. All dark mood lighting, annoying, trendy house music in the background and uncomfortable seating. The kind designed to have you standing all night before you take someone home. And now I understand why my very attentive friends brought me here. It's not our usual go-to place.

"It's like high school or a frat house in here. And definitely not in a good way. I bet all these guys bathed in Axe body spray, gelled up their hair and left their mother's basement to come here and find a 'chick to bang.'" I put air quotes around those words. I have zero interest in being part of that scheme.

"Well . . ." Rina's voice drifts off, scanning the room desperately. "I know I can find you someone worthy."

"Don't waste your brain function. I'm still not interested." I roll my eyes dramatically and finish off my drink, slamming the glass down on the table with a bit more force than I intend. *Oops.* What-ever. I'm extremely satisfied with my anti-men status. Because that's exactly what I am—anti-men—and I'm discovering I'm unrepentant about it. In fact, I think it's a fantastic way to be when you rack up one loser after another the way I have. Like a form of self-preservation.

I've never had a good track record. Even before Matt, I had a knack for picking the wrong guys. My high school boyfriend ended up being gay. I handed him my V-card shortly before he dropped that bomb on me, though he swore I didn't turn him gay. He promised he was like that prior to the sex. In college, I dated two guys somewhat seriously. The first one cheated on me for months before I found out, and the second one was way more into his video games than he was me. I think he also had a secret cocaine problem because he'd stay up all night gaming like a fiend. I had given up on men for a while—are you seeing a trend here?—and then in my final year of graduate school, Matt came along. Need I say more? So as far as I'm concerned, men can all go screw themselves. Because they sure as hell aren't gonna screw me!

"You can stop searching now, Rina." This is getting pathetic. "I have a vibrator. What else does a girl need?" All three pause their search to examine me and I realize I said that out loud. I blush at that, but it's true, so I just shrug a shoulder and fold my arms defiantly across my chest. "I don't need a sextervention. If anything, I need to avoid the male species like the plague they are."

They dismiss me immediately, their cause to find me a "normal" male to talk to outweighing my antagonism. And really, if it's taking this long to find someone then the pickings must really be slim here. I move to flag down the waitress to order another round when Margot points to the far corner.

"There." The tenacious little bug is gleaming like she just struck oil in her backyard. "That guy. He's freaking hot as holy sin and he's alone. He even looks sad, which means he needs a friend."

"Or he wants to be left alone to his drinking," I mumble, wishing I had another drink in my hand so I could focus on something other than my friends obsessively staring at some random creep. *Where the hell is that waitress?*

"Maybe," Aria muses thoughtfully as she observes the man across the bar, tapping her bottom lip with her finger. Her hands are covered in splotches of multicolored paint. As is her black shirt, now that I look closer. "Or maybe he's just had a crappy day. He looks so sad, Halle." She nods like it's all coming together for her as she makes frowny puppy dog eyes at me. "So very sad. Go over and see if he wants company. Cheer him up."

"You'd be doing a public service," Rina agrees. "Men that good-looking should never be sad."

I roll my eyes at that. "You think a blowjob would do it, or should I offer him crazy, kinky sex to cheer him up? I still have that domination-for-beginners playset I picked up at Angela's bachelorette party. Hasn't even been cracked open."

Aria tilts her head like she's actually considering this. "That level of kink might scare him off for the first time. And I wouldn't give him head unless he goes down on you first."

Jesus, I'm not drunk enough for this. "Or he's a total asshole who just fucked his girlfriend's best friend," I protest, my voice rising an octave with my objection. I sit up straight, desperate to make my point clear. "Or he's about to go to prison because he hacks women into tiny bits with a machete before he eats them. Either way, I'm. Not. Interested."

"God," Margot snorts, twirling her chestnut hair as she leans back in her chair and levels me with an unimpressed gaze. "Dramatic much? He wouldn't be out on bail if that were the case. But seriously, that's like crazy psycho shit, and that guy does not say crazy psycho. He says crave-worthy and yummy and 'I hand out orgasms like candy on Halloween.'"

"Methinks the lady doth protest too much," Aria says with a knowing smile and a wink.

She swivels her head to check him out again and licks her lips reflexively. I haven't bothered to peek yet because my back is to him and I hate that I'm curious. All three ladies are eyeing him with unfettered appreciation and obvious lust. Their tastes in men differ tremendously, which indicates this guy probably is hot. I shouldn't be tempted. I really shouldn't be. I'm asking for a world of trouble or hurt or legal fees. So why am I finding the idea of a one-nighter with a total stranger growing on me?

I've never been that girl before. But maybe they're right? Maybe a one-nighter with a random guy is just the ticket to wipe out my past of bad choices in men and make a fresh start? I don't even know if that makes sense since a one-nighter is the antithesis of a smart choice. But my libido is taking over for my brain and now I'm starting to rationalize, possibly even encourage. I need to stop this now.

"He's gay. Hot men are always gay. Or assholes. Or criminals. Or cheaters. Or just generally suck at life."

"You've had some bad luck, is all. Look at Oliver. He's good-looking, sweet, loving, and not an asshole. Or a criminal. And he likes you. You could date him."

Reaching over, I steal Rina's cocktail. She doesn't stop me or even seem to register the action. I stare at her with narrowed eyes over the rim of her glass as I slurp down about half of it in one gulp. "I'm not dating your brother, Rina. That's weird and begging for drama. You and I are best friends."

She sighs and then I sigh because I'm being a bitch and I don't mean to be. I like her brother. He is all of those things she just mentioned, minus the liking me part. But if things went bad between us, which they inherently would, it would cost me one of my most important friendships. And that's not a risk I'm willing to take. Plus, unbeknownst to Rina, Oliver is one of the biggest players in the greater Boston area.

"I'm just saying not all men are bad," Rina continues, and I shake my head. "We'll buy your drinks for a month if you go talk to this guy," she offers hastily, trying to close the deal.

Margot glances over at her with furrowed eyebrows, a bit surprised by that declaration, but she quickly comes around with an indifferent shrug. Aria smiles, liking that idea. Then again, money is not Aria's problem. "Most definitely," she agrees. "Go. Let a stranger touch your lady parts. You're waxed and shaved and looking hot. Let someone take advantage of that."

"And if he shoots me down?"

"You don't have to sleep with him," Rina reminds me. "Or even give him your real name. In fact, tell him nothing real about yourself. It could be like a sexual experiment." I shake my head in exasperation. "We won't bother you about it again," she promises solemnly. "But he won't shoot you down. You look movie star hot tonight."

I can only roll my eyes at that. While I appreciate the sentiment from my loving and supportive friends, being shot down by a total stranger when I'm already feeling emotionally strung out might just do me in. Even if I have no interest in him. But free drinks . . .

Twisting around in my chair, I stare across the crowded bar, probing for a few seconds until I spot the man in the corner. Holy Christmas in Florida, he *is* hot. There is no mistaking that. His hair is light blond, short along the sides and just a bit longer on top. Just long enough that you could grab it and hold on tight while he kisses you. His profile speaks to his straight nose and strong, chiseled, cleanly shaven jaw. I must admit, I do enjoy a bit of stubble on my men, but he makes the lack of beard look so enticing that I don't miss the roughness. He's wearing a suit. A dark suit. More than likely expensive judging by the way it contours to his broad shoulders and the flash of gold on his wrist that I catch in the form of cufflinks.

But the thing that's giving me pause is his anguish. It's radiating off him. His beautiful face is downcast, staring sightlessly into his full glass of something amber. Maybe scotch. Maybe bourbon. It doesn't matter. That expression has purpose. Those eyes have meaning behind them and I doubt he's seeking any sort of company. In fact, I'm positive he'd have no trouble finding any if he were so inclined.

That thought alone makes me stand up without further comment. He's the perfect man to get my friends off my back. He's going to shoot me down in an instant and I won't even take it personally. Well, not too much. I can feel the girls exchanging gleeful smiles, but I figure I'll be back with them in under five minutes, so their misguided enthusiasm is inconsequential. I watch him the entire way across the bar. He doesn't sip at his drink. He just stares blankly into it. That sort of heartbreak makes my stomach churn. This miserable stranger isn't just your typical Saturday night bar dweller looking for a quick hookup.

He's drowning his sorrows.

Miserable Stranger doesn't notice my approach. He doesn't even notice me as I wedge myself in between him and the person seated beside him. And he definitely doesn't notice me as I order myself a dirty martini. I'm close enough to smell him. And damn, it's so freaking good I catch myself wanting to close my eyes and breathe in deeper. Sandalwood? Citrus? Freaking godly man? Who knows. I have no idea what to say to him. In fact, I'm half-tempted to grab my drink and scurry off, but I catch Rina, Margot, and Aria watching vigilantly from across the bar with excited, encouraging smiles. There's no way I can get out of this without at least saying hello.

Especially if I want those bitches to buy me drinks for the next month.

But damn, I'm so stupidly nervous. "Hello," I start, but my voice is weak and shaky, and I have to clear it to get rid of the nervous lilt. Shit. My hands are trembling. Pathetic.

He doesn't look up. Awesome start.

I play it off, staring around the dimly lit bar and taking in all the people enjoying their Saturday night cocktails. It's busy here. Filled with the heat of the city in the summer and lust-infused air. I open my mouth to speak again, when the person seated next to my Miserable Stranger and directly behind me, gets up, shoving their chair inadvertently into my back and launching me forward. Straight into him.

I fly without restraint, practically knocking him over. Not enough to fully push him off his chair—he's too big and strong for that—but it's enough to catch his attention. I see him blink like he's coming back from some distant place. His head tilts up to mine as I right myself, just as my attention is diverted by the man who hit me with his chair.

"I'm so sorry," the man says with a note of panic in his voice, reaching out and grasping my upper arm as if to steady me. "I didn't see you there. Are you okay?"

"Yes, I'm fine." I'm beet red, I know it.

"Did I hurt you?"

Just my pride. "No. Really. I'm good. It was my fault for wedging myself in like this." The stranger who bumped me smiles warmly, before turning back to his girlfriend and leaving the scene of the crime as quickly as possible.

Adjusting my dress and schooling my features, I turn back to my Miserable Stranger, clearing my throat once more as my eyes meet his. "I'm sorry I banged into you . . ." My freaking breath catches in my lungs, making my voice trail off at the end.

Goddamn.

If I thought his profile was something, it's nothing compared to the rest of him. He blinks at me, his eyes widening fractionally as he sits back, crossing his arms over his suit-clad chest and taking me in from head to toe. He hasn't even removed his dark jacket, which seems odd. It's more than warm in here and summer outside.

He sucks in a deep breath as his eyes reach mine again. They're green. But not just any green. Full-on megawatt green. Like thick summer grass green. I can tell that even in the dim lighting of the bar, that's how vivid they are. They're without a doubt the most beautiful eyes I've ever seen.

"That's all right," he says and his thick baritone, with a hint of some sort of accent, is just as impressive as the rest of him. It wraps its way around me like a warm blanket on a cold night. Jesus, has a voice ever affected me like this? Maybe I do need to get out more if I'm reacting to a total stranger like this. "I love it when beautiful women fall all over me."

I like him instantly. Cheesy line and all.

"That happen to you a lot?"

He smirks and the way that crooked grin looks on his face has my heart rate jacking up yet another degree. "Not really. Are you okay? That was quite the tumble."

I nod. I don't want to talk about my less than graceful entrance anymore. "Would you mind if I sit down?" And he thinks about it. Actually freaking hesitates. Just perfect. This is not helping my already frail ego.

I stare at him for a beat, and just as I'm about to raise the white flag and retreat with my dignity in my feet, he swallows hard and shakes his head slowly. Is he saying no I shouldn't sit, or no he doesn't mind? Crap, I can't tell, because his expression is . . . a mess. Like a bizarre concoction of indecision and curiosity and temptation and disgust.

He must note my confusion because in a slow measured tone he clarifies with, "I guess you should probably sit so you don't fall on me again." He blinks, something catching his attention. Glancing past me for the briefest of moments, that smirk returning to his full lips. "I think your friends love the idea."

"Huh?" I sputter before my head whips over my shoulder and I catch Rina, Aria, and Margot standing, watching us with equally exuberant smiles. Margot even freaking waves. Well, that's embarrassing. Now what do I say? "Yeah . . . um." Words fail me, and I sink back into myself. "I'm sorry. I just . . . well, I recently broke up with someone, and my friends won't let me return to the table until I've reentered the human female race and had a real conversation with a man."

God, this sounds so stupidly pathetic. Even to my own ears. And why did I just admit all of that to him? My face is easily the shade of the dress I'm wearing—and it's bright motherfucking red. He's smirking at me again, which only proves my point. I hate feeling like this. Insecure and inadequate. At least it's better than stupid and clueless. Yeah, that's what I had going on with Matt and this is not who I am. I'm typically far more self-assured.

"I'll just grab my drink and return to my friends."

I pull some cash out of my purse and drop it on the wooden bar. I pause, and he doesn't stop me. My fingers slip around the smooth, long stem of my glass. I want to get the hell out of here, but before I can slide my drink safely toward me and make my hasty, not so glamorous escape, he covers my hand with his and whispers, "No. Stay."

Want to find out what happens next with Halle and Jonah? Grab your copy of The Edge of Temptation now!

ALSO BY J. SAMAN

Wild Love Series:

Reckless to Love You

Love to Hate Her

Crazy to Love You

Love to Tempt You

Promise to Love You

The Edge Series:

The Edge of Temptation

The Edge of Forever

The Edge of Reason

The Edge of Chaos

Boston's Billionaire Bachelors:

Doctor Scandalous

Doctor Mistake

Doctor Heartless

Doctor Playboy

Start Again Series:

Start Again

Start Over

Start With Me

Las Vegas Sin Series:

END OF BOOK NOTE

If you haven't read me before, this is the *unedited* part of the book where I try to break it all down for you. I will be honest, I'm devastated this series is over. I absolutely LOVE each and every character I wrote, but more than that, I love them as a unit.

When I wrote Jasper's and Viola's book, I didn't give Henry much consideration. Even into Gus's book. But once Keith's book hit, Henry started forming for me. I wanted him to be more. I liked that he didn't have much of a story that we knew about. I also loved pairing him with Eden because brother's best friend is one of my favorite tropes.

There is just something about Henry that totally got me and I fell SO hard for him!

And Eden. Damn, I just loved writing her. She really flew off the page to me and filled my head with her crazy, fiery ways. She was just too cool for school with the heart of an angel.

I'm not sure what to say about this story. Maybe I'm still too consumed with it, but when I started it, I wasn't sure if anyone would like it. But then as I got deeper and deeper, especially into the Chad in Hawaii scene, I couldn't stop writing it. It was all, I have to know what's happening next, and getting the words on the page seemed vital. I couldn't write them fast enough at that point.

The epilogue was murder for me. I had this whole thing envisioned with them in Disney World and Adalyn is singing as part of some benefit she started. I wrote maybe two pages of it and I just couldn't do it. Adalyn, for those of you who don't know, is the fictional representation of my little one. So to write Adalyn so far in the future... I just couldn't do it. My gut twisted every time. I don't even know why.

So this epilogue, while maybe a touch generic, also closed up the story and the characters for me. I've already been asked if there will be more from these characters and my answer is I don't know. There will not be an Adalyn book for the reasons I mentioned above, but is it possible all these kids will have their own stories one day? Yes. It's possible. Just not right now.

I want to thank my lovely betas, Patricia and Danielle. You ladies really helped me out so much. Especially with the dynamic between Henry and Eden. I am eternally grateful and couldn't do this without your help.

To my adoring husband. Each day with you gets better. You champion me when my confidence is zilch and celebrate my successes as if they're your own. I am truly the luckiest lady on the planet. To my girls. My lovely, sweet, encouraging girls. It's not easy having a mom as an author, but you'd never know it to talk to you. You are my strength, my passion, my happiness, my reason. Being your mommy is the best gig ever.

To all the wonderful people in my reader group, I love you! You're the absolute best and I have so much fun with you. To you, my beautiful readers, thank you!! Every time you pick up one of my books you put your faith in me and I can only hope I live up to your expectations. I love you all!!

XO ~ J. Saman

RECKLESS TO LOVE YOU

Lyric

I can't stop staring at it. Reading the two short words over and over again ad nauseum. They're simple. Essentially unimpressive if you think about it. But those two words mean everything. Those two words dive deep into the darkest depths of my soul, the part I've methodically shut off over the years, and awaken the dormant volcano. How can two simple words make this well of emotions erupt so quickly?

Come home.

I don't recognize the number the text came from. It shows up as Unknown. But I don't have to recognize it. I know who it's from. Instinctively, I know. At least, my body does, because my heart rate is through the roof. My stomach is clenched tight with violent, poorly concealed, sickly butterflies. My forehead is clammy with a sheen of sweat and my hands tremble as they clutch my phone.

It's early here in California. Not even dawn, but I'm awake. I'm always awake, even when I'm not, and since my phone has, unfortunately, become another appendage, it's consistently with me.

It's a New York area code.

Goddammit! I suck in a deep, shuddering breath of air that does absolutely nothing to calm me, then I respond in the only way I can.

Me: ***Who is this?***

The message bubble appears instantly, like he was waiting for me. Like there is no way this is a wrong number. Like his fingers couldn't respond fast enough.

Unknown: ***You know who this is. Come home.***

I don't respond. I can't. I'm frozen. It's been four years. Four fucking years. And this is how he reaches out? This is how he contacts me? I slink back down into my bed, pulling the heavy comforter over my head in a pathetic attempt to protect myself from the onslaught of emotions that consume me. I tuck my phone against my chest, over what's left of my fractured heart.

I'm hurting. I'm angry. I'm so screwed up and broken, and yet, I'm still breaking. How is that even possible? How can a person continue to break when they're already broken? How can a person I haven't seen in four years still affect me like this?

I want to throw the traitorous device into the wall and smash it. Toss it out my window as hard as I can and hope it reaches the Pacific at the other end of the beach, where it will be swept away, never to return. But I don't. Because curiosity is a nefarious bitch. Because I have to know why the man who was my everything and now my nothing is contacting me after all this time, asking me to come home.

Unknown: ***I'm sitting here in my old room, on my bed, and I can't focus. I can't think about what I need to be thinking about. So, I need you to come home.***

I shake my head as tears line my eyes, stubbornly refusing to fall but obscuring my vision all the same. Nothing he's saying makes sense to me. Nothing. It's completely nonsensical, and yet, it's not. I still know him well enough to understand both what he's saying and what he's not.

Me: ***Why?***

Unknown: ***Because I need you to.***

Me: ***I can't. Too busy with work.***

That's sort of a lie. I mean, I *am* headed to New York for the Rainbow Ball in a few days. But he doesn't need to know that. And I do not want to see him. I absolutely, positively, do not.

Unknown: ***My dad had a stroke***

My eyes cinch shut, and I cover them with one hand. I can't breathe. A gasped sob escapes the back of my throat, burning me with its raw taste. God. Now what the hell am I going to do? I love his father. Jesus Christ. How can I say no to him now? How can I avoid this the way I so desperately need to? *Shit.*

Me: ***I'm sorry. I didn't know. Is he okay?***

Unknown: ***He'll live, but he's not great. He's in the ICU. Worse than he was after the heart attack.***

I shake my head back and forth. I can't go. I can't go home. I was there two months ago to visit my parents and my sister's family. I have work—so much freaking work that I can barely keep up. I don't want to see him. I won't survive it. I'll see him, and I'll feel everything I haven't allowed myself to feel. I'll be sucked back in.

Things are different now.

They are. My situation has changed completely, but I never had the guts to call him and tell him that. Mostly because I was hurt. Mostly because I felt abandoned and brushed off. Mostly because I was terrified that it wouldn't matter after all this time apart. If I see him now, knowing how much has changed...Shit. I just...Fuck. I can't.

I don't know what to do.

I'm drenched in sweat. The blanket I sought refuge in is now smothering me. I'm relieved his father is alive. I still speak to him once a month. Wait, let me amend that—he still *calls* me once a month. And we talk. Not about Jameson. Never about him. Only about me and my life. I'm a wreck that Jameson is contacting me. I can't play this game. I never could. It was all or nothing with him.

Unknown: ***I miss you.***

I stare at the words, read them over again, then respond too quickly, ***Liar.***

Unknown: ***Never. I miss you so goddamn much.***

I think I just died. Everything inside me has stopped. My heart is not beating. My breath has stalled inside my chest, unable to be expelled. My mind is completely blank. And when everything comes back to life, I'm consumed with an angry, caustic fury I never knew I was capable of.

Unknown: ***Are you still there?***

Me: ***What do you want me to say?***

Unknown: ***I don't know. I'm torn on that. Please come home.***

Me: ***Why?***

Unknown: ***Because I need you. Because he needs you. Because I was always too busy obsessing over you to fall for someone else. Because I need to know if I'm making a mistake by hoping.***

I shake my head vigorously, letting out the loudest, shrillest shriek I can muster. It's not fucking helping, and I need something to help. Clamoring out of bed, I hurry over to the balcony doors, unlocking them and tossing them open wide.

Fresh air. I need fresh air. Even Southern California fresh air. A burst of salty, ocean mist hits me square in the face, clinging to the sweat I'm covered in. It's still dark out. Dawn is not yet playing with the midnight-blue sky.

I stare out into the black expanse of the ocean, listen to the crashing of the waves and sigh. I knew about him. I would be lying if I said I hadn't Facebook-stalked him a time or twenty over the years. Forced myself to hate him with the sort of passion reserved for political figures and pop stars. But this? Saying he misses me?

Me: ***Seeing me won't change that. But if you're asking, you are.***

He responds immediately, and I can't help but grin a little at that. *You still care about me, Jameson Woods.* When I catch the traitorous thought, I shut it down instantly. Because if he cared, if his texted words meant anything, then I wouldn't be here, and he wouldn't be there, and this bullshit four a.m. text conversation wouldn't be happening.

Unknown: *I'm not asking. Seeing you might change everything. But more than that, I need you here with me. My father would want to see you. Come home.*

I hate him. I hate him. I hate him!

Me: *I can't come home. Stop using your father to manipulate me.*

Unknown: *It's the only play I have. You can come home. I know you can. Are you seeing someone? Before you respond, any answer other than no might kill me right now.*

I growl, not caring if anyone walking by hears. How can he do this to me? How can he be so goddamn selfish? Doesn't he know what he put me through? That I still haven't found my way back after four years? I shouldn't reply. I should just throw my phone away and never look back.

Me: *No. And you're a bastard.*

Unknown: *YES. I Am! Please. I am officially begging. Really, Lee. I'm not even bullshitting. I'm a mess. Please. Please. Please!!!!*

Me: ...

Unknown: *What does that mean?*

Me: *It means I'm thinking. Stop!*

My eyes lock on nothing, my mind swirling a mile a minute.

Lee. He called me Lee. That nickname might actually hurt the most. And now he's asking me to come home. Jameson Woods, the man I thought was my forever, is asking me to come home to see him. And for what? To scratch a long-forgotten itch? To assuage some long-abandoned guilt over what he did? Why would I fall for that?

I sigh again because I know why. It's the same reason I never bring men home. It's the same reason I haven't given up this house

even though I don't fully live in it anymore and it's far from conve-
nient. It's the same reason I continued this conversation instead of
smashing my phone.

Jameson Woods.

The indelible ink on my body. The scar on my soul. The fissure
in my heart.

Unknown: ...

I can't help the small laugh that squeaks out as I lean forward and
prop my elbows on the edge of the railing. The cool wind whips
through my hair, and I hate that I feel this way. That I'm entertaining
him the way I am.

Me: *What does that mean?*

Unknown: *It means I'm getting impatient. Please. I
need you to come home. I know I'm a bastard. I know I
shouldn't be asking you this. But I am.*

Unknown: *Aren't you at least a little curious?*
YES!

Me: *NO!!!!!!! And bastard doesn't cover you.*

Unknown: *Please. It's spinning out of control, and I
need to see you. I need to know.*

Me: *You already know.*

Unknown: *About you?*

Me: *Yes, or you wouldn't be texting me at four in the
morning.*

Unknown: *It's seven here. Does that mean you'll
come?*

Me: ...

Unknown: ...

Me: *Yes*.

My phone slips from my fingers, clanging to the hard surface of
my balcony floor. My phone buzzes again, a little louder now since
the sound is reverberating off the ground. I don't pick it up. I don't

look down. I don't care if he's thanking me or anything else he comes up with. I don't care. I don't want to know.

Because I'm busy getting my head on straight.

Locking myself down.

I'm worried about his father and I want to see him, want to make sure he's okay with my own two eyes.

I'll go home and I'll see him. I'll see him, and I'll do the one thing I was never able to do before. I'll say goodbye. My eyes close and I allow myself to slip back. To remember every single moment we had together. To indulge in the sweet torture that, if I let it, will rip me apart piece by piece. Because I know what I'm in for, and I know that once I step foot off that airplane, nothing will ever be right again.

Find out what happens next with Lyric and Jameson in Reckless to Love You.

Made in United States
Orlando, FL
27 September 2024

52023376R00200